LORD OF DARKNESS

'I am not one of your camp-followers,' Karin spat the words at him, pride and defiance blazing out of her lovely face. Her fingers tightened round the hilt of the knife until he saw the knuckles grow white. With a cry she turned it about so that the blade was against her breast, where the gown had slipped from her shoulder in the struggle.

'What will your King Richard say in the morning when he discovers that a woman killed herself rather than be abused by the man supposedly acting as her rescuer?'

'Stay your hand, girl, I'll not lay another finger on you,' Rollo growled, quickly moving back from the bed. 'And not because of that threat, either. Why should I waste my time with you when there are plenty of willing women waiting for me? This time I shall leave . . .'

'There will not be another,' Karin said, and his eyes gleamed at the tremor in her voice.

'I think there will, my lady. I *know* there will. And the next time, neither your weapon nor your threats will stop me . . .'

Valentina Luellen has been a successful and popular author for some years, and until quite recently she lived in the English countryside with her husband and their son Jamie. However, her husband became seriously ill and she packed everything—including the car, two dogs and five cats—and went to live on a small farm in the Algarve, Portugal. There her husband's health improved, and she now divides her time between the kitchen and the study of her newly-renovated farmhouse.

Valentina Luellen has written sixteen Masquerade Historical Romances. LORD OF DARKNESS is her first longer length romance.

LORD
OF
DARKNESS

BY
VALENTINA LUELLEN

MILLS & BOON LIMITED
15–16 BROOK'S MEWS
LONDON W1A 1DR

First published in Hardback in 1985 by
Worldwide Romance

This Paperback edition published in 1985 by
Mills & Boon Limited, 15–16 Brook's Mews,
London W1A 1DR

© Valentina Luellen 1985

Australian copyright 1985
Philippine copyright 1985
This edition 1985

ISBN 0 263 75130 9

09/0785/104,000

Set in 10 on 12 pt Linotron Palatino

Photoset by Rowland Phototypesetting Ltd
Bury St Edmunds, Suffolk
Made and printed in Great Britain by
Cox & Wyman Ltd, Reading

FOR CARL AND KAY

whose friendship and encouragement have
helped me weather many a storm.

CHAPTER ONE

IT WAS almost sunset over the city of Acre in the year of our Lord 1191. As the blood-red rays of the sun touched the tall spires of the minarets and the golden domes of the temples, towering over flat-topped, whitewashed roofs where men were already beginning to prostrate themselves in the direction of Mecca, the muezzin began the *adán*, the call to prayer.

> *Allah akbar*
> *ashhad an la ilah illa-llah.*
> 'God is great
> There is no God but God.'

A French soldier in the Crusader camp on the slopes of Mount Turon turned his head away to spit into the dirt, but mostly the melodious sound which had become part of the everyday life for the invading army, whose tents had been erected before the city walls for twenty-three long months, was ignored. Few allowed their attention to stray from games of chess, of ball, from the pleasurable pastime of making love to one of the camp-followers, or, for the more serious-minded, training at the quintain.

A steady stream of soldiers had been making their way to Acre since Guy de Lusignan, King of Jerusalem, had pitched his scarlet tent before its walls and laid siege to both city and inhabitants. Welsh and English, French and Italians, together with German mercenaries, now swelled the ranks. The camp was spread in a wide arc before the walls and could not be dislodged by heat or disease or the frequent attacks of the enemy, five miles to their rear on the heights of Tell Keisan. The latter too had been well reinforced over the months with Egyptians, Moroccans and Abyssinians who had flocked to the banner of their mighty leader.

The Crusaders attacked Acre. The Muslims attacked the Crusaders, yet still they stayed before the city walls, and the plight of those within grew more desperate with the passing of each day.

And so it had dragged on until this day in June, which had dawned no differently from any other. But it was—for on the horizon were the sails of many ships, and a fierce undercurrent of excitement ran through the camp, firing the imaginations of tired and disappointed men with new heart. Richard of England had come at last! The king whose courage as a fighting man had earned him the name Coeur-de-Lion. Lionheart! He had come to fight alongside Philip Augustus of France, who had arrived not more than fifty days ahead of him, Guy de Lusignan and Conrad, Marquis of Montferrat. Leopold of Austria, the first to arrive, and the Duke of Burgundy were men whose lives were dedicated to the annihilation of the Infidel and the restoration of Jerusalem to Christian hands.

Reinforcements! Fresh assaults to be made against those thick, seemingly impregnable, walls and the indomitable foe within who, despite the mistaken leanings towards the wrong faith, were to be admired as men of great courage and fortitude. The siege of Acre was all but over.

And then in the path of the King of England's ship was another, a large supply ship flying the flag of his brother-in-arms, Philip Augustus, which confounded the watchers on the shore by turning tail and trying to run for the open sea. It was clear, then, that this was no supply ship but a blockade-runner laden with Muslim sailors who had shaved off their beards and donned Frankish clothes in an effort to sail undetected under the noses of the patrol ships. They had even gone to the extent of allowing pigs to be kept on the upper decks in full view, relying on the assumption that the Christian sailors knew no Muslim ever ate pork!

The engagement was short, but fierce. The Sultan's ship was sunk. The precious foodstuffs and supplies were denied to the besieged garrison in Acre, who watched from the walls with agony in their hearts as another vessel was lost and more men died. Watched too, with heavy dread, the unloading of the English ship and the massive amount of equipment carried from it.

It was an omen, many said that night as they sat around their camp-fires and drank and laughed. An omen to indicate that victory was theirs. God had given his approval of the Lionheart's presence in the Holy Land, and he would do no less for the men who fought with him.

It had taken Richard some eighteen months to reach his destination. He had sailed from the port of Dover on the eleventh of December 1189, planning to join up with Philip Augustus and march south through France to Outremer, from where they would journey to the Holy Land together.

Delays and tragedies at times made many begin to believe no one would ever reach it. The third king who had elected to join them, the Emperor and King of Germany, Frederick Barbarossa, was drowned as he and his men attempted to cross a swollen river in Asia Minor. News came that Philip's wife, Queen Isabel, had died. Richard and Philip argued continually over how the spoils of the conquest should be divided between them. The months passed . . . the Third Crusade did not begin in earnest until the fourth of July 1190, seven months after Richard had left the English shore.

Even then, misfortune dogged the footsteps of the two kings. It was decided that the armies should separate after reaching Lyons, for the countryside was no longer able to provide sufficient food for the massive number of men, some sixty thousand, and the mules and field horses that drew the eleven thousand carts. As the English army was trying to cross the River Rhône, the bridge collapsed under the enormous weight. Another delay of three days ensued, while Philip, who had hired a Genoese fleet to convey him to Outremer, was well ahead of his companions.

Richard reached Marseilles expecting a huge fleet to be assembled and waiting for him, only to discover it had been held up in Portugal, where the king had persuaded the sailors to aid him in his continual fight against the Spanish Moors. This done, the sailors had found other things to keep them in the country, such as the endless flow of wine—and women. Many ended up in gaol. By the time the fleet had been reorganised and sailed to join their king, they found he had already gone on ahead.

Richard and Philip met again to join forces for a brief while in Genoa, where the latter had fallen ill. There were more quarrels on how the spoils of war should be divided, more delays and frustrations as the journey to the Holy Land continued slowly and painfully, with dissent not only between the two kings but among the army as well. From Genoa they travelled to Sicily, where it had been decided to spend the winter. While Christmas was celebrated with much splendour, across the sea in the Holy Land, their ultimate destination, men died in their thousands from disease and starvation, some reduced to eating the flesh of their dead horses to survive.

By February 1191, the army was impatient to be on the move. Richard's continued generosity of gifts to all his troops had averted many desertions over the past months, but now he realised that if he did not continue his journey, he was in danger of losing three-quarters of his men. But he lingered a while longer in order to marry Berengaria, the quiet, shy creature his mother the Dowager Queen Eleanor had brought to him from Navarre. The wedding was celebrated in a small chapel of St George at Limassol in Cyprus, where she was crowned Queen of England by the Bishop of Evreux on the twelfth of May.

On the fifth of June Richard and his fleet left Cyprus for the Holy Land.

The Crusaders were not the only ones whose attention was riveted on the harbour that day. For another, the arrival of more soldiers eager for battle spelled doom for the beleaguered city. More Christians in a Muslim land! Allah give him strength to combat this new foe!

In a tent set apart from the others, three men stood beside a long table looking down at the maps and charts spread out before them. One was small and grey-haired and he wore a magnificent ruby on a long gold chain about his neck. His name was Tamir ibn Dak, and he was one of the favoured astrologers of the regal figure in cloth of gold beside him, Salah al-Din, Yussuf ibn Ayub, Sultan of Syria and Egypt—'Honour of the Faith', the revered title given by his people to a wise and merciful leader. The man the Crusaders called Saladin. Hated by Christians, who considered him an Unbeliever of the true faith, loved by the thousands who followed him as the ruler of the Muslim world. This was the most powerful man in the Holy Land.

He had just dismissed a conference of his generals, called to discuss the disquieting news from Acre brought that morning by carrier pigeon, the only source of communication open since the blockade of the port by Frankish ships. A desperate appeal for help had arrived from Kara Kush, the Governor of Acre. Food, stocks of arrows and Greek fire were exhausted. Morale was at its lowest. If the city was not relieved at once, it would fall to the enemy. Saladin was not known for wasting time. He ordered an immediate all-out assault on the Crusaders, and a Muslim fleet to run the blockade and take supplies to the defending forces. But, alas, his own forces were so depleted by the months of continuous warfare that he knew it would take time to put a strong enough force of men into the field again, capable of defeating, or at least holding back, the Christian army, whose ranks were now enlarged with the arrival of the King of England and his following. Instead of just Guy de Lusignan—may Allah rip out his soul for breaking his oath never to take up arms against a Muslim again—he now had the Kings of France and England and Austria to contend with, and soldiers from Germany. What drew them to this land? Allah, perhaps? His God, not theirs. Brought before the walls of Acre for him, Saladin, to destroy? How he wished it were possible to believe this.

'You are quite sure in your predictions?' He looked up from the heavenly chart at his fingertips, a frown puckering his thin, dark brows.

'I am, my lord. It is as I first told you when the girl was taken. It is written that she will be returned to her own people,' Tamir ibn Dak replied quietly, knowing the pain his words must cause for the third man in the tent.

'No!' Their companion spoke for the first time, his voice vibrating with deep-felt emotion. 'I shall not allow it. I have taken her as my daughter . . . she knows no other father. She has no memory beyond the last four years.' He was a stout man, but of enormous strength which had made him both admired and feared by the Mameluke cavalry he commanded. He was Badir the Great, Emir of Jyira.

'It is time she was told. *Insh'allah*. It is written—and

cannot be changed.' Saladin nodded, and turned away to seat himself cross-legged on a pile of cushions. 'What is to be done? It must be soon . . .'

'If the girl could be found when the city falls . . . if the city falls'—hastily the astrologer corrected himself as two pairs of eyes bored into him—'in conditions which indicate she was a captive . . .'

'She would be released and taken by her own people.' Saladin nodded approval. Not so Badir.

'Returned! To strangers? She is a Muslim now. She knows only our ways. The name I gave her! Me, her father. Ayub, her brother. She is a child! Would you have me hand her over to Unbelievers? Have our women not suffered enough at the hands of these Crusaders? These men who rape and kill for the pleasure of it?'

'Our women—yes,' Saladin agreed. 'She is not of our faith, or of our blood. She is an English girl, taken when Jerusalem was returned to our hands through the will of Allah. You had recently lost your own daughter and so you took her for your own, cared for her, and Allah looked kindly on your foolish but well-meaning act. And on mine, for extending to her my protection. But it is over, Lord Badir. My astrologers predicted four years ago that she would one day return to her own. At that time I warned you I would ensure that it happened. I demand you set her free.'

'I too, have grown fond of her.' Tamir ibn Dak laid a gentle hand on the drooping shoulder of his friend, and felt him stiffen. He sighed. The girl would be returned. Saladin had commanded it! And it had been written in the stars for many years. There would be a void in the lives of them both that time would not be able to fill, nor a woman replace. The laughter—the innocence—the beauty of the treasure they both adored was lost to them for ever.

'Ayub.. . .' Badir began, and was silenced by a look from his master.

'Will obey me—if not his own father.'

'*Insh'allah*.' The Lord of Jyira lifted his mailed shoulders in a shrug of acceptance, pain lining his weatherbeaten features. 'It is written. She must be returned.'

As the white-robed muezzin outside continued to call the Faithful to their prayers, the three men rose and went to the entrance of the tent and knelt on the prayer-rugs laid down for them by Nubian slaves.

Mighty Allah, make me strong against the Unbelievers, was the prayer of Saladin as he touched his forehead to the ground.

Merciful Allah, let Acre not be taken, Tamir ibn Dak prayed.

Badir the Great, who knew with the heightened instincts of a soldier that his time had come to die, prayed to his God that he might die in Acre . . . at the side of the daughter who must live without him.

That night he was aboard one of the Muslim ships which sailed under cover of darkness in the hope of breaking the Frankish blockade. He had no intention of becoming involved in any fighting; at least not until he was inside the walls of Acre. The captain of his vessel made a seemingly suicidal attempt to reach the Tower of Flies which jutted out over the city walls into the harbour . . . then, as enemy ships bore down on him at great speed, veered away towards the open sea. Alone in the vastness of the grey waters, Badir struck out cautiously for the Tower.

It was peaceful within the walls of the House of the Teacher, which was only one of the many smaller buildings contained inside the high walls of the palace grounds. Karin had refused her brother's request to move into the safety of the palace itself. She did not believe Acre would fall to the enemy; if it did—Allah forbid!—she would be far safer where she was. She would pretend she was a mere servant-girl, she told Ayub with a pert smile, and she would be left alone. Her brother had given her a strange look, but to her surprise had not insisted on the move. The entrance was through one of the side gates, the Lion Gate. The house was totally enclosed within high walls pierced by many arches, where bougainvillaeas and roses entwined in a profusion of pink, purple and white. Tall palms sheltered the gardens where fountains continuously splayed water into marble bowls from the mouths of fishes, animals, and horned beasts. The rooms were rich with ceramic tiles which brightened walls and ceilings, and on the walls hung tapestries from Persia and Egypt, silk from Damascus. Gold and enamel work was everywhere, dominating the house, a gift from the Sultan Saladin to one of his favourites.

The House of the Teacher was where Karin always stayed when in Acre, with her father—when he was not away fighting somewhere in the service of Islam— and Ayub, her beloved brother. He, too, was a soldier, fighting against the horde of Unbelievers who had invaded their country, seeking to take from them what was theirs by right. Saladin was slowly driving them back . . . retaking forts and towns they had overcome, razing the castles they had built on soil which did not belong to them. Soon, she told herself with a sigh, soon the country would be at peace again. She would have her father and brother all to herself once more and they could return to their home in Jyira, just outside Jerusalem. Tamir would return to his home as in the old days, and she could continue her studies. How she missed those happy times. She was sick of the fighting, the waste of young lives, the sight of women weeping over their dead, the hospitals filled with injured, the smell of blood.

From the balcony where she stood she could clearly see the camp-fires of the Crusaders around the city. They had fought like men possessed of devils before the massive walls, but always were forced to withdraw out of range of the naphtha and boiling oil poured down upon them, the thousands of arrows hurled into their midst by keen-eyed archers. She could hear sounds of merriment and laughter, which floated to her from the tented army on a strong night breeze. There was no laughter, no time to relax within the walls of Acre. There were the wounded to be attended to, dead to be buried, battlements to be manned, bandages to be made. Not a second could be wasted if they were to survive. She herself had returned from tending some wounded only a short while ago. Even after the luxury of a bath, immersing herself in water scented with jasmine oil, the stench of blood was still in her nostrils, and her fingers felt sticky with it. She shuddered, and lifted her gaze from the enemy camp to the hills where faint lights flickered out of the inky blackness. Saladin's encampment. Tomorrow, perhaps, he would relieve the city and give them all peace and freedom from fear.

She lingered, remembering times past when she had sat with her father and Ayub in the gardens below, beside the crystal-clear water in the pool where she bathed every day, while her servants related the latest gossip from the market-places or friends called to discuss the latest acquisition to their wardrobes. It was a pleasant, easy-going, untroubled way of life. Allah bring down his curse on the Unbelievers who had disrupted so perfect an existence! She had not been able to go outside the city walls for nearly two long, boring years! At first it had been easy to occupy herself, but after six months she found the hours beginning to drag. The only topic of conversation was the wretched war. The sight of the scarlet tent of the King of Jerusalem annoyed her beyond reason. She wished an archer would send a flaming arrow into it, or Allah would unleash a thunderbolt to strike it—and the man within—to ashes.

As the tents beyond the walls grew and grew with each passing month, she occupied her time with the wounded and the needy. She was, after all, the daughter of Badir the Great. It was expected of her. She dressed herself in boy's clothing and rode through the streets offering words of encouragement to the men on the walls, and sympathy to grieving widows, women who had lost fathers and sons; and in her heart she silently wept with them. If she ever lost her

father—or Ayub . . . She could not imagine life without them. They were everything to her, and she to
them.

The exotic aroma of night-blooming flowers floated
up to her from the well-tended gardens, and she stood
quite still, head thrown back, breathing in the heady
perfume as she listened to the call of a bird. Tomorrow
it would be different, she told herself. Tomorrow . . .

'And what does my sister dream of all alone?' a voice
asked softly from behind. Karin turned and smiled at
the dark-haired young man who leaned against a
pillar, watching her. 'Of me, I hope?'

'Always of you, Ayub,' Karin laughed, hurrying to
his side and brushing a light kiss across his cheek. He
caught her to him with fierce possessiveness and
kissed her on the mouth. There were times when he
acted more like a lover than a brother, with his tight
embraces and searching kisses, she thought, quickly
drawing back, but he only laughed when she said she
did not think he should be so demonstrative with her
lest people misunderstood. He had given her one of
his strange looks—she thought of them as strange
because his eyes were suddenly guarded as if his
thoughts were too private to be made known to her—
then laughed and turned the conversation to another
topic. 'You look tired. Come and sit down and tell me
how things are going.'

She took his arm and led him to a couch laden with
cushions. She put one beneath his head, and beckoned a hovering servant to bring them refreshments,
before curling up beside him, an arm tucked through
his.

At nineteen, Karin was fast blossoming into a beautiful young woman. Her hair, which hung past her waist in soft unbroken waves, was the tawny gold of a lion's mane. An Egyptian slave-girl brushed it one hundred and fifty times morning and night until it gleamed with a red sheen. She was tall and slender, but not thin. Already her breasts were firm and well rounded beneath the gold-threaded bodice she wore. Her waist was so small it could be coupled by the two hands of a man, her hips and thighs, shapely and enticing beneath the wide trousers of lilac silk. Her over-robe was of a rose-coloured material and her feet were thrust into dark red slippers of Moroccan leather, striped with gold.

Her skin had darkened considerably in the four years she had been with them, Ayub thought, watching her as she sipped a glass of lemon-juice in which fragrant rose-petals floated. To look at her now, no one would recognise the thin, half-crazy girl he and his father had brought out of Jerusalem. Behind them they left two graves—amid many hundreds of others—those of her parents, killed in the last onslaught before the Holy City fell to Islam once more . . . Left, too, somewhere among the ruins, was the memory she had once possessed, the memory of the name she had once borne, the mother and father whose seed had given her life. Nothing existed beyond the day they had carried her away from the death and destruction and brought her to Jyira and given her the name of Karin, which in the local dialect meant 'Princess'. Soon, very soon, he would have to make his feelings known to her. He could not stand this torture much longer. To be with her, yet not touch her. To kiss her lips, yet not possess her body! He loved her, not as a sister but as the woman he would take for his wife. He knew his father did not approve and would refuse his permission, so there was only one course open to him. He would have to take what he desired so ardently, and when she belonged to him, no one could part them. He had never seen such eyes. Blue like the sky on a summer's day. Blue like the sea—sometimes possessing a hint of green in their depths. Fascinating eyes. He moved closer, roused by the urge to kiss them, to allow his hands the pleasure of exploring the body pressed so innocently against his. She had no idea of the fires which burned in him at her slightest touch, her very nearness.

'Why are you so silent, Ayub? I die for want of news.' Karin said, laying her head back against a cushion. He was dying for want of her! He found his eyes fastening on the small mouth, with a hint of sensuousness—perhaps unknown to her—lingering in the fullness of the red lips. Her eyes were darkened with kohl, as was the fashion, her long fingernails and toenails painted a shade of henna to match her mouth. She was a delicacy fit for a king. It took an enormous effort to draw back from her as she said, a trifle impatiently, 'What are you dreaming of? Your latest conquest—the red-headed woman from Aleppo? Really, Ayub, why don't you take a wife and settle down? It would please father to see you a family man. If anything should happen to you . . .'

'There will be no heir for Badir,' Ayub grimaced. 'I

know. I shall marry—soon. What is it you want to know, inquisitive one?'

'Those ships I saw which arrived yesterday . . .'

'They brought the King of England and his men. Malik al-Inkitar, the one called Lionheart. It is said he is invincible. Already he has his accursed Frankish siege-machines beneath the walls. The one called "Malvoisin". Allah preserve us! It is a veritable machine of destruction.'

'It will be destroyed as all the others were. Will it not?' Karin asked, not liking the look in her brother's eyes. Desperation! Yes, that was what she saw. Desperation! It frightened her.

'We have no more naphtha. Our arrow stocks are gone. The Frankish ships blockade the port, turning back our own ships with badly-needed supplies. It is the end, little sister. We must think of a way to get you out of the city before it falls. Back to Jyira, where you will be safe. Why you ever left it is beyond me.'

'To be near you—and father,' she replied, squeezing his arm. His fingers tightened painfully over hers for a long moment. 'If the walls fall, I shall fight alongside you.'

'The Crusaders would love to see that.' He gave a short laugh, but was then serious again. 'I shall not let them take you, never fear. You will do as you said, dress as a servant-girl and hide yourself here in the House of the Teacher.'

'So close to the palace?'

'It will be safe. It contains the secret room where Tamir keeps his special charts and maps. You will be quite safe there until I can get you out of the city. If I do not come for you, I shall send someone I can trust, bearing my ring.' He lifted his hand and showed her the large pearl set in gold which he wore on his little finger. 'This one, remember it.'

'I shall go nowhere without you,' Karin declared, her chin jutting stubbornly.

'You will obey me—and live. I shall join you when I can. I do not intend to die yet either,' Ayub assured her.

She pressed her face against the smooth fabric of his coat with a soft cry, and the temptation to take her in his arms and comfort her was too great to resist. She hardly seemed aware of his hands moving over her shoulders, his lips against her hair, and he realised that her thoughts were far away on what the uncertain future might hold for them both. As his blood began to boil for want of her, a servant bowed low before the couch. He had brought news of Badir's return to Acre. Ayub's presence was demanded immediately. He had no choice but to leave her.

Why not her? Karin wondered as she sat alone waiting for a summons to join them. Why Ayub alone? What was so terrible that she could not be told? Celine, her handmaid, turned back the silken sheets on the bed in readiness for her mistress to retire, laid out a nightgown of a soft wispy material in pale pink, and waited. Karin shook her head, her expression troubled.

'Not yet. I shall wait a while longer. He must want to see me, Celine. He must! It has been almost a year now.'

'Shall I brush your hair? You know how that soothes

you.' The girl had been with Karin for the past four years, the first servant she could ever remember having. She was an Egyptian, sold into slavery on the death of her mother by a jealous wife who did not want a reminder of her husband's true love about her. She was by far the cleverest and the most trustworthy of Karin's household, which consisted in all of ten servants. Five women, two enormous Nubian eunuchs who guarded her night and day, and another three men who carried out general duties. Karin was watched, pampered and protected from the moment she rose from her bed in the morning until she returned to it at night. Her word was law. Over all of them she possessed the power of life and death, but they were obedient to her commands, well mannered and gave her no cause for complaint. With Celine she enjoyed a closer link, which bordered on friendship, and the girl often accompanied her on her visits to Tamir ibn Dak and remained to learn from his wise teachings.

'I had another dream last night,' Celine said as she brushed the tawny tresses with a heavy silver-backed brush. Her mother had been a famous beauty in her own land, gifted with second sight, who had attracted the attention of her master with her dancing. She had become his number one concubine, and ruled over his harem and his heart until the day she died. Karin knew that Celine had inherited her mother's gift of being able to foretell the future. Already she had forecast the fall of Acre and—Allah forbid!—Jerusalem, but they had kept it to themselves, afraid of Ayub's anger should he learn of the prophecies. For him Jerusalem would always belong to the Muslims. To say otherwise was treason, and punishable by death!

'If it is to do with the city, I would rather not know,' Karin said with a shiver. 'Ayub thinks we have lost the fight. This English King, Richard . . . now that he is here, things are different.'

'I dreamt of you, mistress—a strange dream. You were—different.'

'How so?' Karin asked with a soft laugh.

'Your clothes . . . You were not dressed as you are now, and the man with you . . .' She broke off, and Karin wheeled on her, her curiosity suddenly aroused. Man! Ayub allowed no man to come close to her!

'What manner of man? Celine, why do you stare at me so? What was he like? Was it Yussuf? Malir, Ayub's best friend? He means soon to ask father for my hand in marriage, but I like him not. Tell me, quickly, ere I die of curiosity . . .'

'He—He was a tall man. Big—I mean powerful . . . I could not see his face. He was holding you—here, in this room—making love to you . . .' Karin's cheeks began to flame. She knew of no such man. Powerful . . . big . . . and too forward for his own good! If any man touched her so, she would have him whipped, the soles of his feet ripped raw by the bastinado. Yet she had to hear it all.

'Go on . . .'

'No, mistress. I should not have spoken. I thought it a warning last night . . .' Celine's face was pale. Clearly she was afraid. But why, Karin wondered.

'A warning? Speak! I will know all of it.'

'He was not—a Muslim. I—I saw a huge cross on the tunic he wore, and an emblem—like a bolt of lightning split asunder . . .'

'Enough!' Karin sprang to her feet, blue fire sparking in her eyes.

'A Crusader! An Unbeliever—making love to me? You are mad!'

'It was only a dream . . . It meant nothing . . .' Celine cried. 'Forgive me, I have distressed you. I wanted only to put you on your guard. These men have no respect for women—they are animals. I have seen them with their painted harlots who flock about them, flaunting their oiled bodies . . .'

'We will say no more about it,' Karin said again, shutting her mind to what she had been told. Celine's dreams had a way of always coming true. Not one, that she knew of, had ever been false. Suddenly she was very much afraid . . .

She was called to her father's apartments early the next morning. As soon as she entered the room and went to the side of the man who awaited her, seated beside Ayub, both grave-faced and somehow withdrawn from her and kissed him on both cheeks, she knew something was terribly wrong. She was drawn down beside him. Today there was no casual conversation, as was the usual ritual. No statements of affection, of how he had missed her, how well she looked, how brave she was to bear up so well under the tremendous strain of the past months. Nothing but a voice which came to her as if in a dream, telling her unbelievable things . . . destroying the world she knew and loved. And all the while Ayub sat quiet and still, his eyes locked on her face, offering no word of sympathy or comfort. Nothing!

'I am Karin! I am! I am!' Her voice was shrill, tinged with hysteria. They both looked at her as if she was a stranger. She knew each was adept at concealing his feelings, for in the Muslim world a man did not wear his heart on his sleeve—that was the way of women . . . but their eyes were empty. They held nothing for her. 'Why do you tell me these things? Father, please . . .' She stretched out an imploring hand, but it was ignored. It was Ayub who seized it, despite Badir's frown, and held it fast. For once Karin was glad of that possessive grip, and she clung to him as if to a thin thread of life she saw slipping away from her.

'You are not my daughter. My daughter died four years ago. I replaced her with you, an English girl we found in a burning house. Your father was dead, your mother dying. With her last breath she begged me in the name of my God to spare you. I took you into my house, into my heart, gave you a name, an identity . . .'

'I know no other . . .' Karin almost screamed the words at him, felt Ayub's fingers tighten warningly over hers and fought to control herself. She closed her eyes, shutting out the misery and despair mirrored in their depths, and was still and silent for several minutes. When she opened them and spoke again, both men marvelled at her self-control—and each loved her more for the great courage which had prevailed. 'If I am not . . . your daughter, who am I? Why do I not know my own name? Can it not be a mistake?'

'There is no error,' Badir returned gravely. 'You are the girl I carried from the flames. You were ill for many weeks, always the same nightmare haunting you—the fire . . .' Karin nodded. It was a dream she still experienced, although she had told no one about it. Fire—always fire—separating her from . . . she did not know whom, only that beyond the flames were people calling to her . . . trying to reach her . . . 'The horrors of what you had seen perhaps wiped all memory from your mind. It was a blessing then. Now?' He shrugged heavy shoulders. 'It is the command of Lord Saladin that you be returned to your own people.'

'He abandons me . . . to the mercy of those fiends?' she breathed. 'To be raped? Murdered?'

'It will happen in such a manner that they will think you have been held captive here,' she was told. 'You will tell them who you are, and they will return you safely to your home. Your true name is Alisandre de Greville-Wynter.'

'Return . . . Return where? I have no name but Karin. I am your daughter. I shall not leave Acre without you. If the city falls, I shall fight and die with you rather than surrender myself to them,' she vowed.

'The Governor, Kara Kush, has sent word to King Richard—He wishes to surrender the city. There is nothing else he can do. Tomorrow he goes to meet our enemies,' Ayub said, his mouth tightening into a grim line. 'Within a week, Acre will be in their hands. If we are not dead, we shall be their prisoners. You will not. You will be free.'

'You agree—to this madness?' Karin asked, aghast.
'It is all a plan you have devised between you to get me
safely out of the city, isn't it?' She scanned their faces
eagerly, saw her father shake his head, and hope died
within her. Not his daughter! Not Karin! Celine's
dream came back to her . . . her in the arms of a
Crusader. Merciful God, was he raping her? Was that
to be her fate? She would kill herself before they came.
She would never allow herself to be touched by a
Christian dog!

Celine had taken Karin back to her rooms. She was
scarcely able to walk. She was dazed, shocked, horrified beyond words. She was to be dragged from all
she held dear, above her own life . . . abandoned to
the care of the barbarian Crusaders! Never had she
experienced a nightmare as frightening as this. The
slave girl tried to calm her mistress, but without suc-
cess. Karin threw herself down upon the silken covers
of the bed, vowing vehemently to kill herself before
she would allow herself to be taken from her father
and Ayub, from the life—the only life—she knew. She
was no English girl! How could he tell her such a lie?
She could speak the tongue quite fluently, but, as far
as she could remember, she had been taught it along
with Arabic by her tutor, Tamir ibn Dak. She rolled
over on to her back, staring up at the canopy of pale
blue above her head, a frown furrowing her plucked
brows. No, it was impossible! She had no memory
other than of her father and Ayub, of Tamir and Celine
. . . Why was he doing this to her?

Ayub had sat in silence for almost half an hour after

Karin had left them. He neither looked at his father, nor attempted to converse with him. At length he lifted his head and stared into the impassive face of the man who, he knew, had been waiting for him to make the first move. They had never been close. Now there was hatred between them.

'I will not let you do this. I have devised a plan by which she will escape the enemy if they enter the city. A few days, and I shall have her safely back in Jyira, where she belongs,' he said.

'No!' Badir thundered, and a servant in the shadows trembled at the fury in the one word. The temper of Badir was well known and feared throughout the household. His son was a mere shadow in comparison. A good soldier, but a dreamer, too fond of the women to be strong like his father. Badir had taken many women to his bed, but loved only one, the wife who had borne him a daughter and lost her own life in the process. His son had come into the world not from an act of love, but out of necessity, as his desperation for a male heir grew.

Ayub did not flinch in the face of his father's wrath. His desire for Karin was so strong that it overcame all fear, all caution. He would have her! It had become an obsession with him.

'I will not allow you to . . . sacrifice her,' he said in a low, fierce tone, and Badir's thick brows rose, indicating contempt at this unexpected stand.

'Not allow? You young puppy, you forget yourself. This is not of my doing. It is by command of Saladin. The astrologers have predicted she must be returned—will be returned—to her own people. It was always meant to be so. I shall pray to Allah she remembers us with kindness in her heart.' His gaze narrowed as it centred on the features of his son and saw something lurking in the depths of the brown eyes which he did not like. He had always chosen to disregard it, until now. 'You do not think of her as your sister! You never have . . . You covet only her body,' he accused, and his mouth twisted in disgust.

'The body of the woman I intend to take as my wife,' Ayub retorted bravely.

'I will have you killed first. She goes back to her own. I go to arrange it now. Interfere, and I swear— son or no—you shall die before the sun rises.'

'She is sleeping?' Some while later Badir came silently into the darkened room where Karin lay outstretched on the bed, her face buried in a mound of pillows. Celine came quickly to his side, and shook her head at the question.

'She is plagued by dreams, lord. The fire again. What—What is to happen to her?'

'That is none of your concern,' he hissed, fixing her with a stern look which deterred further questions. 'Give her this. It is a mixture of opiate and water. Put it in some wine so that she suspects nothing. When she is asleep, come to me. There are things which must be done before the morrow.'

'Yes, lord. May I be allowed to stay with her? I am not afraid . . .'

'No. She is alone, now.'

Celine stared down at the small bottle in her hand, and did not move for some considerable time after

Badir had left the room. Then, as Karin stirred restlessly and began to cry out, she ran to the bed to comfort her.

'Hush, mistress, Celine is here. It is only a dream . . .'

Karin started up, wiping a hand across her forehead which was wet with perspiration. Her whole body was damp, her clothes clinging uncomfortably to her skin. Grimacing, she tore them off and pulled on the cool silk robe that the maid had brought to her.

'Open the windows, I am stifling,' she ordered, lying back amid the pillows. She dared not close her eyes, lest the room became filled with smoke and flames again. The heat had been unbearable . . . the roar of the flames licking ever closer to where she lay, trapped by a piece of fallen room-timber, echoed in her ears even now that she was awake and knew it had been no more than the old, familiar, horrifying nightmare. She shivered and wrapped her arms about her body, more for comfort than warmth. The heat—so intense—and yet, for the first time through the haze of swirling smoke and blood-red flames, she had seen a face . . . the face of a woman, her features contorted in agony as she tried to find a way through the fire to where Karin lay helpless, only half conscious. It had been *her* face!

Celine looked towards the windows, thrown open wide to admit the cool night breeze, and decided it was wiser to say nothing. She poured some wine into a silver goblet, emptied the contents of the phial into it and returned to her mistress's side. She had been trained from birth, sometimes painfully, to obey without question, and she hesitated a moment only before handing it to Karin.

'Here is something cool to drink. You are over-wrought. Sit up now and drink it all. In the morning everything will be all right again.'

'Will it?' Karin looked at her dull-eyed. *If I am not Karin, daughter of Badir, who am I?* she wanted to ask, but knew it was useless to ask Celine. If she did know that her mistress had another identity, Badir would have ensured that her lips were sealed. Gratefully she drank the sweet wine from across the water in Cyprus, and lay back, a hand across her eyes. 'Tomorrow, wake me early, Celine. I will not stay here for my father to hand me over to those soldiers outside our walls. I will not! I shall go to the secret room that Tamir showed us once. Do you remember?' The servant nodded, her face betraying no expression as Karin smothered a yawn and then stretched languidly. By the beard of the Prophet, how much of the draught had the bottle contained—she was almost asleep already! She would be incapable of thought, let alone flight, for the next two days, by the looks of it. 'You will come too. I cannot leave you here to face my father's wrath. Ayub will know where we have gone. He will not betray us . . . He will come and take us safely out of the city to Jyira. We are going home, Celine . . . home . . .' Her eyelids drooped . . . she was asleep. Her heart heavy from the deception she had been forced to practise on the mistress she adored, Celine went to find Badir. The instructions she was given, the clothes given into her hands, made her eyes almost pop out of her head in disbelief, but she offered no comment. She did not want to be whipped. Badir was not as tolerant with his servants as Karin, who rarely raised her voice in anger to any of them and treated most of them as favoured companions, rather than chattels servile to her will.

She returned to Karin's room and stared down at the sleeping girl whose face was wiped clean of all anxiety and fear under the relaxing effects of the heavy dose of opiate. There were tears in her eyes as she slowly drew back the covers and removed the robe from the inert body. Karin did not even stir.

'Forgive me, little mistress. He says this will save your life. If he is wrong, I swear by the Prophet that I shall kill him.'

Rollo opened his eyes and stared up at the tent flapping noisily in a strong breeze above his head. There were no sounds from outside, for it was barely light, and so he lay for a while longer, his arms folded beneath his head, wondering what the day would bring forth for him and his men. He had thrown off the blanket in the heat of the night, and lay naked except for a piece of cloth wound about his waist. He had grown used to wearing the minimum of apparel during the years he had spent as a prisoner of the Saracens, and there were times when clothes, especially the restricting chain-mail he was forced to don daily, threatened to suffocate him.

He had been dreaming again. His body was soaked with sweat from the same recurring dream that had haunted him for four long years. Sometimes, now, he experienced it even during the day, reminding him of

the past. What he had once had—and lost! The pain of
it all, the utter desolation of a shattered love that had
driven him that day in Jerusalem into the Church of
the Holy Sepulchre, seeking peace of mind. Seeking
God's grace—his justice! Four years since he had knelt
before the magnificent altar and vehemently decried
the weakness in him, the vulnerability that had
brought him such agony.

Never again! Even though the words were whispered, they seemed to reverberate in the emptiness
around him, as if to mock his show of strength. 'Never
again shall I love a woman. Never again shall I give my
heart. I have done with love. It is a farce—a fallacy. It
brings only pain. There is not a woman born who is
worthy of my trust. I have put weakness behind me.
I shall use as I was used.' The words were branded
into his memory as if stamped there by a red-hot
iron.

The gentle, serene face of the Virgin, holding the
baby Jesus in her arms, continued to smile down at
him, almost compassionately. The silence was unnerving as he rose to his feet, inwardly shocked by the
torrent of words that had come unbidden to his lips.
He had entered this holy place seeking peace . . .
perhaps the vow would give him what he sought. A
life free from entanglements with some doe-eyed,
treacherous woman—and he did not regret it!

'My son.' The voice which came out of the shadows
brought him wheeling about, his hand falling to the
hilt of his sword, but at the sight of the robed figure
who stepped into view, it fell to his side. 'You should
go down on your knees again and beg God's forgive-

ness for such terrible words. Man was not created to be alone. Woman is a necessity.'

'Forgive me, Father, but it is not exactly an area on which you can be an expert.'

'I was not always a man of the cloth. I have known the call of the flesh, and in those days—before God beckoned—I lived a full and satisfying life.'

'Then you were lucky. I was not.' Rollo could remember that day as clearly as if it had been yesterday. The quietness which enveloped them as they stood in the heady atmosphere of frankincense and flickering candles. The sympathy in the voice, the eyes of the middle-aged man who had sought, in vain, to make him retract his statement. 'I shall never love a woman again.'

'You are young . . .'

'And wise, now.'

'Hardly so. I shall pray for you to return, my son, to ask God to absolve you from your vow.'

'If I do, I shall have by my side a woman I love and trust with my heart and soul, every breath in my body.' Rollo's harsh laughter had echoed through the stillness. 'She does not exist! You will never see me again!'

Rollo stretched, flexing his left arm, where a fresh red scar seared the bronzed flesh. It was healing nicely. Thank God it had not been his sword arm! He rose, and crossed to a small table where a pewter bowl filled with water was covered by a cloth to keep out flies and insects. He had learned to be very careful with both water and food in this land where disease raged constantly. Since he had arrived at the camp outside Acre, over fifty people had lost their lives, among them Queen Sybilla, wife of Guy de Lusignan, King of Jerusalem. Fever was prevalent due to the polluted water and fly-blown food. And many others had collapsed beneath the burning sun, unable to stand the extreme temperatures. The dreaded disease called Arnaldia crippled men all about him. Fingernails and toenails dropped off, glands swelled painfully, hair came out in handfuls, skin dried and flaked from face and body. So far he had been spared the dreaded affliction, but then he amused many people by bathing at least once a day.

He stood for a moment surveying his own scarred torso. So many scars . . . but then he had fought in many battles, and somehow survived. No matter how serious a wound he sustained, from somewhere he always found enough strength to struggle back into the world of the living.

Apart from the new scar on his left arm, there were old wounds on both shoulders, etched deep into the brown skin. One on his back, and a long, jagged scar curling around his middle from the axe swung by his best friend! There were scars which could not be seen by the naked eye . . . scars inflicted by pain and loss which had deepened the bitter line of his lean mouth, taken warmth from the pale green eyes which narrowed as he pushed aside the tent-flap for a moment to scan outside. Damnation, where was his squire?

He washed and dressed at a leisurely pace. There would be no fighting today unless Saladin sent down an attack from the heights of Tell Keisan, and that was unlikely. Acre lay before the crusading army, and there was nothing the Saracen leader could do about it! Not now that Richard had arrived. He fastened on his sword and, as an afterthought, picked up his slim-handled throwing-axe. With no one about this early, he could spend an hour at least in practice at the quintain. But first he would rouse Chavo, who had shared his life for the past seven years. There had been a great deal of drinking and carousing the night before, and most of the young squires had had as much difficulty in putting themselves to bed as they had their lords and masters. In fact it had been Rollo who had carried the inebriated young squire to his tent and tossed him unceremoniously down upon his bed. He had been snoring fit to wake the dead as he left.

'Look at him,' Chavo growled, lifting an aching head to stare at the tall figure approaching their tent. 'Half the night drinking and amusing himself with that little dancing-girl, and here he is up and about before any of us. I bet you my next week's pay of ducats that he's already had an hour's practice at the quintain. I don't know how he does it. God's blood! My head. I think I have two . . .'

'I warned you not to try and out-drink him,' Gy Savennes chuckled, and then clutched at his own head with a groan. 'We both have two heads. Stupid heads for attempting such a thing. Why were we celebrating anyway?' He staggered to his feet, cursing a young page who got in his way, almost knocking him over. 'Get out, damn you. Bring me something for this head . . .'

'Wine, sir?' the boy asked in all innocence, and fled

from the tent as a well-aimed boot came after him and caught him a thump on the backside. He took off at a run towards the kitchens, hoping that someone would have a remedy for the hangovers of the two un-gracious squires.

'I seem to remember something about us getting prepared to enter Acre. I'm not prepared for anything at the moment. At least I think that was the reason,' Chavo said, struggling into his underclothes. It had been light for several hours, and he should have been in his lord's tent, assisting him to dress.

'So, you are not dead after all.' A voice heavy with sarcasm drawled from the tent opening. Rollo ducked his head to enter and came to stand in front of the two young men, arms folded over a broad, muscular chest.

He had dressed himself, Chavo saw with a sinking feeling that went right down into the soles of his mailed boots, and he was wearing both his sword and the slender two-headed axe by which he was known, throughout the army, for his deadly, un-erring, accuracy.

He swallowed hard, knowing he was in trouble. As the Duke of Aquitaine's squire, it was his job to be on hand always, to help him dress and undress, accom-pany him into battle, hand him fresh weapons if his own became lost in the mêlée. Carry him if wounded, care for any prisoners he might take, act as subaltern to his retinue . . . as if he, a mere lad of twenty-one, could control the four monsters this man has as a bodyguard, he thought ruefully. They would slit his throat if he looked sideways at them the wrong way! Yet he liked Lord Rollo. They had been together ever

since he was no more than a cub of fourteen, eager to
go into the service of the man he idolised.

'Forgive me, my lord. I . . . overslept. The cel-
ebrations last night!'

'Too much wine—or something . . .' The pale green
eyes dwelt on the anxious features, and then a wide
grin split the fierce countenance and Chavo breathed
again. When his lord looked like this, there was nothing to worry about. 'On this occasion I shall overlook
it. I, too, drank far too much.' It was an unexpected
admission. 'Dress yourself, boy. It is rumoured that
the Governor of Acre would make peace with us
today.'

'Surrender?' Gy gasped, mouth gaping at the news,
until the Duke's amused stare made him realise he was
imitating—and rather badly—a fish out of water, and
he quickly closed it. 'But yesterday . . . there was talk
of another attack on Tell Keisan!'

'Today it's Acre. King Richard's choice. I, for one,
shall be glad to get it over with. Perhaps now we can
move on to Jerusalem.'

Jerusalem! The ultimate goal of all those who had
trudged across Europe to come to this land. The Holy
City. Once they had freed it from Saracen domination
they could return home to their wives and families, the
sweethearts who waited for them.

A fourth man, thin-faced and scowling, pushed his
head into the tent, glared at Gy Savennes and said
curtly, 'Lord Dacre has been calling for you this past
ten minutes. Go to him.'

'Ah, my lord. I'm on my way.' Gy scuttled from
the tent as if a thousand ghosts were after him. To-

day was not going to be the easiest day of his life, he decided.

'I might have known he would be with you.' Hugo de Greville-Wynter's anger was turned now on Chavo. The man at his side was ignored. There was no love lost between them, and they rarely spoke to each other. 'I have told you not to fill that idiot's head with your foolish talk of becoming a knight. He will never reach that stage. He is a clumsy, bumbling fool, and you along with him.'

'A thousand pardons, my lord, I meant no harm. Gy is anxious to be a great knight . . .' Chavo broke off, as Hugo laughed in his face. He was one of the knights attached to the faction of Guy de Lusignan. This was his first time in the Holy Land, and already he had made himself unpopular with his arrogance and bad manners. His men loathed him, his squires feared him. His friends, if they could be called that, constantly talked about him behind his back, and never to the good. He had a big mouth with a loose tongue inside it that had brought him to more than one fight since he had left England. A good fighter he was, with both sword and dagger, when there was an audience. There was a rumour—albeit unconfirmed—that he had knifed more than one opponent in the back rather than face him.

'Don't apologise,' the Duke said coldly, and Hugo swung round on him, his thin face working angrily. 'You answer to no one but me. When you are at fault, I shall reprimand you. I see nothing wrong in encouraging a young man to become a knight. It is an honourable profession. Honour does still count for some people.' The thin face grew purple with rage at the hidden barb.

'I suppose you would have him join your band of mercenaries?' he jeered.

Rollo, Duke of Aquitaine, drew himself up to his full height, which was somewhat over six feet. In the small tent, he dwarfed his two companions. The sunburnt features were bleak, the pale green eyes, unnerving in their intense scrutiny . . . and contemptuous of the way Hugo moved uneasily beneath their gaze, the tiny beads of sweat gathering on his brow.

'My men are professional soldiers, proficient with sword and lance, battle-axe and dagger. They can ride like the wind, lose themselves in the darkness of this heathen land like shadows. You could learn much from them . . . Mercenaries . . . ? Are we not all mercenaries at heart, my lord? Are you not being paid by the King for fighting beneath his banner? I am. So are they. We are none of us much better than each other . . .' He gave a short laugh containing no humour as Hugo gave a strangled cry and rushed from the tent. They could hear him cursing as he strode off.

'Why do you allow him to speak to you that way, Lord Rollo?' Chavo asked in puzzlement, wishing his master had seized his axe and cut down the unpleasant and unpopular man who called himself a knight and a man of honour, and who lost no opportunity in making Chavo's life a misery . . . as he did the lives of all young squires and pages who came near him. 'Our men, I mean your men, are not really

mercenaries—some are from good families. Forgive
me, I say this badly . . .'

'I like to think my men are loyal to me out of respect,
but we both know that respect sometimes is worth
only the gold I pay them each day. My Guard is a
different matter. There I know I have four good and
brave men who would lay down their lives for me,
should I ask. True friends. I have never known truer.
Soon . . .' The pale eyes dwelt on Chavo's face, and
now there was a flicker of warmth in them. 'I have not
forgotten what I promised when you saved my life
here at Acre four years ago. When you are knighted,
so also do you take your place in my Guard.'

'My lord, I did not think! It is an honour . . .' Chavo
could hardly speak for joy. To become one of the
Duke's personal entourage would place him among
the most envied—and most disliked—men in the
whole Crusader army. Proud, fearless, arrogant men
who had earned themselves a reputation for their
fighting skill all the way across Europe, through
Cyprus and into Turkey, fighting beneath the banner
of Rollo, Duke of Aquitaine, Lord of Shah'mat, the
illegitimate son of the Lord of Verduse and a woman of
low birth whom he had loved. In battle they were
veritable devils, giving no quarter to the enemy. Their
leader had earned himself the name of the Lord of
Darkness for his black moods and unpredictable nature. He had gathered no real friends about him
during his years of fighting, save these four men who
guarded him night and day.

He sought no other companionship, nor honours,
yet he was a favourite of the Dowager Queen Eleanor,

mother of Richard Coeur-de-Lion, and had been raised at her court at Poitiers before her imprisonment by her own husband for plotting with her sons against him. Even Richard himself liked the Duke's company, much to the chagrin of many other knights of unblemished birth. Those who sought to be with him, to bask in the glory which often surrounded him and his élite force, soon found their devious reasons discovered and slunk away to other, less particular, company.

The Lord of Darkness was a man alone, yet the men who rode at his side, wearing his colours of white, black and silver, were proud to serve him, jealous of the very special position they held. This, then, was the band Chavo longed to be part of.

'God bless you, Lord Rollo,' he said, falling to one knee, head bent.

'Get up, boy.' His master's voice was almost harsh. 'Find me Piers, Siward and Guyon. Tell them I want them at the quintain immediately. Edred I shall collect myself. After the amount he drank last night, it will need nothing short of Malvoisin to drag him to his feet,' Rollo said with a smile. These were the four knights of renown, although anyone seeing them this morning after the carousing they had all done the night before, Chavo thought, hiding a grin himself, would not give a ducat for their prowess with sword or lance. 'You will not find it amusing when they begin to train you, my young friend. I demand the highest of standards. Should you not reach them . . .'

He spun on his heel and left the tent, reluctant to show that extra little trace of warmth even before him,

Chavo, who had shared much with him during their years of self-imposed exile. He had learned to hide his feelings well—too well. No one ever came close to him these days. The Guard shared his days and his nights, yet knew him not. They fought, drank together, yet always Rollo somehow set himself apart from them. Only Chavo, who knew him better than he realised, saw that withdrawal when others about him did not— and he understood why.

The answer lay amid the ruins of the Castle of Verduse. In the grave of the woman buried there. No woman would ever hold him again as that one had. The bitch! May she be rotting in hell where she belongs, Chavo thought viciously, as he pulled on the quilted gambeson which afforded him some protection against sword and arrow. Until he was a fully-fledged knight, he was not allowed to wear chain-mail of any kind to protect himself. If God sent down an angel, he doubted if even she could melt the ice in Rollo's heart. The Lord of Darkness had chosen to be alone. It was the way it would always be for him . . .

CHAPTER TWO

'LADY, PLEASE! Not so loud, everyone is looking at you,' a voice said quietly, but insistently, in Karin's ear. Somehow she managed to drag open her eyes—the lids felt like lead—and found herself staring up into the grubby face of a young boy of about twelve. The odour which came immediately to her nostrils made her grimace in disgust and she turned her face away . . . and then realised that the terrible smell was coming not only from him, but from the palliasse of dirty straw on which she lay and from her own clothing.

These were not her clothes! Trembling fingers touched the torn, blood-stained dress which barely covered her body, so ripped was it . . . It was of some plain, coarse material, as was the over-tunic of red cloth. Her skin crawled at the harshness of such apparel. She, who was accustomed to wearing silk against her soft skin, chiffon and muslin—only the best—reduced to the state of a . . . a what!

The opiate still dulled her brain, so that it was almost an hour before she found herself able to sit up and take stock of her surroundings and question the cheeky-faced urchin who sat cross-legged beside her, watching her every move. Slowly she lifted blank eyes to the grille door in front of her, forced them to wander around the tiny cell in which she was imprisoned.

Imprisoned! These were the cells below the palace. She had heard terrible tales of this place, but had never set foot in it before now. Imprisoned! Was she going mad?

'What am I doing here?' She turned on the boy fiercely, ignoring the dull thump in her head which made it so difficult to think. Her fingers strayed again, almost in disbelief, to the clothes she wore and were instantly withdrawn with a shudder of disgust. What was happening to her?

'Keep your voice low, lady. Sayid Badir told me to tell you to speak only English from now on, lest the other prisoners betray you when we are released.'

'Prisoners! Released!' she echoed, not understanding, her reply still in Arabic. The boy inclined his head to one side, and she glanced up. The pitifully small cells on either side of her were full of people—dirty, unkempt men who squatted on their heels, staring at her. Women with long, matted hair, torn clothes, young children clinging to their bodies . . . the stench was indescribable! Christian prisoners! Suddenly it was all too horribly clear. This was how her father intended her to be found and returned to her own people! These were not her people! She was Karin, daughter of Badir the Great, and would always consider herself so. She would not allow herself to be taken by Crusader soldiers who would use her for their own pleasure and then discard her. She was a high-born lady and commanded respect wherever she went!

'Lady . . . *Sitt* . . .' the boy said, seeing the rebellion sparking through the dullness of her eyes. 'Do not even think it, or we are both dead! I have sworn to

protect you with my life . . . I would not have one, had
I not,' he added with uncommon honesty. 'I am Omar,
the thief.'

'You sound proud of the fact,' Karin said icily, only
just remembering to keep her voice low so that no one
heard them conversing in Arabic. 'I am not accustomed to mixing with thieves, or . . . or rabble . . . or
Christians . . .'

'Then you will have to get used to it. At least until
the city is taken, and from what I hear, that will not be
long.' The boy gave a shrug, unconcerned by her
high-handed tone. 'And speak in English. Some of
these dogs have ears like desert rats.'

'I am not English—How dare you presume to give
me orders?' Karin snapped.

'You are an Englishwoman taken at the fall of
Jerusalem,' Omar told her solemnly. 'My life as well as
yours depends on your remembering what I tell you. If
the Unbelievers do not kill me, Sayid Badir surely will
if I do not protect you as I promised. And as for Sayid
Ayub . . .'

'Ayub?' she breathed, hope rising inside her. 'He
has been here? Did you see him?'

'They dragged him away, cursing his father like a
madman when he saw you. Luckily everyone else
thinks he was angry because he wanted you for his
harem. None of them has guessed the truth.'

Truth, Karin thought dazedly. She no longer knew
what was true or false! But she was sure of one thing.
She could not, would not, stay in this godforsaken
place. Weakly she climbed to her feet, aware of a
stirring of interest among the other prisoners as she

lurched unsteadily towards the door. Omar caught at her skirt, but she brushed away his hands and beat clenched fists against the solid oak panels until she was exhausted, but no one came. No one answered her pleas, her demands, her threats. Finally she allowed herself to be drawn away, back to the disgusting pile of straw, where she collapsed in tears, not caring if anyone saw her.

'*Sitt*, what am I to do with you?' the boy whispered as she lay weeping silently into her hands. They were bruised and cut from the pounding, and began to throb maddeningly. 'We shall both lose our heads if you go on like this. There is nothing you can do about it, so accept what is to happen to you and allow us both to live a little longer in the shadow of Allah the Merciful.'

'Merciful? He has abandoned me, as my father and brother have abandoned me,' Karin cried. Omar turned to the curious faces directed their way, and made a sign with his fingers against his head to indicate that she was quite mad. She flushed at the gesture and drew back her hand to strike him . . . and then realised what a futile gesture that would be. Accept it, he told her. What other course of action was open to her? If she wanted to live to see Badir and Ayub again, she must carry through the deception. Only when she had been freed from this place could she find them in safety, and demand an explanation for what they had done to her.

She slept, without wanting to, but too weary to fight off the semi-conscious state which overtook her. She dreamed again, and awoke drenched in sweat in the dead of night. The cells were very dark inside. The only light, a faint glow through the barred grille, came from pitch torches on the walls in the passage outside. How long must she bear this indignity—this torture? Omar slept curled up a few feet away from her, his curly head resting upon his hands. He had been set to watch over her—a child protector of Badir's daughter! If she had not been so afraid of what the future held for her, she would have laughed at the situation.

Occasionally a guard stopped outside and peered through at them, but she made no attempt to communicate with him, afraid of the eyes she knew were always on her. How long must she wait before she gained her freedom . . . ?

Acre did not surrender to the opposing forces immediately, as Rollo and the whole army thought it would. Surrender terms were tossed backwards and forwards between the Governor, Kara Kush, and Guy de Lusignan. Between Guy and Conrad of Montferrat, and Philip of France and Richard of England. The first offer, of over two hundred Christian prisoners, was refused. The next offer was an improvement, and received a far better reception. Two thousand Christian prisoners and a handsome ransom for the return of the garrison of soldiers at Acre. Also the wood of the True Cross, lost at the battle of Hattin, when Jerusalem fell.

The terms were agreed. Acre surrendered to the Crusaders, who streamed into the city, banners and pennants flying in the wind. Standards were planted against the thick walls in triumph as thousands of inhabitants left their homes to seek refuge elsewhere, leaving behind them everything they possessed for the invaders to plunder and loot and enjoy for themselves. By the evening of the twelfth of July, the Christian flags flew high over the city and every wall was manned by soldiers from France, or Germany, Italy or England.

On the heights of Tell Keisan, Saladin watched with a heavy heart, suffering a humiliation such as he had never experienced before at this unexpected blow. His fleet had failed to break the Frankish blockade, and with Acre now in Christian hands, he dared not risk an all-out attack, even though he now had the men. He had seen what the siege-machines had done to his troops, had heard of the heavy casualties inflicted by Malvoisin. He would not risk a confrontation now. Let the enemy enjoy their moment of victory. It would be short lived. They would not be content with Acre, these bold warriors who came to take back the Holiest of Holies—the city of Jerusalem—but Jerusalem was a long way off, and Saladin's army would be in front of them, beside them, at the back of them when they emerged from the safety of the city's walls. No, for the moment he would allow his men to rest and regroup. Time was on his side—Allah was on his side—the side of the righteous.

Five days of confinement in this stinking cell. Five days of semi-starvation, being fed swill she would never have given to pigs, let alone human beings! How the others grovelled on their knees, like animals, fighting among themselves to be the first at the plates.

Even the woman and children scrabbled like savages
for a mouthful of slop! Karin turned her face away
from the disgusting spectacle. She was so weak that
she could hardly move. She did not know that the
opiate was still administered to her in the drinking-
water brought twice a day. She had never wondered
why she and Omar had separate drinking-vessels, but
was merely grateful that she did not have to sup from
the same cup as the little thief. Strangely enough, she
was growing rather fond of the scamp. He was rude
beyond redemption, and his manners . . . He was a
street-urchin and proud of it, and even seemed to look
down his nose at her when she reprimanded him for
his atrocious behaviour. But that had been in the
beginning, when she still had a little spirit inside her.
That had long since died from lack of food and the
unsanitary conditions in which she existed. There
were nights when she dreamed she was in her old
apartments, dressed in fine silks, with Celine waiting
on her, another maid painting her toenails and finger-
nails. Afterwards she would go down to the gardens
and swim in the tiled pool surrounded by sweet
jasmine bushes and oleanders. Each time she awoke to
the smell of herself, and the other wretches about her,
she died inside a little more.

She had been abandoned! She accepted it at last.
Accepted also, that she was in no condition to defend
herself against any attack from the soldiers when they
came into the city. To them she would be just another
woman, to be used and abused and tossed to one side
when her usefulness was over. Surely her father and
Ayub had considered this? Did neither of them care?

'Don't cry, lovely lady.' Omar's brown eyes were full of pity as he dragged himself across to where she sat against the wall, tears rolling unchecked over pale cheeks, her head resting against the cracked and disfigured stones. Many bore markings on them. Names, she supposed of other prisoners who had been before her . . . had perhaps perished in this very cell. Dates, too, even poems . . .

'Lovely?' Karin gave a tight smile. 'Your eyes deceive you, boy.' Her hair was loose about her shoulders, unkempt and tangled. One shoulder was bare, where the ill-fitting dress continually slipped away, to reveal a rounded shoulder and the rise of a breast. There was dirt on her face and arms, her hands were caked in it. The night before, she had used the drinking-water to try and wash some of it from her, but it clung to her skin like pitch and now she was parched, for she had not had a drink since then. The guards were late this morning . . . they usually came before this. She would die of thirst before they did, she thought wretchedly.

'It will be over soon—You'll see.'

'No. It will begin.' He looked at her, not understanding, and she shook her head, finding it difficult to find the right words in English. They had conversed in no other tongue for days. Already she was beginning to feel isolated, estranged from the world she had always known, and it frightened her.

'I do not understand you,' Omar said, tilting his head to one side. 'Are you not pleased that you will live? Does life mean so little to you? It is everything to me. I would do anything to keep it—I shall even grovel

at the feet of the Crusaders if it means that my head
will not be parted from my body.'

'It is different for you,' she said dully. How could a
mere child understand?

'Because you are a woman? I should have thought
the advantage was yours. You are not unattractive,
lady. Use the talents Allah gave you not only to
gain your freedom, but to keep it. Most men are soft-
hearted when they see tears in the eyes of a pretty
woman.'

'Be—Be nice to them?' she echoed, eyes widening in
horror. 'You forget who I am.'

'No, *sitt*, you do,' the boy said seriously.

'I don't even remember the name I was given,' Karin
said, with a shrug of a bare shoulder. 'And I care not.'

'You are the Lady Alee-sander de Greveele
Weenter.' Omar had great difficulty in pronouncing
the strange-sounding name, and her brows puckered
in a frown, for she was barely able to understand him.
Wait, now, she remembered . . . but it was so difficult
to gather her thoughts together. Badir's pronunciation
had been quite different.

'Alisandre de Greville-Wynter,' she repeated softly,
almost to herself. What a silly name. She liked Karin
much better.

'As I said, Lady Alle-sander.' She nodded, not
wishing to hurt his feelings further by correcting him
again. 'It is good you remember it.'

There came a loud commotion from the corridor
outside, shouting, and the grating of doors being
opened. People were herded from the open cells on
both sides of her. She could hear some of the women

weeping, the raised voices of children as they were separated from parents.

'What is happening?' she gasped. Omar ran to the door and craned his neck to stare after them. Apart from a very old woman who sat hunched up in one corner, they were alone. She felt an icy hand clutch at her heart. Had the time come? Was the Christian army already in Acre?

'They are being taken outside, lady. It is very noisy in the streets . . . I think Acre has surrendered.'

The door was flung open so violently that Omar was sent sprawling back onto the dirty floor. Two Nubian slaves armed with curved scimitars entered, carrying the limp body of a man between them. Unceremoniously he was tossed on the ground not far from where Karin sat, not daring to move. What now?

'The final touch, for when you are found. They might suspect something if you were discovered with only this little sneak-thief for company,' Badir said quietly from the doorway. Karin tried to gain her feet, but the days of starvation and privation had taken toll of her strength, and the effects of the opiate lingering in her body, had done the rest. With a cry she sank back against the wall, tears of helplessness springing to her eyes.

'Father, I beg you, don't leave me here for them to find. I will do anything you want, or go anywhere . . . Do not do this terrible thing to me!' she pleaded. The hard features before her did not soften. Badir's face remained bleak and pitiless.

'I have done what has to be done. The rest is up to you and this little sneak-thief here. He will try to stay with you and guide you over the first days . . . they will be the most difficult . . .'

'Father . . .' Her voice was hardly audible. Tears welled down over her cheeks, leaving pale streaks on her dirty skin. She did not even attempt to wipe them away. She no longer cared. Omar had said that most men could be swayed by the tears of a woman, but he did not know Badir!

'I have no daughter. May the shadow of Allah remain over you until you are safely back among your own, child.'

The door slammed behind him. She heard the massive bars thrust home across it. Her eyes finally forced themselves to look at the still figure of the man on the dungeon floor. He had been young in life, perhaps twenty or a little more. There was a gash on one side of his head, and the blood had welled into the material of his pale grey surcoat, and dried. It was clear that he had been dead for at least a day, for his limbs were stiff. One hand was curved into a grotesque claw.

Omar began to search through his clothing, and she watched for several minutes before realising what he was doing. 'Stop it, you little fiend! Get away from him! Do you rob even the dead?'

'He's a Christian, lady. They always have gold on them!'

'Leave him in peace, or when we are freed I shall tell the soldiers you murdered him when he awoke and caught you trying to rob him,' she threatened. 'Then you will surely lose your head.'

'And so will you, if I betray you,' Omar returned,

his small eyes narrowing to pinpoints. She merely shrugged, and he realised that she did not care what happened to her. With a sigh, he withdrew to another wall and squatted on his heels, watching her. 'When we are found, there will be no one to dispute your story,' he said, motioning with his head to the empty cells on either side of them. 'Sayid Badir has thought of everything.'

Yes, Karin thought bitterly, wishing it was dark so that she could not see the dead Crusader. Everything to be rid of her . . .

The noise from outside grew. She felt herself beginning to grow faint as the heat intensified. This, together with the terrible strain on her nerves, brought them to snapping-point. Voices from the corridor! What now? More corpses to give substance to her claim she was some English girl, a prisoner of the Saracens for four years? She would never be able to carry off the deception.

'In here, my lord! A woman and a boy . . .' someone shouted, and faces peered through the grille at her. She closed her eyes and found herself praying to Allah to guide her through the next few moments . . . She was so terrified she could not move, or speak.

'Lady . . .' Omar murmured warningly in English as the door swung open, and figures in chain-mail poured in. She screamed as someone caught hold of her and pulled her to her feet. 'Don't hurt her, gracious lord, she has suffered enough. Her brother lies dead at her feet!' he cried, horrifying Karin with the blatant lie.

'A pretty wench, beneath the dirt . . . Sweet Jesus,

the stench in here . . . Get out before we are suffocated!' an English voice close by Karin's ear ejaculated.
She twisted around to stare at the face of the man who
held her. He towered over her. She could see little of
his features, for the protective coif of mail which
covered his head also obscured most of his face. His
skin, what she could see of it, was deeply tanned. One
of the many who had been a long time in the Holy
Land, she surmised. It was a hard face, with deep lines
etched either side of the lean mouth. But it was the
eyes which arrested her attention and caused a
shudder to run through her weakened body. They
were the palest green she had ever seen, and as cold as
ice. A humourless smile twisted the mouth for a brief
moment.

'You are in no danger from me, girl. Besides, I like
my women to smell a little sweeter than you do,' came
the barbed insult which was the final injustice
wrought upon her and broke the last thin threads of
her self-control. She screamed at him and raked at the
exposed part of his face with her nails. He swore as she
drew blood, and cuffed her sharply on one side of the
head. She folded in his arms like a rag doll, barely
conscious.

'Kill me,' she moaned. 'I care not . . .' She felt
herself swung up into a pair of strong arms. The links
of his chain-mail were rough against her bare skin, but
she scarcely noticed the pain as she was borne quickly
away from the dungeons, up the winding flight of
stairs which led to the upper part of the palace. She
could hear the man who held her calling for the boy to
be brought along too—and the body of the dead

Crusader to be removed for burial. He was someone of importance, which was probably why he had not handed her over directly to his men. Knights and officers always had the first pick of the women.

She tried to move, but was held too tightly. Her head fell back against his shoulder, and for a moment those green eyes bored down into the depths of her very soul.

'Poor little thing, you've had a hard time, haven't you?' The gentleness of his tone took her completely by surprise, for it did not go with the grimness of that dark face. She fought against the confusion his words evoked, reminded herself he was the enemy, and did not warm to them. That was what he wanted . . . to throw her off her guard so that she would be more receptive to his advances when he chose to make them.

'Omar—The boy,' she whispered, using the tongue in which she had been addressed. 'He . . . He was good to me. He bribed the guards for food . . . for us . . . my brother . . .' Her voice faltered and broke. She did not know how to lie. It had never been necessary before. The man gave a curt nod.

'He will not be harmed. No more will you. None of my men will lay a finger on you, so you can rest easy on that score.' He halted for a moment, and stared about him. They were in the gardens, Karin saw, and his gaze was directed at Tamir's house. 'Chavo, over there! Bring the boy. It will serve to house us until we leave.' Another Crusader, following close behind, wearing the same colours of black and silver on his white surcoat with the traditional red cross on his left shoulder, was ordered, 'Siward, my Guard will mount a personal watch about the place. Once this has been done, the rest of the men will encamp near by. We shall go to greet the King when he enters the city. Tell them it is a fine city, and the women are some of the choicest in the land, but they will not have the chance of either until I give the word. Anyone who disobeys me . . .' The sentence was left unfinished, and again Karin felt a shudder run through her. Already his thoughts were of women and booty . . . What chance would she have against him?

She raised her head as they neared the house. From beyond the garden walls came the sound of shouting, then cheering, but nothing to indicate if the remaining garrison of Muslim soldiers had attempted to put up a fight. Where were Badir, her father, and Ayub? Never would she be able to think of them as anything but her family, no matter what happened to her. Where would she be taken? England? A strange land where she knew no one. She wanted to stay here.

A scream rose in her throat. The man carrying her shifted his hold suddenly, caught her by the back of the neck and thrust her face against his surcoat—so that her cheek rested against the Crusader cross sewn on one shoulder of it—but not before she had seen the dead bodies of her servants scattered before the house. Little Jina, the newest addition to the household, who always attended her at bath-time. Datu, the Nubian, his sword still in its scabbard at his waist, cut down before he could even draw it . . . and others, lying where they had fallen.

Then there was a darkness, until she recovered to

find herself lying on a divan in one of the lower rooms.
The knight who had carried her from the dungeons
was forcing a goblet against her lips. She gulped at the
cool wine, drank thirstily, and then pulled back from
him, her expression accusing.

'Murderers! How could you? Women . . . slaughtered! You are all animals!'

'You are mistaken. This was not our work, though
why you should be concerned for the very people who
have held you in captivity is beyond me.' He stepped
back from her with a frown, poured more wine into
the goblet and drank from it himself. In the smallness
of the room he was even taller and broader than she
had at first thought. He reached up and swept back the
coif to reveal hair as black as a raven's wing, cropped
short about his head and neck, contrary to the fashion
which favoured it worn considerably longer. His gaze
searched her pale face. 'Perhaps you were not always
so badly treated. I have known of women taken
prisoner who have made life easier for themselves
by becoming—shall we say—accommodating to the
enemy . . .'

Karin stared at him for a full minute before understanding, and then her cheeks began to burn with the
insinuation that she had sold her body for momentary
comfort. That might be the way of Christian women,
but it was not hers!

'Lord, she is as innocent as the day she was born.'
From the back of the room, Omar came sliding down
on his knees before the tall Crusader. 'It was because
she would not agree to go into the harem of a mighty
lord that she was confined in such conditions. And her

poor brother, in trying to defend her . . .' The boy lifted his shoulders meaningfully. Karin hid her face in her hands, unable to watch him and his convincing performance. Not only a thief, but a skilful liar . . . once again forced to resort to living by his wits. But this time he was helping her, and to utter one word in retrospect would cause the death of them both, she had no doubt. 'Do not speak harsh words to her! Can you not see the distress she is suffering? Her poor brother dead . . . Her own life in jeopardy . . .'

'How so, boy? From us? Have we not just rescued her from the pit of hell?'

'Yes, gracious lord. But your men are not like you— a knight, a man of honour! This is a great lady, and I wish only to be her servant—to serve her, now that she is free, and repay the kindness shown to me during our long months of imprisonment together.'

'Lady?' For the first time, Rollo considered the evil-smelling, wretched creature he had carried from the palace dungeons. A lady beneath the dirt and grime? Perhaps, but it would take three hours' soaking to reveal anything closely resembling a woman. Her hair was matted, her face streaked with tears, her finger-nails caked with dirt and sand. His eyes narrowed fractionally as they considered the broken nails, still bearing traces of henna, as did the toenails protruding from worn leather sandals. He knew it had become the custom for some Christian women while in this land to follow the traditions of their counterparts, the Muslim women, and one of these was a great desire to paint their nails and blacken their eyes with kohl. By heaven! They were both lying to him! 'Does the lady

have a name? No, let her speak for herself. I have
never met such a reticent reception—Not even a
"Thank you" for saving you from harem life . . .' His
voice was heavy with sarcasm.

Karin straightened on the couch. There was something lurking in the depths of those eyes she did not
like—something that roused her from her stupor. She
was supposed to be an English girl, and the English
were a proud race, their women haughty. She fixed
the man with a cold stare, and said bitingly, 'My name
is Lady Alisandre de Greville-Wynter, and I am not
accustomed to being addressed as if I was a servant-
girl at your bidding. And you?'

Rollo's eyes gleamed, but he kept a tight rein on his
temper, despite the bitter memories which arose in
him at the sight of her haughty look. It had been a long
time since any woman had dared to speak to him in
such a fashion or glare at him as if he were a nobody. It
reminded him of what he was . . . of the past which he
successfully kept in the deep recesses of his mind . . .
She would soon learn, if she did not take care with her
words, that he was not a man who took kindly to the
arrogance of a fickle woman.

'Rollo, Duke of Aquitaine. Lord of Shah'mat, my
lady. De Greville-Wynter, did you say? A coincidence,
of course . . .'

'Coincidence?' Karin felt Omar's eyes fasten on her,
the look in them warning her to take care in what she
said.

'Yes. There is a Hugo de Greville-Wynter with the
army of King Richard. A relative, perhaps?'

'I—I . . .' Karin raised a hand to her eyes, suddenly

growing very hot and uncomfortable. She began to sway . . . It was no act, although it did have the lucky effect of completely diverting Rollo from his line of questioning. He wheeled about on the silent squire standing behind him.

'Take two men and go through the house, Chavo. Find rooms for Lady Alisandre. The boy can stay with her—for the moment. Rooms for us, too. See if there are any servants alive who can tell us what happened here. Join me with the King when it is done.' He turned back to Karin, who lay watching him in silence, her head supported by a cushion Omar had tucked solicitously beneath it. Like a pair of conspirators, he thought. What was it he did not know about them both? Perhaps someone among the other prisoners could enlighten him.

'When Chavo has found somewhere for you, I suggest you bathe, and then rest until I return. Have no fear that anyone will intrude on your privacy. My Guard are about the house and will allow no one to enter.' *Or leave,* she thought, inwardly trembling at his words. She was still a prisoner, but at least she had Omar. She was not alone, and perhaps somehow they could devise a way to escape from the city and get to Jyira. She had no intention of leaving her father or Ayub or the land where she belonged. It was unthinkable even to consider it.

'You are most thoughtful, Lord Rollo,' she murmured. 'If—If my manner has been . . . somewhat strange, please forgive me. To be free again! I cannot believe it . . .'

'Of course.' He did not believe her, but his tone did

not betray the fact. 'Until later, then.'

He did not wait for an answer, but turned on his heel and left her. Alone with the realisation of what had befallen her, Karin wept, and nothing Omar could say or do gave her comfort.

It was dark outside the house. From the direction of the streets came the sound of revelry, shouting and laughter; noises which indicated that heavy carts and wagons were being brought into the city. The Christian army was making itself at home, Karin thought, her heart sad as she surveyed the flickering lights in the distance. These came only from the bivouacs of the soldiers who remained outside the city walls to combat any unexpected attack from the army of Saladin. Did they know that he was no longer a threat to them, she wondered, at least not for the moment? Beyond their encampment, the countryside was dark, with no sign of any other fires. Saladin had melted away into the vastness of the countryside about him. Taking Badir and Ayub? She prayed not.

Gradually she was beginning to recover from her ordeal. Unknowingly, the squire had brought her to her very own rooms. It seemed an eternity since she had last stood on the balcony and breathed in the fragrance of the night flowers, she thought, but in fact it was little more than a week. Seven days since she had stood with Ayub and discussed the surrender of Acre. She remembered her brave words, that she would fight at his side rather than be parted from him. *Oh, my brother, how I need your strength now*, she murmured.

'Did you speak, my lady?' Chavo looked across at her. He had arranged a bath for her, and while he had been doing this she had 'found' the assortment of clothes in the closets and pretended great excitement at being able to don fresh, clean apparel. She had been careful in her choice. A sleeveless robe in saffron yellow with an over-mantle of deep blue, edged with gold, and golden sandals. As she lazed in the scented water, it was difficult to forget that she was no longer Karin but the Lady Alisandre de Greville-Wynter. More than once she had had to bite her tongue to stop herself calling out to little Jina to bring more hot water, for Celine to come and dry her and brush out her hair.

And then, as she was drying herself, she heard a commotion in the other room. Karin stepped out, swathed only in a large towel, to find Celine thrust to her knees before Chavo, begging for her life. She had hidden when the soldiers searched the palace, she cried. She had been abandoned by her master and was in fear for her life. And then, seeing Karin, she screamed at her to help her, swore to serve her faithfully if she would intervene . . . Karin needed no prompting.

'I shall take the girl as my maid,' she told Chavo in a tone that belied argument. 'After all, I have no one to care for me.'

The look on the squire's face told her that he was in a quandary as to what to do, and without Rollo to give him explicit orders, he overcame his natural dislike of anything and anyone not Christian like himself and agreed to the request. Or was it a demand, he wondered, as he looked into Karin's set features? But it was a blessing in disguise, he decided, when Karin was ushered back into the other room for her toilette to be completed. She was a lady, after all, and a lady required servants. Even a Muslim one was better than none, and so long as she gave no trouble he saw no harm in it—at least until Lord Rollo returned.

They had no chance to converse, for Chavo remained close at hand until Karin showed herself again. She tried to compose herself, calm her wildly beating heart as she stood on the balcony looking out over the palace gardens. Yet how could she hide her emotions! She was bursting with anger and hatred for the men who roamed at will throughout the palace and gardens, staring at her with rude eyes whenever she showed herself. Only the presence of the Guard of the Duke of Aquitaine kept them from becoming bolder, she was sure. Had she not been protected . . .

Chavo came to her side, frowning as he saw her shudder. 'You are cold, my lady. Come inside. Will you have a little wine to warm you?' He could hardly believe that this elegantly robed young woman was the same pathetic creature his lord had carried into the house. She was beautiful! Her hair shone in the lamplight, her skin still glowed from the hot bath. She moved now with grace and confidence, and her eyes had lost that terrible hunted look . . . it had reminded him of a trapped animal.

'No, I want nothing, except to know what is to happen to me,' Karin said, determined not to allow herself to like this helpful young man. He was no older than she was, but so much more experienced in the ways of the world, she suspected. But he did not look at her with the same boldness as his master had done. He sympathised with her plight. Perhaps she could make use of that—and of him—if it became necessary. She was appalled at how deviously she had begun to think. Omar never stopped warning her of the consequences if it was discovered she had been living as the daughter of Badir the Great for the past four years. If she was not used as a hostage to be ransomed, another use would be found for her—especially now that it could be seen what a prize she was.

'Happen to you? That is up to Lord Rollo, my lady, but you have nothing to fear. He means to speak to the King—King Richard. Before long you will find yourself on a ship going home. How I envy you! Back to England—to the green fields, reasonable weather . . . your own people.'

If she heard those words 'your own people' again, she would scream, Karin decided, her small mouth tightening. Chavo looked at her perplexedly, not understanding why she showed so little excitement at the prospect. And then he thought he understood, and sought to reassure her further.

'Ah, your brother. He will have a Christian burial tomorrow. I am sure Lord Rollo will allow you to pay your last respects to him—if it will not upset you too much. It would be better to try and forget the misery of what you have endured, my lady, if that is at all possible. It is over now. Think only that you are going home . . .'

'I—I cannot remember it . . .' Karin said brokenly, and Chavo's face registered astonishment.

'Not remember England? What of your family? Mother? Father?'

She searched her mind for the things Badir had told her, and turned away, as if confused. 'I have no memory beyond the day Jerusalem fell. No family . . . they were killed in the fighting. I remember only a terrible fire . . . my name being called . . . and then . . . that awful dungeon. Not that one at first,' hastily she corrected herself, as he frowned. 'Nothing is very clear, even now. My brother and I were imprisoned with many other people . . . to be ransomed, I suppose. Since we were not, I must suppose we have no family to do so. We might have rotted in that cell to our dying days . . . He did. Messire, forgive me, I cannot talk of it more. Not now . . .'

'Indeed you must not. Rest, and I shall come back later. Are you sure you wish the girl to remain? I do not trust her willingness to help. She may wish you harm . . .' He lingered by the doorway, staring across at the olive-skinned servant turning back the covers of the bed.

'The will to survive can be very strong. I think she will serve me rather than throw away her life—as the boy now does,' she returned, forcing a smile to her lips. It was the first time she had felt like smiling in seven hellish days, but now she had a reason. 'But you may leave me a weapon, if you like. A dagger will suffice.'

Chavo hesitated, but Lord Rollo had not given orders she was not to be allowed to protect herself— and he was already beginning to have fanciful dreams about this vision of loveliness. When he became a

knight, in two or three days, he might find the courage
to ask if he could wear her colours. Every knight had to
have a lady to protect. The Duke would not desire the
honour—his opinion of women was not repeatable,
and his treatment of the majority of them left much to
be desired. He was too bitter and full of malice towards
every one of them. But he did have good cause . . .

He gave her the silver-hilted dagger he carried, bade
her good night and left her. Karin waited a full minute
before throwing herself across the room into Celine's
arms. They cried unashamedly on each other's
shoulders, while Omar kept watch to ensure they
were not disturbed and turned up his nose at such a
disgusting show of emotion. For the past hour Karin
had been forced to hold back her questions, and show
no signs of relief at the miraculous escape of her
friend. She had almost betrayed herself with joy when
they came face to face again.

'Tell me again,' Karin insisted, pulling Celine down
beside her on the bed. She reverted to Arabic, and kept
her voice low. 'My servants . . . What happened to
them? Where is Lord Badir, and my brother, Ayub?'

'He is not your brother, mistress,' the woman
began, and then was silent as Karin fixed her with a
stern look.

'I will know no other . . . nor any other father. As
soon as an opportunity arises, I shall escape from here
and return to Jyira. You may accompany me if you
wish, or stay here with these animals who call themselves men.'

'It was on the orders of Lord Badir himself that your
servants were killed,' Celine whispered, and Karin

gave a cry of disbelief. 'He thought it necessary. No one who knew who you were was to remain alive. When I overheard him discussing it with Lord Ayub, I ran and hid myself in the secret room—as we had intended to do, do you remember?'

Karin nodded. 'Before you drugged me and I was taken to that horrible place. How could you do such a thing to me, Celine? You have no idea what it was like . . . the filth, the smell, the wretchedness of those other poor creatures down there . . .' She broke off, realising for the first time that she did not feel hate for the other Christian prisoners, but pity. Would they have felt any for her, had they known her true identity, she wondered? She doubted it.

'Lord Badir would have had me killed and someone else administer the draught to you had I not agreed. I would have found you, I swear it. I saw you brought out of the palace, and that is how I came to be here. I could not leave you, mistress.'

'Thank you. I am in need of a true friend. I know not where to turn any more.'

'And that one?' Celine looked at the boy hovering by the silken curtains. 'Are we to trust him?'

'With our lives, as he trusts us with his,' she answered. 'He intervened with the Crusader who found me, this Duke of Aquitaine. I like him not. The way he looks at me . . . I did not know what to say to him. It was Omar who spoke up for me when fear took my tongue.'

'Do you think you are believed?'

'I do not know. Celine, tell me true, what do you know about me? Am I Badir's daughter? I can remember nothing before my illness four years ago. Tell me,' Karin pleaded.

Celine withdrew from her, a troubled look on her face. What to do for the best? The truth or more lies? Pain—or destruction of the world in which she had lived . . . among people she thought to be her own?

'Tell me,' Karin insisted. 'I will know.'

'Four years ago, a month after Jerusalem was returned into the keeping of Allah's servants, the Lord Badir brought you home to Jyira. Earlier that year he had lost his only daughter, whom he worshipped. He was heartbroken; no one could console him. And then, that day, he carried you into the house, half-dead and feverish, calling out strange names in your agony. You had not a hair on your head.'

Karin gasped, shutting off the sound behind her hand. She remembered none of this. Celine looked at her, seeking confirmation to continue, and she nodded.

'For three long weeks you hovered between life and death. He rarely left your side. You became the daughter he had lost. He gave you the name "Karin", and swore everyone to obedience to your every wish as if you were indeed his daughter. When sanity returned to your mind, he told you you had been ill and that was why your memory was affected.'

'I could not remember my name—or speak my own tongue . . .'

'Yes, that you could do, for it was English, the tongue of your parents who had died in their blazing house in Jerusalem. Arabic was taught you by Tamir ibn Dak. You had a quick mind and soon mastered it. The Lord Badir grew so proud of you. Before long it was as if two images merged in his mind—yours and hers. You were as one. You became Karin, daughter of Badir the Great, sister of Ayub . . . although *he* has never thought of you as such.'

'Why do you say such a thing?' Karin asked, a frown puckering her brows. 'Ayub has always been kind to me, and loving . . . Do not hesitate now, but tell me what you mean?'

'The Lord Ayub wishes to have you for his wife. His father refused permission time and time again. Once they almost came to blows over you. I heard them arguing while you were imprisoned, and then Ayub stormed out of here . . . It was the night before the city surrendered.'

'And my father?'

'Who knows? Among the many captives to be ransomed, perhaps. I shall try to discover his where-abouts, if you still wish to know.'

'Of course I do! It seems I must accept, whether I like it or no, that I am indeed English, Celine, but by birth only. My heart is not, and I have no memory of any other life except the one here. This is the way I wish to continue living.'

'Do not say so before the soldiers, or they will treat you as all other women in the city,' Celine warned. 'Even now they scour the streets in search of amuse-ment. No woman is safe without an escort. At least this lord who found you seems to be a man of in-fluence. He will protect you.'

'He will have his price, like all men,' Karin retorted,

remembering the way those pale eyes had dwelt on her. What would he think, now that she was clean and presentable?

The sound of voices outside made them draw apart. When Rollo entered the room with Chavo close on his heels, Karin was reclining on the bed, while the maid sat on the floor, apparently asleep.

He had discarded his armour and put on clean breeches and stockings, the latter bound with strips of leather. His surcoat was grey, this time, with the same coat of arms emblazoned in silver on the front. The Crusader cross was omitted. He still wore his long sword, she noticed, but at least he had discarded that deadly-looking axe before presenting himself again. *Caution*, a voice within her warned. *You cannot treat this man as you do all others. He owes no allegiance to Bakir, and is no friend of Ayub. He is master of himself and will take orders from no one, save perhaps his king.* As he came to stand by the bed, there was an arrogance in the dark face that re-aroused anger in her, and brought her to remember what was happening outside the safety of this house. His men would be among those carousing in the streets, making free with the women, looting and destroying property. All in the name of their Christian God!

'I am pleased to see you have recovered so quickly from your unpleasant ordeal,' Rollo said with a pleasant smile, but the eyes held no warmth, and indeed Karin saw a hint of suspicion lurking in their depths. At a single glance he took in her new clothes, his gaze lingering on the bareness of her arms and shoulders, the shapely ankles visible below her skirts.

She looked more like a harem woman awaiting her
master than some refined English rose who had just
gone through four years of suffering and grief. The
Saracens were not renowned for their humanity to
prisoners. Men were worked until they died under the
whip. Women—the pretty ones—found their way into
a harem or the bed of a wealthy merchant, and were
often sold off after a few years to someone new. They
aged quickly. This girl looked fresh and startlingly in
control of herself. During one year of imprisonment,
he had aged three.

Karin lowered her gaze before the unasked question
in his eyes. 'Your squire has cared well for me. Would
that I could reward him in some way, but as you know,
my lord, I have no possessions of my own to part with,
except this bracelet I wear. I cherish it dearly and
would hate to part with it.' She fingered the silver
filigree bracelet about one wrist.

Rollo had noticed it when he had first found her in
the dungeon, and wondered why someone had not
stolen it from her. Even with many of its stones
missing, what remained should have caught the eye of
a guard or a sneak-thief. It was only one of the many
things about her which troubled him. *What you had to
bargain with was used a long time ago*, he mused, allowing his eyes to dwell once more on the firm swell of her
breasts beneath the silken robe. She flushed and
looked away again, momentarily confusing him. She
acted the innocent well enough . . . Could he be
wrong? He gave Chavo a bleak look, as the young man
said quickly,

'I am pleased to serve you, my lady, after all you

have been through. No task is too great. You have only to command me.'

So she already had the gullible Chavo under her thumb. If she intended to try the same thing with him, she would be disappointed with the result!

'You have eaten, Lady Alisandre?' Rollo asked in the same polite tone, and she nodded. 'A pity. I was hoping you would join me tonight. Perhaps another time, when you are not so fatigued.' His mouth tightened as she deliberately smothered a yawn, indicating that his presence was no longer required. She acted the lady, all right! 'The woman goes with Chavo.' He saw Celine start, confirming his suspicion that she was not asleep.

Karin, too, was disturbed by the news. She sat up, demanding, 'Why? I need her.'

'The boy can stay, but not she. I do not trust her. My squire will see she comes to no harm, and she will be returned to you in the morning.'

Celine quickly scrambled to her feet and hurried towards the door, while Karin watched helplessly. She had the feeling that Rollo was waiting for her to protest more vigorously. Why should she, who had suffered at the hands of these people, care what happened to the woman . . . or to Omar? She must take more care—be more careful in the choosing of her words. As Celine drew level with Chavo, his hand fastened over her arm to hold her fast. Without a word he led her from the room. So that was the way of it, and she was beginning to like the squire! He was no different from the rest of them . . . no different from his master. No doubt he would do his share of celebrating with some women tonight . . .

'I do not possess the hatred for these people that you do, my lord,' she said, slowly rising to her feet. She had to stay in command of the situation and allay any suspicions he had of her, even if it meant being nice to him. The thought revolted her, but she was aware that she had not shown nearly enough gratitude to the man who had rescued her. 'Perhaps I should, but I know what they are suffering now, as I once did. It gives me no satisfaction to know that that poor woman will be abused.'

'A truly Christian attitude, but one which escapes me. I have seen too much death and bloody warfare to share it with you. But as for hating the enemy? No, I do not hate them. I respect them as a fighting force. I expect no mercy from them should I fall into their hands, and they receive none at mine.'

'How callous! What kind of man are you?' she cried, aghast, and he stepped towards her, catching her by the shoulders. She winced at the fierceness of his grasp and struggled to free herself, but was like a child in his hands.

'The kind that finds you attractive, my lady . . . and expects some kind of thanks for my gallant rescue. Come, now, have you nothing to offer me? Not even a kiss? Or have you expended all your charity on those who have gone before me?'

The insult cut deep. She threw back her head to challenge it, her eyes burning with blue fire. As he bent his head towards hers, Rollo found himself thinking he had never seen the like of them before. They

were the blue of the sea, the richness of sapphires . . .
Her mouth was stiff and cold beneath his. She twisted
and squirmed in his arms until he tightened his hold
and the pain forced her to be still.

His lips ground into hers in a kiss that shocked her
to the very depths of her soul with its passion and its
demands, and forced them apart with a ruthless pressure. She felt as if she were being suffocated, and
sagged weakly in his embrace, her limited strength
gone. Sensing the change in her, he eased her backwards until she felt the bed against her legs. Karin's
senses reeled as he lowered her onto it. Celine's dream
. . . it had to be. No! No, she would not allow it to
happen to her! If only she had something with which
to defend herself.

The dagger Chavo had given her—it was beneath
the pillows. Rollo felt her go limp beneath him, and
raised his head to stare down at her, surprised to see
she was smiling.

'Do you always make love to a woman wearing a
sword?' she enquired, her voice tinged with amusement. 'Am I such a danger to you, my lord?'

'Not to me,' he chuckled, releasing her to reach for
the fastenings of the girdle which held the sword
about his left hip. Karin waited until it fell to the floor,
then sent him reeling with a foot against his chest. It
was not a powerful thrust but it took him off balance,
and by the time he had recovered and lunged towards
her again, she had the dagger in her grasp. Drawing
herself back against the pillows, she held it before her
threateningly.

'I shall kill you if you touch me again . . .'

'You will try . . .' Rollo came closer and saw the fear which sprang to her eyes. They both knew that, if he chose, he could disarm her with ease.

'I am not one of your camp-followers!' She spat the words at him, pride and defiance blazing out of her lovely face. That did halt him in his tracks, and wipe some of the fury from him. It was a long time since he had thought any woman beautiful . . . longer still since he had considered their feelings above his own. He had been taught many years ago never to show that kind of weakness. Yet this woman before him was not only excitingly beautiful, but desirable, and Rollo was not usually a man to allow a show of resistance to deter him from his objective. A small trinket, a few sweet words, wine or a coin usually had the desired effect.

Yet now he was hesitating when he had only to reach out and pluck the weapon from her. He suspected she did not have the courage to use it, despite her brave words, and she certainly did not possess the strength to put up a great struggle.

Karin's fingers tightened round the hilt until he saw the knuckles grow white. With a cry she turned it about so that the blade was against her breast, where the gown had slipped from her shoulder in the struggle.

'What will your King Richard say in the morning when he discovers that a woman killed herself rather than be abused by the man supposedly acting as her rescuer? A grand knight—Duke of Aquitaine. A man of honour! Do you know the meaning of the word?'

'Stay your hand, girl, I'll not lay another finger on you,' Rollo growled, quickly moving back from the bed. 'And not because of that threat, either. Why should I waste my time with you when there are plenty of willing women waiting for me.' Retrieving his sword, he pushed aside the curtains, then turned and stared back to where she sat, hardly daring to believe she had won her fight. 'This time I shall leave . . .'

'There will not be another,' Karin said, and his eyes gleamed at the tremor in her voice.

'I think there will, my lady. I *know* there will . . . And the next time, neither your weapon nor your threats will stop me . . .'

'My lord.' Chavo stood by the couch where Rollo sat. He had been staring into the contents of his silver goblet for some ten minutes, unaware of the squire who came and went from the room. 'Are you joining the men? They expect it. In fact they are waiting for you.'

'Soon. Tell them I shall join them.' Chavo had the feeling that his lord cared not whether he joined them or not and that was unusual. Each enjoyed the company of the other. He did not understand Rollo's black mood this night. He had the pick of the choicest women in Acre, yet he made no move to select one. Until he did, his men would not make their choice. Chavo glanced over his shoulder towards the curtained area behind him.

'She sleeps?' Rollo questioned, his eyes narrowing at the movement.

'Ay, my lord, like an angel.' He ignored the twist which deepened Rollo's lips. 'Such a fine lady, do you not think?'

'A lady is not defined by the demureness of her smiles,' came the ungracious answer. 'I am not sure of this one. She looks to be half-starved, and mistreated. She has suffered the loss of a brother—or has she? Why should we take her word, Chavo?'

'Why should we question it, lord?'

'Why indeed? Something here . . .' Rollo laid a hand against his heart. 'No one expects a woman to have the courage of a man, or to fight against the Infidels as we would. Yet this one . . . It is a feeling, no more. We know their ways, do we not?'

'Ay, lord, better than most.' Chavo's nod affirmed that they had shared much together.

'So has she—or so she says. Yet, deep within me, I feel something is wrong. Watch her for me, every minute of the day. I rely on your judgment. You are young, Chavo, and she is pretty. Nay, beautiful, beyond the expectations of most men. Do not allow her to turn your head . . .'

'My lord,' the squire protested in indignation, and Rollo smiled at his pink cheeks.

'I know she will not persuade you with her smiles, but there is another here, one you have taken a fancy to, perhaps . . .' The young man's colour deepened, and Rollo nodded. 'Be careful. Take heed of what I say. Trust no woman.'

'I shall heed her, my lord, but I—I shall not treat her as others do. Must I abuse her because she is weaker than I? Must I make her afraid of the True Faith? How

can we convert others, when they are afraid of us? I
will not do it!'

Rollo looked at the stubborn expression, recalled
how Karin had looked with the knife against her
breast, and felt disgust at what he had become. Yet he
was unable to change. He looked into the face of his
squire and saw perhaps a chance for a new beginning.

'Go to her,' he said quietly. 'Try gentleness and
patience. Are we not all God's creatures?'

For several hours afterwards he sat in the darkness
of his rooms. Below somewhere he knew his men
were waiting for him to join them. He was tired of it all!
The killing in the name of God! The plunder, the
booty, the incessant desire to change one man's faith
to another's. Did it matter by what name God was
called? In the mosques of Islam he was Allah, and
Muhammad was his prophet. In the Christian world,
God, and Jesus, his son. He had not forgotten the wise
old man who had sought to teach him the 'true' faith
when he was a prisoner. At first he had listened,
because it took him away from the nightmare of the
work-parties that toiled under the excruciating heat—
and then something else had crept into his mind. A
desire to learn. To know more of the Infidel, the
enemy, in order to destroy him. And yet, in time, even
that had taken second place to the urge for new
knowledge. With it could he not teach his own people?
Could not two faiths live in peace? One God shared
between them?

He was a fool! Richard had showed him that!
The Infidels cared nothing for any other faith. The
prisoners they had released were shadows of

men, pitiful creatures who could scarcely see after being imprisoned in dungeons below ground since the fall of Jerusalem—or Acre, when most of them had been captured.

Yet *she* could see. Lady Alisandre de Greville-Wynter could see! He thought of the slender form encased in diaphanous silks, and anger began to rise within him. She was not what she said—he would stake his life on it! Yet, tomorrow, he was to go before King Richard and plead her cause. What cause? A name . . . that was all he had!

His men were waiting. He thought of Karin, and the knife against her golden skin, and wished with all his heart he had taken it from her and made her his. In over six years he had not looked at a woman and desired her as he did this one! The heat had affected him, he thought, as he rose to his feet and girded on his sword. What else could make him want a woman so? Half the camp was down with some malady or other. Why should he be different? Yet he was not one to desire just another woman—They came and went from his life without meaning, without memory. This one was different. He had looked at her and liked what he saw, yet he had left her to sleep alone.

He was mad! The sun had affected him. He had need of the company of his men and a willing woman. Tomorrow he would be himself again. Tomorrow he would deal with Lady Alisandre de Greville-Wynter, if that was her name. If not, it did not matter. She was a woman, and women mattered not one iota to him!

CHAPTER THREE

'YOU SAY she has no memory of anything before her capture?' Rollo drawled. 'How convenient.' He ignored the dusky-skinned woman vainly trying to distract his attention from the tiled pool below and the solitary swimmer diving and surfacing in the translucent water. He could see every curve of her body from where he stood—So could the men of his Guard on duty in the trees a few yards away, he mused, a tight smile tugging at his lips. Yet she did not seem to care who gazed on her.

His head ached from too much wine the night before. It had been dawn before he tumbled into bed with the woman at his side—and promptly fell asleep. He had been awakened by a veritable man-eater, who had left the marks of her long nails on his back from where they had made love. Still, she had kept his thoughts from Alisandre de Greville-Wynter for a short while at least. Now she was back in his thoughts—and in his vision . . . He liked what he saw, there was no denying that! How many had gone before him, he wondered? Saracen and Crusader? Wherever she had been for the past four years, it was not confined in the kind of place in which he had found her.

Neither her wrists nor her ankles bore any kind of chain marks. His still did, from the months of being manacled like an animal. Unconsciously his fingers strayed to his scarred wrists, running the calloused tips over the deep indentations. Yet not one blemish on her soft skin!

'Did you manage to find out anything from the other prisoners?' he asked at length. Leila the dancing-girl had given up trying to entice him and had gone back to the couch, where she lounged invitingly, her lower lip pouting as she stared at his broad back. He had made love to her, and she knew she had satisfied him. Had she not been trained to please a man? Yet now his mind was full of this unknown Englishwoman.

'I could find only two or three that remembered her; the others have all been dispersed among the camp. They said she had been brought to the dungeons a few days after they themselves were put there. Most had come from Ascalon and Jaffa.'

'Where did she come from?' Rollo asked, eyes narrowed against the glare of the mid-day sun as he stepped further out onto the balcony to watch Karin emerge from the water. Immediately she was swathed in an enormous towel by the waiting maid. Coincidence again? Only one of the household left alive— this woman called Celine. Was he imagining things, or was there an intimacy between them which would not have been possible had they just met, as each would have him believe. There was a possessive manner about the maid's actions, like a lioness guarding one of her young.

'No one is really sure, my lord. One man thought he heard her speak to the boy in Arabic, but he is old and rather confused,' Chavo said, following him. Below them, Karin had stretched out on some coloured cushions, and Celine was drying her hair. She was totally unaware of the two men above her.

'Did he now! How interesting. Have you heard her converse so, with either the boy or the maid?'

'No, Lord Rollo.'

'Then listen well to what passes between them. I want to know if she speaks their tongue—and, if so, how well.' Rollo returned inside and stared at the dancing-girl. 'Join the other women and come back tonight,' he ordered.

'I have pleased my lord, then?' Leila asked huskily, relief sweeping over her that she was not to be handed over to his men. This man was a knight, and a powerful one, from all she had heard. It would be good to keep his protection.

'You would not be coming back if you had not,' came the dry retort. She rose and came to him, and her lips lightly brushed across his. And then, with a soft laugh, she ran from the room in a swirl of dusty pink organza, leaving behind her in the air the heady scent of musk.

Karin sat up as a shadow fell across her, and instinctively clutched the towel round her more tightly. Celine continued to brush her hair. It was almost dry, and lay about her shoulders in soft ripples.

'I'm glad you are acclimatising yourself to a normal life again,' Rollo said, his tone heavy with sarcasm. He could not help himself. She aroused so many conflicting emotions inside him. A pale flush, not caused by the heat of the sun, tinged her cheeks. The blush of

colour on the golden skin was most becoming. Any
other man would have been speechless before her
beauty, a slave to her every whim, but Rollo was not
any man . . . He was a hard, embittered soldier, who
had seen much death and killed more men than he
cared to remember, including a man he had once
called friend, who had sought to take his life with an
attack from behind. Even badly wounded, he had
been more than a match for the treacherous cur! His
solitary existence, without close friends, or wife and
the joys of knowing a family, were of his own choice,
and he had no intention of altering the way he lived.
There were times when even Chavo, who had been at
his side through many battles and saved his life on
more than one occasion, was shut out of his empty
world. There was a part of him he could not share with
anyone . . . He did not know how, any more.

'I would hardly call this normal,' Karin retorted,
bristling inwardly at his tone. 'There are men—your
men—watching me from behind the trees.'

'They are there for your protection,' he told her
coolly, unperturbed by her manner. 'And to ensure
that no unauthorised persons gain entry to the palace
gardens now that the King and Queen are there. This
afternoon I am to present you to them, and to King
Richard's sister, Joanna. They are all curious about
your miraculous return among us and would have you
tell your story to them in person. But, I was forgetting,
you remember very little about your imprisonment. A
loss of memory, my squire tells me.'

'Yes. Apart from my name, I know nothing about
myself . . . only that my parents were killed in

Jerusalem,' Karin said, selecting her words with the utmost care.

'Did your brother not fill in the—gaps for you?' Rollo interrupted, a gleam stealing into his eyes.

She hesitated for a moment only, realising how foolish she had been to forget that she was supposed to have had a brother. Somehow she managed to stay calm and poised beneath the scrutiny of his green eyes.

'I thought him dead. We were separated for almost a year after our capture . . . and then kept in separate cells, when he—when he . . .' She muffled what sounded like a sob, and lowered her head as though in distress. 'If any of the guards so much as looked at me, he would fly into a rage and attack them . . . We were very close, you understand? I did not even know he had been brought with the other prisoners until they threw him into my cell. He had been wounded while trying to escape. He lasted a few hours only . . .'

'My poor lady, how you have suffered,' Chavo murmured, and received a glare from his master. There were times when he wished Lord Rollo still had a heart. This delicate little creature had been subjected to indignities and humiliation that would have broken a man, let alone a frail woman. Her courage was magnificent. He smiled at her, allowing her to see he, at least, was in sympathy with her. He smiled at Celine too, Karin noticed. A rather shy smile. She wondered what had taken place between them last night. Her maid's lips had remained sealed on the subject, and none of her own efforts to find out had succeeded.

'How—How long am I to remain in Acre, my lord?'

Karin asked, thinking it prudent to change the subject. She looked up into Rollo's dark features and was suddenly struck how handsome this man was. The aquiline bone structure betrayed noble blood, despite the rumour Celine had told her—that he was the illegitimate son of a great lord in France, but his mother had been nothing more than a village woman who had caught his eye.

The deep brown of his sunburnt features complemented the thatch of raven-black hair. She found it difficult to judge his age: somewhere in his middle thirties, or a little younger, she imagined. A much travelled man, she had heard, with a notorious reputation when it came to women. She could see why he would never have trouble finding one to accommodate his needs, Karin mused, watching him as he looked about him, acknowledging the four watchful men on guard with a nod of his head. Arrogant, masterful, so sure of himself . . . some women liked men that way. She hoped he would not consider her by the same standards as all his others conquests. She was the daughter of an Emir—no man touched her unless she wished it. No, she was forgetting . . . She was not Karin!

His pale eyes came to rest on her face again, and the sudden warmth which stole into her cheeks had nothing to do with the fierceness of the sunshine pouring down on her. When he looked at her, it stirred something in her . . . a feeling she had never experienced before with any man. She neither understood it—nor welcomed it from such a direction. It would be dangerous even to smile at him, for fear he mistook it for an invitation. Yet she could not deny what she experienced each time she found his gaze on her. It was like the flickering of a flame somewhere deep inside her—the beginning of a fire she must not allow to be fanned until it was out of control. Not with him! Not with the Lord of Darkness!

Rollo had been considering his reply. 'The army remains here until Saladin ransoms the Muslim garrison, and then we shall most likely move on towards Jerusalem. You will be sent back to England on the first available ship. Unless, of course, you are planning to remain out here . . . The King's sister and the Queen will be remaining, and there are several other ladies . . . some of the knights have their wives with them. Plenty of feminine chatter, should you require it . . .'

Karin was silent. She did not want to be sent to England, but how could she avoid it? Rollo was watching her closely, and sensed the indecision inside her. The thought of leaving worried—even frightened—her.

'I could speak with Queen Berengaria, if you wish. I am sure she would understand your desire to grow more acquainted with your own world once more before going home. All this must seem very strange to you after so long an imprisonment.'

'Indeed it does,' she quickly snatched at the bait he offered. Too quickly, he thought. An abandoned whore from someone's harem, or a spy, carefully planted among them? It was the first time he had ever considered that she might be something more deadly than just a wanton seeking to hide an unsavoury past in some Infidel's bed. 'Thank you, my lord, I would be

most grateful for your help. With my—my brother
gone, I have no one to turn to. I am so alone . . .'

'Consider yourself under my protection, Lady
Alisandre,' Rollo murmured with a smile. If she intended to remain in the vicinity of the army, he
wanted to know where she was every minute of the
day. 'Now I must try and find something more suitable for you to wear this afternoon. While the clothes
you have been wearing are most becoming, they
might tend to make—shall we say—the wrong impression on the King and Queen. We must present
you as a lady.' *Even if you are not*, he added silently to
himself.

Karin gave him her hand, and for a moment he laid
his lips against her fingers. After he had gone, she
found herself trembling. His touch had brought vividly back into her mind what had passed between
them the previous evening. Her lips still felt bruised
from the fierceness of his kiss, and there were small
dark smudges on her shoulders where he had held her
in his tight grip.

He was playing some game with her this morning.
He was too nice, and far too obliging. What did he care
what she looked like—He sought only to get her into
his bed! Behind her, Celine breathed a sigh of relief as
Rollo disappeared from sight, and she slipped the
dagger she held beneath a cushion, where Karin had
placed it earlier. She had vowed never to go anywhere
without it!

'What are you going to do?' Celine asked quietly.

'What can I do? I must meet this King Richard and
his Queen, and continue with this deception. Some-

how I have to make them like me—and after them—
him!'

'The Lord of Darkness? That's what he is called. He
has a terrible reputation with women, mistress. You
are not safe with him. I thought he meant to take you
last night when he sent me away.'

'He did, but I had other ideas . . . and my dagger
was all the persuasion he needed to change his mind,'
Karin answered, lying back on the cushions and closing her eyes against the bright sunlight. How wonderful it was to laze here after her imprisonment . . .
somehow, with the feel of the sun on her body, she
was not so afraid of what the future held for her. 'But I
have to make him trust me too, Celine. That should
not be too difficult—he is only a man. Arrogant and
brutish, like all Franks, but I shall win him over. When
he leaves Acre, I must go with him, and somewhere
along the way we shall melt into the night and return
to Jyira. Let me rest awhile. I must prepare myself for
this afternoon's encounter.'

'My Lord King, Queen Berengaria, Queen Joanna, this
is the Lady Alisandre de Greville-Wynter, of whom I
have already spoken to you,' Rollo said, bowing low
before the three seated figures. The room was full of
people grouped around the King and the two Queens,
and standing on both sides of him and the woman
whose hand he tightly held.

Alisandre heard the murmur which ran through the
onlookers as she went down into an elaborate curtsy
that she had practised time and time again before the
mirror. She had hardly recognised herself when

Celine had finished dressing her. The gown she wore was of flame-coloured silk, with a jewelled girdle about her tiny waist. The sleeves, tight from shoulder to elbow, widened suddenly until they became so long that they almost touched the floor. Her hair had been secured into two thick plaits and bound with scarlet ribbon. On her feet were red shoes of leather, decorated with gold. Her head was covered by a white wimple, which accentuated the pallor of her cheeks.

Rollo felt her tremble, and darted a quick look into her face. If this was an act, it was a good one. She looked as if she was about to faint. He, too, had been taken aback by the woman who had been waiting for him. She looked every inch a lady in that brilliantly coloured gown which moulded the contours of her figure and fell in sweeping folds about her feet. She straightened, and he saw her shoulders stiffen; he sensed that she was steeling herself to remain composed. She was no coward!

'Ah yes, the mysterious beauty you have been hiding away for yourself,' Queen Joanna murmured, pushing back a stray lock of her own bright red hair. 'I now can see why, can you not, brother?'

'Indeed I can.' Richard, King of England, leaned forward in his velvet-padded chair to gaze at the man and woman before him. He was now in his thirty-fourth year, married for only a few months to the quiet figure of Berengaria of Navarre seated on his left. He was a tall man and well built, with striking red-gold hair and moustache and brilliant blue eyes. Eyes that now held a hint of amusement as they rested on Karin. 'I hope this knight finds favour in your eyes, my lady.

He is a surly character and too solitary by half. I would bring some warmth and laughter into his empty world. Perhaps you are God's instrument to do so? I believe he found you imprisoned in the dungeons below this palace. Is that so?'

'It is.' Her! And the Duke of Aquitaine. The sooner she could escape from him the better, or this English King would have them wed! Rollo did not appear in the slightest put out by the statement. In fact he was smiling as though the King's words amused him. They did not amuse her! 'Would it had been possible to take the city a day earlier, so that my poor brother might have also lived.'

'Yes, Lord Rollo has told us of your sad loss,' Richard murmured, nodding in sympathy. 'God moves in mysterious ways, my lady. We must accept the sometimes painful burdens he lays upon our shoulders. But you are alive, and looking well. Queen Berengaria has voiced a wish that you should spend some time with her, and I have readily given my permission.'

'Perhaps she would prefer to spend her time with another,' Joanna whispered in his ear, but not so quietly that the men and women near by did not hear and exchange amused looks. 'I am sure she feels quite indebted to the man who plucked her from such a hideous existence. Do you not, Lady Alisandre?'

'I am in the Duke's debt.' Karin almost choked over the words, aware of him watching her, and of the broadening smile on his face.

'Then we must think of a way in which you can repay him,' Richard said. The friendship which had

developed between himself and this protégé of his
mother, the Dowager Queen Eleanor, was a firm one,
and he did not want some artless woman depriving
him of Rollo's company for too long. A week or two,
and he would have her sent back to England out of
harm's way.

'Would it be possible to trace Lady Alisandre's
family in England?' Rollo suggested, and Berengaria
laid a hand on her husband's arm.

'We must at least try to do this for her. She must stay
with me until it is time to return home, then we shall
do all in our power to return her to the bosom of her
family. Failing this, we shall find a suitable husband
for her . . . a knight of some substance who will care
for her.'

Karin's cheeks flamed as Richard nodded. How
dare they discuss her as if she was not present. She
would not be palmed off as wife to any man not of her
choice!

'I—I rather fear I have no family,' she said, as
Berengaria smiled at her. 'My parents as I recall were
killed in Jerusalem. Now that my brother is dead, I
have no one.'

'The lady could not be more mistaken!' Hugo de
Greville-Wynter came from behind some knights at
the back of the room and bowed before his King. His
eyes dwelt for a long moment on the slender figure in
red, his expression betraying none of the anxious
thoughts running through his mind at that moment. 'I
do believe we are related. My own father lost his life in
Jerusalem four years ago, along with his brother and
sister-in-law. Their daughter, a young girl of about

fifteen, was with them at the time. It was supposed she died with them in the blazing inferno of their house. Now . . . I do believe the Lady Alisandre is my cousin, come back to life!'

Karin swayed. Immediately Rollo's hand was beneath her arm, steadying her. She caught at it with nerveless fingers. Her touch was like ice. Cousins! Related to this thin-faced man who undressed her with his eyes. She felt quite sick with fear and apprehension. This was not turning out at all as she had expected—or hoped!

'Of course,' Hugo continued, with a faint shrug of his bony shoulders, 'she may be some impostor who is using the name of a dead girl. The claim will have to be investigated. I am quite prepared to be patient and abide by the final decision that you come to, my Lord King.'

The cunning sand-snake, Rollo thought. Hugo acknowledged her, yet in the same breath planted seeds of suspicion in the minds of all listening. 'As you say, there must be an investigation to the lady's claim,' he said aloud. 'Until such time as it is proved—or disproved—may I ask that she be placed in my care?'

'Is she not already?' Joanna asked sweetly. Richard silenced her with a look. This matter did not interest him. He wanted to get back to his plans for the assault on Jerusalem. If only Saladin would hurry and pay him the rest of the two hundred thousand gold talents in ransom for the release of the Muslim garrison at Acre, and free the remainder of the Christian prisoners, some two thousand still to come. Then he could

leave this place and finish what he had set out to do
. . . to return the Holy City to Christian hands.

'I should have thought the lady would be better in
the hands of Lord Hugo,' Berengaria murmured. She
did not like Hugo any more than Rollo, whose reputation she liked even less. If Rollo had seduced the girl
already, there would be mortal combat and bloodshed
between the two men.

'She will be safe in the hands of the Duke of
Aquitaine,' Richard assured her, the use of his title
telling her and everyone else of his trust in this man
most considered little more than a mercenary, and a
ruthless one at that!

'Do I have no say in this?' Karin asked breathlessly,
as they were dismissed, and Rollo led her to one side
of the room. She could feel Hugo's eyes following her,
and not only his. She had not been unaware of the way
other men had stared at her. Neither had Rollo, but
with his Guard to protect her, they would never reach
her . . . neither would she be out of his reach.

'The King has spoken. Are you not pleased you are
to stay, and that you may have a cousin? Perhaps the
shock has upset you,' Rollo said solicitously and beckoned to Chavo to come and escort her. 'Return Lady
Alisandre to her apartments. Stay within call until I
return.'

'Yes, lord. My lady . . .'

Inwardly seething, Karin left him. There was
nothing else she could do.

Rollo stared after her, a frown creasing his thick
brows. He sensed someone at his elbow, and turned to
find Hugo there, also watching the departing girl.

'Quite a handful, that one, even for you. I suspect hidden fire beneath that icy exterior,' he chuckled. 'Not my type, of course.'

'No,' Rollo said drily. 'I believe your taste runs to boys. At least my appetite is healthy.'

'If not voracious.' Hugo's eyes glittered warningly. This man always rubbed him up the wrong way. 'I suppose I should thank you for telling me about her.'

'Do you really believe she is your cousin—the girl who was supposed to have burned?'

'I'm sure of it. Did you notice the bracelet she was wearing?'

'She had it on when I found her, hidden beneath her sleeve.' He was referring to the filigree bracelet on Karin's left wrist. Once it had been a work of great beauty, the dozen or more rosebuds in the design set with precious stones—diamonds, emeralds, sapphires—but over the years she had lost many of them. Ayub had promised her a new one, a replica of the old, for her birthday. 'The boy told me he used to take one jewel from it at a time, to bribe the guards for food or clothing, sometimes medicine.'

'A most resourceful little thief. I have heard about him. My uncle gave that to his daughter on her twelfth birthday. It came from Jerusalem, brought back from an earlier crusade by one of his ancestors. I recognised it at once. My aunt wore it before it passed on to the daughter. I saw it on her many times.'

Rollo stood quite still, his face an unreadable mask. Then she *was* Alisandre de Greville-Wynter, this man's cousin! He had been wrong.

'Why were you so willing to step forward and

acknowledge her?' he demanded. 'As there was no other living relative, you inherited your uncle's estates. By right, they are hers. You will be left with nothing.'

'I'll wed the girl, and she will be so grateful to me that she will let things stand. All the possessions of a wife belong to her husband, do they not? Grateful to me as she has been to others before me,' he added meaningfully, and watched a slow flush steal into Rollo's skin. He wanted her for himself!

'Others?' he repeated tersely.

'Alisandre was an only child. I don't know why that man was with her in the dungeon, but he was not her brother!'

'Mistress, come quickly. Look!' Celine cried, and Karin sprang from the couch and ran out onto the balcony to see what had brought about such excitement. For almost a week she had been in the Little Palace of Dreams, watched over night and day by a conscientious Chavo. In the grounds outside, the Guard of the Lord of Darkness kept everyone away from both the palace and the grounds. She was a virtual prisoner in the small house, her only comfort an occasional visit from Queen Berengaria, who brought her clothes and accessories and sent a magnificent black horse for her to go riding, but Rollo had withheld both the horse and his consent from her. She scarcely saw him, except for a glimpse of his tall figure as he came and went from the house. Leila, the dancing-girl, she had seen lying naked beside the pool one afternoon, and had sent Celine down to her with orders that she should confine herself to the interior where she belonged.

The answer which came back was not repeatable, and Leila continued each day to flaunt herself before the eyes of the men on guard. None made any attempt to touch her. She belonged to the Duke of Aquitaine, and no one took anything that belonged to him unless they wished their life expectancy suddenly to shorten drastically.

The liaison disgusted Karin. At least he could have chosen better for himself from among the women who remained in Acre. This painted, voluptuous creature was clearly of the lowest order, as were most of those who accommodated the ordinary soldiers of the army. Had he gone straight to her when Karin had repulsed him? Leila would not. She knew the advantages of having a powerful benefactor. When Acre was retaken by Saladin, as Karin was sure it must be some day, the girl would pretend she had suffered the most awful atrocities at the hands of the Crusaders in the hope of escaping the fate meted out to common whores who blatantly paraded themselves unveiled for men to gaze at their bodies.

Not to have her face covered was, for Karin, the hardest thing to grow accustomed to. In the presence of anyone other than Badir or Ayub, her features had always been veiled. Nowadays she was on view for anyone to stare at, and at times it unnerved her, especially when that person was Rollo.

Celine caught her wrist, and dragged her to the edge of the wall. Below them, lines of men, fettered hand and foot, were being herded towards the palace and the dungeons waiting to receive them. Crusaders stabbed at them with the hilts of swords. Some were not so kind, and used the flat of the blades to urge the unfortunates on when they faltered or stumbled. The heat was oppressive. Many were calling out for water, but none was given, only curses and more blows. She knew that Christian prisoners had been treated as harshly, but still the sight appalled her.

'Look . . . at the back of the line. Is that not the Teacher?'

'Tamir?' Karin whispered, her eyes searching the sea of faces. It was. Tamir ibn Dak, the gentle old man who had instructed her in so many things, was among the new batch of prisoners. Each day more and more swelled the cells to bursting-point. Why did Lord Saladin not ransom them? 'What is he doing here? We left him safe in Jerusalem.'

'I heard it said that he has been with the Mighty Saladin himself,' Celine answered, leaning up on tip-toe to watch the lines of men shuffle by. 'He looks ill, mistress. See, he falls. Mistress, no! You must not go down there!'

Her words fell on deaf ears—Karin was already on the balcony steps. By the time Celine caught up with her, she was on her knees beside the grey-haired man who had fallen to his knees on the ground.

'You! Bring me some water. Do you want to kill him?' she ordered the nearest soldier. When he hesitated, taken aback by the sight of this Christian woman cradling the head of an Infidel in her lap, she cried, 'Do as I say, or I shall speak of this to the Duke of Aquitaine.'

'That will not be necessary, my lady.' One of Rollo's Guard, Siward, a fair-haired giant of a man whose Viking ancestors had raided the shores of England and carried off the woman who was to give him life, bent to hand her a horn containing fresh water. 'Give him this, and then let us take him. Lord Rollo would not like to see you thus.'

'I care not what he likes,' she retorted with a toss of her loose hair. Tamir moaned as she trickled the water between his parched lips, and his eyes opened. In his weak condition he was unable to hide the amazement in his eyes at the girl who cradled him so gently against her.

'My Princess . . . I have found you!' He had always called her this. Thanks be to Allah he had spoken in Arabic! Karin hoped that none of the soldiers understood what had been said.

She laid a finger across his mouth and shook her head, indicating that he must say no more. She herself dared not speak for a full moment, so overcome was she with anger and remorse at the pitiful state in which she found him.

'What is happening here?' Men fell back as Rollo strode through their ranks. Siward acknowledged him stiffly, aware that he had failed in his duty in allowing Karin even to get near the prisoners. 'This is a strange situation to find you in, Lady Alisandre.' His tone was cutting.

He stood with his hands on his hips, staring down at her, and his face was bleak and unsmiling. 'Get up, girl. You forget who you are.'

'As you do, my lord.' Karin climbed to her feet, after

slipping the horn of water into Tamir's hands and
motioning Celine to take her place. But the maid was
hauled roughly away by Siward and held fast. 'You
call yourself a man of honour?' Her scornful tone had
the force of a mailed fist behind it, and she cared not
who heard what was said. 'How proud you men must
be of what is done here! Look at these wretched
creatures? Half starved, nearly dying of thirst, every
one of them. Where is your compassion for your
fellow human beings?'

'Speaking for myself, I have none left. It deserted
me on one battlefield or another as I watched my
comrades-in-arms cut down and mutilated by men
just like these.'

'Like him?' Karin pointed to Tamir, her eyes blazing
with contempt.

'He was young once. He will have killed in the name
of Allah,' Rollo snapped. 'Did you learn nothing during your days of captivity? Saladin is waging a jihad
against us—a Holy War. Men like this live only to kill
Christians, to erase from this land any faith other than
their own. And we are here to stop them.'

'To kill and butcher them, rather. Is there any differ-
ence between you?'

'Perhaps not?' He shrugged mailed shoulders. He
was tired and dusty after riding in with these men, and
in no mood for pleasantries with this infuriating little
wench over the rules of warfare and non-existent
virtues of the Infidels. He wanted to bathe, and have
Leila massage the aches from his limbs, and to sleep
for at least four hours.

'You are wrong.' Karin was so incensed by the

unjustness of his words that she did not stop to think. 'This man has killed no one. His name is Tamir ibn Dak, and he is an astrologer, a man of learning. A gentle man, not an animal as you are. This is one man who does understand the meaning of the word honour.'

'And how would you know that?' Rollo's gaze narrowed as she bit her lip, suddenly afraid of what she had done. Even Siward and Chavo, behind him, were staring at her with open suspicion on their faces. She saw Celine's eyes imploring her to take care. Rollo stepped to her, thrust his fingers under her chin, and pushed back her head, forcing her to look up at him. 'I asked how you know his identity? Did you perhaps favour an old man with your company in order to make life easier for you?'

She gasped at the suggestion. She knew that he had been suspicious of her from the very beginning. Had this been in his mind all along?

'Well?'

'He—He was kind to me once . . .' she stammered. What did it matter what he thought of her! As soon as she could get out of the city, she would be free of him. Free to find Badir and Ayub, and return to her home.

'Kind?' Rollo gave a short, humourless chuckle. 'Now that's a new word for it. That being the case, you had better think about being a little more pleasant to me unless you want to find yourself back with the rest of the whores and camp-followers.'

'It was not like that. I told you, he is a teacher. I—I was made to work from time to time . . . He took me into his house when his daughter was ill. I helped to nurse her.' She lied frantically, praying that Tamir would not deny her words.

'These people have skilful, knowledgeable physicians. What use were you except to offer comfort of a different kind?' Rollo snarled. He released her, aware of the many eyes watching the encounter. 'Get these men where they are going. Not the old man. Siward, you and Chavo take him inside. As for you,' he rounded on Karin again, 'go with them, but save your concern for one who will appreciate it more than him.'

She needed no further encouragement to hurry back into the house, her cheeks burning with embarrassed colour. It was only too clear what he meant, and everyone listening knew it as well as she did. Ignoring grinning faces, she pushed her way through the soldiers and followed Siward and Chavo, who supported Tamir between them, shutting her mind to Rollo's inference. It was too late to consider the consequences. Whatever he did to her, Tamir was alive, and she would fight tooth and nail to keep him so. Besides, she still had her dagger. If he dared to lay one finger on her again . . .

'So you are a teacher. Of what, old man?' Rollo demanded, as he sprawled in a large high-backed chair beside the bed where Tamir lay. The old man was clean now. His hair and beard had been washed in rose-water, his tattered clothes removed and clean ones put on him. He had taken a little soup and more water. Rollo had to admit that he must once have been handsome. He was old enough now to be Karin's father . . . but then some women preferred the experience of years. His eyes flickered to where she stood beside the bed. She looked ill at ease and uncomfortable. And so she should, he thought, remembering the scene in the courtyard. A brother who was not her brother, and now an aged Infidel with whom she had shared some kind of relationship. What kind? That was the question hammering at his brain.

'Languages, the stars, the study of the heavens and the mysteries hidden there.' Tamir was not intimidated by the scowl on the knight's face. He did not fear death, and was too old and tired to seek to avert the hand of fate. 'Life.'

Rollo gave a laugh, and reached for the silver goblet at his fingertips. He drank thirstily, and Chavo refilled the vessel held out to be replenished.

'I am sure you know much of life, but it is hers that I am interested in.' The goblet full of wine was directed at Karin. She had not left Tamir's side since he had been brought to this room. With Celine's help they had ministered to him, and tried to assure him that he would come to no harm.

'She was among some Christian prisoners in Jerusalem. How long ago . . . three years, if my memory serves me correctly. I took pity on her. Compassion is not unknown among my people, my lord, as it seems to be among yours.'

'Watch your tongue, dog,' Chavo growled warningly, but Rollo waved him to be silent.

'Let him speak. Worse has been said to me.' He was looking at Karin as he spoke, and she quickly averted her gaze from the boldness she saw there. He had every intention of making her pay for his moment of generosity, she suspected.

He smiled at her discomfort, and a shadow passed over Tamir's face as he watched them. Was this the one? he wondered. A strong man, but too arrogant . . . with bitterness in his heart. Allah watch over his little Princess in this one's company!

'She remained in my household for over a year. Then, when Acre was besieged, many of the Christian prisoners were shipped here—as bargaining power, if you like. She was among them. I have not seen her from that day to this.'

'What did you teach her during that time, old man?' Rollo asked softly.

'She has a quick mind. I found her company quite stimulating. She is fluent in French, which made it possible for us to converse. We would sit many nights together, watching the stars . . .'

'The pastime of lovers,' Rollo growled. To his surprise, Tamir managed a weak smile.

'It pleases me that you have experienced a little romance in your life, my lord. From what I have heard of the Lord of Darkness, he has shut out all pity, all love, all weakness from his life.'

Karin watched dark colour steal into Rollo's cheeks at the words. Had he once felt warmth, appreciated beauty, known love? She could not imagine him in love, nor the woman who would give herself body and soul to this hateful, cruel man. She knew so little about him . . . She hastily reproved herself for allowing her thoughts to stray in such a wayward direction. She hated him! She was not concerned with anything about him, she told herself fiercely and with strong conviction. Even so, she still wondered what manner of woman could love him . . .

'And deals harshly with all those who oppose him,' came the biting answer. 'Or seek to make a fool of him.'

'One cannot make a fool of a man when he is already a fool, blinded by bitterness and ignorance to the true meaning of Life. Fulfilment, my lord. One day, when Allah smiles on you, you will understand what I mean.'

'Brave words, old man. Do you realise I have the power of life and death over you?'

'You cannot kill him,' Karin cried, her eyes widening in alarm. 'He is old and helpless . . . Oh, you monster!'

'Hold your tongue, or I'll have you gagged, woman,' Rollo ordered in fury, and she relapsed into silence, knowing full well he would do so if she spoke again. 'I will hear no more of your lies!' He returned his attention to Tamir. He was steadily drinking his way through the pitcher of red wine which sat on the table beside him, but it did nothing to improve his temper or to dull the anger inside him. On the contrary, it was beginning to inflame both. 'Can you foretell the future, old man? Tell me how long it will be before we ride into Jerusalem again. Tell me that.'

'You will never take Jerusalem, my lord. It will remain in Allah's hands,' Tamir replied quietly, and Rollo stiffened in disbelief. No one in the whole army believed that their quest would be in vain! After all

these years, the terrible loss of life, the endless
battles . . .

'You lie!'

'As you wish. I answered your question—I can say
no more than that.' For a long moment Tamir considered the angry face before him. At length he said,
'You were born under a dark star, my lord. Your name
suits you well.'

'Tell me something I don't know. It has been dogging my footsteps since the day I left my mother's
womb.'

'A woman will be your salvation. The right one, this
time . . .'

'Wrong, astrologer. I want no female complicating
my life.'

'But you are not a hermit, surely? You have women?
I have heard . . .'

'Sweet Jesus, no!' Rollo laughed harshly. 'And I
shall continue to do so. But one woman? Someone
special? Never! I prefer to be alone.'

'No man is truly alone, or wants to be, if he is honest
with himself. Besides, it is too late—it has already
begun.'

'What has?' Rollo demanded, with a fierce frown
darkening his countenance.

'Your journey to Paradise with the woman who is to
be your eternal companion. It is written. There is
nothing you can do about it. Accept your fate, my
lord,' Tamir murmured, his eyes closing tiredly.

'*Insh'allah!* What is written is written. Then, for her
sake it will be better if we never meet,' Rollo muttered.

'Perhaps you have . . . Perhaps not . . .' came the

quiet murmur from the bed. 'There are some things the stars cannot foretell.'

He was lying, Karin thought, watching him as he drifted into sleep. He knew everything! Why had he not been more explicit?

Rollo looked across the bed at her. His head was pounding . . . She saw a moment of naked hunger in his eyes before he got up from the chair and left the room without a word. He dared not remain close to her a moment longer!

As the days passed, Rollo no longer commented on Karin's friendship with Tamir ibn Dak. The old man was allowed to remain in his own home. She collected papers and charts, and at night would sit with him and Celine and Omar, making sure no guards were close by, or Chavo lingering in an ante-room—and they would discuss what had taken place, and make plans for the future. Karin was still determined to make her way back to Jyira, and she now included her old teacher in this plan, never once realising that Tamir did not include himself in any schemes. He lived from day to day, content that his life had been spared by the Duke of Aquitaine. He amused the soldiers by drawing up their horoscopes, and impressed them with his wisdom of the heavens. A few more learned knights even approached him to discuss more serious matters, but never again did Rollo question him about the future . . . or on the strange words spoken to him that first night.

Neither did he make any attempt to force himself on Karin again, and she was beginning to believe her fears had been misplaced, until he came upon her one night in the gardens as she bathed. For a whole week she had been having the fire dream, so that she was almost afraid to go to bed, knowing that, the moment she slept, it would return to haunt her again with terrifying clarity. The face of the woman still lingered in the flames. Now there were voices, calling to her in English . . . and then Ayub was holding her, telling her it had been a dream. Then he, too, would vanish and she would awake to find Celine shaking her.

Dreading the thought of another disturbed night, she went down, very late, to the pool. She knew Rollo's Guard were lurking among the trees, but she had grown used to them by now and forced herself to ignore their presence. Besides, apart from the torches burning along the wall beside the water, it was quite dark. She slipped into the water and immediately felt herself begin to relax. It had been a pitilessly hot day and the water was still quite warm. She swam slowly about, her long tawny hair trailing out behind her like a cloak.

She knew Celine had gone to Chavo's room, as she did every night when she thought her mistress was asleep. She would be gone for an hour, or sometimes longer, and would return to sit at the foot of the bed until sunrise. So now it was Omar who sat cross-legged on the blue and red mosaic tiles and watched over her, biting enthusiastically into a large plum he had just plucked from one of the many fruit-trees growing in abundance near the water. The boy had become Karin's eyes and ears for what went on about her. He was allowed to move freely within the grounds and in the streets beyond. She suspected that Rollo might be having him followed, and had warned him to be on his guard. He had given her a cheeky grin, and said that no one who had not been born to the life he led could ever follow him through the narrow, twisting streets and keep him in sight for more than five minutes.

He brought her word of the growing impatience of the Crusaders to leave Acre and press onto their ultimate goal, Jerusalem. Leopold of Austria had left the country soon after the city fell, following a brief but ugly quarrel with the Lionheart. And now the Christian camp seemed to be dividing. Those for Richard and Guy of Jerusalem included most of the nobles from all the countries involved, and Guy's brother Geoffrey, together with the whole of the English army. Siding with Conrad of Montferrat and Philip of France were, of course, the French soldiers, many of the Knights Templar and the men under Conrad's command from Tyre.

After great debating, with many red faces and tempers white hot, Omar related, it had been agreed that Guy should remain King of Jerusalem until his death, upon which Conrad and his new wife, Isabella, would reign, passing the crown onto their descendants.

Now Philip of France was growing restless, and talking of returning home. He had been ill frequently since his arrival and was constantly waging a war of words with Richard of England over one thing or another—often over the amount of booty to be attributed to him. He had vowed to remain three years on this crusade, but already he was tired of it. The

rumour was rife among the soldiers that he intended
to go home very soon, perhaps even before the end of
this month of July.

What then? Karin wondered as she swam. Would
Richard fight on alone? He would be outnumbered by
the mighty armies of Saladin, and cut down before he
had gone half-way to Jerusalem. More fighting! More
dead! Perhaps Rollo, Duke of Aquitaine, among them.
Why had he come into her thoughts? No matter how
hard she tried to shut him out, he was always there,
intruding on her peace and solitude. He must not die,
because she needed him to get her out of the city, but
this was the only reason she wished him to live. Had
he not humiliated her at every turn? He insulted her
with every look, every word and every touch until she
dreaded meeting him even for a second. Never before
had anyone reduced her to such a state of tension and
confusion. In his eyes she was less than the lowest
woman in the city, and he made her feel his contempt in no uncertain manner. He was despicable!
Detestable!

She swam to the edge of the pool as voices drifted
to her from beyond some oleanders. As they grew
nearer, one was instantly recognisable as that of the
last man in the world she wanted to encounter at this
moment. There was much laughter as Rollo came into
view, accompanied by Siward and two others of his
Guard, one of them carrying a flagon of wine. Both
Omar and Tamir had given her to understand that he
did not often seek the company of his men, yet he
looked content enough tonight. They parted, only
Siward following him towards the house, for he had a

room next to that of Chavo. As they neared the pool,
she slid beneath the water and held her breath until
she felt she would burst, and was forced to surface
again. Soft laughter brought her head jerking up in
horror as she pushed the clinging wet hair from her
face and eyes. Rollo stood on the edge of the pool,
watching her.

'I was wondering how long you would be able to
stay down there. The water looks most refreshing. Are
you coming out, or shall I come in there with you?'

'Must you always be so unpleasant?' Karin snapped, already beginning to feel agitated by the way he
looked at her.

He looked surprised as he bent to pick up her robe.
Omar was nowhere to be seen! Karin made no move to
rise out of the water and take it from him. He gave a
broad smile, dropped it onto the tiles and turned his
back long enough for her to clamber out and wrap it
firmly around her dripping body.

'At least you do have some manners.' An eyebrow
rose at her haughty tone. He followed her as she
turned towards the house—and sanctuary. As she
reached the whitewashed pillars which supported
graceful arches before the long windows, and gave
blessed shade during the extreme heat of the day, he
caught up with her and stepped ahead to block her
way. Karin caught her breath as his hands went to
either side of her head against the pillar behind her,
imprisoning her.

'Would you be so loath to be here if it was your
teacher with you?' he mocked, wicked lights glinting in the green depths of his eyes, and her own

blazed anger in return. 'Close your eyes, pretend it is he!'

'Stand aside, or—or I shall speak to Queen Berengaria about these constant insults,' she cried defiantly, throwing up her hands to ward him off as he moved closer.

'Insults? Truth, my lady. You show a strange preference for all things alien to me, and I am not the only one to comment on it. A thief for a daily companion. An Egyptian slave-girl. An astrologer from Jerusalem. Yet the man who saved you from spending the rest of your life in a dirty, stinking dungeon is thought of as the lowest form of life.'

'You have been deliberately rude to me since the first day we met,' Karin protested, stung by the unjustness of his words. If only he had showed even a little consideration! 'Of course I am grateful to you . . . I realise I owe you my life.'

'Which is in my hands until your claim to the de Greville-Wynter estates is either proved or known to be false,' Rollo murmured, and felt her stiffen with shock. What was he saying? It had sounded like a threat! 'Consider it a warning,' he added, as if her thoughts had been open to him. 'Do not continue to antagonise people with these friendships.'

'Just because you deny yourself the friendship of others, is that any reason to demand it of me?' How she wished someone would come along so that he would be forced to release her! His nearness was beginning to be frightening. The weight of his body was pressing hers against the pillar, so that she could not move even when he took his hands away from her

face and began to caress her through the robe that
clung seductively to her still wet skin. Despite the
dampness, and the fear rising in her, his touch burned
like fire. At home, if a man had dared to look at her as
he did, let alone attempt to touch her body, she would
have screamed for a guard and had him whipped.

'I demand no more from you than you seem to have
been willing to give to others,' Rollo said in answer.
His fingers brushed away strands of wet hair from her
cheek and stroked the side of her neck, following the
edge of her robe down to where her breasts rose
beneath it. His words told her that he considered her
no better than the dancing-girl he kept for himself
upstairs, and memory of that brazen woman forced
back the waves of faintness which threatened to over-
take her.

'Are you tired of your toy already, my lord?' She
tried to turn her face away to avoid his lips, but they
found her cheek, her eyes, her mouth, cutting off her
scornful comment.

She struggled in silent humiliation at the lips which
took hers by storm, first bruising them with angry,
searing kisses, then cherishing them gently with an
expertise which rendered her incapable of resistance—of thought—of hatred . . . How could she fight
him when he made her feel so exhilarated . . . so alive!
She did not even move when she felt him slide the
robe away from one shoulder and cup a breast in his
hand. A scarred thumb teased the pink rosebud nipple
with growing confidence, until her skin tingled with
pleasure at the intimate caresses.

He thought her to be willing, she realised—sanity

suddenly thrusting its way through the haze of pleasure and unreality—like Leila, or any of the other camp-followers who tagged after the army to accommodate lonely soldiers. No doubt he had had his fill of them, too. He ignored the clenched fists which began to pound against the hard muscles of his chest, and in desperation she threw back her head, and pleaded.

'No, I beg of you, my lord. You are wrong about me! I am not what you think . . .'

'Indeed you are not. I have known that from the beginning. So at last we begin to understand each other. Have no fear that I shall betray you, for I am not a vindictive man. If others are deceived by the charade, they have only themselves to blame,' Rollo replied, knowing a moment of triumph at her confession.

She sagged weakly in his embrace. He had misunderstood. So long as she was pleasant to him, he intended to continue with his protection! Karin was dumbfounded—and lost. For some reason, she had no more defences against this man.

Rollo frowned as he saw the tears which sprang to her eyes, flooding them like shimmering crystals. 'What game are you playing now, girl? You'll not sway me with those,' he said warningly. Weakness was one luxury he could not afford. To do so might mean the shattering of the protective walls he had built round his heart, so thick, so massive, that not even Malvoisin could batter them down. They were there to stay until he drew his last breath. Yet—how he wanted to believe in this trembling little creature he held, to believe in her innocence, her virtue, the cry for mercy on her lovely face! How could he? Even as she fought against his kisses, her lips answered his. Her resistance was a sham, a farce, as was everything about her.

Too late he heard the soft footstep behind him and caught the flash of alarm, swiftly changing to sheer relief, that crossed Karin's face. Even as Rollo released her, his hand snaking down to the dagger in his belt, Tamir brought the stone he held down across the back of his skull. A thousand coloured lights exploded before his eyes as, with a groan, he sank to the ground at her feet.

'Quickly, child! Run to your room before he recovers,' Tamir urged as she stood stupefied, staring at the unconscious Crusader. 'I will fetch his Guard and tell them he has had too much to drink. I do not think he will admit that he was so intent on making love to an unwilling woman that he was attacked from behind by an old man!'

'You do not know him,' Karin answered, growing afraid for her friend. 'But he did not see you, and he will not get your name from me.'

'Do you know him, little Princess?' Tamir asked softly, and she felt her cheeks burn as she gathered her gaping robe around her. 'Be careful—he is a dangerous man. The stars have predicted a dark force in your life. Mayhap this is what they meant.'

'I would rather die than let him touch me again!'

'That was not the impression I had when I saw you together. However, this is no time to discuss such matters. Go! Leave this to me.'

CHAPTER FOUR

THE NEXT MORNING it was all over the house how the Lord of Darkness had celebrated a little too vigorously and collapsed beside the pool, where he had been found by two of his Guard. Celine was surprised that her mistress did not share her amusement at the thought of the incident. But the smile faded from her face when she was told the truth.

'Mistress,' she gasped, a hand going to her mouth. 'Tamir! What will he do to him?'

'Nothing, I shall not allow it,' Karin assured her fervently, yet in her heart she knew there was nothing she could do if Rollo decided to vent his anger on the unfortunate man. Perhaps if she went to him, and spoke for Tamir? No, that would only deepen his belief that she had been the man's mistress. How could he be so blind? Tamir was older than her own father would have been, had he lived. Was he to suffer because Rollo could not understand simple friendship?

That morning she was to accompany Queen Berengaria on a trip into the streets of Acre. Queen Joanna had returned from the bazaars accompanied by three pack-horses laded with purchases, and Richard's wife was eager to see for herself the wonders offered. She was a very shy person, Karin had come to realise, and often felt overshadowed by the vibrant personalities of her warrior husband and his attractive sister, who, it was rumoured, was to be found a husband soon from among the many eligible knights and nobles in the army.

Berengaria longed for Richard's company, or a show of affection, but he was always more at ease with the men he fought with than his new bride, and it hurt her deeply. She found Karin easy to talk to, sensing her unhappiness. But she never spoke of what troubled her, and there was no way the Queen could draw her out.

Karin at last rode the horse which had been Queen Berengaria's present to her. This was only the first of many, for as the days passed, she had been sent fresh fruit and sweetmeats, bolts of cloth and many accessories to complete her wardrobe. If there were men among the King's following who had taken a dislike to Karin, an even deeper dislike developed of her friendship with the Queen of England. But Richard was pleased with the friendship which had developed between them, and stated so quite openly to all about him. In some quarters, this heightened the intensity with which suspicion surrounding Karin grew and grew, multiplying beyond all proportion. No one ever knew how the rumours began: some said she was a whore who had escaped from some harem; others, that she had sold her body in return for her life and would be damned to the eternal fires of hell for such a sin. One or two of the more daring ones even hinted that she might be a spy, but made sure they did not say so within the hearing of the Duke of Aquitaine or any of his personal entourage.

Rollo was well aware of their mutterings, and of the tide turning against Karin. He knew that the whole malicious scheme had been instigated by Hugo de Greville-Wynter. Before confirmation ever came back from England as to her identity, Hugo would have her branded as either an outcast or a spy. As Rollo rode through the streets that morning, three of his Guard behind him, he knew he would have to kill the man before his plans succeeded. Why he should even care what happened to the girl, he did not know, and it angered him that his thoughts were still of her, even with an aching head which she had brought about. It had been a long time since he had allowed his guard to drop so drastically . . . and all for a few stolen kisses. His men were still smirking behind their sleeves over the rumour which had quickly spread. He had growled ungraciously at Chavo when he attempted to confirm it, and snapped at the next man he saw with a smile on his face. That was what was expected of him. He would return to the house and throttle the life out of Tamir, that grey-haired dog!

He found the Queen's entourage in the Street of Silversmiths. Servants were already carrying armfuls of brass and pewter plates, and goblets studded with all manner of precious stones. Chavo hovered beside Karin, who was shaking her head at the Queen's insistence that she buy something. Rollo swung himself from his horse and stood for a moment, watching her smile and repeatedly refuse the offer. She wore a gown of pale lilac silk and a surcoat of purple edged with gold. The girdle about her waist was gold, with fringed tassels. Her hair was loose today – he suspected she preferred it this way—with a circlet of fine gold holding the white wimple in place. A breeze stirred it away from her face, and he saw her eyes glowing with pleasure at this outing. More colour than he had seen for weeks—healthy colour, he noted, recalling how easily she blushed beneath his gaze—resided in her cheeks. The image was suddenly marred by the memory of painted nails, and a soft expletive exploded under his breath.

'You spoke, my lord?' Siward asked, very carefully. Rollo's mood was not improving. Why, when he had this desirable creature all to himself, and the undivided attention of Leila, was beyond the men of his Guard. Each one would have sold his soul for an evening alone with either.

'Stay with the horses, and stay alert. We may be negotiating with the Infidels, but that won't stop them putting a knife in your back, given the chance.'

Karin looked up as he pushed his way through the crowd of merchants and beggars clustered about them, and quickly looked away again, pretending she had not seen him. Her heart began to race. Why did they have to encounter each other here? Had he followed them to spoil her day deliberately?

'Lord Rollo, this is an unexpected pleasure.' Berengaria gave him her hand, which was touched politely to his lips. 'I hope you are not about to tell me we must return to the palace, as I am just beginning to enjoy myself. What do you think of this material I have brought? It is for the King.'

She indicated a bolt of dark green damask held by a servant. Rollo pursed his lips as her eyes rested on him amusedly. He was a soldier, not a ladies' man, and well she knew it. They had taken a dislike to each other on sight, neither knowing quite what caused the irritation which arose whenever they were together. She considered him rough and rude. He thought her pale and insignificant to be the queen of such a man as the Lionheart.

'It is the King's favourite colour, I believe.'

'You know him well. Better than I, I think,' Berengaria replied, turning away to ask the price of a gleaming silver platter being held out for her inspection. The shopkeeper thrust it under her nose, pointing and jabbering so fast that she threw up her hands in dismay. 'I cannot understand a word. Can anyone? I like it. I shall have it.'

'Look, it is a calendar,' Karin explained, 'but he is asking too much for it.'

'How clever of you . . . Yes, I can see now . . .' the Queen exclaimed, bending forward to examine the platter more closely. 'What shall I offer him?'

Karin dared not look at Rollo. She had spoken without thinking! She should pretend ignorance now before she betrayed herself further, but Berengaria was asking her again about a price.

'Ha—Half of what he is demanding,' she replied.

'Even that is too much,' Rollo drawled. He spoke quickly in fluent Arabic to the shopkeeper. A price was agreed, and the money handed over. 'I told him the Queen of England intends to hang the plate in her palace and show everyone what craftsmen exist in the world of Islam. He begs me to convey to you his appreciation of your good taste.'

Faces blurred suddenly before Karin's eyes. Voices faded, then returned more loudly, accompanied by a pounding which threatened to burst her eardrums. She swayed unsteadily, and heard the Queen exclaim anxiously, 'Look to the Lady Alisandre, someone!'

Karin knew whose arms went about her and supported her against a hard body until the giddiness had passed. When the mists cleared and she looked up into his face, she saw that his eyes were cold and accusing. This time she knew no excuses would be accepted, yet heard herself stammer, 'Forgive me . . . The heat . . .' Without his assistance, she would have fallen, for her legs were trembling and scarcely held her.

'What a fool I am! This is your first venture out,' Berengaria declared. 'We shall return at once. Where are the horses, messire Ambrose?'

'At least two streets away. Shall I bring them here?'

'That will not be necessary. If you will consent to ride Siward's horse, Lady Alisandre can have mine,' Rollo said with a smile.

'An excellent idea. The poor child could not walk another step.'

The Queen was helped to mount Siward's enormous horse, not without some difficulty. As he led it away and servants streamed past them after the royal figure, Rollo swung Karin up across his silver-mounted saddle. She reached for the reins, but he caught them up with a look which indicated that his trust and his patience were both at an end. What was she to do now? she wondered frantically. Perhaps she could pass the incident off lightly to the Queen, explaining that she had been taught Arabic by Tamir ibn Dak while a prisoner, as Rollo had learned his while in captivity. If he thought her to be a spy, she would be handed over to the King and his nobles for trial! She could lose her head! She felt faint again, and clutched at the high pommel. As Rollo's eyes momentarily searched her face, she recalled what he had said to her the night before: I shall not betray you . . . I am not a vindictive man. Only so long as she obeyed him would she have his protection. Suddenly she was indifferent to what could happen to her. Badir's whole scheme had gone wrong, and she was tired of it, and frightened of what would now become of her. He could never have envisaged that she would fall into the hands of a man like the Duke of Aquitaine. If she were to throw herself on the mercy of the King? What was she, after all . . . ? The daughter of an important general in Saladin's army. She would be held for ransom, and when that was paid she would be released, and free to return to him and to Ayub.

Yet there was talk among the army that Saladin had no intention of paying the ransom already agreed for the garrison at Acre. An even worse story hinted that he had massacred all the Christian prisoners in his possession. She was appalled at such a lie, but could say nothing to dispute it. But if, by some quirk of fate, no money changed hands, she would have confessed everything for nothing. She might still be in the hands of the Lord of Darkness.

She stole a look into the face of the man walking beside her. His hand was on his sword, and his eyes

constantly searched the alleys they passed, scrutinis-
ing the faces of men passing by. He was careful and
suspicious and dangerous—Tamir was right. Dangerous, indeed, but for a far different reason from the one
she had first harboured. Dangerous to her as a
woman. There was no use denying that, for a brief few
minutes while he held her, she had thrilled to his
kisses, and the caresses of his hands. No man before had ever made her feel like that . . . she had
allowed no man such liberties. Still less had she per-
mitted Rollo to be so bold. He was the kind of man
to take what he wanted! She would have no say in
the matter, and now his hold over her was even
stronger.

It was almost mid-day, and the sun beat down upon
her head until she thought she could bear it no longer.
Before all this, she had never been troubled by the
heat, but being too long confined indoors, deprived of
the freedom she had always enjoyed in Jyira . . . and
these last months in Acre had driven her to desperation. She had forgotten how narrow the streets were,
how they smelt. Life in the city had made her grow
soft.

They reached the place where the other horses
waited under close guard. Without a word, Rollo lifted
her to the ground. As his hand remained on her arm,
she stared at him, and then said cuttingly,

'How far do you think I could run, my lord?'

'From me? Not three steps,' came the chilling
answer. 'You and I have a reckoning this afternoon.
Who hit me, by the way?'

'Hit you? You were drunk, my lord. You fell and

banged your head. I hope it hurts,' she added vehemently, and he gave a tight smile.

'That's better. I prefer you with more fire. This milk
and water act begins to bore me. You forgot yourself
back there, didn't you?'

'How? Oh, because I understand a little of their
language . . . as you do. Omar taught me, to make the
days less long and dreadful. Where did you learn
yours, my lord? In the bed of another dancing-girl?'

'First in the galleys, shackled to the man beside me
day and night. Then, when I was sold to a merchant,
from his wife who took pity on the starved skeleton
they had bought. They worked me like a pack-mule
from dawn to dusk, but I was fed well and had a bed of
sorts to sleep on. This is how I know you were never
their prisoner, my lady Alisandre, or whatever your
name is!'

Pushing back his sleeve, he revealed the leather
guard about his wrist. She knew that the other wrist
was similarly bound. She had seen them, and thought
nothing of it, as soldiers often strengthened weak
joints in such ways. Her eyes widened as he unlaced
the leather and pulled it open for her to see the scars
which seared the skin, twisting this way and that in a
hideous pattern. What agony he must have endured
in trying to free himself from his shackles in order to
make such terrible marks, she realised. His face ex-
pressionless, he fastened the guard and adjusted his
sleeve.

'No words of sympathy, my lady? No excuses for
the fact that you have no signs such as these on your
skin? Look at them!' He snatched her hand and the

material fell away from a flawless wrist. 'Sweet Jesus, there was a time last night when I found myself wanting to believe in you. As if I had not learned my lesson the last time!'

'I—I don't know what you mean . . .' she whispered.

'Nor will you—now!'

They rode through the streets in silence, past vendors of vegetables and fruits who ran into the paths of the horses to show their produce, past stalls of fish, already beginning to smell in the heat. Metals were being polished by the side of the road, silver and gold of the most intricate designs. All were hastily abandoned as from a minaret high above the riders, a white-robed muezzin began the mid-day call to prayer.

The sound tore at Karin's heart, for it reminded her of a life she must now abandon. Whatever happened to her in those years, what she could remember of them, were lost for ever. Men touched their foreheads to the ground, oblivious to the riders passing by. Many of the servants and bodyguards stepped around the prostrated figures in disgust; others deliberately cannoned into them, sending them sprawling. Such cruelty! Why was it not possible for all persons to choose the way they worshipped God? God . . . she had not thought of him as Allah! A small band of riders wearing the cross of the Knights Templar waited respectfully for the Queen and her party to pass, then spurred their horses down the street, sending pots and pans, fruit and people scattering in all directions.

As she turned back in the saddle, her expression

registering contempt, she saw Rollo watching her. She cared not that he saw the anger on her face. There could never be peace between these two peoples when such acts of unwarranted aggression took place. She closed her eyes, and prayed to the only god she could ever remember to free her from her predicament.

The attack came without warning. The Queen was riding some way ahead, surrounded by soldiers, as they passed through the narrow streets just before the palace, and in places riders were forced to follow in single file. From doorways and alleyways, men threw themselves at the men and horses. She cried out as a dirty, bearded individual caught her bridle and wrenched it from her hands and attempted to pull her mount into a side street. From behind, she heard Siward utter a bloodcurdling yell, and caught a glimpse of him bearing down on the man. Then there were two between him and her, and he was slashing at them with his sword. She fought to regain control of her horse. Were they to be robbed? Murdered?

'Alisandre!' Rollo's voice. He had never called her that before. She half turned, to see him fighting violently with a man who had leapt up behind him and was attempting to stab him in the back with a dagger. Sunlight flashed on the curved blade, and she screamed again, and in doing so, averted what might have been a fatal blow, for his eyes were for her alone in that fleeting second as he uttered her name.

'Karin, in Allah's name, woman, ride!' A voice shouted close by, and she found herself staring down into Ayub's grimy features. He was dressed as a beggar, so it was not surprising that she had not

recognised him as the man who had grabbed her reins.
'Ride! Or do you enjoy the company of this lord so
much that you wish to remain with him?'

A horse cannoned into hers, almost throwing her off
balance. Rollo! He had disposed of his opponent and
come to her aid. If she did not do something, he would
kill Ayub! She kneed her mount forward, allowing the
reins to slip from her hands. As she bent to gather
them up, she appeared to lose her balance and cried
out as she fell heavily against the stone wall of an
archway. She heard Rollo cursing blindly as he came
after her, but in the narrowness of the street it was
impossible to push past and pursue her seeming
attacker. She reeled in the saddle, clutching at her raw,
bloody arm, torn by the harsh stones.

Rollo grabbed the reins in one hand, and urged both
horses on out into a place where the road widened.
Men were rushing back past them, in obedience to his
orders. Karin moaned in pain as he tore away her
sleeve and ripped some of the beautiful material in
pieces to bind the grazes which reached from shoulder
to elbow.

'A life for a life,' he said, cupping her chin between
fingers of steel. 'I shall not forget.' His face was closed
to her, with not one flicker of emotion in his eyes.

As she sat, not comprehending his words, he told
Siward to look after her and rode after the attackers,
but returned in less than ten minutes. Of the five who
had sprung out on them, three were dead, one a
prisoner and one had escaped. The man at liberty was
Ayub!

*   *   *

At the house, Rollo gave her into the keeping of Celine, and left her. His attitude puzzled her. He had bound her injury as if he were concerned, yet when he departed, his face was as black as thunderclouds, his manner curt. Omar came from behind a chair as Rollo strode out of the room, assured himself that he had gone, and then came back to where Karin's arm was being bathed and dressed by the maid.

'Did you see him? The Lord Ayub?'

'What do you know of this? Speak, boy, or I shall box your ears! Where do you go when you disappear? Last night, for instance. One moment you were by the pool, the next you were gone.'

'He came last night, to see you. He was not pleased to find you enjoying the kisses of a Christian dog,' Omar returned saucily, and ducked out of range as Celine reared up to throw a wet sponge at him.

'Ayub, here?' Karin whispered. Alive and well, but believing the worst of her! Surely he did not believe she welcomed Rollo's kisses? 'Tell me everything.'

'He went away again. I was to say nothing to you. He hoped to waylay the Queen's party and sneak you away. He almost succeeded, too . . . But for that Christian dog, he would have.'

'Enough of that, or you will lose your head for such talk!' They were Ayub's words. To him all Crusaders were dogs . . . mongrels of the devil. 'What of my brother? Where is he? Is he safe?'

'He is here,' Omar replied, grinning at her. 'Outside in the garden. He was not sure if you would want to see him. He did not think you over-anxious to leave the Duke of Aquitaine's side this afternoon.'

'Oh, the fool! Here? If he is caught! Celine, leave my arm. Go and make sure that Chavo does not come in here. Omar, you little wretch, fetch the Lord Ayub here. With care, mark you. If he is caught, your head will roll with his.'

'And yours, lady. And yours.' He scuttled away into the darkness outside, leaving Karin hardly daring to breathe. If Ayub were alive, perhaps Badir was, too. How wonderful that would be!

She stared at the cold-faced man who came into the room, ran to him and put her arms about him. For a moment Ayub did not move, then, as his desire for her rose up to overcome the anger which had been eating at him for four long hours, his arms enfolded her. He kissed her long and ardently, whispering her name in a fever.

'Oh, my love, I have been so afraid for you. I did not know what to think . . .'

The Lord Ayub wishes to have you for his wife, Celine had said. Karin knew it now to be the truth. The way he held her and kissed her . . . This was not the way of a brother! His possessiveness alarmed her, and she struggled against his hold. He drew back with a contemptuous oath.

'You did not fight him last night!'

'Ayub! That is unfair and untrue. He—He forced himself on me . . .'

'Is that why you saved his life today? I want him dead for daring to lay his Infidel hands on the daughter of Badir . . . the bethrothed of Ayub, Lord of Jyira.'

'My . . . Badir is dead?' she gasped, and he nodded.

'He did not want to live, with you gone. No more do

I. That is why I am here. Omar has told me all the news. Soon the Crusaders will leave here, and I shall take you somewhere on the way to Jerusalem. Home to Jyira to be my wife.'

'Ayub . . .' she began to protest, but he silenced her with more kisses. She was horrified to realise that the thought of being his wife sickened her. She loved him, but not in that way . . .

'I shall come for you. Wait. Trust in me,' he urged.

'I do, but . . . these were not the wishes of your father.'

'Our father you should have said, Karin. Do you now regard yourself as one of them?' Ayub's eyes blazed with a feverish, almost unhealthy, light.

'No . . . I don't know. It is so different here now.'

'With him?'

'I am under the protection of the Duke of Aquitaine until my claim to the estates of my parents can be proved in England,' Karin said icily, and he sat back on the couch and stared at her.

'So, you accept you are this Christian woman. I thought you might. It matters not. You belong to me. I shall come for you, Karin, and I shall pluck you from under his very nose. You shall be my wife. I have vowed it shall be so.'

'And—And if I refuse? I cannot think of you as anything but my brother Ayub,' she replied tremulously.

He caught her to him so savagely she winced in pain. 'You will be what I want. I shall teach you to forget him. You shall see.'

She sat dazedly on the couch after he had gone,

hardly aware of Celine's questions. It could not be happening to her! Deserted by Badir, she was not expecting to return to Jyira as the wife of his son but as his sister, as she had always thought herself to be. She laid her aching head back against a cushion, and her pallor so alarmed Celine that she ran to fetch something cool for her to drink. Rollo came unannounced into the room as she was drinking the sherbet-water.

'Leave us,' he ordered the two hovering servants. Both looked at Karin for confirmation, and to their surprise she nodded.

'Your maid has caught the eye of my squire,' Rollo said, waiting until they withdrew to speak again. 'But I expect you already know that?'

'She speaks little of it to me. I do not think she wishes to upset me with such details.'

'She was well used before Chavo took her.' He helped himself to some wine from the glass decanter on the table beside her, and as he straightened, goblet in hand, his gaze swept over the loose robe she was wearing, the tawny-gold hair framing her face. The chalk-whiteness of her cheeks was the only indication of the shock she had suffered over what had happened. Even now, he was not sure of what he had heard in those brief, jumbled moments—or seen. Her horse was being dragged away by one of the Arabs. As he went to help her, she appeared to lose her balance and fall heavily against the archway wall. The robe was sleeveless, exposing a bandaged left arm which lay upon a cushion.

In the shouting, he had thought he heard a name— Karin, imagined that he had seen the bearded man thrusting his face up to hers, urging her to ride like the wind. Karin meant 'little Princess'—the astrologer's name for her! That was what he had been trying to remember. That meant she had known the man. Had she fallen, or was she seeking to prevent anyone pursuing him?

'I believe him to be a kind young man . . .' Karin faltered, not liking the way he was staring at her.

'Not rough and ill-mannered like my men—or me?' he challenged, and a faint tinge of colour stole over her skin. 'Forgive me, I did not come here to cross swords with you again.'

She was quite taken aback by the admission, but sensing an ulterior motive to this change of manner, said stiffly, 'Why have you come, then, Lord Rollo?'

'To thank you for saving my life. Believe me, my life is of the utmost importance to me! Although words of gratitude do not come easily to my lips, I am aware I owe you a debt which must be repaid.'

Until that moment Karin had not even considered that she might have saved his life. She had seen the upraised dagger, and screamed instinctively . . . Yet she was glad he lived—she could not deny it. How she wished she could!

'Consider it paid. Did you not rescue me from prison? There will be no more talk of debts between us. I would not like you to be in mine, or I in yours.'

'How honest we are this evening,' Rollo remarked with a frown. What was she admitting? That she feared him as an enemy—or as a man? 'A little more, if you please. Go on,' he urged, when she put aside her drink and her expression became hostile. 'It is for your own good I say this. I cannot extend my protection to you for ever unless you tell me the truth. Who you are. What you were doing in those dungeons. Why other prisoners have no knowledge of you before you suddenly appeared there one day with the thief, Omar. How you come to claim a dead man as your brother, when Hugo de Greville-Wynter emphatically states that Alisandre was an only child?'

She gasped as if he had struck her, totally unprepared for this onslaught of questions. For one mad moment she considered confiding in him . . . then it passed, as she realised the consequences. To be completely in his power! It was unthinkable.

'He was not your brother, was he?' Rollo demanded harshly, and she shook her head. She expected anger, but none came. 'Tell me,' he insisted, more gentle in his tone, but she could not. She was too afraid. There was only one person she could trust, and that would be Richard, King of England. He was said to be a chivalrous knight, well-loved by his men for his fairness to all. As Saladin was. How alike those two men were. They fought each other perhaps because they were so alike. Stubborn—dedicated—religious fanatics when it came to one essential matter . . . who held the Holy City of Jerusalem.

She could recall it so clearly in her mind. Pale Judaean hills intersected by stony roads where pilgrims toiled from all over the world to the shrines of their faith. The Wailing Wall of the Jews. The al-Aqsa Mosque of the Muslims. Could that place not be shared as in the past? Could no one reach Richard and his counterpart, plead with them, reason with them?

They were men of intelligence and honour. She thought of the acres and acres of orchards—groves of olives, oranges and lemons in abundance. Above them the tall minarets and domes of the mosques. The Golden Dome of the Rock, the Tower of David. So many places she had walked in and marvelled at, without knowing why: Gethsemane . . . the Church of the Holy Sepulchre . . . Now she found herself beginning to wonder why these places had held such meaning for her. Could she have been there before . . . ? Before when? Before the start of her memory four years ago, when she was not known as the daughter of Badir and had another name, another identity?

A cold chill swept through her, and Rollo, watching her face, saw a fear so startling, so consuming, engulf her that he himself grew alarmed and dropped to the divan beside her.

'Tell me, woman. Your thoughts now—this minute . . .'

'Of Jerusalem . . .' She was too shaken to deny what had been in her mind, and he stared at her, amazed.

'What do you know of the city? Have you been there?'

'I lived there.' Why did she state that so emphatically. She had no knowledge of living there, yet knew she had. It was no lie, he knew it at once. Yet what was she? Daughter of Islam or of Christianity? 'I do not understand . . . there are images in my mind . . .'

'Go on, I am listening. But I have been there, so I shall know if you lie,' he warned, and the eyes that regarded him were dark with anger.

'Lies! Are you surrounded by so many enemies, my lord, that all you can think of is that every word spoken to you will be a lie?' she scorned, and he had no answer, for that was the way he lived—had lived for many long years. And then this girl had come into his life to begin a slow, deliberate dismantling of his defences, his chosen way of existence. He would not—could not—allow it to happen, or he would be doomed for a second time to the fires of hell . . .

'You little fool, will you not let me help you?' he muttered, grasping her by the shoulders. She cried out as his fingers dug painfully into her injured skin, and he released her with an oath. 'Always I bring you pain, and you . . . I cannot believe a word you say.' He sprang to his feet, the greenness of his eyes once again darkened with suspicion and mistrust.

'Do you not understand?' Karin cried, 'I cannot trust you—or anyone.'

'Except your maid, the boy Omar, and the astrologer and the man who attempted to steal you away from me today,' Rollo returned, grave-faced, and she sank back on the divan, trembling. He knew. Not everything, but enough to demand her death if he so chose. What alternative would he offer—his bed?

'*Insh'allah*,' she said, her voice hardly audible to him, and his mouth tightened. That one word condemned her!

'As you say . . . If God wishes. Your God or mine?'

'Are they not the same? Have you seen him to tell me otherwise?'

'Sweet Jesus, do you know what you are saying?' he ejaculated harshly, and she shrugged slim shoulders.

'I shall deny it, if you demand more of me than I am willing to give. I am not what you think, as I tried to tell you last night, but you would not believe me.'

'No, and I paid for my foolishness. I shall have someone watching my back the next time,' Rollo said, with a humourless smile. Thank God, he had not left a guard outside, or her words would have been heard by others besides him. Why did he care? She was what he had thought her to be! He should have been jubilant in his triumph, yet he felt no satisfaction from her admission. Rather a strangeness that saddened him. Sadness! At the confession of a whore, or worse, who had sought to distract his own attentions by a false portrayal of virtuous innocence!

'My lord!' Chavo stood breathless in the doorway. 'They are murdering him! The old man! Everyone has been told that Saladin has massacred his Christian prisoners, and Piers's brother is among them. He has gone mad! He swears to kill the astrologer, and her too,' he gasped, indicating Karin, who had leapt to her feet at his words. Tamir! They meant to kill Tamir? She rounded on Rollo accusingly.

'He is one of your men! Was it your intention to keep me here while they take the life of an innocent man? You are beneath contempt!' She spat the words at him, evaded the outstretched arm Chavo flung out to hold her back and fled along the passage towards Tamir's room. As she ran, she could hear Rollo swearing profusely, and the sounds of great violence ahead. Sounds which slowed her steps, and made her sink weakly against the wall—blows, laughter. More blows, the sounds of breaking furniture. Allah protect him from these men! she prayed.

From in front of her came three men, two carrying blooded knives. She flattened herself against the wall still more as they neared her, and heard one cry, 'Look! 'Tis her! The spy.'

'You fool, don't touch her, she belongs to the Duke of Aquitaine,' another cried, rushing headlong past him, almost knocking him over in his haste.'Not for much longer!'

She saw the knife begin to descend towards her body and could not even scream, though she was petrified with fear. Torchlight glittered on a sword-blade as Rollo's weapon sank deep into the man's heart. Behind him, men of his Guard were pouring into the corridor, cutting down the second and third men who fled from Tamir's apartments.

Tamir! She reeled through the open doorway, saw him lying in a pool of blood on the floor and threw herself beside him, oblivious to the men behind her.

'No!' Her cry rang through the chaos of the room. She sat amid wrecked chairs and overturned tables, shattered porcelain and glass, cradling the head of the old man against her breast. His blood soaked her robe, but she did not notice it or heed the insistant order to leave him. Leave him? Why should she? This gentle man had shown her mercy and kindness, love! Treated her as his own daughter, as Badir had done. Men not of her faith, yet her life had been spared. She had been treasured among them.

Why were her thoughts so? How confused her mind was . . . nothing seemed real in her mind any more!

'Promise me . . .' Blood seeped from Tamir's mouth as he tried to speak. She wiped it away from his lips with the material of her gown. Rollo bent to stay her hand, conscious of the onlookers to this scene, but she shrugged his hand off and he drew back. Siward took one look into the black expression and knew great uneasiness. He exchanged glances with Chavo, and they moved forward simultaneously to block the way to where Karin sat with her dying burden. 'Do not tell . . .'

'I have done with deception.' Karin's voice was low, but clear to those who listened.

Rollo's hand tightened over the hilt of his great sword, and warned his Guard with a look to act when he did, if it became necessary. One look was enough. They needed no verbal order. If he wanted this woman and sought to take her from under the very nose of the King of England himself—whatever she was—they would support him because their allegiance was to this man alone! To no other, and they would die before they turned against him. The memory of the dead guard outside was like dust in their mouths, choking them. A traitor. He had died by the blade of his lord. It was as it should be. Had Rollo not killed him, he would have died by their hand. The Guards of Darkness were always one to a man behind their lord and master . . .

'Karin, for the love of Allah, listen,' Tamir pleaded, fighting for breath. 'Think only of yourself now—You are in good hands . . .'

She gazed down into the face of the man who had taught her all she knew of life, of literature, of the arts and the beauty of the world. To die thus, at the hands of—one of *his* men! Ordered to deprive her of the most important person she had to depend on at this time, isolating her so that she would perhaps turn in her misery to *him*. And she had been beginning to trust him. To like him! To like him! More than like him . . . How traitorous was the weak body of a woman to fail her so miserably! But now she knew what manner of man lurked behind that half-smile, that pretended concern!

'I am—and always shall be—Karin, daughter of Badir, sister of Ayub, Lord of Jyira,' she declared defiantly in English. It was done!

'Strange words for the daughter of an English lord,' a voice declared, and Karin slowly raised her head and stared into the mocking features of Hugo de Greville-Wynter. 'More like those of a spy!' The faces around him registered agreement, yet she hardly noticed them. She had eyes only for Rollo, who was staring at her impassively. No one knew what the Lord of Darkness was thinking!

'I demand she be taken before King Richard to answer for this treachery.'

At this, Rollo turned to look at Hugo, and the look should have shrivelled him to a cinder!

'Demand?' snarled the Duke of Aquitaine. 'This woman is under my protection. Or have you forgotten that, in your desire to see her dead? Do your estates mean that much to you, my lord?'

Onlookers gasped at the deliberate insult. Hugo grew pale, and then his cheeks flamed as he realised the full extent of the jibe. It was a challenge.

'An accommodating wench, my lord Rollo? Why else would you defend her?' he sneered.

'A matter of honour, if you comprehend the word. She is in my care,' Rollo answered with a smile. A terrible smile which invited death, Karin thought. He wanted a challenge—a fight! But why? Only then did she realise that her final words had been in English, not Arabic, and had been understood by all! Rollo held her life in his hands. If he wished, he could now denounce her as the spy he always suspected she was, yet he was choosing to defend her instead. She did not understand.

'I do not have to answer to you.' She glared at Hugo, and then at the Duke of Aquitaine. 'Or you! I am not answerable to any of you.'

'But you will be answerable to the King of England, who will be most interested to know how you speak the tongue of the Infidel so fluently,' Hugo sneered. 'The old man spoke to you—and you answered—in Arabic! We all heard you!'

'I have been their prisoner for four years,' she cried, and saw a look of disbelief on every face. Only Rollo betrayed no emotion. What was he thinking as he looked at her? If only she knew!

'Siward! Chavo! Take the lady to her room and remain with her,' he ordered. 'She is in my charge, my lords,' he added, as there was a murmur of dissent and faces grew angry. 'I shall answer to the King—as she will. Let all grievances be settled in his presence. Would you allow the jealousy—nay, the perverted desire—of one man to avert true justice?'

Hugo was deserted! They had clamoured around

him in his call for help, but few would go with him if he
sought to challenge Rollo. At least *his* appetites were
healthy! And she was beautiful! Some cared, others
did not. It would be for the Lionheart—who at this
moment was incapable of giving a decision about
anything, for he lay sick in his tent, as he had for the
past four days—to say if she was guilty or innocent.
But none had the power or the desire to challenge the
authority of the Lord of Darkness!

Siward caught Karin by the arm and dragged her to
her feet. She fought against him like a woman de-
mented . . . yet she knew that Tamir was dead and no
longer needed her. Rollo came to her and confronted
her, but did not touch her. His eyes bored into her very
soul.

'Go with them,' he ordered. 'They will take you,
willing or no. Stay until I come.'

'For what reason?' she demanded, pale-faced.

'If you do not know that, then you are a fool.' His
voice did not carry beyond them, and his words left
her speechless. What should she read into them?

Outside in the passage, two of Rollo's Guard held a
third man, who clutched a sword-cut on one arm.

'My lord, mercy,' he cried as Rollo approached.
Karin struggled in the arms of her captors, trying to
linger to hear what was being said. 'There was a
Saracen with the old man . . . we saw him enter.'

Her knees almost gave way. Ayub! Who else could
it be? He had left her and gone straight to Tamir,
and only Omar could have told him that the Teacher
was a prisoner. The little thief had much to answer
for!

Slowly Rollo came to a halt and faced the man. There was a growing anger in his face which made her very afraid.

'They were spies, my lord. For the love of heaven, we were but doing our duty!'

'I gave no order to kill an old man,' came the chilling answer.

'First he came from *her* apartments. We followed him!' The man indicated Karin, and she steeled herself to meet the gaze which turned on her.

'This is true? Be careful, girl, there is little I can do for you now. Take great care with your words.'

'He did not come to see Tamir. He came to see me! He was my brother Ayub.' How controlled was her voice. No trace of the fear in her heart or the tumult in her breast as his eyes narrowed with contempt. His hatred of her she could bear, but not his kindness, this willingness to help her, for then it laid bare the weakness in her . . .

'Stay with her,' Rollo ordered, sliding his sword into its scabbard. 'I shall come when I have spoken with the King. Ill or not, he has to hear what I have to say before Hugo and the vultures gather in earnest.'

Siward urged her on towards her rooms. Chavo followed, grave-faced. Omar was immediately removed to another room under guard. Lest he carry messages for her of which they did not approve, she suspected. She felt too wretched even to argue when he was propelled, cursing and struggling, from the room. She could offer him no comfort, or allay his fears that he was about to be put to death for helping an enemy to gain access to the palace grounds. Because of him, Tamir was now dead. She could not forgive him yet—if ever.

Both Chavo and his companion looked at her as if she had betrayed them. Them? She had betrayed herself in her moment of grief, and she would pay for it, but she no longer cared. The look in Rollo's eyes had wounded her more deeply than any accusation of treachery, or spying! Merciful Allah, give me courage for what lies ahead, she prayed, as they left her alone with Celine.

Courage for what? she wondered, as she lay outstretched on the divan. What did life hold in store for her now?

CHAPTER FIVE

THE KINGS of France and England were quarrelling again. Philip wanted to go home. The Crusade, for which he had promised solemnly to stay three years, no longer meant anything to him, and home he went, leaving Acre at the end of July, departing from the port of Tyre for his homeland in the first week of August. Richard was left in command of his men.

The heat was oppressive. Tempers short. The King of England himself was slowly recovering from a bout of sickness which had sapped his strength and denied him to his army for three long weeks.

Three long weeks, during which Karin was confined to her apartments and saw no one save Celine and Rollo, and, of course, his personal Guard who were assigned to keep her safe. Safe! She was a prisoner. They were everywhere—on the balcony and below it, in the gardens and about the pool. There was nowhere she could go alone and eventually she kept to her rooms, tired of seeing the same faces following her and watching her every move. Everything she said or did was reported back to the Duke of Aquitaine. He was her master in every way! And she hated him all the more for the power he had over her. Hated herself, too, for the weakness in her which cried out that she should confide in him whenever they were together, and beg his help. She never did. Pride forbade her to abandon herself to this devil!

Yet, while she hated him, she knew that he alone stood between her and the wrath of Hugo de Greville-Wynter. She had not liked him from the beginning. Now she knew the kind of man he was—an upstart knight who preferred young boys to women, and boasted of it to his followers. She was not sure what they thought of him yet . . . she only knew Rollo's opinion and that of his men. They loathed the insignificant little man with a mouth so large that it was compared to the ears of a donkey by the Arab servants around him.

For days she went in fear for her life. Every sound made her jump . . . His voice made her catch her breath, yet there were times when he did not even enter the room to ask how she was. It was his way of humiliating her still further, she decided, and he did it so well.

His voice was the one she wanted to hear most. To bring her reassurance. Why should she trust him? She did not know. Yet who else was there? His Guard protected her against all-comers . . . for him? They also protected her against the spite of Hugo de Greville-Wynter. To all he was now the injured party, wishing to believe in her innocence, yet fearing that he was mortally wrong and could be admitting an Infidel spy into the midst of his family. She almost laughed aloud at the thought. He had looked at her and desired her, despite his other leanings, and now he had denied her because he knew she was, in truth, his cousin.

Such fear on that thin face. He knew something she did not! He feared the loss of his estates in England; but why, if she was an impostor? As the days passed, Karin came to accept that she was indeed Alisandre. She liked it not, but the feeling grew more and more. This woman was a stranger to her, would be accepted more by the men around her if she acknowledged the fact openly, but she could not. She knew, yet could prove nothing. She still had no memory, save that of Badir and the gentle Tamir who had died still trying to protect her—and Ayub, who wanted her for himself. This terrified her almost as much as what might happen to her when she appeared before Richard and his knights to face Hugo's charge of treason.

She knew no life other than that which Badir had given her, yet while in the company of Rollo, a change had overtaken her . . . a very frightening change! Her dreams became more intense, yet when she awoke she could never remember them. She felt differently in these Christian clothes, although she saw by the way men looked at her that they considered her in no way changed. She could not explain the way she felt, yet she accepted that something had happened to her since the day the Duke of Aquitaine had found her in the dungeons below the palace. This was how Badir and Tamir had said it would be. But how could she abandon all those dear to her for the new, strange life?

When *he* was close to her, nothing was strange. Frightening—yes! In his hands he held her life! But, more than that, he had awakened something in her she did not understand and could not accept, and her hatred of him deepened because of this puzzle. She was not like Leila, the dancing-girl, or any of the camp-followers or the women who came nightly to entertain the Crusaders, yet when *he* looked at her she became a different person.

'Have you no word at all to say to me?' Richard demanded with a frown, staring at the silent woman before him.

Berengaria laid a hand on his arm, and his frown grew, to indicate that she should not try to interfere. For the past hour she had been intervening for the prisoner, and it was beginning to annoy him. Women knew nothing of such matters. Hurt, she drew back and received a sympathetic smile from the King's sister, sitting on his left. There were times when Joanna did not understand her brother's strange moods . . . at times, he was so insensitive. Could he not see that the little Princess from Navarre loved him, and wanted to be his true wife—his Queen? He showed more affection for his comrades-in-arms than for her. She sensed disappointment in him, and despair in Berengaria.

'Say, my Lord King?' Karin answered in a quiet, but perfectly clear, voice. Her head ached abominably, but no sign showed on her serene features. She was controlled and poised, and her proud bearing brought glances of admiration from many of the men surrounding the dais where King Richard sat with the two Queens. Whatever she was, she was no coward. They appreciated that—and the contempt with which she refused to be baited by the insults and innuendoes flying at her. Nothing seemed to ruffle her, yet the

Duke of Aquitaine at times had trouble in controlling his temper.

Rumour had it that she was his mistress. No one blamed him for bedding such an attractive morsel, and many envied him, but this show of concern was out of character. If it were any other man but he, one might think that he was bewitched!

'What would you have me say? That I am innocent? I am. That I am a spy? I am not.'

'Liar! What are you then? A whore?' Hugo growled, and the men at his side, who had been drinking with him earlier, muttered encouraging words in his ears. They were French soldiers under the command of an old enemy of Rollo—the Lord Bois-Gilbert—and had already taken bets on the outcome of the hearing. The odds against the woman losing her head before the end of the day were nine to two. 'Admit you killed the real Alisandre and took her place!'

'Why should I want to do that? This is my home. I am quite happy here. I do not want to go to England. I hear it is a cold and unfriendly place.'

'Take care with your words, girl,' Rollo hissed. He stood a few paces to one side of her, marvelling at the stamina which kept her on her feet, facing the gathering unafraid, but frustrated by her lack of spirit in defending herself.

'Do they not want the truth?' she asked, forcing herself to meet his burning gaze. She did not understand why he stood beside her in this, against his own friends and comrades.

'The truth could lose you that pretty little head,' he muttered, and for a moment her courage faltered. She

had not considered death. Surely she would be held
for ransom?

'You ask who I am?' She faced back towards the
dais, to gaze into the stony face of the King of England.
Berengaria gave her a faint smile, but she dared not
return it. 'I do not know. I have no memory, apart
from the four years after the fall of Jerusalem. For
those years I have lived in Jyria, not far from the Holy
City. Until a few weeks ago, I thought my name to be
Karin, and that I was the beloved daughter of Badir.'

'I know of this man,' someone in the crowd shouted
out. 'He has the ear of Saladin himself. He is a devil
. . . He would not spare a Christian life if he had the
chance to take it.'

'His daughter had just died,' Karin interrupted,
struggling to maintain her composure. She must not
break before them, yet the past hour had been a
nightmare and she was beginning to feel weak and
faint. 'He told me my mother's dying words had been
to beg him to save me, and he did.'

'And you lived with the butcher who killed your
parents?' Hugo taunted. 'Do you think us fools? He
took a fancy to you, and you were spared to share his
bed.'

'You acknowledge that she is Alisandre, then?' Rollo challenged, and Hugo's face reddened with anger.

'That is what she would have us believe. I shall
never accept her. She will weep next to get our sympathy. Shall I tell you what happened? Perhaps it is
true that she lost her parents in Jerusalem and that she
has lived with this Badir. Why? Because she is one of
them. Her mother and father were accursed Infidels.

Does it not make more sense to believe that she seeks vengeance for their deaths and has come here to spy on us? She speaks the tongue as one of them. Her servants are Muslims. The old man who died was one of them, too.'

'You will be saying I am one, next,' Rollo gave a grim chuckle.

'You make a pretty pair,' Hugo jeered, old resentments for this man rising up to goad him on recklessly. 'You also have knowledge of their ways—and their language. Men have died in their chains as prisoners rather than lower themselves to acknowledge the Infidels and their faith. You, I hear, took the easy way out. Did you convert, my lord of Aquitaine? Is that why the pair of you are so friendly?'

'Sweet Jesus, you shall die for that.' Rollo wheeled on him, his hand on his sword, forgetful of the royal presence.

'Stay—not an inch of blade will be shown in the presence of your King,' Richard shouted, and both men fell back. 'This matter will be settled now.'

'I demand justice, my King,' Hugo said, falling to one knee before him. 'This woman cannot be allowed to live—nor will I suffer the humiliation of not being allowed to defend myself against this man.'

'Then it is easily settled. Tomorrow the two of you will meet in combat—after this woman's innocence or guilt has been decided. We need a champion, a gentleman to fight for her against Sir Hugo. Who will step forward?'

What was happening? Karin wondered dazedly. Champion? Fight?

'I ask no one to risk his life for me,' she said, stepping forward.

'It is our way,' Richard returned. Not one man had moved in the crowd. 'Come now, are there no gallants among you to be her champion? Will no one prove her innocence before God and man?'

'I will!' Every head in the room swivelled around to stare at the Duke of Aquitaine. Karin felt herself sway. Him! He would risk his life to save hers! The buzz of excited conversation was cut short as Richard rose. It was no combat. Rollo against Sir Hugo! At least no unnecessary time would be wasted.

'You have your wish, Lord Rollo. You accept, Sir Hugo?'

'With pleasure.' Hugo did not look as pleased as his answer indicated. He was no match for Rollo, and he knew it—So did everyone else, damn them!

'Tomorrow, then, before the heat becomes too intense. Shall we say at eight, my lords?'

'What is happening?' Karin asked for the fourth time as she was escorted back to the house. ' I demand that you tell me.'

'You are in no position to demand anything, Lady Alisandre—or do you prefer Karin?' Rollo retorted. He did not release her arm until they were in the privacy of her sitting-room. Pouring out wine for them both, he handed her a goblet. 'Drink it.'

'Your concern touches me, my lord.' The sarcasm in her tone stung him, as she intended. How she would dearly have loved to lay her head on his firm shoulder and give way to tears! She only sipped at the wine, and put it to one side. 'I ask yet again, what is this talk of combat?'

'It is the way we settle matters. If I am killed, you will be judged guilty and executed. If I kill Hugo, you will be innocent.'

'And free?' she cried, hope springing to her face. 'Free to leave Acre and return to Jyira?'

'You will not lose your life, is what I should have said.' Rollo drained his vessel, and watched her sink, ashen-faced, onto a divan. 'I do not do this out of the goodness of my heart. Hugo and I are old enemies. It is good to have this chance to settle with him. Besides, if he is dead, you will be a very rich young woman. There will be no claim on the estates in England, except yours.'

'If I live, I shall not go there. I intend to stay here—in Acre, if I must, but I shall not leave these shores.'

'You will do exactly as I tell you. For your own sake, do not go against me in this.'

'What is it you want?' she said tremulously, her eyes widening at his words.

Reaching down, he pulled her up against him, holding her fast to his chest. His eyes began to glitter at the open fear on her face. Now she understood!

'I want you,' he answered calmly. 'Before the sun sets tomorrow, you will belong to me.'

She moaned as his lips descended on hers in a wild, primitive kiss that fired her senses to an uncontrollable response. She was tired and frightened and in no condition to resist the skill this man imparted into every kiss, every caress of his hands on her body. She heard him laugh in triumph as her lips parted, and answered his for the first time, and the room reeled so unsteadily that she closed her eyes to stem the giddiness upon her.

'Until tomorrow,' Rollo murmured, easing his mouth from hers.

She had not expected him to leave her, but prepared for him to exact payment from her, now! She fell back onto the couch, stunned and shocked at the feelings he had aroused in her. This could not—must not—happen . . . but it had. She knew it that moment, with no uncertainty, that she was in love with him!

The combat between Rollo and Hugo was fast being turned into a full-scale tournament. Long before eight the next morning, carpenters began erecting a makeshift arena surrounded by rows of seats. The King, passing by with several of the Knights Templar, was about to question what was being done, but seeing the enthusiasm with which the preparations were under way, he changed his mind and moved on without speaking a word. The men were bored, restless. This would occupy them for a few hours, and allow old grudges to be settled, hot tempers cooled on the field of friendly battle. Sometimes not so friendly battle. More often than not, this was the way to deal with an enemy, an annoyance—all in all often a most amusing time, Richard mused. Perhaps he himself might even participate . . . the men would like that.

A tournament mêlée was an engagement between two groups of knights who fought each other on horseback. This was very popular with most of the soldiers, for it allowed all to engage in the rough and tumble which relieved the monotony and frustration which had been building up since the fall of Acre. Fighting men were not accustomed to sitting around day after day, getting drunk every evening and growing soft in the arms of a woman. Rollo insisted on his men practising each day at the quintain, as he did himself. He took them out on skirmishing raids and demanded from them the highest fitness. If they got drunk at night he did not care, as long as they appeared ready to do his bidding the next morning. He was as ruthless with himself as he was with them. He asked them to do nothing he would not do himself.

Nothing worried him about meeting Hugo in combat. The man was treacherous; but in an open arena, before everyone, there was nothing underhand that he could do. The tournament would be good for his men and for him, Rollo thought, as he strode through the lists. He had bet Siward fifty ducats that he would be unseated in the mêlée, and another fifty that Chavo would best him in single combat. The winner would also have Leila the dancing-girl, should he want her. Even if Siward were unhorsed, he would have the attentions of that tigress, he mused, a smile tugging at his mouth as he thought of his young squire's deepening affection for Celine. A pity he did not believe in true love, for that was what Chavo proclaimed it to be. It was his intention to take the girl with him when the army moved on. Rollo had not objected. Karin would need a maid, for she too would be accompanying them to Jerusalem.

He did not try to analyse what he felt for her. The emotions were too complex, and each time they were together, more confusing. There was only one way to get her out of his system, to place her in the natural order in his life—which was somewhere after his men, but equal with his horse—and that was to have her. There was no mystery about her. She was just a woman to be used for his pleasure, like so many others before her. She would have to accept that that was how it would be between them until they returned to England. He had not considered any further. Possibly he would be killed . . . that was the only way she would ever gain her freedom, he had decided.

Chavo was waiting for him in the tent set up at one end of the arena. Outside was tethered his white charger to be used in the mêlée. Combat with Hugo was to be single-handed and on foot, by agreement between them. The squire had brushed the animal's coat until it shone in the sunlight, and he had already placed on it a white caparison edged with black, emblazoned with the coat-of-arms of the Duke of Aquitaine.

'All is ready?' he asked, stroking the silky mane of the animal.

'Ay, my lord. Siward will bring the lady in half an hour.' Rollo nodded. 'Forgive me, Lord Rollo, I am confused . . .'

'For what reason?' Rollo's eyes wandered about the compound. On either side of his tent, with his flag fluttering in a strong breeze, other tents were being hastily erected. Squires and pages were busy grooming horses, polishing swords and axes, and cleaning mail and shields. Groups of men stood around talking, making predictions on the outcome of this joust or that. There was excitement in the air, and it made him feel good. He did not think of Hugo or the fact that he was going to kill him. He would not allow himself to dwell on that until a moment before they faced each other.

'Why did you offer to champion the lady? Is she not what you have always suspected?'

'Yes. She could hardly accept the challenge herself, could she?' he returned with a grin, which told Chavo that he did not object to the question.

'The King would have found someone . . .'

'It suits me to fight, Chavo. Let us leave it at that.'

'But she's just another woman . . . Why risk your life for her?' Chavo was thinking of the graves at Verduse as he spoke.

'It is a matter of honour. You forget that Hugo insulted me. As you say, she's only another woman. Or is she, Chavo?' Rollo's tone grew unexpectedly harsh, and the squire's eyes widened in surprise at the pain he heard there. 'What if I am wrong?'

For the first time he considered the possibility, and it brought a vehement oath to his lips.

'You are to sit beside Queen Berengaria, lady. It is her wish,' Siward told Karin, motioning her to go up to the raised dais where the two Queens sat with the King in their midst. He acknowledged her with a nod, nothing more. Joanna was busy talking to a young knight who was pleading to wear her favour in the tournament. With an amused laugh, she undid the scarf at her waist and gave it to him. Blushing profusely, he hurried back to his friends to show them this symbol of acclaim.

'My dear child, how pale you are,' Berengaria exclaimed, drawing Karin down to the stool beside her.
She wore dark red silk, which complemented her
brown hair and eyes. Karin had selected the first gown
in the cupboard, heedless of her appearance. She felt
numb, as if in a dream. She had not slept at all, and
there were dark grey shadows beneath listless eyes.
The gown was dark blue, edged with silver thread,
and left bare her arms and shoulders. Her hair was
loose, crowned with a simple gold circlet. Despite the
intense sunlight, she had not worn a wimple. She
thought them quite unnecessary, and irritating about
her face. 'Do not worry. I hear the Duke is an excellent
fighter.'

And he would win, Karin had no doubt of that. Her
innocence would be established before everyone – and
then she would have to account to him for his action.
She shivered, and the Queen frowned.

'Are you ill? This whole place is rife with disease.
You must take care.'

Karin smiled wanly, grateful for her concern. She
was genuine, not like Rollo. He would fight for her,
not because he believed in her innocence, but because
it suited him to have her still deeper in his power. He
was the spawn of the devil and she hated him, but at
the same time she knew she loved him. How was it
possible for the two to be so closely interwoven?

'Who is ill, Majesty? Not you, I hope?' Rollo came up
behind them, and acknowledged Richard and his
sister before standing close to Karin's seat. His eyes
searched her face. 'You, my lady?'

'Do you think it strange that she should feel unwell?' Berengaria demanded icily. 'The child has to sit here while two men decide whether she lives or dies. How do you think she feels, my lord?'

'She should place her trust and her life in my hands,' Rollo returned, unperturbed by the tone. He would allow no one to rouse his temper today. He needed a cool head and a clear mind for what had to be done. The only way Hugo might win against him was if he were to be wounded in one of the earlier jousts. He would have to keep his wits about him.

'Have I not done that already?' Karin asked. 'Against my will . . .'

'Your stubbornness might well have resulted in your losing your head, had I not accepted Hugo's challenge,' he reminded her. She had to admit the truth of that. Everyone was so confident he would win—but what if he did not? Her life would be forfeit. 'Give me something of yours to wear. Am I not your champion?' he added, with a one-sided smile as she stared up at him in amazement, which told her that the gesture was for the sake of the eyes watching them, no more.

'I have nothing . . . Wait, take this. It is the only thing of value I possess.' She pulled the silver bracelet from her wrist, and held it out to him. 'Small recompense for your help, my lord.' He ignored her jibe.

'A man of honour demands no payment,' Berengaria murmured, lowering her voice so that Richard would not hear her. 'Your thanks will be sufficient, child, when you are proved innocent of these ridiculous charges.'

Nevertheless Rollo took the bracelet and placed it inside his hauberk.

With a bow that acknowledged both Karin and her royal companions, he moved away in the direction of the tents. Karin was aware of one of his men positioning himself to the rear of her, and as trumpets blared to announce the start of the mêlée, she locked her hands in her lap, looking neither to the right, nor to the left.

The mêlée, which began in an atmosphere of friendly rivalry, ended with one man dead and two of Rollo's Guard wounded, together with another eight men from the opposing camp suffering injuries of some kind. No one seemed to know quite what had happened, as was often the case at these tournaments. Horses and lances had been abandoned, and hand-to-hand combat was in progress when she saw Rollo under attack from five men who were pressing him back towards a barrier. To her, it appeared as if they had deliberately closed in on him, abandoning previous opponents. They were trying to kill him! This was no game played out for the amusement of the spectators, who were on their feet, urging on this man and then that as the intensity of the fighting grew.

Siward and Chavo were trying desperately to reach their master. The squire broke through first and took up a position to one side of him. Siward followed close behind. Three against five now. Karin realised that she had been holding her breath. Rollo's huge sword dispatched the man nearest to him. He attacked with great ferocity, which brought roars of approval and loud cheers from the onlookers, who realised they were getting more than they expected this morning, and were enjoying every moment of the blood-curdling spectacle. If this was any indication of things to come, the combat between the Duke of Aquitaine and Hugo de Greville-Wynter would really be something to remember.

Another two men down. Rollo and his men were pressing home with the advantage. Another threw down his sword, and ran . . . He would never be able to show his face in camp again! And then it was over, and Karin closed her eyes, thanking God that Rollo was still alive.

'Courage,' the Queen whispered in her ear, misunderstanding her anxious countenance. 'It will be over soon.'

There were several short combats in between, but none of them gave the excitement or brought the crowd to its feet as the mêlée had done. And then it was time for the main event. Both knights presented themselves before the royal dais, whereupon Richard asked them if they could not settle the issue without shedding blood.

Hugo's eyes locked on the figure in blue, and narrowed to angry slits of pure hatred. He was on his own! Those fools he had hired to kill the man at his side had failed miserably.

'I do not wish to take the life of an innocent woman, my Lord King,' he replied. 'However, this claim to my estates must be withdrawn.'

'What say you, my lady?' Richard asked, looking at Karin. 'Are you prepared to do as is asked, and prevent the combat?'

'No, she is not.' It was Rollo who answered before

she could even open her mouth. 'I have been chosen to represent her, and so I answer for her in this matter. The combat stands. And I ask that no quarter be given. *Tout à outrance.*'

Hugo's face went a sickly grey at the request, hearing the low murmur of approval from people about them. A fight to the death! Looking into Rollo's chilling eyes, he realised he knew about the mêlée. He was going to kill him!

'So be it. Continue . . .' Richard waved them away.

No quarter! Men nudged each other and grinned. The Duke did not want to lose his precious possession. Perhaps he was bewitched, after all. Karin shut her ears to the titters and crude remarks, and ignored the stares and rude looks which came her way. When she had been imprisoned in the dungeon, she had known uncertainty and fear which she had thought never to know the like of again, but she knew them now. She could hardly breathe, and it was not the growing heat that caused the discomfort, but the sight of the tall mail-clad figure with his black surcoat bearing the huge bolt of lightning, split asunder, which brought it about. He fought like a man possessed of a great anger. For this encounter he used not his sword, but his deadly axe. The newly-sharpened blade gleamed in the sunlight, and brought cries from the crowd as it narrowly missed Hugo's legs, then his head. Now it sliced through one of his arms. It was horrible!

The two men were mortal enemies—Rollo had admitted that much to her—so why had he waited so long for this confrontation? Surely there had been many opportunities to fight him before this day? She sensed an inner conflict in him which she did not understand. One as confusing and terrible as that tearing her apart at this very moment, perhaps. She did not want him dead, but if he lived, what then? What would be demanded of her?

Her head jerked up as a throaty roar ripped through the people. Hugo lay sprawled at Rollo's feet. The latter went down on one knee beside him. A moment later he rose and came slowly towards King Richard, who had been leaning forward in his seat, eagerly watching the combat. It was clear to see that he had enjoyed it as much as the four lances he had broken with men from the Duke of Burgundy's contingent earlier.

'He is dead, my King,' Rollo said simply. 'I am satisfied.' He did not look at Karin. She could not take her eyes off him. His face was streaked with dust and sweat. As he wrenched back his coif, she saw that his hair was wet and clung to his head from the mighty exertions of the fight. There was a streak of blood on one arm and across his right temple, but he had sustained only minor bruising and very few cuts. Hugo had been unable to close with him for most of the time, as Rollo swung his axe in a wide arc about his body. He was a formidable foe. Now she began to realise why he was hated by most, respected by some, feared by others. He was a man of honour, but it was of his own making, with his own code, his own laws. His Guard understood this, obeyed him and respected him. Of all men, these would be the ones who gave him love and companionship . . . the friendship he seemed so determined to deny himself.

'As I am.' Richard stood, and gazed around him. 'Let it be known that the charges laid against this lady are considered to be judged false. We will hear no more of them, or the King's anger will descend on the culprit. As to the estates of the Lady Alisandre'—he paused, allowing the name to sink into the mind of every man and woman about him—'we have decided they will be in no better hands than those of the man who has defended her so valiantly. Do you agree, Lord Rollo?'

Rollo looked taken aback. He had scarcely been listening to the King. Hugo's words still rang in his ears, making a mockery of what he had tried to achieve. 'Tell me the truth,' he had urged the dying man. 'She is your cousin, is she not? The bracelet— You said you remembered the bracelet . . .'

In his dying moments, Hugo had smiled at him. 'I lied. I fancied the wench. Did I not say I would marry her? She is not Alisandre.'

Not Alisandre! Then she was some Saracen wench—and he had held back from her. He blinked several times, and shook his head as if to clear the sounds of battle from his brain.

He said in a brusque tone that made even Berengaria glance at him sharply, 'Ay, sire. If you wish it.' He neither sounded, nor looked, pleased.

'We are agreed, then. As for the lady herself, until we return to England, she shall remain in your care. Now let us go and wash this dust from our mouths. I am parched.'

*   *   *

Chavo winced as a heavy goblet sailed past his ear as he entered the tent where Rollo was. His master had not yet even taken off his mail. He would soon have to find him another squire. His own duties were now ended, for the King had taken this opportunity to knight him for his bravery outside the walls of Acre during an attack by the enemy. They had attacked unexpectedly at night, and only his sharp ears had averted a disaster. As it was, the Crusaders had been driven back, suffering heavy losses. He did not want to leave Rollo's side after all they had shared, but he longed to don the silver mail and surcoat with its crest, the livery of the favoured Guard.

'The lady has been returned to the house, my lord. Siward watches her. Let me help you out of your mail . . .'

'No!' Rollo rounded on him, eyes glittering. 'Damn you, leave me alone.'

Just another woman, Chavo mused. This one was like an open sore. If it was not treated soon, the infection could be fatal.

'As you wish, but the King is expecting you.'

'Stay, Chavo, I am in a foul mood—and it has nothing to do with Hugo's death. Yes, get me out of this; I feel like a butcher after today's spectacle. He paid them to kill me, you realise that, don't you?'

'The moment I saw your old enemy Bois-Gilbert making for you, I expected some trick. That one always hated you.' Chavo stripped off the mail, brought a bowl of water and towels, and bathed his master's body. There were several welts across his chest, where Hugo's sword had bounced off the close-linked mail. It had not penetrated, but there would be bad bruising in that area for days.

'You and Siward did well. We must celebrate your elevation to my Guard tonight. Would that please you?' He would get beautifully, blissfully drunk, Rollo decided, wrapping a towel about his hips. 'Here, give her this when you see her again—or to her maid. I care not.' He tossed him the bracelet Karin had given him. He had spent the last half-hour closely examining it, and knew without a doubt that it had been made by skilful Arab craftsmen. She said she had always worn it. With each word she had condemned herself, and he had chosen to ignore the facts because he wanted her as he had never wanted any woman. It had not been this way before, even in Provence!

Chavo stared at the ornament, and then into Rollo's closed face. An idea began to form in his mind.

'Do you not think the lady might be—shall we say—grateful that you saved her life, my lord? She may wish to—thank you later on, when she has had a chance to recover from her ordeal.'

'You always were a romantic fool,' Rollo growled, but not unkindly. 'Give me some fresh clothes and let's join the King. I wish to hear no more of her, do you understand me?'

'Oh, yes, my lord. Very well.'

Karin slept for the whole afternoon, awakening as the sun was slowly dipping behind the distant hills of Tell Keisan. Did Saladin and his men wait somewhere behind them for the Crusaders to leave Acre? she wondered as she returned to the coolness of the room behind her and the tray of food and fruit-juice Celine had just brought. Some of the tenseness had gone from her, but too much still remained. If he did not soon come and tell her her fate, she would break under the strain.

'No, he has not been here, nor sent word of any kind,' Celine assured her when she asked, not liking to remind her mistress that it must have been the fourth time in ten minutes. The latter was not exactly true.

Chavo had come back to the house and had pressed a handful of ducats into her palm. From the Duke of Aquitaine, he told her with a broad smile. She was to go to the markets and buy her mistress's favourite foods and prepare her a fine meal. He had sent a bottle of wine, too. However, on no account was Celine to tell Karin where the fare had come from. Lord Rollo thinks she might throw his well-meaning gesture back in his face if she knew he was behind it, Chavo had said, and she had to admit that would probably be the case. She was astounded by such a show of concern, and said as much, whereupon the squire reprimanded her for her hasty judgment of his master, who was a generous and fair man in all things.

'Ensure that Lady Alisandre has an enjoyable evening,' he said, kissing the tip of Celine's nose. The powerful aphrodisiac he had administered to the wine would weave its powerful magic on the unsuspecting young woman. Perhaps by the time he manoeuvred Lord Rollo back to the house, she would be in a more receptive frame of mind. She *was* different! Rollo, with his longing for her, had made it so. 'When they next meet, perhaps they will not act like combatants on a battlefield. Neither wishes to give way to the other; yet have you seen the way my lord looks at her?'

'He lusts after her, that is all. She is only another pretty woman to him. His gifts will not change how she feels about him.'

'You know nothing about him.' The wine would achieve what nothing else could, Chavo thought. 'And little about her, if you have not seen how her eyes follow him, too. Why, she stands every day on the balcony just to see him pass. Deny me that if you can,' he challenged.

Celine could not disagree, for it was the truth. Karin did spend a great deal of time out on the balcony which overlooked the gardens. And always she was there when Rollo returned from a hunting trip, or from a council of war with the King. Did her mistress truly harbour some tender feelings towards this terrible man? She was so young and innocent—surely she would not allow her head to be turned by a man of violence? Hard, unpredictable and totally ruthless, he was not for her. Yet who was she, a mere slave, to say what had been written? Tamir ibn Dak had spoken of a strange, dark force in her life . . . Celine had no right to argue with the destiny already charted for Karin.

She had nodded and said she would do as Chavo asked. Now, as she watched Karin enjoy a sweetmeat, she was pleased to see the lines of fatigue fading from her young face.

As it grew dark, Celine prepared a bath for her mistress, scenting it with oil of jasmine and rose-petals. Karin lazed in it for almost an hour, while the maid sat beside her and sang with her lute. It was reminiscent of her life in Jyira, and brought tears unbidden to her eyes.

'You are tense and over-wrought,' Celine said, wrapping her in a towel. 'Come, I shall give you a massage and rub some oil into your skin. You have been sadly neglected of late.'

'That is not your fault,' Karin replied with a smile. 'Yes, I would like that. It is good to be still alive, Celine. I should be grateful to him.'

The maid looked at her sharply, but the remark was an innocent one with no hidden meaning.

'He has protected you,' she admitted reluctantly, removing the towel as Karin stretched herself out on the divan, and she began to knead the rigid muscles. 'There now, is that not better?'

'Pure heaven! I had forgotten what is it like to be pampered.' Karin relaxed beneath the insistent pressure, her arms folded beneath her head, and within minutes she felt all tensions slipping away. She was almost asleep by the time Celine had finished and gently began to smooth perfumed oils into her skin. This had been part of her daily routine at Jyira. Petted, pampered and thoroughly spoilt. How drastically life had changed for her, and would change again when she accompanied the army from Acre. There would be none of this luxury then.

She stared at the clothes Celine had laid out on the bed ready for her to put on, recognising them as part of the wardrobe from those other days. A slender tawny eyebrow rose in appreciation as she regarded the short black brocade jacket threaded with gold and silver.

The trousers of Cyprus silk, dyed a most becoming shade of jade green. The matching slippers. Lastly the sleeveless over-robe of Persian cloth of gold. Her favourite outfit!

'As you said, mistress, it is good to be alive,' Celine said quietly, and Karin offered no protests as the woman began to dress her. For the first time in many long weeks she felt a woman again! The softness of the materials was bliss against her skin. She remembered the coarse gown she had worn in the dungeon, and inwardly shuddered. Even the gowns Berengaria had sent her she had found restricting. Nothing gave her the same sense of freedom as her own attire.

A thought struck her as she was staring at her reflection in the polished wall mirror. Who was this woman who faced her? Infidel or Christian? Karin or Alisandre? The clothes told her nothing! She was not even sure what she felt inside any more.

'What is this, a celebration?' she asked with a laugh, which was a little too high-pitched to Celine's way of thinking. As if she saw two images, she thought, and both of them frightened her! Celine had clapped her hands and several servants filed into the room carrying trays of food. She drew a table up in front of the divan and motioned Karin to be seated. 'I have not seen food like this since . . .'

'Since the night before you left Jyira,' the maid murmured, pouring deep red wine into a glass and handing it to her. 'Anchovies, roast fowl with grapes. Sliced chicken-breasts. Sugared cakes, your favourites. Grapes, dates, figs and oranges. I scoured

Acre to find all this for you, mistress. Say you are
pleased with my efforts?'

'Pleased? Oh, Celine, you are a treasure. What
would I do without you?' Karin sipped the wine she
held, and gave a smile of approval. 'This is nectar.
Never have I tasted better. I shall be eternally grateful
to you for this kindness. I feel—I feel I can cope with
anything.'

'May I go now?'

'To your Chavo?' Karin asked, popping a juicy black
grape into her mouth. 'Will you not stay here with me
and enjoy all this?'

'He celebrates his knighthood with his lord; but I go
to prepare my own celebration for his return, with
your permission,' Celine said, almost shyly.

'Of course. There is no need for you to return. When
I have eaten my fill, I shall go to bed and, I think, sleep
soundly for the first time in many weeks. Thank you,
my loyal friend.'

She had been right to do this, after all, Celine
considered. Perhaps the Duke was not as black as he
would have everyone believe. Was it possible that he
possessed a heart like everyone else? On impulse she
bent and kissed Karin's hand, and then ran from the
room. Her mistress was happy, and so was she. She
would apologise to Chavo for her unkind words, and
show him how much she loved him when he returned
to the house. She would think more kindly of his lord
in the future.

What was that perfume, Karin wondered some time
later, and then, glancing about, found tapers of frankincense burning all round the room. The sweet,

heady smell made her feel drowsy after all her food.
What a feast! Dear, dear Celine! They must never be
parted. But for her constant loyalty and friendship,
she could never have endured the past weeks. How
relaxed she felt, almost languorous. She had drunk too
much wine, she thought. No! The bottle was still
half-full. What did it matter? She stretched, and looking down at the clothes she wore, smiled to herself.
Thank goodness Rollo could not see her attired thus.
She would have liked to have seen him, though, to
thank him for saving her life. His non-appearance had
taken her aback, but with his contempt of the female
species it was understandable that he would pefer to
spend time getting drunk with his Guard than being
with her. Yet he had given her to believe otherwise.
Had she, in her fear of him, been mistaken?

The atmosphere in the room grew stuffy, and she
climbed slowly to her feet and wandered out on the
balcony. Sounds of revelry came from the direction of
the palace and beyond the garden walls, as on most
nights. Crusading knights and ordinary soldiers
swelled the taverns to overflowing, drinking the
cheap wine thrust upon them, competing for the
attentions of the whores who flocked to such places
and often fighting each other before the night was
ended.

Above her, the sky was bright with stars. She knew
most of them by heart, after the teaching of Tamir.
Andromeda was her favourite. Somehow she had
always identified herself with this strangely formed
cluster, spiralling like a mis-shapen ball in the velvet
sky. Tamir gone! No more would she sit at his feet and

listen to his words of wisdom. Badir was dead, but the
love she had for him would never die. And Ayub—he
would always be her brother. To think of him in any
other way was not possible, especially now.

She watched a reddish-brown lizard climb over the
white wall beside her, stare at her impassively as if to
question her presence in his domain, and then disappear into a crevice without a sound. A soldier with
his arm about a woman came into view, embraced and
disappeared into the sanctuary of the trees. She suddenly felt very much alone and reproved herself for
being so silly.

Celine had provided her with a feast and wine to
chase away her aches and cares. She was dressed in
the most expensive of materials, chosen with great
care from the many that had been presented before her
by the merchants. And she was safe from Rollo, who
was getting drunk with Chavo. Safe? Was that what
she really wanted? If he had shown her one indication
of kindness, would she not have welcomed his arms
about her and tried to heal the breach between them?
If she could convince him of her sincerity—her
honesty . . . But that was not possible. He would not
listen to one word she had to say, and his arrogance
would provoke her to say angry things, and unleash
both their tempers.

He was there in the gardens below her with Chavo,
looking up to where she stood, and she gasped and
quickly stepped back. But it was too late, for he had
seen her and was climbing the steps to stand before
her. One hand went instinctively to her breast, against
her wildly pounding heart. How handsome he looked!

Over a linen shirt he wore a tunic of dark grey, edged with black braid, the sides fastened with decorative clips. His breeches were of some light material, his shoes of leather.

His sword-belt was heavily jewelled, and there were gold rings on his fingers and gold buckles securing the half-cloak flung carelessly about his shoulders. As her eyes devoured him, so his did her, from the top of her shining red-gold hair to the tips of her pointed slippers. She felt her breath catch even more in her throat as she waited for the sarcastic comment. None came.

Chavo glanced from one to the other, and said quickly, 'My lord, I am for my bed ere my legs desert me.' His voice was no steadier than his gait as he bowed low, almost toppling over as he lost his balance. Rollo's hand grasped his arm and steadied him. His eyes did not leave Karin's face. 'Before I go . . . forgive me, I still have this.'

He pushed something bound in a piece of leather into his master's hands and tottered off, barely avoiding the table where remnants of the food still remained. Frowning, Rollo unwound what lay in his hand, and froze. The bracelet he had tossed so contemptuously to his squire lay gleaming with a muted glow of silver and precious stones. All the missing ones had been replaced. The worn, scratched silverwork had been polished to a high degree. The young fool! Was he playing matchmaker now?

Without a word, he held it out to her. Karin came to him and took it from his palm, and then, as she saw what had been done, a cry of pleasure escaped her lips. 'Oh, my lord, thank you! It is as it once was . . .'

'You have had it a long time, then?' he asked in a hollow tone, and she nodded. Bright lights danced in her eyes. His head swam from too much wine. That was it, he thought. He was drunk. No woman could ever do this to him again!

'I have always worn it . . . at least as far as I can remember.' She slipped it onto her wrist. His eyes followed her hands, continued up over the smoothness of bare shoulders, and down to where the robe of gold parted to reveal the embroidered jacket beneath, which barely covered the firm swell of her breasts. When he returned them to her face, he found it to be crimson. She pretended embarrassment, yet she appeared before him in this attire? 'I—I was about to retire . . .' His bold gaze made her stammer nervously, yet she realised that her fear of him no longer remained. 'But—if you have a moment . . .' She pointed to the abundance of food she had left. 'Celine made a fuss of me tonight, and there is wine . . .'

'I have had far too much already, but one more . . .' Rollo shrugged, and followed her into the room. He tossed his cloak aside and sank onto the divan at her side, watching as she poured wine for them both. Had she been waiting for him? No! She could not know that Hugo had refuted her claim, thus proclaiming her to be what he had always suspected.

Karin was aware of him observing her every move, but it did not un-nerve her, as at other times. She offered him some sliced chicken, which to her surprise he accepted, and afterwards more wine and fruit. She drank with him, and grew more and more relaxed.

Why was it not always this way, she wondered, as she refilled his glass. Perhaps now she could talk to him, make him understand . . .

'Why did you do this?' She touched the bracelet against her skin, still wondering at such an act of kindness. He would have paid a ransom for the jewels. She knew that the Arab merchants in the city extracted every ducat possible from the enemy who came to trade with them, demanding their finest silks and satins for their women, their best lodgings, weaponry, horses.

'Does it matter? It pleases you, does it not?' She nodded, not understanding his distant manner. She leaned forward, reaching for the plate of fruit, and the oils of her skin, warmed by her body heat, drifted to him. His fingers fastened round her wrist. 'Should a thing of beauty not be decked with jewels, appreciated by all who gaze on her?' he laughed softly.

His touch sent a tingling sensation along her spine. The look in the depths of those green eyes transfixed her. Ayub, who had said he loved her, had never looked at her in this way. Desire—longing—passion— they were all there, and something else, too—pain! Always, when he looked at her, it was there some- where in his expression.

'I think you are a little drunk, my lord,' she said, but she did not move away from him, could not . . . even if he had allowed her to do so.

'Not too drunk to know that I have wanted you from the first moment I set eyes on you . . . And from the way you are tonight, I suspect you have the same hunger in you demanding to be satisfied.'

She stiffened at the harshness of his voice, but his hands began moving over her bare skin. As light as a breath of wind his fingertips eased away the robe, explored the smoothness of her creamy shoulders, the soft skin rising above the short jacket.

'I think you and I are well matched, Karin.'

She tried to protest as he drew her against his broad chest. This was not why she had invited him in! She wanted to banish his suspicions about her before they left Acre, and make him trust her . . . His lips touched her cheek, her eyelids and the smooth line of her throat, and each kiss rendered her more and more incapable of thrusting him away, of resisting the demands being made on her. Never had she felt this way with a man . . . It was frightening, exhilarating, promising fulfilment of something deep inside her she had never dared acknowledge before—passion!

With a soft cry she pulled free of his embrace. She expected a show of annoyance, or that he might try to grab hold of her again, but instead he leaned back against the cushions and regarded her with narrowed eyes.

'I *am* not—*will* not—be another of your conquests!' she said fiercely, and one dark eyebrow rose quizzingly.

'Why should you think I consider you so?'

'You do, I know it!' she declared. 'You think of every woman in that way. I have heard what kind of man you are!'

'I do not recall any complaints so far,' Rollo drawled, and his mocking tone brought colour surging into her cheeks. He held out his empty goblet, adding, 'Pour

me some more wine, and let us see if we cannot dispel
this image you have of me.'

Karin's hand trembled visibly as she obeyed.

'And for yourself, I do not like to drink alone,' he
said when she drew back, and slowly she refilled her
own goblet. His hand covered hers as she sat down,
and his fingers began to caress the back of the smooth
white skin, explore the long, slender fingers. He had
large hands, she noticed, with scars in several places.
Seeing him dressed in such finery, it was easy to forget
he was a professional soldier, the leader of a band of
mercenaries. Or so they were called by many. But the
marks reminded her.

'Why do you frown?' Rollo asked, as her brows
drew together. He sipped his wine, appreciating its
depth. It put to shame everything else he had drank
that evening.

'I think you enjoy to fight,' Karin said with sudden
boldness, and looked surprised when he chuckled
loudly.

'I do. There's nothing I enjoy more than a good
fight!'

'Why do you invite death?'

'I don't invite it, my lady. If my time has come, it will
find me wherever I am, whatever I am doing. I shall
not be able to avoid her sting. *Insh'allah.*'

'Are you not afraid?' She was amazed that he could
accept the end so calmly—almost with amusement.

'Only of the manner in which I die. It would be good
to end my days with a sword in my hand, facing an
enemy. Or in bed, making love to a beautiful woman.'
The deep chuckle rose once again in his throat to bring

more colour to her cheeks. She did not know how irresistible it made her look. 'What do you fear?'

'Many things, after—after what has happened to me.' She broke off, cautious about confiding how terribly afraid she was of—him! Of her present predicament. Yet she was finding it easy to talk with him tonight. That in itself should have made her more afraid, but it did not. 'You—You are different tonight.' The words tumbled out before she had given them thought.

'As you are. I was just thinking how enjoyable the evening has become.' He lifted a hand and touched her cheek, aware again of the perfume of her oiled skin. He had been drinking all evening, but he was not drunk; yet what other explanation was there for the way he was feeling now towards her? He wanted her so badly that the pain was like a knife twisting in his stomach. Oaf! He had made no secret of his desire and had probably frightened her with his boldness. He had only to look into those lovely blue eyes to know she was no harlot!

Tonight he found it impossible to accept that she was anything but a beautiful woman in fear for her life. He could put her mind at rest, and reassure her she was no longer in danger. He would continue to give her his protection.

Her skin was satin smooth beneath his fingers. They lingered for a moment before lifting to remove the jewelled combs which secured her hair on the crown of her head in a profusion of curls. It tumbled past her shoulders like a mane of burnished gold. He caught several silken strands and marvelled at the texture.

She was by far the loveliest creature he had ever encountered.

Lisette! Verduse! He tried to conjure them to mind as protection against the fire surging through his loins—but he could see only Karin.

'Please, don't!' Karin whispered, but she did not move as he drew closer, and laid his lips against her cheek, trailed kisses which seared her skin, her very soul, down over her shoulder to the rise of a breast, now cupped in strong brown fingers.

'You have no reason to fear me,' Rollo whispered.

'Have I not? You have made it quite clear to me—to everyone, that you regard me as your property. You said I would belong to you. Is that why you are here? To claim what you consider yours?'

Rollo looked up into her face, reproach in his eyes. 'They were my words and, when spoken, I meant every one. But no, I did not come here to claim my due for saving your life. If it had been my intention to do so, I would have been here far sooner and, believe me, I should have accomplished my aim by now.'

'By force? Rape? It is the only way you will ever have me!'

'It is not, and well you know it. Must I remind you I am here at your invitation? If you are so afraid of me—of what I may do to you—as you would have me believe, why did you extend such an invitation?'

Karin had no answer. She did fear him, for so many varied reasons. Most of all for the effect he had on her whenever they were together.

'Shall I tell you?' He brushed aside the mane of red-gold hair to plant kisses behind her ear-lobes, against her temples. She closed her eyes, not daring to look into his glittering eyes. Why did she not slap him—push away the fingers insistently squeezing her breast, the hand caressing her thigh, that burned her skin through the thin material covering it? His breath was heavy with wine, yet she did not want to turn her face away from his, or stop his lips from parting hers in a kiss that left her weak and breathless—and wanting more! 'It is not me you fear. It is yourself. I can feel the hunger in you. Deny it if you will, but it is there, and only I can satisfy it!'

The heavily drugged wine had done what it was intended to do. She offered no protest as he unfastened the jacket and pushed it away from her breasts. She gasped as his mouth took hers again with sudden, explosive, overwhelming passion. The skilful, knowledgeable hands continuing to explore her body had excited many women, some as unresponsive as she had been when first he touched her. Rollo no longer cared why she had been up at this late hour, dressed like some harem woman. He wanted her blindly, and that was the way he made love to her—heedless of what the morrow brought. That would take care of itself—it always did! If she had not wanted him, she would not have invited him in, fed him wine . . . She had waited for him!

Karin caught her breath as his lips devoured her bare flesh. No part of her was sacred to him as his lips followed the downward caresses of his hands—over firm breasts, the rosebud nipples now taut with desire, proclaiming her surrender, the flat, smooth stomach—the secret place between her thighs where no man had ventured before. She was shocked by his boldness and yet excited by it. Shy to have his eyes devour her body—yet, strangely, not ashamed.

And then, as he drew back from her to strip of his clothes, she found herself staring for the first time in her life at the unclothed body of a man. It was the body of a soldier—hard, toughened by years of fighting. Scarred in many places, chest, shoulders, back, and along one long sun-bronzed leg. A tight smile tugged at his mouth as she laid a tentative finger against one of the fresh weals on his chest made by Hugo's sword. These!—for her! He had killed for her! Impulsively she pressed her lips against each one in turn.

Winding a length of loose hair around his fist, Rollo tugged back her head and once more took her mouth. He sank over her, his weight pressing her down on the couch. Karin gave herself up to his embraces without restraint, surrendered herself to the exquisite pleasure beginning to flow through her body. Every tiny touch, caress, kiss brought her closer to the final surrender of her innocence.

Only once did she attempt to twist away from him, and that was when he pulled away the last of her clothing and sank deeply into her. The sudden unexpected pain penetrated even her dulled senses, and she cried out. Immediately he was still, and her eyes flew open in alarm, afraid he was leaving her. She clutched him to her and he began to move inside her again, slowly, gently. His lips covered hers, silencing her tiny cries . . .

The light awoke Karin next morning. Although it was early, bright sunlight filled the room, blinding her

when she first opened her eyes. She turned her head
on the pillow to avoid it—and froze . . . There was a
man beside her, watching her. Rollo! One hand was
against her breast. A leg was thrown across hers. For a
moment she stared at him in sheer disbelief, then, as a
smile began to spread across his face, memory flooded
back and with it the realisation of what she had
allowed him to do to her!

She tried to jump from the bed, but he caught her
and flung her down again. A hard leg was thrust
beneath her thighs, roughly parting them. She protested feebly, still not fully awake, and heard him
drawl mockingly in her ear:

'Be still, woman. You were willing enough last
night. I'll leave you in peace soon enough.'

Shameful recollection of the easy way he had overcome her slipped back into her mind. Bright colour
surged into her cheeks, then receded, leaving them
ashen. He had not been this way with her last night,
why so now? She had known such happiness in his
arms, such contentment and pleasure. He was looking
at her now as if he hated her! He had tricked her! He
had come with his soft words and persuasive kisses
and done exactly what she had accused him of—
claiming her as a possession. If he had raped her
without pity she would have felt the same as she did
now—unclean! Used!

She fought against the arms trying to hold her
down, the body pressing against hers, determined to
subdue her again. He caught both her wrists in one
hand above her head, while the other began to explore
her breast. His mouth bruised hers cruelly. How could

she have welcomed his advances so readily before? She had drunk too much wine, allowed him to overcome her fear of him with his gentleness. Wine! Had she been drugged? It was the only explanation for his victory over her. *He* had done it! She did not know how, but somehow *he* was responsible for what had taken place, and he alone!

Her limbs felt like heavy stones, confirming what she suspected. She had no strength to throw him off and was forced to endure the long, tortuous assault on her already weakened body. As a few hours before, there was no part of her that was sacred to him. Tears welled into her eyes as pain penetrated the aftermath of the drug which still numbed her senses as he thrust deeply into her, and then he was drawing away, pulling on his clothing. She lay unmoving, shocked that this had happened to her. Without a word, he left her.

Her mouth was dry from the wine and whatever had been in it. She stumbled from the bed, shielding her eyes from the bright sunlight in the room. The place was chaotic. Her clothes were scattered over the divan and on the floor. The wine bottle was overturned on its side. Half-empty plates of food still littered the table. She found some fresh water in a pitcher and gulped back great mouthfuls. From the ante-chamber came a loud cry. Celine's voice raised in anger! No—extreme hatred! She grabbed up a robe, flung it around her, and reeled towards the curtained doorway.

Now a blow, and the sound of someone swearing furiously. Before her, on the ground, Chavo was nursing a bruised jaw. Blood seeped from a cut at the side of his mouth. Rollo still stood over him, fists clenched, his face terrible to see. Celine was raving at him in her own tongue, calling down all the curses of Allah and his prophet Muhammad on the heads of them both. If he did not take their lives, then she would. Karin leaned against the wall, too dazed to take in what was happening. Rollo raised his head and saw her, and his face changed. Pain again, but more heartrending than she had ever seen before. It was as though his heart were being torn from his body.

'I did not know! I swear it!' he said heavily. 'I thought you to be willing. My God, I've never taken an unwilling woman in my life . . .'

'They had me drug you. Sweet mistress, forgive me, I did not know.' Celine threw herself at Karin's feet. 'He . . .' She glared at Chavo, wishing that all the demons of hell would pluck him from this earth to where he rightfully belonged. 'He said his lord wished to make amends for his rude manner. He wished there to be a new understanding between you, now that you had been proved innocent before the King and his knights. The food, the wine, it all came from him! He lied to me. They lied to me.'

'No!' Chavo cried. He scrambled to his feet, stepping well back as Rollo's fist rose menacingly before him. 'Lord Rollo knew none of what I did. Forgive me, lady,' he gazed wide-eyed at Karin's gaping robe. Hastily she clutched it together, remembering that she was naked beneath it. When she found her voice, her tone shocked both men with its harshness.

'You would do anything for him, would you not, messire? Would that I could believe him innocent of this, but I cannot. He has made his intentions towards me too plain from the start. It will make a fine joke among your friends, will it not, my lord? But do not expect me to hide my face in shame or condone your lies! This morning I shall go to the Queen and tell her what took place. I shall demand to be taken out of your hands. If not, I swear I shall kill you for what you have done to me.'

'Done to you?' Rollo echoed softly. He stepped across the space separating them, his eyes glittering dangerously. 'I care not if you believe me, woman.' It was a lie. He did, and he hated himself for hurting her still more. Drugged . . . Yes, he could see it now in her eyes. But last night he had been drinking, and the sight of her in those alluring clothes, the softness of her against him when he touched her, seemingly as eager as he to satisfy the hunger in her . . . He knew what he must do, and it did not sit easily on his shoulders. He had sworn never to give another woman his name—But what other choice had he? And he must speak to the King before she had a chance to tell her side of it. 'You were eager enough, drug or no. I felt it in you. And this morning . . .'

She gasped at the insinuation. He knew she had not . . . Not that way!

'Keep them both here,' he ordered Chavo. 'I shall send someone to relieve you later. They are to contact no one. See no one.'

'Yes, my lord.'

'I shall deal with you later also,' came the departing threat.

'I hope he slits your throat,' Celine whispered fiercely, as she helped Karin back into the bedroom.

Chavo made no answer. He had never seen Rollo so furious. No matter how black his mood, how fierce his temper, he had never struck him before. He knew he had made a terrible mistake. If his life was forfeit, it was no more than he deserved.

'Wed the Duke of Aquitaine?' Karin repeated in a hollow tone.

Berengaria nodded. She had just been told of Rollo's visit to the King two days before, and of the royal permission given for him to take this girl as his wife. She looked as if the idea appalled her. And so it should, if he were as cold-hearted a man as rumour had it. He had fought for the girl, so now he supposed he could marry her and lay his hands permanently on her estates. That one had a shrewd brain!

'There is nothing I can do. I talked with the King, but he is all for it. You do need someone to care for you, my dear. Why, the lands you have in England are vast and need a man's firm hand.'

'Marry—him?' Karin said again. 'Dear heaven, why did he not leave me where he found me? Life there would have been better than with him.'

'He is not a pauper, you know,' the Queen said, trying to reassure her. Heaven forbid that she should ever consider it! 'He has accumulated much wealth since he came to Palestine, and he has a castle here, and land. The King thinks highly of him.' She laid a hand on Karin's shoulder, and felt her tremble. 'You will want for nothing. In a year or two, when you have a family, it will all be different for you.'

A family? Bear him a child! Never!

CHAPTER SIX

'YOU WANTED to see me?'

Karin leapt to her feet as Rollo's voice behind her brought her out of deep thought. She had not heard him enter. She had not seen him since that night, nor had he made any attempt to see her. All communication had been through Chavo or Siward. The marriage between them would take place on the twenty-third of August. Just like that! And he expected her to obey like one of his servants!

She had gone several times to his rooms, but had been refused admittance by the Guard, and told he was not there. Not for a moment had she believed the excuse.

As she turned to face him, she felt the colour begin to rise in her cheeks. She did not know the effort it cost him to remain unmoved at the sight of her. He had fought against coming to her, making her believe that what had happened had not been a cold-blooded plan to seduce her and reduce her to the level of other women he had known . . . Fought and won the battle raging inside him. But it had taken four long days during which his men feared to go near him, and he hated himself for the black mood which overshadowed him and brought back memories of the past. Memories of that other woman who had once lain in his arms and whispered sweet words of love in his ear. He had believed her, for he had worshipped the ground she walked on. He had given her his love, his name, his wealth, his very soul—and she had betrayed him . . .

He would never be that vulnerable again, nor that weak—no matter what it cost him.

Karin looked into the hard face and knew that her words would fall on deaf ears. Why was he doing this to her? 'I have been told we are to marry,' she said stiffly. She was dressed in a gown of yellow which set off the sheen of her hair to perfection, but also accentuated the frightful pallor of her cheeks. He wondered if she had slept at all since that night. Why would the words of remorse not come to his lips? They were in his mind. Was that other memory to haunt him for the rest of his life? 'By the Queen and by your squire. However, I have not heard it from you.'

'I have the King's permission to wed you—yes. You are prepared? It is to be quite soon.' His tone showed indifference, and it shocked her.

'Prepared?' Karin gasped, staring at him as if he had taken leave of his senses. 'You expect me to obey you!'

'No, the King,' Rollo replied, grave-faced. 'You have no say in the matter. It has been decided. We are even, now. You gave me my life—I have given you yours.'

'I shall not marry you,' she cried, her face blazing defiance. 'I shall defy King Richard! You! All the knights in Christendom and all the demons in hell if I have to! Do you hear me? Why are you doing this? You do not want me as your wife.'

'No.' He gave her a piercing look. Ruthlessly she

quelled the fluttering sensation it aroused deep inside her. For her own sake she had to remain immune to any gesture, however small, on his part, for it would be as false as he was, meant to win her over to agree to this preposterous idea. 'You are quite right. I do not want another wife.' Another! Her eyes widened at his words. He had been married before? She had not heard of this. 'I swore many years ago that I would never give another woman my name. However, circumstances have determined otherwise. I have wronged you, and therefore I must do what is right by you.'

'How kind of you, gracious lord. Why me, and not one of the many others you have had in your bed?' she taunted, and was surprised to see a slow flush steal over his face. Was it possible that he did regret what had passed between them? That Chavo had spoken the truth? 'You cannot force me into this match.' Her voice held no conviction, for she knew that the King's word could not be gainsaid.

'You are not like them—I admit that now—but you will never hear it again from my lips. You will wed me on the twenty-third of this month, and when you have my name you will behave as a wife should. You will obey me in all things. Should I hear one whisper of scandal about you again, I shall not hesitate to kill you. My name shall not be bandied about among my men for low comments a second time.'

'Are you so ambitious that you really intend to marry a woman you detest?' Karin cried, frightened by his words. What frightful secret lurked in his heart to give vent to such a threat?

He looked at her with a frown, and she hastened to add, 'My estates in England. It has been proved that I am the Lady Alisandre de Greville-Wynter. The Queen says I am wealthy . . . that they are vast . . .'

'By all the saints, do you think I care about your paltry little dowry?' To her horror he laughed in her face. It was not a pleasant sound. 'I have more gold than you could count in a year; jewels, land, a castle here in the Holy Land which I bought from the Knights Templar. With it went my solemn oath to destroy it before I allowed it to fall into the hands of the enemy, but that is unlikely. It is manned by the toughest of my fighting men, mainly European mercenaries, aided by some very competent German pikemen. They defend it whenever I am away, and defend it well. Shah'mat will never fall to the Saracens! And I have lands in France . . .' He broke off, a shadow crossing his features. 'Nay, not there. I have renounced those for ever . . . But to think I want your estates? You delude yourself. If you have nothing more to say, I have an engagement . . .'

'With your dancing-girl?' She flung the words at him bitterly, although she knew he was not going to her, for he had on his chain-mail and she could see two armed guards hovering outside the curtained alcove. She hated herself for the pettiness of the remark as a smile tugged at the corners of his mouth. There was no humour in his eyes, however, which held a warning as to the consequences of a repetition of such foolish defiance.

'Rest assured, I shall find time for you. I shall see

you at our wedding,' was the parting taunt as he left her.

If only she could get out of the city, Karin thought, as she paced the room throughout the hours of daylight. Darkness found her exhausted, and Celine was unable to comfort her as she continued to contemplate the awful day which was growing inevitably nearer. Three days more until she was bound to the Lord of Darkness for ever. The next morning the maid found her dressing herself in a feverish haste.

'But he will not allow you to go riding by yourself!' Celine protested when Karin explained the plan she had in mind.

'Then he can send someone with me, I care not. Should a bride not be allowed to shop for her wedding day? The Queen would think it most strange if I told her he had denied me this request,' she returned. Her plan, such as it was, entailed a simple journey to the markets to buy materials, trinkets, a present for her husband on this joyous occasion. She had seized on any excuse. Somewhere in one of those twisting, cobbled streets she would take flight and ride for her life . . . or run, whatever came first.

'Am I to come with you?' the maid asked hesitantly. Her mistress had made no mention of *that* night, and she was afraid she was still held to blame for what had happened. How could she have been so stupid as to have believed Chavo's lying tongue! Even when they had lain together after his return, she suspected nothing. While she was enjoying his kisses and promises, her mistress was in the arms of that devil! Subjected to Allah only knew what indignities. Her silence on the subject had served to increase Celine's unhappiness.

'Of course! Do you think I would leave you behind? It was not your fault, Celine. If anyone's, it was mine. I wanted to trust him . . . I liked being near him. I wish I had never met him, yet I ache when I do not see him. I love him, yet I hate him.'

'Mistress, do you realise what you are saying?' Celine gasped.

'I wish I did not, but I am not drugged now. If he came to me, and made love to me, I would fight him with every breath in my body because I know I mean nothing to him. But in the end I would allow him his way, because my body would desire it. I have no weapon against him.'

'Except his own desire for you,' Celine murmured, and Karin looked at her questioningly. 'Chavo told me of a woman in his past—He loved her very much. I do not know what happened, only that she is dead and he has never loved another since. Neither has he hungered after one, as he has after you! Deny him what he wants. That will bring him to heel!'

'What I am not willing to give, he will take,' Karin answered, recalling the morning when he had taken her without one moment of thought for her own feelings. So different from those dream-like hours when he had held her in his arms, taught her the pleasure and delights of the act of love, shown her skilfully, yet carefully, after that initial lovemaking on the divan, the dizzy heights to which he could lift her. Time and time again she had asked herself whether, if she had not been drugged, she would have responded as she did.

Siward shook his head as she attempted to leave her apartment, folded his arms across a massive chest, and stood fast.

'I demand you allow me to leave. Fetch Lord Rollo, then.'

'That is not possible. He is in council with the King and others. You must wait.'

'Must I? Send word to Queen Berengaria. Ask her to provide an escort for me to ride into the town. There are things a bride must purchase before her wedding day, sir knight. Not that I expect you have ever met a true lady before!' Karin said scathingly.

'Siward's father was Cormus, a great Viking warrior. His mother was Isoldan, daughter of a king. If you were a man, he would kill you for those words,' Rollo said, coming into the room in time to hear her. 'What is it you want?'

'To go into the town. Surely you realise that I have nothing to wear for my wedding? Are you such an unfeeling creature that you expect me to appear in one of the gowns given to me by the Queen?' Karin said, and instantly his eyes narrowed suspiciously.

'You gave me to understand that you care little for what is to take place.'

'I have my pride. You will not take that from me. I will not be married in someone else's clothes and be sniggered at by other women. Would you like it said that you are too mean to provide for me, my lord? Everyone knows I have nothing of my own, so it is expected of you . . .'

'What you expect and what you may receive could well turn out to be quite different,' Rollo warned, but to her great relief he nodded.

'Go with her, Siward, and heed not her viperish tongue. It will soon be curbed. Take two more men with you, and return her here before noon.'

'Three men to guard two fragile women?' Karin jeered.

'It will show everyone how much you mean to me,' he mocked, and she had no answer. 'Should she give you trouble, Siward, tie her to her horse and bring her back that way. That will also show everyone how I treat shrewish women.'

Karin swept past him, cheeks flaming. He was insufferable. Was every encounter between them to be like this? Taunts, innuendoes, baiting remarks. She had to escape . . .

But she had no chance. The three Guards who flanked them allowed her horse to take not one step out of line, and when she walked on foot through the bazaars, Siward was beside her, one man in front, and the third brought up the rear with Celine. If she ran, her maid would be held, and she would not go without her. Yet if she did not . . . More than once Celine cast an appealing glance towards her, her eyes silently urging her to take a chance if it came. None did. The men were trained professionals, and they knew what would happen to them if they allowed their charges to escape.

Maintaining the pretence to the last, Karin bought several rolls of satin and a bolt of scarlet velvet from Spain. She handed it over to the soldiers with malicious glee. She would weigh them down with so much stuff that they would regret this day for the rest of their lives. She purchased slippers of Moroccan leather, brilliantly dyed ribbons and linen undergarments. Siward handed over whatever payment was required without questioning any of the items. How much money had Rollo given him? she wondered. She intended to spend it all!

As she continued, selecting necklaces of amber and coral, a heavy gold ring set with an enormous amethyst and various other items of jewellery, she became aware of the smile spreading across the Nordic features. As if to say—Spend what you will— I have plenty—My lord is a wealthy man. She had lost her battle. Silently she admitted defeat, and announced that she was tired and wished to return.

Riding back, she knew that she should be happy with what she now possessed. She could hold her own against any woman in Acre. Why, with her new materials, her gowns would be as spectacular as those of Queen Joanna herself, yet the thought gave her no pleasure. It meant nothing to her. The rich clothes and the jewels were of no importance.

She wondered all of a sudden why the streets were so crowded. People jostled past them, heading in the direction of the main gates of the city. Knights Templar strode through the throngs packing the narrow alleys, rudely shouldering their way and pushing people aside. Veiled women, too, slipped cautiously from houses to sidle along in the wake of everyone else. What curious spectacle brought so many people flocking to the walls? She looked at Siward, but he shook his head.

'I want to know what is happening,' she insisted. Perhaps the hostages were being released at last. She knew some of the men who had fought with Ayub over the past twenty-three months. If they saw her alive and well, they could tell him . . . perhaps they might devise a scheme to save her. But not before the twenty-third, and if she was lifted from under the very nose of the Duke of Aquitaine, it would be to become the bride of the Lord of Jyira. Two men who wished her for their wife! 'It is not yet noon.'

He shrugged and motioned her to continue. They rode in silence until they reached the mighty gates of Acre which now stood wide open with people streaming through. Crusaders lined the walls, she saw when she looked up at the ramparts, and there were archers at every arrow-slit. Had Saladin returned? If not, were the people leaving? She saw, and wished she had not, so gruesome was the sight which met her eyes on the plain beyond.

Earlier that morning, by the order of Richard, King of England, the garrison hostages had been rounded up and taken outside the city walls and there they were put to the sword. None was saved but a few high-ranking officers who would still fetch a good ransom. Beheaded by men who slew them with great gusto, relishing in this act of butchery, Karin thought, turning her head away. The stench of blood was nauseating. Already birds of prey were gathering overhead. Arab men watched stony-faced. Women wept behind their veils.

From a distance, Richard and his officials watched the slaughter of over two thousand six hundred men. Ugly murmurs ran through the Arab crowds, silenced by the prodding of the swords or lances of the Franks. The latter considered the sentence on the prisoners just, for was it not rumoured that Saladin had murdered hundreds of Christian prisoners while he negotiated the release of his own men? Had he cared for them at all, he would have paid their ransom within the time set.

'Come, my lady, this is no place for you,' Siward said. She did not even hear him. He took her horse's bridle and led her away.

Rollo was awaiting their return in the garden. Karin stopped before him, her features pale despite the heat of the sun. She felt sick and faint. Nothing could ever erase the memory of what she had seen. Another nightmare to haunt her. She was still trembling from the ghoulish spectacle.

'Butcher!' She spat the word at him, and felt Celine take her by the arm, and press it warningly.

'You saw? Damn you, man, why did you take her there?' he shouted at Siward. 'Am I surrounded by fools, of late?'

'Like you, my lord, I expected their release, not a massacre,' came the gruff reply.

Karin gave a short laugh of disbelief. 'Butchers, that is what you all are! Let me tell you this. There were men there who have defended this city for nearly two years. Gallant, fighting men, as brave as you any day, my lord Rollo. They were Ayub's men . . . an élite force of Turkish archers belonging to my brother, the

Lord of Jyira.' She ignored the look of fury which came into his face at her deliberate reference to the other life she had known. 'He will not let this rest. He will have your head severed from your body and pinned to the Jerusalem Gate for this atrocity.'

'And you would like that,' Rollo said heavily. He could have hit her. It took every ounce of self-control not to clench his fist and strike her.

'Yes, I would like that! Take me inside, Celine. The stench of death is out here, too, and I like it not.'

'Wake up! Sweet Jesus! Wake up, woman, or I'll drag you from the bed,' Rollo ordered for a second time, and Karin's eyes, dazed with sleep, slowly opened. She gasped, and reached for the covers that she had thrown back from her body in the heat of the night. He snatched them from her grasp, caught her wrist and pulled her into a sitting position. 'Get up. Quickly! Ask no questions. Put these on.'

She wore only a thin nightgown, totally transparent, yet he did not even look at her as she turned away to stare in amazement at the garments he had tossed down on the bed. A link-mail hauberk, undershirt, pants and a white burnous. He expected her to wear those? She would look like a boy!

'One more second, and I shall rip off your clothes and dress you myself,' he threatened, a hand reaching for the material covering her body.

'Send Celine to me. I will not change in front of you,' she cried.

'No. I shall give my reasons in a moment, if you are quick. Besides, what have you to hide from me?'

The taunt stung her into action, and she slid the silk from her shoulders. As it fell to the floor in a huddle, he looked at her for the first time, and she felt as if the floor moved beneath her feet. His eyes wandered over firm, rounded breasts, such a tiny waist, shapely hips and long, slender legs. He had not forgotten an inch of her loveliness. He took a step towards her, saw the fear which entered her eyes as she thought he meant to touch her, and stopped again.

'Hurry. My men are waiting below!' he snapped.

'Waiting—Why? Where are we going? Tomorrow . . .' Tomorrow was the twenty-third. Was there to be no wedding? Had he ever intended that there should be?

He read the unspoken question in her eyes, and said with the same brusqueness, 'You will have to wait a while longer to become my devoted wife. We are leaving the city with the rest of the army. Richard marches for Jerusalem!'

'Leaving?' she echoed. She knew nothing of this! He came forward, brushed aside her trembling hands and fastened the laces of the linen shirt, helped her to don the mail hauberk and, over it, the surcoat bearing his arms.

'You will be my new squire,' he said humourlessly. 'I would have taken the boy, Omar, but I do not want a knife in my ribs. He will be safe here.'

'And Celine! I cannot—will not—leave her behind.'

'She stays. It is necessary to allay suspicion. For the next day or two, until we are well away from here, it must be believed that you have remained in the city. Don't worry. She is under the Queen's protection, and nothing will happen to her.' She looked at him, not understanding, yet aware that something was terribly wrong. 'Well, I suppose you will pass,' he added, stepping back to inspect her. 'Put on your burnous and pull the hood well over your face.'

She did as she was bid, and he nodded in satisfaction.

'Better. You will pass, until we are out of the city. Siward and Chavo will ride with you. No one will challenge you, for you wear my colours, but should you be stopped, you will allow them to do the talking.'

'I go nowhere until you tell me what this is all about,' Karin insisted. 'There never was meant to be a marriage, was there? You intend to bundle me off, now that you are leaving, to be used when the fancy takes you . . . Like the rest of the camp-followers with the army.'

'The King is allowing only the laundry-women and those who have lost their men to accompany the army from Acre,' Rollo replied grimly. She had seen such women scouring the streets of the city for captured Saracen prisoners. These they mutilated horribly in revenge for the husbands, lovers or sons they had lost in battle. They fought alongside the men with equal ferocity, in hauberks and carrying weapons, but were greatly despised for their brutality. Many had fallen before the walls of Acre, screaming to be avenged. 'For your own sake and mine, you will not betray your identity.'

'Why should I believe you?' she whispered.

'Queen Berengaria tells me there is a plot against your life. Some still do not believe you to be as innocent as you would have them think. Had they heard the way you have spoken to me, they would know you are not. However, I have decided that you shall come with me. As my future wife, it is my duty to protect you. The Queen and the King's sister, and the other ladies, remain here until we reach a new haven. Jaffa, perhaps, or Ascalon. Then they will join us.'

'Surely it would suit you for me to die, my lord,' Karin suggested. 'Then you would have my estates without the bother of an unwanted wife.'

Rollo's eyes gleamed with unspoken mockery. Before she could move, he caught her to him and bruised her lips beneath his for a long, tortuous moment. He gave a soft chuckle as he released her. 'Whatever made you think I did not want you? Surely someone has told you that I have an eye for beauty? Whatever else you are, Karin, you are beautiful—and desirable. This time alone together will give us time to get to know each other properly. Perhaps by the time we reach my castle at Shah'mat, you will not find marriage to me such an unpleasant proposition.'

She stepped back from him, rubbing a hand across her lips as if to erase his kiss, and his eyes narrowed angrily.

'It is time to leave.'

'But Celine!' she cried. 'Give me five minutes to say goodbye—I beg you?'

The anguish in her voice reached him, and he nodded and strode out. A moment later Celine came into the room and stared unbelievingly at the mail-clad figure before her.

'Mistress! He really does mean to take you with him?'

'Yes. He says my life is in danger. I know not whether to believe him. What is to happen to you?'

'I am to go to the Queen in the morning and stay with her. Don't worry, I shall be quite safe. It is you I fear for—alone with him.'

They hugged, each seeking comfort from the other. Karin's face was wet with tears when she drew away, conscious of Chavo hovering in the doorway. She had not said a civil word to him since that night!

'I shall pray for you,' she whispered.

'May Allah guide your footsteps,' Celine replied, holding back her own tears, knowing they would only add to her mistress's distress. 'Go, quickly! We shall meet again soon.'

The days which followed were unreal for Karin. She rode in the midst of Rollo's Guard. Never was she without a man at her side, even when they stopped to rest. Rollo himself was always riding to and fro among his men. He was a hard taskmaster, she came to realise, and demanded the best from everyone—even her, who had never had to endure the rigours of an army march before.

Past Haifa, over the ridge of Mount Carmel and on past Caesarea. Had the wagons accompanying them not been stocked full with supplies, Richard's men would surely have starved, for the land they covered each day had been burned by the Saracens ahead of them. No crop was left for the enemy. Castles and fortifications were razed. Any type of shelter had been demolished, and at night they camped beneath the stars. By day they sweltered under unbearable heat. Flies and mosquitoes brought disease and discomfort at every turn.

Because of the hilly terrain, a direct route to Jerusalem was impossible, and so Richard decided to make for Jaffa. On one side the fleet, with fresh supplies and assistance when required, on the other the army of Saladin—following, waiting. It was a game of nerves, one which he played well, but not so the men with him, who became more and more anxious to engage the enemy as the days passed. Still he held them back, keeping them in tight formation, ordering no man to break ranks. It was not an easy command to maintain.

Saladin's élite Turkish horsemen, agile and skilful with their bows as they rode, were matched against heavily armoured men with shields and lances . . . their was the advantage, the Crusaders discovered in skirmish after skirmish. The arrows sank into the close-linked mail, but barely penetrated the skin. Even so, wave after wave of attack, of arrows flying through the air and descending on men sweating inside their mail, cursing the order which kept them in line and unable to take out after the enemy, made tempers run short. Sunstroke began to account for more casualties than arrows.

Three weeks later, the King of England ordered his army to encamp on a plain to the north of Arsuf. He had come to realise that he must commit his men to a full-scale battle, or morale would worsen.

A parley with Saladin was asked for. In his place came his brother, al-Adil, from whom Richard demanded the whole of the Holy Land. Less than two days later, men were roused to march again, groaning at the short break that had brought them little respite from the intense heat and discomfort they endured day after day.

Rollo and his men marched behind the Normans and English who guarded the royal standard, and in front of the French, with the Hospitallers bringing up the rear—the position of greatest danger. The army of Saladin had camped in a forest east of the Crusaders' route. That morning Rollo had insisted that she ride behind him, with two men on either side, and two behind her. He had also given her a basilard, a dagger with a double-edged triangular blade, with which to defend herself if they were attacked, he said. Attacked! He had on his strongest armour, carried lance and shield, and rode his strongest war-horse! He smiled somewhat grimly at her anxious features.

'Perhaps one of your friends will kill me,' he said humourlessly.

He had not touched her since they left Acre some three weeks before. By day she rode among his Guard, who knew her identity. To the remainder of the two-hundred-strong force which followed him—among their ranks, Frenchmen from Provence and the Pyrenees, the latter fighters of exceptional ferocity, a few English and German mercenaries—she was simply his new squire. There were jokes on the pretty appearance and soft complexion of the newcomer, but they were mostly given in a friendly manner. A few who had envied Rollo's acquisition at the tournament in Acre muttered that he had found himself a boy who looked more like a girl, to make amends for leaving his woman behind him—but they did so out of earshot of their lord and his Guard, not wanting a challenge thrown down.

Karin did not understand why she had been left alone. At night, when they made camp, she shared Rollo's tent, lying a few feet away from him on a makeshift bed. While on the march, he had no more comforts than his men. He slept on the ground as they did, his only concession a covering above his head. She wondered if he would have bothered with that had she not been with him. Sometimes, when they stopped, she was so tired that she would almost fall from the saddle. No one ever dared to come to offer her help, though several times she was aware of one of the Guard watching her with sympathetic eyes. The life of a squire was a hard one, Rollo had told her that first day. It was meant to be. It was to train him for life as a knight. His duties were many, the hours long . . . and whenever there were people about, she was forced to fetch and carry for him, remove his boots, sometimes even his mail. She polished that, together with his weapons . . . He had treated her as a stranger for all this time. She knew it was for her own good, but she did not like him for it, and stubbornly refused to carry out the more intimate tasks required of her, like bathing her master.

She ached in every limb. In the mornings she was so stiff that she could hardly remount her horse, a huge brute far too big for her. Although an excellent horse-woman, she was accustomed to an Arab mount, well trained and docile, who obeyed her every wish, not some courser of fifteen hands. There were days when she sat on his back and compared herself to a tiny olive, lost on a mountainside. How she stayed on, she never knew. Rollo never allowed her to see him watching her, or the admiration he felt at her stamina. The march was a gruelling one, but she had endured it well. He never allowed her to know how he felt by a kind word, a smile, even a tiny compliment. He intended to continue as he had started out—as her master!

'If we are attacked, you will ride like the wind,' he told her. 'You will be on your own. I shall not send men with you, for they are honour bound to stay and fight.'

'Are you not afraid that I shall ride to my friends?' She spoke of the waiting Saracens, as he had, and saw his face darken.

'They will take one look at you, dressed as you are, and an archer will put an arrow in you before you can get close enough to call to them.'

'Why did you not leave me in Acre? I was safe there.'

'No, you were not. Hugo, believe it or not, did have friends. They were conspiring, with others who also believe you to be a spy, to kill you the moment I had left. It would most likely have been made to look like an accident, so that the Queen would not suspect, but she is more intelligent than they realised. I, too, underestimated her worth,' he added. 'It was she who warned me of the conspiracy. She did not agree with my decision to bring you along, and so I did not ask her approval. You are here, and still alive . . . How many lives do you have, *Kutti*?' She coloured as he used the Arabic for 'cat.' 'One spent in Jerusalem . . . one in the dungeons at Acre. Another at the tournament. I would not run, if I were you. They are going fast!'

The beginning of the attack on the Crusader columns almost frightened her to death. Towards midday, as all about her men toiled under the heat and she clung to her saddle feeling limp and drained, the air was suddenly full of arrows. They whistled through the air to find their marks in the ranks of the foot-soldiers, who dropped into the sand, screaming and groaning, as with a great clashing of cymbals and beating of drums Saladin's army came out of the trees to do battle with the army of Malik al-Inkitar. The Turkish cavalry came pounding towards them, reinforced with coal-black Nubians and black-robed Bedouin, all magnificent horsemen. They were faster and more agile than the Crusader cavalry, who relied on a massive charge in strength to break the enemy ranks and then over-run them.

Hold fast, Richard had ordered, and hold fast was what the men did under tremendous pressure. Karin, in the confusion, was thrown from her horse as she wheeled him about and tried to race away from the carnage. She had no thought of heading towards the Saracen forces at that moment, only of avoiding death. As she lay stunned on the ground, Rollo bore down on her, swept her up behind him and galloped off towards the baggage carts. Without a word, he dumped her behind one, and rode back into the midst of the battle, his axe swinging above his head. Through the swirling dust and sand kicked up by the horses on both sides, she could see that the Hospitallers had broken ranks and charged—and Rollo and his men were close behind them, disappearing into the haze and confusion of men and bodies.

Ayub was a soldier. He had sometimes spoken to her of war, and she had often seen Christian prisoners being brought into Jerusalem or Jyira, but it had never been like this. The noise—the utter carnage—the sunlight glinting on swords, lances, polished bucklers, the spiked helmets of Saladin's Turkish cavalry.

'God and the Sepulchre!' The cry rang out close by. The King of England raced past in full pursuit of those who had broken ranks to charge, followed by Bretons and Templars, Guy de Lusignan and his men from Poitou bringing up the rear. Leaning her head against a wheel, she closed her eyes and prayed it would soon end.

'Stir yourself, boy.' A mailed boot thudded into her side, winding her. She looked up to see a bearded soldier staring down at her. 'Hurt, are you?'

'My—My head . . .' she stammered, then flinched as he reached for the coif covering her hair. 'No . . . No, I am all right, just stunned for a moment. I can go back now . . .'

'By the look of you, you'll be more help here with the women. Help the wounded . . .' He moved away, leaving her to turn her attention to the men being deposited all around her. Bloodstained mail had sunk into flesh as arrows penetrated it at close range. She gulped for air, and turned away. A woman from the laundry wagons who had brought bandages shook her head, and said matter-of-factly, 'Don't waste your time with those three, they are dead. Come with me.'

Rollo found her when it was over, tending to the injured and dying. Gently he took her by the hand and raised her to her feet. Tears welled into her eyes . . . She wanted to lean her head against his shoulder and weep, but knew she could not. A squire did not cry like a woman on his master's shoulder.

'Come, my men have need of you, too,' he said gruffly, and she followed behind his horse to where he had made camp.

There was much celebrating that night among the Crusaders. First Acre, now Arsuf. Two major defeats for the great Saladin. Perhaps he was not so great after all. The Frankish cavalry, led by the Lionheart, had won the day. The Turks fled before them. Richard made no mention of the Hospitallers' charge against his orders. They had merely anticipated what was to come, and nothing had been lost by it, thanks to his skill in regrouping his men and breaking off the assault when the object had been achieved. Now they could continue on to Jaffa, where they could all rest. Perhaps Saladin himself might come to the next negotiations, he mused, now that he had witnessed at first hand the superiority of his enemy!

The chirping of crickets, and the laughter of the men outside who were grouped around the many fires, retelling accounts of their encounters, followed Karin into the realms of sleep. She had been housed in a tent away from the others. Rollo had left her, as soon as he had assured himself that she bore no injuries, to see to his own men. She had wanted to offer to help, but the remembrance of those other soldiers she had nursed that afternoon would not allow the words to pass her lips. She had been streaked with blood on her hands, arms, face. Her clothes were covered in sand, the surcoat a brilliant red instead of white where the blood of a dying Frenchman had spurted as someone removed the arrow from his chest. Alone in the tent, nausea had overcome her. She had lifted the cloth, thrust her head outside and been violently sick. Even though the noise of it all still clamoured in her brain afterwards, she gradually managed to compose herself.

She was brought food and wine, but had no stomach for either and left them untouched to stretch out on the hard mattress which had been put down for her. She had removed the uncomfortable hauberk and the boots that crushed her feet, and flung them away from her in disgust. The smell of blood would always linger with her, she thought, as she covered herself with her burnous. She left the lamp burning very low. The soft glow comforted her. She did not want to dream tonight.

She did not think she would be able to sleep after what she had seen, but soon her eyes began to close and she sank into an exhausted slumber. She was rudely awakened by the sound of someone swearing as they blundered over Rollo's bed, which was always placed across the opening of the tent so that he would be awakened instantly if anyone came near. In the blackness, she could not accustom her eyes at first. Rollo? If it was, he was drunk.

Fearfully, she sat up, demanding, 'Who is it? Who's there?'

'I seek Lord Rollo. I am Lord Dacre. Where is he, boy?'

Karin realised that he thought her to be Rollo's squire. Trying to deepen her voice, she answered, 'I know not, my lord . . . I was asleep.'

'Asleep? On a night like this? What's the matter with you? No stomach for a good fight. Get up . . .' The man jeered, and reached down to grasp her arm. She flinched away as rough fingers coupled her wrist. A bearded face was thrust close to hers. 'What the . . . !' His free hand had touched her breast. 'Judas priest! A woman! So Lord Rollo isn't as lonely as we all thought . . .'

She gasped as his fingers fastened in the front of her linen shirt and ripped it from neck to waist. The weight of his body bore her backwards onto the ground, as his mouth, reeking with wine, sought hers.

'In times of war, he will not mind a comrade-at-arms appreciating you too,' Dacre chuckled. He pulled back her head and forced his mouth down on hers. Karin nearly fainted with horror. Where was Rollo? Or the men he always had protecting her? She screamed, and he cuffed her roughly on the side of the head, all but stunning her. She heard the shirt rip again, and her senses began to fade. In a last desperate effort to be free of the tremendous weight holding her down, the cruel hands ravishing her body, she gathered what little strength she possessed and thrust a knee upwards. There was a loud exclamation of pain, and

Dacre momentarily released her, jerking himself backwards. The arm he flung back to strike her again hit the low hanging lamp and scattered flaming oil over his clothes and as far as the walls of the tent. Within seconds, a sheet of flame leaped up beside Karin. Roaring like an enraged bull, the man sprang towards the entrance and disappeared into the night, leaving her . . .

The flames were separating them again . . . She could see the face so clearly, and this time she could hear the voice plainly . . . calling 'Alisandre'. Her mother! The woman was her mother. Why could she not move? She looked down. There was a beam across her legs, trapping them . . . the flames were coming through the doorway now, and the face was gone. She could hear nothing but the roar as they flared closer, feel nothing but the heat . . . She screamed again and again . . .

'I think she is coming round, my lord,' Chavo said quietly. Rollo did not even hear him as he crouched over the prostrate figure he had carried from the burning tent only an instant before it collapsed. She had been hovering between consciousness and unconsciousness for almost two hours, during which time she had cried out time and time again for someone to save her mother and father. She drifted between Jerusalem and Jyira and two different worlds. Would he ever know the whole truth about her he wondered.

The eyes which opened onto his face at once registered fear. She started up, then clutched at her head and fell back, her hands over her eyes.

'Stay with her until I return,' Rollo ordered, and left the tent without speaking a word to her.

Karin gazed after him, her mind in a state of great confusion. Where was she? This was not Jerusalem? But there had been a fire . . .

'Try to drink a little wine, my lady,' Chavo urged, and held a horn drinking-vessel to her lips. No sooner had the sweet wine touched them than she pushed it away, her expression accusing. He shook his head. 'It is not doctored, I swear it. Dear heaven, will you never forgive me for what I did? I thought if my lord's hunger for you was satisfied, that would be an end to it. But you are not like the others. I saw it in his eyes when he struck me. Would that he had taken my worthless life! Drink, I beg you.'

Her throat was parched and sore from the heat and smoke. Karin raised herself and drank thirstily. 'Where are my clothes?' She had just realised that she was naked beneath the burnous covering her. She remembered now. Dacre! The lamp! She fought to calm the wild beating of her heart.

'There was little of the shirt left. Lord Dacre's filthy hands had nigh torn it in two . . . and one sleeve was alight when Lord Rollo carried you from the blaze. See, he has bandaged your arm.'

Slowly Karin felt life beginning to return to her numb body. One leg felt very sore, as did her injured arm and one side of her face. She touched her loose hair and found many singed strands. Her breasts hurt, too, from the rough hands which had clutched at them. Closing her eyes, she lay still, absorbing Chavo's words. Rollo had run into the blazing tent to drag her to safety! He had ministered to her! He had undressed her and smoothed salve on her tender skin.

Thinking she had drifted into sleep again, Chavo quietly left her. She heard him speaking to someone outside before moving away, and knew that guards had been left to watch over her. How had Dacre managed to enter Rollo's tent without being challenged? She felt physically drained by the whole thing. Her head began to swim as she sat up, hugging the burnous about her . . . She needed air. She felt as if she was still suffocating, and her eyes were stinging from the smoke. The soldier stared at her curiously as she stepped out. She could hear voices raised in anger from the direction of one of the camp fires, and the sound of blows . . . In the flickering light, she saw Rollo standing over the body of a man on the ground at his feet.

'It is best you go back inside, lady.'

'I cannot.' As he gave an understanding nod, she motioned to some rocks several yards away. 'I shall be there. You can still see me.'

'For my sake, stay there! I do not want to end up like Edred.' The man lifted a hand in the direction of the inert figure. 'The sentry on duty when Lord Dacre attacked you, lady. I have seen my lord in many rages, but this one! The devil would not fight with him tonight.'

Karin hurried past him to where four massive rocks were half-buried in the sandy earth, and crouched beside them. The cool night breeze began to alleviate the unpleasant feeling in her stomach, and after a few minutes of deep breathing the sickness threatening to rise in her throat had also gone. She laid a flushed cheek against the roughness of one of the stones, her eyes riveted on the fire in whose glow Rollo still stood. He was angry—she could see that, even from where she sat. The firelight flickered over blazing eyes, taut mouth, the features moulded like a granite mask. Every man about him looked uneasy. Had she not known otherwise, she might have believed his outward show of concern was genuine. It appeared that they were receiving the unleashing of the full fury of his temper.

All this because she had been attacked? Or because the knight Dacre might return to his friends and tell them that Rollo had disobeyed the King's command and brought a woman with him? He would be disgraced, and she would most certainly be sent back to Acre, where, if there was indeed a plot to kill her, she would exist in the shadow of death. Karin had come to believe he had spoken the truth. If she had been forced to accompany him purely for his pleasure, he would have taken advantage of the situation long before this. Every night when they were alone, he had the opportunity to make love to her again, but, if anything, he deliberately went out of his way to pretend she was not there. Unless, of course, other men came to see him, in which case she had the humiliating experience of having to pretend to be his squire, at which times he took great delight in telling her how clumsy she was, how unsuitable to the life chosen, how awkward and stupid. His performance each time was so convincing that she knew no one had ever suspected his squire of not being what 'he' appeared to be. Now, her presence had been revealed. What would tomorrow bring for her?

Discovering she was not in the tent where he had taken her, Rollo followed Karin to where she sat. She was clasping her hands about her knees, her forehead resting on them. He stood for a moment watching the wind stir her hair, touched by the pathetic pose.

'Are you all right?' he asked quietly.

'Yes.' She did not look up at him, and he moved closer, dropping on one knee beside her. Tilting back her head, he stared down into flushed cheeks which told their own story—eyes haunted with memories and sadness. 'I could not stay in there any longer. I was not trying to run away . . .' This was added with a touch of defiance in her tone.

'I know.' Her skin was unhealthily hot to the touch, almost as hot as his own, he thought. She was in a state of shock; he was fighting to ward off an attack of ague. Even before the battle he had felt it upon him. Tomorrow or the day after he would be out of his mind with fever.

'That awful man—the one who . . .'

'Philip Dacre. He will not be a trouble to you any more. Nor to any other woman,' Rollo told her gravely, and her eyes searched his face. 'He is dead. He attempted to ride away after he had left you—to burn . . .' He felt her shudder, and silently cursed himself for the careless words. 'My sentries have orders to shoot anyone leaving without my authority.'

'What will you do?' She was horrified. 'What will you tell the King? Is—was—Dacre not one of the commanders of the men left behind by the King of France?'

'He was.' Rollo shrugged, as if the problem was of no importance. 'Riding alone at night is very hazardous. He was warned . . .' he said meaningfully. 'Do not concern yourself with him. If he had not died in that way, I would have called him out and he would have taken his last breath by way of my axe.'

'How easily you talk of killing.' Karin drew back from him, frightened by the calmness with which he always spoke of death. 'What will happen now?'

'We proceed to Jaffa. At least, perhaps we do . . . I may change our destination. My castle at Shah'mat is not far away. You would be safer there, and I have adequate men to watch over you, should you think of leaving me.'

'Which I shall do at the first opportunity,' she declared. His castle! No wonder he had been so patient! He could afford to be—she would be his prisoner!

'That would be unwise. I shall bring you back from wherever you go,' he threatened, bending his dark head towards her face. 'Have you forgotten that we are to be married?'

Her sharp intake of breath and the widening of her eyes told him that she had not expected that decision still to be in force. He lightly touched her shoulder, felt her recoil, and tightened his fingers so that he held her fast.

'I did not think—I mean . . .' Karin shook her head. 'I do not understand you. Am I not to be imprisoned in your castle for your pleasure?'

'What a mistrusting little wench you are,' he said

shortly, knowing that he had only himself to blame for
the way she was thinking now. He could feel the
sickness in him beginning to drain him of strength. He
needed sleep, but he wanted her. Deuce take the fever
to come upon him now! Tonight he suspected that he
could have given her the comfort she desperately
needed; shown her he was not the *bête noire* she
believed. 'But then I have given you little cause to trust
me. The fault is mine.'

Karin could only stare at him in astonishment. Was
this the arrogant man who had made love to her?
Stripped her of all dignity? Rollo, Duke of Aquitaine,
who a moment ago had spoken so calmly of the death
of the man who had tried to rape her, was now, with
gentleness in his voice, telling her he was to blame for
the mistrust and enmity between them?

'I think you are either drunk or ill,' she retorted.
'What has changed your mind, my lord?'

'You are closer to the truth than you realise,' he said,
getting to his feet and drawing her up after him. 'As to
the reason for my change of heart, I do not know . . .
Perhaps the sun has addled my brain.'

'Oh, you are impossible!' Karin exclaimed. The
wind snatched at her burnous. Before she clutched it
to her again he glimpsed the rise of her breasts, a long
leg and a well-tapered thigh. It was as well he could do
nothing about it, he thought, as he took her arm and
led her back to the tent.

'Here—You take the bed.' From a heavy chest he
took several woollen blankets and tossed them to her.
'Do you want something to help you to sleep?'

'No!' His mouth tightened at the swiftness of her

answer. It was in her mind that any wine given to her would be drugged, and he knew it, and liked it not. Perhaps she would never trust him, he thought, as he extinguished the light and removed his outer clothing. Why did it matter? He was giving her his protection and his name, and many women had sought that over the years. In France she would be received at the court of the Dowager Queen Eleanor, also at Richard's court in England. His money would give her everything she wanted. So long as she accepted him as her master, he would be fair with her, and as kind as the past allowed him to be.

Karin stiffened in alarm as she felt him lie down beside her and pull the blankets over him, waiting for him to turn and take what he already considered his.

'Go to sleep, *Kutti*. After a battle, do you think I have the strength for what you are thinking? You have no idea how much I need sleep . . .' His voice came out of the darkness, mocking her fears. Moments later his deep breathing told her he was sound asleep. Involuntarily she also began to doze as the day's events took their toll of her. She awoke only once, in the grey light of morning, to find her head pillowed against Rollo's shoulder. He still slept soundly, the satanic features not relaxed even now. A thin film of sweat had gathered on his brow and cheeks and covered his bare shoulders.

She dared not move for fear of wakening him and perhaps provoking him into the action he had denied himself the night before, for the burnous had parted from her body as she tossed and turned restlessly, and one of his hands lay against her breast, cupping it between calloused fingers. Her skin burned like fire. Even asleep, his touch had the same effect on her, she thought, as she drifted back into the realms of peace.

Only in the morning, when she woke again and lay remembering how close her body had lain against his, did she grow ashamed that she had not pulled as far away from him as possible. Would she have fought him had he made any demands on her? She told herself Yes, but was not truly sure any more. When she was his wife, she would not be able to refuse him anything. He would have total power over her, and the estates in England she had never seen. What would life be like for them? Berengaria's words came back in to her mind, and she lay with her hands over her face . . . 'In a year or two, when you have a family, it will be different for you.' A child! The idea had horrified her then. Now . . . !

Chavo brought her new clothes, another hauberk and boots and a clean linen shirt. How she longed for the touch of silk against her skin again! He told her that Rollo had sent a messenger to the King requesting permission to go first to his castle before journeying to Jaffa, as he was concerned for its safety and the lives of the inhabitants. With Jaffa almost in sight, the permission came back within a few hours.

So they were not to go to Jaffa yet. Karin felt a strange kind of excitement rising inside her as she rode that day. Perhaps from this castle at Shah'mat she might learn more of the man who was soon to be her husband, perhaps receive some insight into what troubled him so deeply, made him turn his face from friendship, and scorn the love of women. He was handsome and rich and powerful, she reasoned. Many women would have sought to be his bride over the years, yet he had never married again. How he must have loved his first wife to prefer life alone rather than seek someone to take her place! Why had he chosen Karin? Sometimes she was sure he did not even like her, yet she was to be his lifetime companion.

Not a faithful companion, she suspected. His wife and bedmate, but he would still have other women who might mean even more to him. Why, then, was he marrying her? If only she had the courage to demand an answer from him.

The journey to Shah'mat would take three days. She saw little of Rollo at first. That night, when they made camp, he did not share the tent with her, and she fell asleep realising that she had seen little of him all day, and that what she had seen had puzzled her. He was unusually silent, delegating the task of heading the column to Chavo and Siward. She noticed often he swayed unsteadily in the saddle as if the sun was bothering him. She thought he had been joking when he said the sun had addled his brain, but now she began to wonder if he was indeed suffering from its overpowering effects.

She had barely finished dressing the following morning when loud voices drew her outside. Chavo came running to her, his face pale with anxiety.

'Lord Rollo, my lady! Come quickly! I cannot wake him . . .'

CHAPTER SEVEN

KARIN KNEW the signs at once—feverishness, ramblings, moments of extreme cold and then heat. She had watched Tamir once tend Ayub when he was struck down in the same way. A high fever had developed on the third day, and they had sat beside the bedside of the sick man all night and all the following day until it broke and he began to recover.

Rollo lay where he had slept the night before, a few feet from the ashes of the fire. His face and body were soaked with sweat, and his shirt clung to him. One arm was outflung, the fist tightly clenched. Men drew back as Karin knelt at his side and laid a hand against a wet cheek.

'He is alive . . . I can feel a heartbeat, but he will not wake!' Chavo cried.

She thrust a hand inside his shirt and felt the steady throb of life there . . . But for how much longer? For a strong man it might take two weeks for him to die. She shook her head, not knowing what to say. Every eye was on her, as she looked up at the young knight.

'All we can do is pray. Has he had these attacks before?'

'Twice, the last time only just before Acre fell to us. There was a physician with the army who had medicines . . .'

'If Tamir was alive, perhaps he could cure him. In

sacrificing his life, perhaps that of your lord will also be in peril.' He could not die. He *could* not! If only she could remember the potions Tamir had used. A part of some tree . . . made into a liquid and fed to the patient every four hours before the fever was at its height, every two after that. An ugly murmur ran through the Guard standing over her. If Rollo died, she knew her life would not be worth one ducat.

'The old man was an astrologer.' It was Siward who spoke, and she nodded affirmation. 'What is it you seek to know that he could have told you?'

'He had a leather pouch with him always, containing medicine. If I only had that . . . Lord Rollo must be made comfortable and kept warm at all times.'

'Warm,' someone said jeeringly. 'Can you not see he has a fever, woman?'

'There will be a time when he will feel extreme cold,' she replied, not allowing herself to rise to the taunt. 'We shall be here for several days, messires, perhaps longer, so I would suggest that you prepare yourselves for a long wait. Chavo!' She had never called him that before, and he dropped to one knee beside her, eager to do her bidding. She needed his help! This was his chance to prove the remorse he felt for that night. 'When I say comfort, I mean exactly that. A comfortable bed, clean bed-linen. Lord Rollo will most likely need a change of personal clothing every few hours. We shall need something to cover the bed and keep away insects, or he will be bitten to death. And he must have hot drinks hourly, for he will be unable to take solid food.'

'And where did you learn all this, eh? During your

time with the Infidels?' a bearded man with a scarred cheek demanded, and she rose to her feet to face him, aware of the hostility radiating from every man around her. They did not like her—they never had. She was safe only so long as Rollo lived!

'Yes.' She gave him the answer without hesitation. 'I learned from the wise old man whom one of you murdered. He could have saved your lord.'

'Perhaps it has been willed that you may also heal him.' Siward stood beside her, a battered leather pouch in his hands. He held it out to her. 'We are not all stupid men, lady, men with big mouths who boast of our achievements as we seduce countless women. I, too, am interested in the art of healing, though I have had little chance to try it in this accursed land. I found this after the astrologer was killed. I guessed it to be what you say—herbs and remedies—and I kept it to examine and perhaps use when the opportunity came.'

'Without knowing the correct proportions, you might have killed someone had you tampered with it!' Karin snatched it from his grasp. The power to save Rollo was in her hands! She should have revelled in this moment. He was ill, perhaps dying, and it was possible that only she could save him. Rollo would never know why she sought to save his life, believing perhaps that she was afraid of what would happen to her at the hands of his men should he die. He would never know she did it out of love! She would never have the courage to tell him, and have that love rejected. For him, love did not exist. He could neither give it, nor accept it.

'Are you going to allow *her* to tend our lord?' the bearded man demanded. 'She will poison him!'

'Then she will be buried in the same grave with him after I have slit her treacherous throat,' Siward said. 'Believe me, lady, I will do it if he dies!'

'He may die, anyway, even with what little help I can give him,' Karin faltered, and the bearded man laughed harshly.

'You see? Already she is afraid for her own life. Treat him yourself, Siward. We all trust you.'

'No!' Karin clung to the pouch stubbornly. She looked up at the tall Norseman, a strange calmness settling over her. 'I shall tend him. Chavo, do as I ask. Erect a tent quickly, and let us make him comfortable. As for you,' she smiled, unafraid of the hand resting threateningly on the dagger in his belt, 'if your lord dies, I have no reason to live. You may do as you wish with me,' she said quietly. A look of understanding passed between them. He wheeled away, issuing orders which sent men running to the baggage cart to unload the tents that were erected when a long stay was in prospect. Karin sank to her knees beside Rollo, pillowing his head on her lap. She remained, stroking his forehead, until they came to carry him away.

She had not slept in two nights. Every limb ached, and her eyes barely managed to stay open. Karin jerked herself back into wakefulness and inspected her patient. Rollo lay tossing in a large bed. They had been removing his garments and taking them away to wash every hour, for if they were not soaked with sweat, he had vomited upon them. He lay naked beneath clean sheets. She wondered how long he could keep down the drink he had taken not ten minutes before. His fever was rising to an alarming pitch, and no matter what she did, it continued to mount. She had sat for a long while over Tamir's pouch, selected what she thought were the right phials, mixed them, and administered them to the sick man. Patience, Tamir had always told her. Allah cures in his own good time. But she was so impatient to see some change. She did not mind that outside were men eager and willing to take her life if he died. She cared because she loved him, sought to make him well and keep him by her side. She, who was his prisoner! Yet, at this moment, was he not hers? It should have given her pleasure—even satisfaction. She gained neither from the sight of his thin, drawn features.

'What have you given him?' Siward stood at her side, demanding an answer.

She blinked tiredly. He was her constant shadow. She had no doubt that if Rollo died, so would she. Yet she had spoken the truth when she said the end of his life would also mean the end of hers. The love–hate emotions confused within her predicted it.

'I have already told you,' she answered tiredly. 'It's a part of a tree. It comes from some far-off place— India, perhaps, or China. It is something Tamir learned from an old man, a healer like himself who was journeying on a pilgrimage with one of the caravans that passed through Jyira. He was always seeking new ways of healing. He told me he had spent four months listening to this old man, and had learned many things from him. Be thankful he did! I do not know how the remedy is named, only that I have to mix these three powders . . .' She showed him the different wooden bowls which lay before her. 'One is the part of this tree, the others . . .' She lifted her shoulders. 'I am not Tamir, but I watched him many times. I know what I am doing. He will live, never fear!'

'It is you who should fear, lady, should he not,' came the grim answer, and her eyes sparkled with unexpected defiance at his manner. Climbing to her feet, she ran a hand through her dishevelled hair, sweeping it back from her face.

'*If* he dies, then you may do as you wish with me. I shall be powerless to stop you,' she said bitterly. 'But until that happens—if it ever does—stay out of my way! Did you not know the Lord Rollo and I are to be married?'

By the amazement which crossed his face, she knew he did not.

'Do you think he will take kindly to the things I shall tell him? The threats I have endured during my efforts to cure him?'

'Cure him,' Siward said in the same tone. 'Or you will answer to me. When he lives and opens his eyes and tells me how wrong I have been, I will apologise to you. Until then . . .'

He left her, shivering, even though it was mid-day and the blistering heat penetrated the tent despite all they had done to keep it cool. A long piece of cloth had been hung over the bed to try to keep Rollo free of flies and the deadly mosquitoes whose bites were said to produce such terrible ailments among all the men.

When she was able, she dozed by his side, and would then return to put her arms about him and hold him as he shivered and trembled like a child. He was strong, she told herself. He would recover!

Two days became four. Then five and six. The strain was beginning to show in the thinness of her cheeks, for she ate little in those long hours of tending her patient. His need was her only concern. How much longer?

Chavo became her constant companion. When she dozed from sheer exhaustion, she would awake to find him watching his master, and there was no reproach in his eyes. When Siward or any of the other men looked at her she saw either hatred, mistrust, or, in the former's case, total disbelief! What was it about Rollo that bound his men to him? They both feared him and loved him.

Yet they were no different from Karin, who dreaded his touch after that wild night, yet had grown to long for it again as the days passed. She was a wanton to want him so! He had a way about him that commanded respect and obedience, yet she could give him neither of these. She did not know him. Soon he would be her lord and master, too, and he was still a stranger despite the hours they had spent together.

Would he ever consider her feelings above his own as he had the night he made love to her, or would it be as it was the following morning between them, when he had taken her roughly, painfully, seeking only to satisfy himself?

He was helpless now as he lay sick in his bed. His

men, brave soldiers that they were, would do nothing one way or the other until he lived—or died. She sat alone with him, apart from the short hours when Chavo shared her watch. It was hard to be civil to him, recalling what he had done; yet hard not to, when he was at hand to be of assistance to her when she needed it the most.

The fever must break soon—It had been seven long days. Rollo was weak and drained, and his strength was fast ebbing from him. The next two or three days could see him live—or die. She said this to Chavo only, and the young man's face grew white. This was the only person who could tell her of the man she was to marry, she thought, and laid a hand upon his arm when he was about to leave her.

'Stay,' she entreated. 'We need to talk.'

'My lady, I can apologise no more . . .' he began, but she held up a hand to silence him.

'I want not your apologies. Tell me about your lord. The truth! I want to know why he uses me so.'

Chavo stared at her aghast. To divulge such a confidence would be a betrayal of all he held dear. Yet this woman he had wronged . . . he owed her . . . and she was to be the wife of Lord Rollo.

'Tell me,' Karin urged. 'You fool, I care not for my own life, only his. Because of you I now belong to him, but I admit to myself and to you that it would have happened sooner or later. It is written . . . Do you not understand that? No more do I. I am living in two worlds . . . I have two names . . . I know not who I am.' She looked at him, her blue eyes wide and appealing, and he was lost. 'For the love of God—or

Allah . . . If I am to love him, let me do so, knowing what I fight?'

'A ghost, my lady.' Chavo was slow to answer. His eyes were fixed on Rollo's inert form as though he could hear every word, unconscious as he was. 'He will surely kill me for this!'

'As I shall surely kill you for the humiliation you heaped on my head that night,' she swore. 'If I do not, then I will seek another to do it for me. Tell me!'

Chavo swallowed hard. He had lost Celine through his stupidness, and he wanted her back. A bargain, perhaps . . . He said so, and watched Karin smile slightly.

'I shall ask Lord Rollo, when the time is right, if you tell me all I want to know.'

'There was another woman . . . she was very beautiful. No, she was—perfection. She was everything any man could wish for. My lord saw her, wanted her . . . but he was nothing . . . a bastard, you understand.'

'No, I do not.' Karin shook her head in bewilderment. In the Muslim world, the one she remembered best, many sons and daughters were thus sired, and they were not discarded, or abused, or ignored. The daughters were married to influential families, and the sons trained in the art of war, or learning, or medicine. Why did Rollo feel so strongly about his birth?

'It was different for him,' Chavo explained patiently. 'His father was a great lord in Provence. He fell in love with a village maiden, but she was betrothed to another—A simple man from the village. It was his right . . . the *droit de seigneur!*'

'The right of the lord?' she whispered. 'To take a

bride on her wedding night?' She knew this law, yet did not know how. Chavo nodded.

'The woman was willing. She did not wish to marry anyone but her true love, and that was impossible. She bore a son, Rollo. But she died, and several years later he married a woman of his own rank. My lord was brought up in the castle as the rightful heir, for the wife produced no children. It was like an omen. He hated his childhood. He speaks little of it to me, but I was there, and I remember the sour face I always used to see. I was young, then, a mere boy, but I always remember how proudly he rode among us, how he encouraged us in our efforts to rise above our lowly station. His father did not thank him for it, but he forgave him. They were very close. Secretly, I think he not only admired, but loved, his son.

Lord Rollo was desolate when he died, though he hid it from all but me. I had hunted with him, caught fish in the stream by the village, tumbled the village maids . . .' Chavo broke off, colouring hotly as Karin's gaze turned on him. 'It was expected of him—They would not have thought him a man, had he not!'

'And his wife,' she insisted, gently laying another wad of wet cloth against Rollo's feverish forehead. How many before her? How many had been important before his wife? Or after?

'She was perfection, as I have told you. So many men sought her . . . yet she held herself aloof. Then Lord Rollo approached her, and it was as if she became a willow stem bending in the breeze . . . She was his. They married, and then . . . My lady, do not make me tell!'

'Go on.' She would not allow him to stop now.

'I know not what happened between them. My lord was absent from his estates—at court, and fighting. He did not want it this way, but he is a knight . . . he spent little time with her, but when he came home . . . It was as if he had never been absent, so happy did they always seem together. I know he was.'

'What took place?' Karin would not allow him to withdraw without finishing the story.

'She took other men—many. Whenever he left the castle, she had a different man in her bed. Grooms, men from the village . . . great knights from the court. And when he came back, she ran to him like some innocent virgin! Holy Mother! I could have killed her myself. And when he discovered it—found she had lain with his best friend—he went mad . . . No one knows what happened. The servants said there was a terrible quarrel and he pushed her down the staircase. It would not have mattered had he done so; she was in need of killing!'

'Do you think he did?' she asked. Her hands were locked tightly in her lap, and she carefully unwound her fingers and tried to calm herself.

'I care not, my lady . . . No! I do not think so. Only the night before, he had told me he intended leaving her to her own devices and coming to the Holy Land. I was to be his squire . . . When the King—King Henry—heard, he banished him. My lord was not liked, for he was a friend of Queen Eleanor, as his father had been before him. In recognition of the old Duke's loyal service, the Queen had Rollo taken to her court at Poitiers. He was raised alongside King

Richard and his brothers. I think that is why they remain so close now. It was a very different atmosphere there from the boredom of the English court, he used to tell me. There were troubadours, and chivalrous knights who knew how to woo a lady fair.' Again Chavo coloured as Karin's eyes centred full on him enquiringly.

'So many people came to Poitiers, my lady. Educated people, such as scholars and poets. And there was music to gladden the heart every day of the year. It was not all play, of course. There was the hard lesson of how to become a knight. Only men of extreme courage and skill ever achieve the perfection that Lord Rollo has done.'

'Why was he not liked by King Henry?'

'The royal couple had long since ceased to be in love. The King devoted all his time to his mistresses, and the Queen to her sons. How she adored them! My lord has often spoken of her wise counsel. More of a friend and adviser than a mother, if you understand me. She was capable of giving so much more than love. The King would allow none of his sons the slightest power, and this frustrated them, and they sought to take it for themselves. My lord Rollo was riding with the Queen, disguised as a man, to join her sons in Paris, but they were accosted by one of the King's patrols and she was arrested. My lord was sent home in disgrace, his father heavily fined for his part in the affair, and neither was allowed at court again. The poor Queen was imprisoned for the rest of her husband's reign.'

'How dreadful!'

'He was but a lad of fifteen then. Two years later, his

father died and he became Lord of Verduse. A heavy burden for one so young, but he never complained. He was loved by every serf who worked for him, and respected for his fairness and honest dealings with all men. The King should not have taken everything from him. It was unjust!'

Karin nodded agreement with the man's vehemence.

'We have travelled far and wide, and the sickness is still in him. I do not think any woman will ever have his trust—his love—again,' Chavo said gravely, and Karin shrugged her slim shoulders.

'She did not want him.'

'And you do?' His face was suddenly alight with joy. 'Oh, my lady, when I tell him!'

'You will say nothing. You owe me. Stay silent! I shall fight this battle alone.'

He stared for a long moment into her stubborn features.

'It shall be as you wish.'

Rollo's temperature continued to rise. Karin's anxiety grew, and outside the tent the mutterings of his guard did nothing to alleviate her fears. Siward stared down at her as she pulled the covers over Rollo's sweat-soaked body. There was no more she could do, and she said so.

'If he dies . . .' the knight said, and she glared at him despite her fatigue.

'Leave us!' she ordered, and her tone was such that he found himself moving towards the opening before he realised what he was doing.

Karin rose from beside the bed. Her fingers reached

for the lacings of the shirt she wore. He was shivering so violently that he would die of cold if he did not have warmth. She doused the light, shed her clothes and climbed into the bed alongside him, gathering his shaking body against hers. It seemed an eternity before he grew calmer. But it was only a few minutes before another spasm shook him. She entwined her arms about him, holding him as tightly as she could against her own body . . . Her lips touched his wet hair where it curled about the base of his neck, lifted to his red-hot cheek, and finally to his mouth.

When he lifted the flap some hours later, Siward stared in silent surprise at what he saw . . . and marvelled at the woman who had brought about a miracle.

Rollo, Duke of Aquitaine, who was known far and wide as the Lord of Darkness for his ferocious temper and manner in battle, lay curled on his side, his head pillowed on the breast of a woman. How tenderly she held him, he thought, remembering her brave words that first day. She had no reason to fear him . . . Her love had sustained her through this crisis. Would it could sustain her through all the crises to come, when their lord was on his feet again and his old cynical self? A smile touched Siward's scarred face as he stepped away and left Rollo sleeping like a babe in Karin's arms. He was glad he would not have to kill her!

Rollo awoke, and lay wondering where he was. He had been dreaming of Lisette and Verduse. He had come home to find her in the arms of yet another man whom he had been forced to kill to protect her non-existent virtue and his name. She would do anything to sully his name, he had realised, soon after they were married. It was a game with her. Find a man, seduce him, entrap him and then degrade him, but she had failed with him! Her lovers often died beneath his sword, or were beaten and frightened off by his men. Her hatred of him grew each time until he came to understand that she wanted him dead. She longed for his wealth and his estates, to be a grieving widow—but without the demands he made upon her.

For a long time after he had discovered her unfaithfulness, he had made love to her out of spite and hatred, and she had revelled in his anger, his brutality with her. But soon he left her alone, choosing to seek his pleasures with village girls, or women at court whose morals were as depraved as hers—as his began to be. Any woman was better than none, he told himself, as he lost himself in the arms of whore after whore and gained no satisfaction.

God, he was hot! Yet he was naked . . . He pushed aside the covers and turned—freezing as he found himself staring at the woman lying beside him. For a moment he did not recognise her. Long red-gold hair lay about softly tanned shoulders, concealing the rise of a breast. With his leg he pushed the covers to the edge of the bed, and allowed his eyes to appreciate the long legs and lithe hips, feeling, as he did so, a hunger rise in him that could not be denied.

She stirred as he laid a hand against her skin, but did not wake. The Saracen woman! Here . . . willingly! Or had someone pushed her into his bed to keep him company while the fever raged? She hated him, and would not come willingly to his bed!

Her skin was satin smooth beneath his touch. He lifted his head and felt it swim for lack of food. How long had he been half dead? Two days, or four as previously? Where had they been going? Jaffa. Now he remembered! No! Shah'mat! Richard had given him permission to go to his castle and prepare it against siege. It stood between Jaffa and Jerusalem, and could be a stepping-stone for the army. A place to rest and regroup, to plan for that final march.

Karin sighed, and moved beneath his hand. His fingers stroked her thighs, upwards to her waist, to the uplift of her breast. Ignoring the throbbing in his head he eased himself forward, laid his lips against a pink nipple and at the same time thrust a leg over her so that she was pinned beneath him.

She came awake almost at once, her body stiffening beneath his. He moved his mouth to hers, not as before with a rough command, but gently, seeking rather than demanding, and to his surprise felt an involuntary response. Spurred on by this, his hands became bolder on her body. She moaned as he shifted his weight over her, yet did not attempt to resist him. Parting her thighs, he sank into her, exhausting himself in the wild moments which followed.

When he rolled away from her and fell asleep again, Karin lay with tears flowing unchecked down over her cheeks. Tears for the assault on her body that meant nothing to him. Tears of relief that his strength was returning! He was going to live!

*   *   *

'How long?' Rollo asked. He was sitting up in the bed, supported by a mound of pillows. He was pale and drawn, but since he had woken an hour before and summoned Siward and Chavo to him, weak or not, his voice held the same authoritative note. Karin was nowhere to be seen. He wondered why!

'Eight days, my lord,' Siward answered.

'The woman . . .' Had it been a dream? Her body entwined with his—such pleasure—such fire . . . It had to be a fantasy of his imagination. To know such exquisite pleasure . . . Weak as he was, his mind was still quite lucid, and the memory shocked him. She had offered no resistance, nor encouraged him in the act, yet the culmination had been beyond anything he had ever experienced . . .

'She has not left your side since you collapsed, my lord.' It was Chavo who spoke. 'She treated you with some concoctions left by the astrologer.'

'What?' Rollo started up, but then sank back again. Despite his indignation, he knew the arts of some of these healers, and silently he had respected the grey-bearded Tamir ibn Dak . . . while also disliking him for his association with Karin.

'She knew what she was doing, my lord,' Siward muttered. 'I swore to slit her throat if you died, and she cared not. And now you are well, and we all thank God for it.'

'As I do,' Rollo said. 'Bring her to me, and then leave us alone.'

Karin came into the tent apprehensively. After what had passed between them earlier, she was not sure how Rollo would act towards her. Arrogant again, mocking that she had been so easy for him to master? She had been half asleep and exhausted. Barely an hour's sleep before she had been woken by his hands on her. She had dreaded them, yet they had brought her nothing but pleasure, and that alone made her ashamed. He could use her at will, and her love made her vulnerable, unable to thwart his intentions . . . Yet, she told herself, he had been ill for so long that he did not know what he was doing. That he could have been making love to any woman, because the need was in him, did nothing to ease her discomfort. Did he even remember?

'I owe you my life, so Siward tells me,' he said quietly.

'You could have died. I am no physician.'

'That is not what I have been told. Both he and Chavo have been singing your praises since I recovered my senses.' He frowned at her answer. Why were there no recriminations for what had happened earlier? 'Tomorrow we move on to Shah'mat.'

'It is too soon!' Karin protested. 'You are weak—You need at least three days' rest.'

'I shall rest at Shah'mat. We both shall,' he told her, and she knew it was useless to protest further. She had made up a bed for herself of cushions and blankets on the other side of the tent. His eyes followed her as she went to it and sat down. If she did not have sleep soon, she would drop. Behind her, Rollo drawled, 'The bed is still comfortable. I shall not disturb you— again.'

Her cheeks flamed. He did remember! Not answering, she turned on her side and closed her eyes, the stiffness of her back proclaiming to him she had no intention of passing any comment.

Shah'mat was a Crusader castle in the hill country outside Jerusalem. It was small in comparison to Beaufort or Margat in the Lebanon, but it suited Rollo's needs. He loved this place above all others, even Verduse, where he had been born and raised and fallen in love . . . and been betrayed—or any of the other places he had seen during his years of wandering.

He was reeling in the saddle with fatigue as it came in sight an hour before dusk on the fourth day of travelling. Karin had been right, he acknowledged; he had been too weak to travel, but somehow he had stuck to his horse and refused all offers of help, stubbornly refusing to stop and rest at hourly intervals as was asked of him, knowing that, if he did so, there would come a time when he would be unable to remount his horse. As he fought to get through each new day, he found his strength slowly beginning to return. Tonight he would sleep in a comfortable bed, with cool linen sheets over him, he mused, as he reined in, waiting for Karin to draw level with him. He would drink good wine and partake of some of the best food in this part of the country. Most of his servants were Arabs. They had been with him from the beginning, and gave him the same loyal service as his other men. Had they not, they would have been treated with the same harsh justice as their companions. He had one law for both, and he never wavered from his responsibilities.

'Shah'mat.' He waved a hand at the outline towering on a hill before them. 'We shall be there within the
hour. Siward, send someone ahead to make preparations for our arrival. We shall want hot baths and
lots of food . . . and a little entertainment, I think.
Tonight you shall wear silk against your skin again,'
he murmured to Karin, and she shrugged as if it no
longer mattered to her. Instantly there was anger in
his eyes. Her manner was deliberately offensive, and
had been so since the start of this journey. No matter.
Once at Shah'mat, when she was forced to accept their
union, she would settle down. If she did not, and
continued with this act of defiance, he would have to
show her his displeasure. Recalling how pliable she
had been in his arms that morning, how responsive to
his demands, he did not want to arouse antagonism
between them again. He liked her the way she had
been then . . .

Karin's eyes remained fixed on Shah'mat as they
drew nearer. Behind them, somewhere among the
ranks of the men, there came singing. They, too, were
happy to be returning to a safe haven. Tonight others
would stand guard, while they slept or made merry
with the castle women.

The fortress itself stood on the spur of a hill. A road
carved out of the hillside was the only approach,
winding up and up towards the grey stone edifice like
a dusty yellow ribbon. The hill itself sloped steeply
away from the walls, making approach from all other
directions impossible. There were four large square
donjons, which were all of a hundred and twenty feet
high and at least forty feet wide.

Out of the corner of her eye she saw Rollo straighten in the saddle as they approached the main gate, shedding the tiredness upon him. They passed through massive gates, where heavily armed guards saluted the return of their lord. Above them on the ramparts, archers and cross-bowmen kept a constant vigil. To Karin, entering Shah'mat was just like entering a small town. She had never seen anything like it before. People milled about her, occupied in a multitude of different jobs. In the long building which housed the horses, a smithy worked sweating over a roaring fire, shouting at the apprentice who was late bringing the next mount to be reshod. Washerwomen chattered over the laundry, while children played near by. From the direction of the bakery came the appetising smell of freshly-baked bread, and she felt her stomach growl with hunger. Wheat bread, still warm from the oven, dripping with butter made in the castle itself, and home-made cheese. How she used to love such things as a child. The blood drained from her face so suddenly that Chavo kneed his horse close to hers, and said quietly,

'Are you all right, my lady?'

She nodded, conscious of Rollo turning curiously to see what was amiss. She could remember nothing of her childhood, yet suddenly she knew, without doubt, that she had done these things before—and it had not been in Jyira. Rather, somewhere like this place . . . Why, oh why, could she not remember? Was she to spend the rest of her life not knowing who or what she really was?

'I—I am tired, nothing more,' she stammered.

'We all are. Bring her inside, Chavo. Siward, see to
the men. I leave them to you,' Rollo said, dismounting. He came over and lifted her to the ground,
releasing her quickly as if aware of the many eyes on
them. 'See that she has everything she needs in the
solar, until the rooms are made ready.'

Karin watched him stride away, acknowledging the
greetings from all sides, to disappear into a building
across the far side of the courtyard.

As she followed Chavo she took a long look about
her, still marvelling at the amount that was going on.
Granaries were set back from the courtyard and
ammunition-houses. The cellars for storing all manner
of things, he told her, seeing her curiosity. At
Shah'mat they were self-sufficient, and had enough
food to withstand a year-long siege. It was a proud
boast, for not many castles could hold out so long
without reinforcements of some kind from outside.

Lord Rollo had his apartments in one of the donjons, which also housed the guest-rooms and solar.
Below were two of the many guard-rooms. Always
occupied, Chavo added. There was a kitchen inside,
and another outside to cope with the three hundred
men, women and children who might live here all at
one time. There were servants' quarters, accommo-
dation for the married families, a chapel high up in
another of the donjons, and a loggia.

'A veritable fortress,' he finished with a smile, as he
bowed her into a pleasant room where the window
arches in the Byzantine style gave a magnificent view
of the surrounding countryside. There were sheep-
skin rugs in many different colours scattered over the

wooden floor. Deep, comfortable sofas, reclined low
to the floor in the way favoured by the Arabs, covered
with bright cushions. With a sigh she sank onto one to
lay her head back and close her eyes. She did not care if
she never moved again.

'I will send someone to you with refreshments, my
lady,' Chavo said, retiring to the doorway. She was
almost asleep before he reached it. 'And I shall see if
some of the women can find clothes for you. If you
like, that is?'

'More than anything, I want to get out of these
clothes,' Karin replied, grimacing as she stared at her
dusty hauberk. 'Please, find me a dress . . . anything.'

The room was very pleasant, she decided, rousing
herself after a few minutes to look around her. Rollo
lived well. It was circular, and slightly smaller than the
interior of the donjon itself, for a spiral staircase
wound its way round the walls to all the storeys—four
in all. The last of the late afternoon sunshine streaming
through the window embrasures bathed the wooden
furniture in a muted glow. Everything was spotless,
she noticed, admiring the gleaming silverware on an
enormous dresser to one side of the room.

Tapestries hung from the walls, depicting hunting-
scenes with horses, men and dogs, and sometimes
falcons. A set of exquisitely carved jade chess-pieces
were laid out on a table of Arabic design and structure,
a game still unfinished. She had not considered Rollo
to be a man with such patience! A brightly plumed bird
sat high on a perch just inside the door under the
watchful gaze of a plump black kitten curled up on a
cushion on the sofa.

Stretching, she rose to her feet and went to the window. In the far distance she was sure she could see the shimmer of the sea. Closer to the fortress, brown and white goats like small dots on the parched earth grazed beneath the sleepy gaze of the herdsman. Almost directly beneath the walls were cultivated orchards of olive and fruit trees, their boughs hanging heavy with a good autumn crop. Shah'mat was indeed self-sufficient! From another window, she sat and watched the activity going on in the courtyard below as she drank hot coffee served in the Arabic way—very strong and sweet, in a small porcelain cup, and ate the wedges of bread and slices of thick cheese which accompanied it.

The pretty girl who had brought it reminded her of Celine. Was she safe in Acre? Surely Rollo would not have left her behind to face the wrath of the vengeful knights—friends of Hugo de Greville-Wynter who had sought to take her life? She smiled and thanked her in her own tongue, and saw the girl's face light up with pleasure and astonishment.

The maid who came to remove the tray an hour later was not at all pleasant. Her manner was sullen, and the eyes which considered Karin were rude in their inspection of the new arrival who stood before her in boy's clothing.

'Come with me. I shall take you to your rooms.' She was somewhere in her late twenties, with thick brown hair braided into one plait over her left shoulder. The neckline of her gown was deliberately pulled low to expose the rise of full breasts, and when she walked she had a way of lifting her skirts to show her ankles.

Remembering Rollo's reputation with women, Karin wondered if this was what the castle women thought was expected of them. Did they compete for his favours when he was home? she wondered. It was not a pleasant thought. Would he send for her when it was her *turn*?

'Anything you want, ask Berta there,' the woman said before she left Karin, and pointed to a plump middle-aged woman standing by the carved velvet-draped bed with a pile of clothing in her arms. 'She's an old fool—a little mad in the head, you understand, but good enough for the likes of you.'

'That's enough, you insolent girl. How dare you speak to a lady like that?' the woman cried, her face burning red as she dropped the clothes and started towards the door. 'My lady, forgive her, she has no manners.'

'Lady? Her? Not from what I hear about her. Some woman Lord Rollo found in a dungeon at Acre . . . One of them! He's been amusing himself with her during the journey.' A pair of hard brown eyes turned on Karin, and she saw hatred in their depths and sensed a jealousy in this woman she could not understand. 'But now he is back and he is mine, do you hear . . . harem woman? I shall warm his bed tonight, and for all the nights he is here, as I have always done!'

Embarrassment gave her tongue the venom of a viper, as Karin said calmly, 'You are welcome to him, for I do not want him. If I did, you would stand no chance against me. A harem woman is taught how to please a man, and how to keep him interested with a thousand and one little tricks of which you know nothing. I could pluck him from under your very nose if I chose. Leave me! I am tired.'

'The spectacle of seeing two women fighting like alley-cats does not appeal to me.' Rollo stood in the open doorway. Karin caught her breath, knowing he had heard the spiteful remark. The glitter is his eyes told her he had not only heard, but believed, her words! 'There are hungry men waiting downstairs, Lina. Go to them.'

'Shall I come to you later, my lord?' As she passed him, Lina laid a hand on his arm. He shook it off and she stepped back, knowing she had gone too far. Quickly she stepped round him and disappeared.

'And what prompted that little scene?' he asked drily, advancing into the room. At the foot of the bed, he paused to inspect the pile of clothes Berta had tossed there.

'Your woman thought I was a rival. I have told her otherwise.'

'My relationship with Lina is none of your concern, and mine with you, none of hers,' he snapped. He had to fight to keep his eyes open, so exhausted was he now. Karin's blue eyes flashed, challenging his statement. His relationship with her? So he did intend it to continue!

'In a day or two, when I have rested, I intend riding on to Jaffa. You will remain here until I return. There will be things you need, so give Berta a list and I shall bring them back for you.'

'Things?' she echoed, hesitantly. 'What kinds of things?'

'Feminine things—You reminded me once that I am

supposed to provide for you, so I shall do so. Until
your dresses and effects can be brought from Acre,
you will have to go on wearing other people's clothes
unless I bring you some materials. There are perfectly
good sewing-maids here who will make anything you
want—within reason,' he added, as if to indicate that
he would not permit her to wear the things she most
preferred, as she had done that first night he came to
her. 'Remember that you are about to become my
wife.'

'You speak of this again, yet I see no ring,' Karin
said suspiciously. 'I am here in your castle, at your
mercy, with no friends, no one to turn to as I had
in Acre . . . At least the Queen tried to protect
me against you. When she knows what you have
done . . .'

'She will thank God you are still alive,' Rollo intervened. 'Still your tongue, *Kutti*, and think on that! You
are alive. You would not be had you stayed there, of
that you can be sure. You are tired. We both are. It is
no use trying to discuss anything with you now. Trust
Berta. She was born in this land, and perhaps she will
understand you better than any of us. Trust her—If it
is in you to trust anyone.'

'And who is to blame if I cannot?' she accused, and
his mouth tightened.

'If you need anything, you have but to ask her, and
if it is possible, you shall have it,' he said, turning
towards the door.

'My freedom?' she called after him, and saw his
shoulders stiffen.

'Would that were possible,' he answered heavily as

he passed through the door, leaving her to puzzle over the strangeness of his words.

Berta, Karin was soon to discover, was a combination of a fussy mother-hen and a protective lioness. No one who came to see Karin was allowed to reach her before she had vetted them. Even Chavo and Siward bowed to her will. On the odd occasions when Lina came to attend to her needs, she was very quiet and subdued and never again gave way to the rudeness of that first day, although Karin was well aware of the malicious-ness of her gaze. It made her shudder. Wherever she went, she seemed to make enemies . . . and it was never of her own doing!

A week passed. She wanted for nothing, and Berta's protective companionship soon washed away all seeds of mistrust, even the suspicion that she had been planted by Rollo to spy on her every move. For days all she did—all she wanted to do—was eat and sleep, or laze on a divan in the solar listening to tales of Berta's childhood. Sometimes they played chess. Her parents had been wealthy, but not rich, people by the standards of the man she now served, who had come on a pilgrimage to Jerusalem, fallen in love with the country and remained. As her own parents had done, Karin thought, only they had remained and died, consumed by fire. Again a corner of the veil over her memory was lifted. Each day there was something—a name . . . a face . . . the snatches of a song . . . a lullaby. Had her mother sung it to her as she cradled her on her knee in Jerusalem? Or where?

In an impulsive moment she told the woman all

about herself—or as much as she knew, including
Rollo's intention to marry her. The more intimate
details she had left out, but she sensed from the way
Berta sometimes looked at her that she had heard
them from other sources . . . The Guard perhaps, who
knew everything that happened—and what they did
not know they made up with colourful additions, no
doubt, or from the other men who rode with him.
Soldiers grouped around a camp-fire, relaxing as
many did in the courtyard below her rooms at night,
enjoyed telling of the exploits of their lord as well as of
their own, for it made him more human in their eyes.

Berta had been most sympathetic and understanding, and Karin had warmed still more towards her as a
friend. Yet she longed also for the companionship of
Celine, and even the little rogue Omar with his cheeky
tongue.

Shah'mat began to have a strange, almost frightening, effect on her. She began to like being there. Once
she had recovered from the long journey and the
sleepless nights encountered when Rollo was ill, she
found herself relaxing and almost beginning to feel a
part of this enormous castle. That was the frightening
part—To feel as though she belonged. This was not
the life she knew—the life she wanted—or was it?
Karin wanted something far different, in another
place, but the part of her that was Alisandre found
Shah'mat very pleasing. Even the servants no longer
overawed her in their scarlet and green livery, with
each tabard bearing Rollo's coat of arms to proclaim
that they worked for the Lord of Aquitaine. There
were so many of them. Servants to wake her in the

morning with her breakfast. Servants to bathe her,
dress her, walk with her in the grounds and along the
allure behind the battlements. She was never alone. If
Berta did not accompany her every minute of the day,
there was a silent man or woman dogging her footsteps, or standing silently some feet behind her chair.
Did they think she intended to fly from the place? she
wondered.

She grew accustomed to the stares and whispered
comments, sometimes the sniggers and giggles which
accompanied them. She learned to ignore them and
conduct herself in a cool, aloof manner that soon had
people remarking on the change in her. The ladylike
manner in which she conducted herself—why, she
had to be born to it! It could be seen in the proud
bearing of her head and carriage. No words of reproach or anger passed her lips at the uncouth manners of some, who were eventually silenced by their
own companions—forgetful that they themselves had
uttered the same, or worse, comments in days gone
by.

Rollo recovered his strength and, as he had said he
would, left with two of his now three-man Guard, one
having been killed at Arsuf, and half his men to ride to
Jaffa for supplies and to learn how the main army was
progressing. They would not have left for Jerusalem
yet, he told her the night before he left. They would
most likely remain in the town for some considerable
while to regather their strength and make new plans.
He had attempted several times to coax her down to
the Great Hall for meals, but she stubbornly refused
and always ate in her room or in the solar, which she

used frequently because of its sunny position. He knew he could have insisted, but he was not yet ready to force a confrontation. That would come when he returned, if her attitude towards him did not change. She gave him her list, by design very short, and said she would be grateful for whatever he could find. Other things could wait until her estates were settled and she had money of her own, as she did not wish to be obligated to him. The remark angered him, as she knew it would, and he left her abruptly. Karin was aware of Berta's reproving gaze on her afterwards, and knew she had been wrong to bait him, but what other choice did she have? Surrender? To throw herself into his arms and admit her love? He would make the most of the advantage that would give him, she suspected, and would avail her naught. There would come a time when he would turn from her, tired of her as he tired of all women, and go to someone else. Perhaps someone at Shah'mat! Lina, perhaps, eager and waiting? She would not be used and tossed aside. When she was his wife, she would submit to him because she would then be his by law, but he would never know of the agony in her heart. Such a weapon in his hands could surely destroy her. Would he use it? Had that other woman so destroyed his faith in goodness and love that he would deliberately seek to crush her for so foolishly loving him?

To her surprise Chavo accompanied him, but not Siward, who became her escort when she began to go riding several days a week. To his chagrin and the amusement of many of the castle inhabitants and the tuts and frowns of a good few more, she asked Berta to find her a pair of trousers and a man's shirt and boots. Thus attired, she galloped enthusiastically about the countryside, experiencing a feeling of freedom lost to her since Acre. She recaptured the pleasure of the sun on her face, the feel of a sturdy mount beneath her. Between them emerged a silent, unacknowledged truce.

Returning to Shah'mat one afternoon, she found the whole garrison grouped in the bailey, and knew at once that Rollo had returned. Men stepped aside to allow the two horses passage. She reined in before the steps of the inner entrance, and Siward swung himself from the saddle and came to help her dismount. She thanked him with a smile and, turning, found Rollo standing before her, hands on hips and a frown of disapproval on his face. Surely he could not be jealous? She immediately dismissed the thought as ridiculous, and moved towards him. The ride had brought a flush of colour to her cheeks, and her eyes had a brightness in them he could not recall seeing before.

Karin felt excitement rise unbidden inside her at the sight of him. She could not deny that she was glad to see him again. She had missed him over the past two weeks, even though she had seen little of him—a decision of her own choosing—before he went away. He looked tanned and recovered from his illness. No doubt he had been well cared for in Jaffa!

His gaze fastened on her appearance as she came to stand before him, and his mouth deepened into a mocking smile. 'Have you so little to wear, that you parade yourself in that attire?' he asked, raking her from head to toe with bold eyes. The shirt clung closely to her breasts, and was tucked into the loose trousers accentuating her tiny waist and flared out about her ankles, reminding him of those she had worn in Acre. The look she gave him was almost as mocking as his own, and his gaze flew to Siward, wondering if he had given her this extra confidence, but his stare was returned levelly and he felt ashamed for what he had been thinking. It had happened before, and he thought it might happen again? He was still vulnerable!

'If you remember, you gave me no chance to pack when we left Acre,' she reminded him.

'That is true. I have remedied that on my trip to Jaffa.'

'How goes it with the King and the army, my lord?' Siward asked, and men craned their necks to hear his answer.

'Not good. The Saracens had razed Jaffa. So badly destroyed was the town that the army is encamped outside in olive groves until rebuilding is completed. The King has carpenters working round the clock— not that there are any complaints, believe me. It is quite pleasant outside the walls, and women have arrived from Acre to—shall we say—make up for any discomforts?'

There were guffaws of laughter from those listening. She was right, Karin thought. He had enjoyed his visit.

'I have brought the supplies we need. See to them, and then partake of the casks of ale in the last cart. Tonight we shall eat and drink and forget war, for it will be upon us again all too soon. We shall have word when we are needed, never fear. Until then, Shah'mat is the first concern of us all. Forget not that we stand between Jaffa and Jerusalem. If we fall, the way of the army will be blocked by the enemy. I have sworn to the King that this will not happen. Are you with me?' Rollo cried, and a great cheer went up which almost deafened Karin. To a man, they knelt before their lord and pledged allegiance.

She saw the pride which came into his face. He nodded in satisfaction, waved them away, and grasped her by the hand, pulling her after him through the doorway.

'I have missed you,' he said roughly, and before she could guess his intentions had swung her back against a wall and kissed her. She was too startled to resist in the first few minutes as his mouth explored hers, hungrily, with a passion that shocked her. Then, as his body flattened against hers, pressing her against the cold, hard stone, a fire rose inside her and her lips answered his . . . He stiffened and drew back, and she saw that his eyes were dark with suspicion again. Just as he had looked outside in the courtyard . . . 'It would seem you have been lonely, too, although it did not look that way when you returned from your ride.'

'I have not been bored, if that is what you mean,' she returned, wishing her lips had not been so eager to answer his. 'Berta has become a good friend, and, as you have seen, Siward accompanies me when I ride. I am watched at all times, my lord. Doubtless you left instructions to that effect. I cannot turn round without finding one of your servants behind me.'

'Would you run—if you could?' Rollo asked quietly, brushing a wisp of loose hair behind her ear. She had not been out of his thoughts for one day—or one single night. She haunted him like a desert mirage—there, but inaccessible. Now he was back, and the very nearness of her drove him to the very point of dragging her upstairs and settling things between them there and then . . . but he restrained the temptation. He had come like a suitor bearing gifts, and that was how he would present himself to her, impatient or not!

'Well?' he demanded when she gave no answer, and he saw a shadow cross her face.

'I do not know any more,' Karin replied, and it was the truth. 'Where would I go? To Ayub? To Jyira? I no more belong there now than I do in England. I do not belong anywhere . . .'

'You belong with me,' he told her, gripping her tightly by the hand again. 'Come and see what I have brought for you. A bride should look a bride, and you will!'

He led her into the Great Hall, where boxes and trunks were being deposited by the servants. He threw back first one lid, then another, and beckoned her to see. She gazed in astonishment at the array of materials, gowns, underclothes, jewellery. There was even linen for the bed and curtains, and tapestries for the walls. More drinking-vessels of silver, beautifully engraved, and eating utensils. Six exquisite drinking-glasses in cut glass, which caught the sunlight as he held one up for her to see. She was stunned. Was all this for her? She tried to thank him, yet no words

would come. Why? To make her accept the forth-
coming wedding more readily?'

The wedding—She had forgotten that!

'Where is the priest that you bring to marry us?' she
asked indifferently, and Rollo laid down the glass with
a frown.

'We are to be married in Jerusalem, before all the
court, with the King of England and Queen Berengaria
as our guests. What more could you want? Why do
you look at me so, *Kutti*?' The nickname he had
adopted for her brought an uncomfortable flush to her
cheeks. 'I thought you would be pleased.'

'Take me to Jaffa—Put me in the care of the Queen
until we are married, and I shall be pleased. Then I
shall believe you,' she cried, and he swore at her so
violently that she flinched.

'Believe me? I care not what you believe! What do
you think all these things are? Gifts to pacify you? You
are mine, and I shall take what I want—when
and where I choose. Do not forget that I am master
at Shah'mat,' he thundered, eyes blazing at her
stupidity.

'I knew it.' She backed away from him towards the
stairs. 'You never intended to wed me. Why should
you, when—when . . .'

'When you have nothing new to offer me?' he
finished bleakly. 'I, too, am beginning to ask myself
the same question. I marry you as a matter of honour.'
Turning away from her, he gazed out of the window,
his arms folded. 'These things will be brought up to
your bedchamber within the hour. Tonight I shall
expect to see you down here to eat with the rest of us.'

'I prefer to eat in my room,' Karin retorted. 'I will not be stared at and made fun of by your men.'

'You will do as you are told.' He wheeled on her, and his face was that of the devil himself, black and murderous. Gone was the tenderness she had glimpsed there when he had kissed her and shown her the many presents he had brought back. A fortune lay at her feet. The man she loved stood before her, yet she could reach out and take neither. 'If you do not come down of your own free will, I shall come and fetch you. Dress you, if necessary. As you seem to prefer force to gentleness, you shall have it.'

'I—don't . . .' Karin cried tremulously, and his eyes narrowed at the break in her voice.

'Then do not bring it upon yourself. Let there be peace between us,' he said stonily.

She turned and ran from him, up the winding stairs to the sanctuary of her bedchamber. Several trunks had already been deposited on the wooden floor, and Berta and another woman were unpacking them. Karin swayed in the doorway, breathless, doubting her own eyes as a figure rose to greet her. Celine!

CHAPTER EIGHT

SHE COULD NOT believe it! Celine at Shah'mat! But not
Omar. When she questioned his absence, she was told
he had grown bored with his continued confinement,
the Guard who continually watched him night and
day. He would not believe they were there to keep him
alive! And so, one night, he had stolen away, returning, Celine suspected, to the alleyways whence he had
come and was once again engaged in his old profession of stealing. Karin regretted that she had been
unable to see him again, to thank him for his aid in
those first turbulent days when she had been 'released' from the cells below the palace in Acre. To tell
him she no longer held him responsible for the death
of Tamir. His allegiance, such as it was, Ayub held,
and the little thief had helped him in those last moments of the Teacher's life, not only to meet with him,
but, she suspected, to help her 'brother' escape to
safety.

Celine had journeyed with the Queen's entourage,
heavily guarded, she told Karin . . . and never far
from Berengaria's side. There had been rumours that
there was a plot to kill Karin as soon as Rollo and his
men had left the city. The Queen herself had con-
firmed it, and although the maid had been taken aback
at her mistress's sudden departure, she had at last
accepted that the Lord of Darkness had saved her life!

All their lives! She had accepted that, with him, Karin would be safe.

Queen Berengaria had sent Karin many clothes and gifts—and wedding presents, together with a message that she would be at her wedding, the day after Jerusalem was returned to Christian hands. Karin sat on the edge of the bed, holding a jewelled girdle and a mirror backed in gold and encrusted with jewels, and there were tears in her eyes. Tears for her own foolishness which made her reject Rollo's kind gesture. Why he had made it would always be a mystery to her. And now, perhaps, because of her rejection, it was too late to heal the breach between them.

He did not love her. He would never love her—but she loved him. A little happiness was better than none. A few hours, days—she prayed for weeks, even months—in his arms, was better than a lifetime of denying the love within her that was crying out to be satisfied.

'You are not happy,' Celine declared, watching her mistress's face, and Berta gave a snort.

'She is as happy as she deserves. No woman ever rejects Lord Rollo twice, my girl,' the older woman muttered. She always spoke to Karin as if she were her daughter, and in need of much instruction. She had reproved Lina for her forward manner, but of late she talked to Karin how she pleased: as a mother would lecture a child, or offer advice to a young girl seeking reassurance. Without her company, and her brief spells of outdoor recreation, Karin knew she could never have endured the weeks she had been at Shah'mat. She felt as if she belonged, but she knew she must not. She was afraid to come to terms with what she had discovered in her heart. 'You love him, yet you send him away. You treat him like a love-sick boy. It's a wonder he does not put you over his knee,' Berta added, and Celine looked at her in astonishment.

'You allow her to speak to you in such a manner? Have you forgotten who you are?'

'That is it, Celine, I don't know who I am any more,' Karin answered miserably. 'I try to be Alisandre, but I know so little of her . . . A little more than I did in Acre, for my mind plays strange tricks on me of late, giving me glimpses of the past, yet I can put no order to them. When I try to be Karin,'—she shrugged her slim shoulders—'I no longer have the confidence Karin once had. If you were rude to me, I could no more have you beaten than I could send you away because you are a Muslim, an enemy. You are not my enemy, any more than Berta is, yet you two are from different worlds and you are both my friends. I am confused, and it frightens me.'

'He frightens you,' Celine retorted. 'He always has. I have not forgotten what he did to you . . .'

'I am to be his wife,' Karin interrupted. 'I wish it, and I will have no more said about it.'

'At last you begin to show some sense. Let us see what we can find to make you shine tonight,' Berta said, with a smile of satisfaction at her words. 'This?' She held up a gown of watered silk, shot with silver. 'No, something to hold his attention, something a little more daring!'

'She does not need clothes to have a man's eyes on

her, especially his,' Celine said, stepping back from the trunks. 'I have brought your own clothes, mistress, should you prefer them. He will notice you in those.'

She produced the flimsy garments and laid them out on the bed. Berta gave a cry of horror, bringing a smile to Karin's somewhat pale features. How she wished she had the courage to wear something like that to go down to the Great Hall, but if she ever donned them again, it would be in private, for Rollo alone to see. She wanted no other man to gaze at her body.

'Put them away, Celine, and find me something plain. Lord Rollo brought me many things . . .'

'What about this, to go with your eyes?' Berta suggested, holding out a dress of blue muslin. It was sleeveless, and cut low, with a very full skirt that fell to the floor in graceful folds from a tight waist. There was a tunic in the same colour, in velvet, its dagged sleeves edged with gold braid on which were sewn hundreds of tiny seed-pearls.

'That will do nicely. Find some slippers to match, and then put away everything else. I am going to rest for a while, then take a bath,' Karin instructed, beginning to unbraid her hair. Tonight she would wear it loose, with the gold circlet the Queen had given her . . . and be very selective in her jewellery. She did not want Rollo to think she was trying to impress him, or to enjoy too much her moment of capitulation.

She found herself growing quite excited as the time drew near for her to bathe and dress to go downstairs. For the first time she would be sitting with him among his Guard and other men who ate in the Great Hall.

Seated at his side—which would be her place always, when they were married. Would he take her to England and leave her there to roam again, expecting to find her eagerly waiting each time he returned, she wondered, as she undressed and stepped into the huge bath being filled with water. She enjoyed this time, when she could relax and unwind after the day. Or would she accompany him, as the Queen did King Richard? Would he want her, or would she be an unnecessary encumbrance to his dalliances elsewhere?

'Have you seen Chavo?' Karin asked, as Celine took a pail from one of the maids and carefully poured more hot water in. 'His room is below. All the Guard have their rooms there, and the other men below that.'

'I do not want to see him.'

'I have forgiven him, Celine. Can you not do the same? Do not allow what happened to me to spoil what was between you. I thought it was something rather special?'

'It was. Now there is nothing,' the maid replied with an indifferent shrug, but Karin saw the pain in her eyes before she looked away, and knew that love had not died in her. Wisely she refrained from comment. Like her, Celine would find that love could not be denied for ever. It was stronger than hatred, stronger than fear. It would be heard!

She washed herself all over with soap impregnated with oil of jasmine, remembering as she did so the night Celine had massaged fragrant oils into her skin, dressed her in her favourite clothes, and left her to go to Chavo, while her mistress had eaten delicacies specially prepared and drunk of the doctored wine the young squire had sent. And then Rollo had come to her, not knowing she was drugged, seeing only a desirable woman who did not refuse his kisses or the bold advances upon her body. Tonight she intended to present herself before him—just as desirable as she had been that night—but this time in full control of her faculties. If anything happened between them again, it would be because she wanted it!

The door opened behind her, and she looked up expecting to see Celine with towels to dry her. Enjoyable as the water was, she knew she must not linger, or Rollo would think she was deliberately disobeying him and come to fetch her. She wanted no ill-feeling between them this night. If he saw that she had accepted her fate, perhaps he would be kind again and she might then grow to know the true man, the man beneath the cruel exterior—the gentle man who had brought her gifts from Jaffa.

Lina stood before her, holding another pail of water. The look of hatred on the olive-skinned face shocked Karin, and instinctively she slid beneath the water until only her shoulders showed, glistening wet in the lamplight.

'I have brought my lady more water.' Her tone was insolent; the eyes which stared down at her were contemptuous of the body she had seen.

'Take it away, I have no need of it. You may go. Send Celine to me,' Karin ordered in an authoritative tone, and the woman's smile grew even more derisive.

'Do not think because you have been in his bed once you can talk to me like that, harem woman,' she snapped. 'I am Lina . . . his woman. Did I not follow him from my island of Cyprus? Have I not been here, at his beck and call, for the past year? He will tire of you as he tires of all the others, but never Lina. I stay—always.'

Karin gasped. Her mouth compressed into a tight line, she climbed to her feet, and the woman stepped back at the anger sparking in the depths of her blue eyes. Her tawny hair hung about her wet shoulders, scarcely concealing the firm, uplifted breasts. She was beautiful!

'When Lord Rollo and I are wed, and I am mistress here, you will not remain,' she said coolly, marvelling at her own audacity. But she knew that if she allowed this woman to win against her this time, the next would be worse, and the time after, she would have no defences against her hateful words. The battle had to be won now. 'I shall ask him to send you away—and he will. He will refuse me nothing.'

'Bitch!' Lina hurled both the word and the contents of the pail at her at the same time, and ran from the room with Karin's screams echoing behind her.

The water had not been hot. Not even luke-warm. It had been ice cold! As it doused her, something snapped inside Karin's head. She could hear herself screaming, but was unaware of the people in the room with her trying to calm her. She was naked, and so cold! She wrapped her arms about her shivering body, but could find no warmth. How cold the wind was . . . When would her mother let her put on her clothes? Everyone was looking at her. Not only at her, but all the other young girls who stood beside her, as naked and freezing in the wind as she was.

'In God's name, what goes on here?' Attracted by her terrified cries, Rollo had run from his rooms, still only half-dressed himself. He passed Lina in the passage, but had no time then to wonder at the strange smile on her face. In two long strides he had crossed the room to where Karin stood, with Berta and Celine trying unsuccessfully to calm her, snatched up a towel and wrapped her in it. She sagged, near fainting, in his grasp as he lifted her clear of the bath and carried her to the bed.

'Wine, quickly,' he ordered, and Berta waddled to do his bidding as fast as her legs would carry her. Knowing there was always some in his room, she fetched a stone jug filled with some of the wine he had brought back that very day from Jaffa. He had been sampling it after his bath, and she had also grabbed up the pewter goblet alongside it.

Rollo snatched the vessel from her and ordered roughly, 'Fill it.' Then he lifted Karin into the crook of his arm and forced it against her stiff lips. She was shivering so violently that the wine spilled over the towel wrapped about her, staining it a vivid red. Berta stepped back with a gasp, and crossed herself. He glared at her.

'Leave us. Both of you!'

'My mistress will have need of me,' Celine said stubbornly, and he stared at her bleakly.

'She has me! Go!'

'A cover . . .' Karin begged. She clung to him with nerveless fingers, rolling her head against his arm, her eyes still tightly closed. Mother of God, what demon possessed her, he thought, as he gathered her close against him, rocking her as if she was a small child who had woken in the night and needed comfort? 'Please, mother, may I not dress now? I am so cold!'

'Hush! Soon you will be warm,' he whispered, his lips against her hair. He pushed the wet strands away from her face and laid his mouth against hers until he felt an involuntary response, then drew back. 'Where are you now, *Kutti*?'

'On the Hill of Calvary. It is so cold . . .' Slowly her eyes flickered open. 'Rollo—how . . . ? I thought . . .' She turned her face into his shoulder and found he was not wearing a shirt. Puzzledly she lifted her head. 'Your skin is damp . . . have you too been on the mountain?'

'No, little one, I had just finished bathing when your screams brought me in here. I thought the devil was trying to abduct you,' he returned with a half-smile. She seemed in no hurry to move away from him. He was in no hurry to release her. Calvary—Jerusalem again! Why had she been wet and without clothes? And then a memory rose from the back of his mind to give him the answer—confirming, too, once and for all, her true identity. He would never doubt again that she was Alisandre de Greville-Wynter!

'He already has,' Karin murmured, freeing a hand from the confines of the towel to push more hair away from her face. 'I am so very cold. May I have my clothes?'

'First you must drink more wine, and then I shall

have a fire lit in your bedchamber. You are in no condition to go downstairs tonight,' Rollo said, and she drew back from him in surprise.

'But it is what you want . . .'

'I do not want you to get a fever. You are still shivering.'

'That is because your—Lina—threw a pail of cold water over me. Deliberately, I think, although I have no way of proving it. She does not like the thought of my taking her place.' Karin did not dare to look at him as she spoke, but he slipped a finger beneath her chin and tilted back her head. 'I shall be sure to take a fever if you keep me here like this,' she added.

'I can think of a better way to warm you than hiding that body beneath dull clothes,' Rollo replied with a wicked grin. 'But I know it would not be to your liking . . . Besides, I want some questions answered. The coldness of the water apparently produced some kind of shock to your memory. You thought yourself somewhere else—not here at Shah'mat.' He left her to go to the door and shout for a servant. When one came, with Chavo close on his heels, he ordered wood to be brought and a fire started. Then food was to be served to them in Karin's bedchamber. 'Tell the others I am not joining them tonight,' he added to the waiting knight. 'Lady Alisandre has need of me. Let them make of it what they please.'

He came back to the bed where Karin sat staring at him in bewilderment—yet secretly pleased at the unexpected concern he was showing for her. She wrapped the towel more firmly around an exposed shoulder, ignoring his searching look, and sat in silence until the fire began to crackle in the hearth and a table had been drawn up close to her on which was laid out wine and food.

Throwing down a heap of cushions before the fire, Rollo lifted her and carried her across to them, planting a brief kiss on her lips before he went to fetch another towel. Her astonishment grew as he proceeded to dry her hair, but her protests were brushed aside. Although she was still cold, the fire was warming and the wine had comforted her from the inside. What a terrible few moments those had been . . . so vivid and so real . . . as if it had been happening to her at that very moment.

He poured more wine for them both and sat down behind her, easing her back so that she was resting against his drawn-up knee. Now that she was herself again, she realised he had no shirt on, only a pair of breeches. Even his feet were bare.

'Drink,' he ordered, 'and then we shall talk of this strange nightmare that is capable of haunting you even in the daytime.'

'Must I?' She drained the goblet and put it quickly aside, not wishing to relive it all over again, but he nodded. 'Lina . . .' The spite on her face! She would never forget it. Yet, in a way, that woman had done her a favour, for she had released another small part of her memory . . . 'I told you, she threw cold water over me.'

'And she will be whipped for it,' Rollo said. She twisted round to look at him, her eyes widening in disbelief.

'If you would do that to her—who is someone

special to you—what would you do to me, my lord?'
she asked with a faint smile. 'In Jyira it would be the
bastinado, or my feet plunged into boiling oil. What
little trick would you think up for me?'

'Do not ask,' came the chilling reply, and as she
paled he caught her to him with a soft expletive. 'Do
not change the subject. Tell me what happened.'

He could sense that the incident had not only frightened her but also drained her, for she sank against
him, laying her head against his chest. Several times,
as she spoke, he felt a tremor run through her body.
He knew she was no longer cold, for her skin was
warm to his touch, but shocked. He had envisaged an
evening far different from the one they would now
spend together, he thought, remembering the food
growing cold behind them, but it did not matter. He
felt a change in her, and it pleased him. And, in this
moment of stress, she needed him! It was a feeling he
had never known before. Women had wanted him
and he supplied their needs, often satisfying his own
also, but he had never had need of them, nor they of
him.

This creature curled in his arms sorely needed
understanding, and consideration—and affection.
Not the kind he gave other women, but honest,
genuine affection. The kind he had shut out of his life
for so many years.

'It is not clear now in my mind . . . but I remember
my mother taking me up to the slopes of Calvary.
Many other young girls—my friends—were taken
there. It was an act of penance, you understand.' Rollo
nodded, but did not speak. 'Our—Our heads were

shaved . . . and we took cold baths. Saladin and his army were at the gates of Jerusalem. Celine told me that when Badir first brought me to Jyira there was not a hair on my head . . .' She gave a shaky laugh. 'How ugly I must have looked! How desperate we all must have been, and it availed us nought. The city fell . . . My parents died. I do not understand why God allowed it to happen. Why could the city not be shared? It is such a beautiful place. Why do you want to marry me there?'

The question brought a frown to Rollo's face. How could he tell her of the vow he had made in the cathedral there—the vow which had drastically changed his life? Before he could confess what had overtaken him, he must ask God to free him. Only then could he give her the honesty she demanded, and spend the rest of his days as a man, not an empty shell.

'I have my reasons. Are you afraid I shall desert you before then?'

'Your reputation would suggest that you tire easily of your toys, my lord,' Karin murmured, not raising her head from his chest. She was being too bold. Or was she? The truth could not harm either of them. 'I doubt if I shall last any longer than the others.'

'You do not try as hard as they did,' Rollo chuckled, and she felt her cheeks burn. He really was arrogant beyond words! 'Perhaps, if you did, you might be surprised at your own potential.'

He stroked her hair, now almost dry from the heat of the fire, and slipped a hand down inside the protection of the towel against her breast. She quivered at his touch, and protested feebly as he tilted her head back against his shoulder—but not too much, for already she was dying for him to kiss her, to hold her and shelter her from the outside world. She had felt safe at Shah'mat for a whole week. Now she felt safe with him.

'What do I call you?' Rollo murmured, as his lips caressed hers and nibbled at her ear, while his hand became bolder beneath the towel. She clung to him, desperate for the comfort he offered to shut out the hideous memory of Lina and the spasms of coldness which had sent her mind spinning back into the realms of darkness. But, even as she did so, she knew it was not just comfort she wanted—or needed. She wanted to belong to him, and to love him in what small way she knew how. 'Karin? Alisandre? I now know that you are indeed she. I have heard tales of the strange rituals that took place before Jerusalem fell. You must have been there.'

'Then call me whatever it pleases you to call me. Wife, perhaps? No, that you will never do, for that would mean I have your heart, and you do not have one to give.'

'Do not ask for what I cannot give, then, but take what is offered,' Rollo whispered, pulling away the towel and pressing her down onto the cushions. Cupping her face between his hands, he gave her an odd smile. 'My name I gave to another woman, and my trust and—my love. That will not happen again. I give you the here and now . . . and my promise that if you are honest with me, so shall I be with you. Let there be peace between us, *Kutti*? Yes, I shall always call you

''Cat''. Perhaps I may need to borrow one of those extra lives in the future! Who knows?'

'They are yours . . . all of them.' She lifted her arms, no longer embarrassed by his eyes on her, and entwined them about his neck, bringing his mouth down to hers. She felt the surprise in him at her boldness.

For a long moment he lost himself in the exploration of her mouth, aware of the eagerness in her response. Lifting his head, he asked quietly, 'If you had not been so frightened by what happened earlier, would you have welcomed my kisses as you do now?'

'I—I don't know.' Why was he spoiling it? Could he not see—feel—the fire in her? 'Yes, I think I would. I have come to accept our marriage . . . whenever it is to be.' The last words told him that she was still vexed at the delay.

'Never fear, I shall wed you.' Rollo sat back on his heels, staring down at her. The flickering firelight turned her pale skin the colour of honey, introduced a red sheen into the burnished gold tresses in disarray about her head. Her eyes were wide, the blueness of them as deep as the sapphires he had brought with him from Jaffa, which would grace her throat on their wedding day. Instinctively her fingers gathered the edge of the towel to her, drawing it over her exposed breasts as he continued to look at her in silence. Was she so shy—so demure—in Siward's company? It was not the first thought to strike him when he saw them together, nor the one which entered his head now, to wipe away the pleasantness of the moments before.

'For a woman, you do not lie well,' he said dryly.

Karin sat up, grasping the towel about her properly,

angry and embarrassed at his refusal to accept what
she had offered. She had never acted so with any man
before.

'Would you have me a liar—and a bold hussy like
the women who come from Acre to accommodate the
army?' she demanded.

'Never lie to me, *Kutti*, for I shall know it. As for
being bold . . . you are different tonight, and I am not
sure if I like it or not. No, I do not think it becomes you
as it does others I have known. But then you have not
had their experience of life—of men. Or that is what
you would have me believe.'

'Why will you not admit that you know I am not
the—the whore you thought me?' Karin cried, her
agitation growing. He was deliberately trying to provoke her, she thought, as if afraid to acknowledge his
victory. She did not understand him. It was what he
had wanted from the start.

'I was wrong in that, I admit. There, are you satisfied?' Rollo asked as he rose to his feet.

'You are too generous with your apologies, my
lord,' she said scathingly, and watched his eyes
narrow.

'Don't anger me!'

'Anger you? Am I capable of that? Annoyance,
perhaps, but not anger. I am a mere chattel, to be given
what you can . . . when and where you please. Were
those not your words? I suppose I should be grateful to
you. I have my life—I shall have your name. Why
should I want anything else?' She flung the words at
him recklessly, deeply injured by his rejection. Was
she so clumsy, so inexperienced, that she could not

hold him even for one short hour? Bright tears flooded her eyes, and she turned her head away so that he would not see them. 'I will not live in her shadow,' she muttered fiercely.

'Explain yourself,' Rollo demanded curtly. Damn the girl, she sounded like all the rest. Position, money! Were these all she thought of, too? Was he cursed with greedy women?

'Your wife!' She flung back her head and stared up at him, and saw his hands clench at his sides. 'I will not be treated as if you expect the day to come when I shall act as she did. I will not!'

'If you did, I would kill you. Who the devil told you about her? Siward? Just how close have you two become?'

'Did—Did you kill her?' she faltered, ignoring the cruel taunt.

'She is dead. That is all you need to know. Go to bed. I may come to you later . . . if I am not otherwise diverted.'

'By Lina—or a flagon of wine?' Karin said cuttingly, and he threw her a slow, ugly smile from the doorway, his eyes stripping her of the towel, reminding her of the touch of his hands on her . . . and of how much she still wanted them.

'You enjoyed it the last time,' came the insulting comment before the huge oak door slammed after him.

Karin got up and dragged herself over to the bed, shivering again, yet she was not cold. He frightened her when he was in these strange moods. Was there nothing she could do to reach him? Must she go down on her knees and confess her love and place herself totally in his power? Yet, was she not already!

Wearily she curled up beneath the bedcovers, the towel still wrapped firmly about her body. Would he come to her, and take her as he had that first time? With a sob she turned her face into the pillows and allowed the tears to flow. She had been so sure of herself tonight . . . And now he had made her feel awkward and clumsy—and very foolish. How he must despise her!

'My lord, we did not expect to see you.' Chavo rose to his feet as Rollo came striding into the Great Hall. 'Is Lady Alisandre not with you? She has recovered from her fright?'

'She has gone to bed.' Flinging himself into a chair, he beckoned a servant to bring him ale. The food placed before him was thrust away again. Chavo and Siward, seated on his right, exchanged frowns. On the lower tables, the rest of his personal Guard and a few selected men lowered their voices at the sight of the scowl on his face. More glances were exchanged. He had been in a good humour on the way back from Jaffa, and not just because he was returning to Shah'mat. The wench had something to do with it. Most of them had seen the gifts he brought, and had joked about the Lord of Darkness suddenly seeing the light! Yet now here he was, looking as black as thunder and drinking heavily. She had sent him away . . . No, he would not allow that!

As Rollo sat drinking throughout the evening, consuming ale and then wine without appreciation, many

conjectures were passed among the lower tables . . .
all well out of earshot of the dour-faced man who
stared sightlessly down the Hall, lost in his own
thoughts. By the end of the evening, as they began to
drift away to their beds and the women who awaited
them, the majority had decided that the Duke needed
a good battle to take his mind off his troubles. The
sooner they left to join the main army, the better.
Siward was delegated to broach the subject.

The hall was quiet now that most had departed.
Servants were clearing away the mass of platters and
drinking-vessels, while the dogs roamed beneath the
tables gobbling up the scraps of meat. Rollo, with his
booted legs stretched out before him, was staring
moodily into his drink. He had pulled a chair close to
the fire when Siward went to join the Guard and
Chavo had cautiously slipped towards the stairs. Fool,
he had thought, his lip curling wryly. Still mooning
over the Arab girl. What a pair they made! He knew
that if he went to Karin now, in his present mood, his
love-making would be selfish and undoubtedly sav-
age. He had promised himself it would be that way no
more. He had tried! And then she had answered him,
her body arching up towards his with a hunger to
match his own, and it had shocked him.

Lisette had lied to him for a full year before their
marriage, and for another afterwards, and love had so
blinded his eyes and his mind that he had thought her
innocent of the many rumours which circulated at
court. He had killed two men and seriously wounded
another, which brought him under the eye of King
Henry, who already had no love for him as he was a

close friend of the exiled Queen Eleanor. As a lad in his teens he had been instrumental in trying to help her to escape to Paris to be with her sons, Richard, Henry and Geoffrey, who were aligned against their father in a power struggle. She had been arrested before reaching the city. The King had a long memory, as Rollo was soon to discover!

Lisette! He could not think of her without a red mist rising in front of his eyes. When he had found her with a stable-boy he had killed him, and hated himself for months afterwards when he grew to accept that it was she who had lured him to her bed, not he who had pursued her—as she had made him believe at the time. There were others, too countless to remember. The last lover, his best friend, had challenged him after her death—prompted by the King, he suspected. He had killed him, too, in a deadly fight which had almost cost him his life. To his dying day he would bear the scars.

He had been banished from Provence. His estates and title forfeit to the Crown. As a final, defiant act he had razed the castle to the ground and ridden away without a backward glance, young Chavo at his side. When he had returned to the land of his birth again, Queen Eleanor was a free woman once more and welcomed him . . . and Richard restored his lands and title, and made him Duke of Aquitaine on his mother's insistence. But he had never returned to Verduse. Even five years later, the pain was still too great.

It would never leave him, he decided, reaching for the wine again. How much had he drunk? He still felt too sober. Siward took a chair beside him.

'The men are anxious to be on the move again, my lord. There is talk of riding to Jaffa to join the main army. I think you should talk to them.'

'We shall leave when I say so. Any man who deserts me now will not ride with me again,' Rollo growled. He looked into the Norseman's bronzed features, and asked slowly, 'Are you anxious to leave, my friend?'

'It is preferable to growing lazy, my lord. Do not misunderstand. I have a great feeling for this place, as you have, but I am a soldier. I am paid to fight.'

'Then find something to occupy them. Let them take out their boredom on each other. Offer them money. Such an inducement never fails—with anyone!' Rollo answered with a shrug.

'As you wish. I shall speak with them in the morning. My lord, is anything wrong? Siward stared unflinchingly into the hard face which turned on him. How bleak the eyes were as they searched his face. What did he seek to discover?

'Should there be?'

'You are . . . unusually morose. The journey home tired you, perhaps, after your illness?'

'Why don't you say what you mean? Why am I not with her?'

Siward nodded, preferring this bluntness between them. At least, then, he knew where he stood. He had the feeling that Rollo harboured some grudge against him, yet for the love of heaven, he could not imagine what it could be. He had not been like this before he went away. And then he recalled the cold green eyes which had focused on him as he rode into the courtyard with Karin that afternoon, and she was laughing at some joke he had just made, her cheeks glowing, eyes shining. He sighed and shook his fair head.

'My lord, you do me a deep wrong. She is yours. I but obey your orders. I have watched her or had her watched while you were absent. When she grew bored in the castle and asked to be allowed to ride, I saw no harm in it. I could not trust her in the care of anyone else . . . Would you have had me do so?' Rollo shook his head, and Siward shrugged. 'She rides like the wind . . . as well as any man. Almost as well as you, I think! And she has an eye for good horseflesh. She longs for the mount Queen Berengaria gave her. You brought it with you, did you not?'

'Ay. I have not told her.' There was much he had not—could not—tell her.

'A pity. It might have cheered her.'

'I saw no trace of sadness in her when she returned this afternoon,' Rollo remarked heavily, hating himself for this jealousy in him which he neither liked nor understood. 'You have become—friends.'

'As far as that is possible, yes. I am nobody—just the man who rides with her—perhaps she finds it easier to talk to me. Forgive me, lord, but you are not the easiest of men to converse with . . .'

'Do not tell me my faults—I know them well enough already,' Rollo interrupted, draining his goblet. He would go to her! He began to rise, then sank back into his chair with an oath. No, not this way, while he was laden with drink. The slightest word would inflame his temper, and she would suffer for it. 'I begin to think I know her not. In Acre, she was just another woman. Here, I find myself beginning to act like . . . like a love-sick dog about her. Yet I love her not,' he added, as a smile touched his companion's lips. 'Do not think that she is any different for me . . .'

'Then why do you sit here with me, and look at my ugly face, when you could be looking at something far more lovely?'

'If I knew that, I would not be here! Forgive me, Siward. My black thought will be the death of me one day. When I saw you together . . .'

'I do not take from my lord. If I wanted the woman, and knew you did not, I would ask for her. Fight for her, if you refused to give her to me. But she means nothing to me, except as a friend. Not many men like me can be blessed with such friendship . . . We enjoy each other's company, my lord. That's all. If she betrayed you, I would kill her, as I once threatened to do when the fever took you. That has not changed.' Siward rose to his feet, and took his leave. When he reached the door of the Great Hall, he looked back, hoping that Rollo had decided to go upstairs. But he still sat by the fire, and a servant was replenishing his empty goblet.

'I hear you like to ride,' Rollo said, coming into Karin's room the next morning to find her sitting up in bed. She was enjoying some fruit, and nodded, lost for words. Even Celine was looking at him nonplussed, knowing what had passed between them the night before. Yet here he was, coming unannounced into her mistress's room before the hour of eight as though nothing amiss had taken place. 'Perhaps you would care to come hawking with me this morning? I want to see if you are as good a horsewoman as Siward tells me. I've had your horse brought from Acre—the one Queen Berengaria gave you.'

It was a challenge he knew she could not refuse. Even so, a stubborn expression registered on her features, and he motioned to Celine to leave. When the door had closed behind her, he said stiffly, 'I am trying to apologise, *Kutti*. Do not make it difficult for me.'

'For what? It is always I who am in the wrong, not the great Lord of Darkness.' Karin turned her head away, only to have it jerked back by ruthless fingers. His eyes were blazing.

'Last night, because of you, I got very drunk, and still I could not erase you from my memory. Usually wine is most successful.' He did not sound very proud of the fact, Karin thought, as she forced herself to look up at him. Immediately her limbs felt weak. She wanted to reach out and clasp him to her. Tell him— entreat him—to believe she was not the wanton his wife had been, but she dared not. She wanted to run her fingers through his thatch of black hair and whisper words she had never said to any man. Yet she dared not. He had repulsed her once, and would do it again. While he did not believe a woman could be true and could love him, he was safe . . . secure against another invasion of his heart. He did have one. Would he otherwise have brought her so many beautiful gifts?

'I thought my lord found me very insignificant,' she

whispered. Throwing himself down beside her, he placed his hands each side of her head so that her face was imprisoned between them.

'Last night I acted like a fool. It was not the first time, nor will it be the last. It is something you must learn to bear with me . . . I give what I can,' he added, and it was a cry from the heart. Karin was touched by the desolation in his voice, and a look she had never seen before in the depths of those green pools. She lay breathless, unsure of herself and of him, and yet filled with a sudden sense of hope—of possibilities. He need not have come to her . . . 'Too much has happened. I can give you no love.'

'I have never asked for anything from you,' she said quickly, and he nodded, his brows drawing together into a tight frown.

'No, you have not. I have judged too harshly, and too quickly. We know each other—yet we know not,' Rollo replied with a half-smile, and she felt herself surrendering once again to the charm he could exercise at will. Was this another act meant to disarm her or a genuine attempt at reconciliation?

'I—I have not thanked you yet for all your gifts, my lord,' she said in a small voice. 'I was taken aback yesterday . . .'

'Liar! Did I not tell you I would know? You thought I brought them to buy you. No?'

She nodded, ashamed at the thoughts that had passed through her mind when she saw them.

'Honesty at last. It is a beginning,' Rollo murmured. Bending his head, he kissed her gently on the lips. She waited for his hands to lay claim to her body, but he drew back. 'We leave within the hour. Will you be ready?'

'May I dress as I please?'

'To ride, yes. Within the castle, you will dress to please me.'

'I am at my lord's command,' she replied meekly, and he frowned again.

'Would that you were. You are too meek again, *Kutti*.'

'Can I never please you? Too meek, or too bold. You are never satisfied.'

'Be yourself. I shall wait for you below.'

When he had gone, she flung aside the bedcovers and called for Celine to dress her. Neither she nor Berta agreed with the apparel Karin chose, a laced shirt and loose, harem-style, silk trousers, and boots as before, but it suited her, for it gave her the freedom she needed astride her horse. Siward had not exaggerated when he said she rode like the wind, as Rollo found out that morning and in the days which followed, as they rode and hawked among the foothills. Both were careful in the things they said when in each other's company, and more so when she joined him in the Great Hall, as she did that night and for every night afterwards, until she came to realise that not only he expected it, but his men did, too. Within a month there was no trace of antagonism from any of them.

She was no longer bored. When she did not hunt with Rollo or ride at his side through the olive groves, past trees laden with the last juicy oranges and bright yellow lemons, she sat with Celine and Berta in the solar, making her new gowns, inspected the kitchens, or toured the castle, making herself known to the servants.

As they accepted her, so now did Rollo, yet he had not come to her bedchamber again or sought to touch her, apart from what was necessary in the course of lifting her from her horse or guiding her to the dinner-table at night. She wondered at his strange attitude and knew he was aware of her curiosity, but he did not enlighten her until a long time after that frightening night when Lina had doused her with cold water. She saw little of the woman these days, and learned from Chavo that she had been reduced to a kitchen-maid by Rollo's order. No longer was she allowed anywhere near the donjon where Karin lived.

Riders came and went frequently from Shah'mat, bringing messages from the army and the King himself. One night over their meal, Rollo told everyone of the negotiations now under way between Richard and Saladin, of the former's plan to marry his sister Joanna to the Saracen's brother, al-Adil. Karin heard the murmur of disapproval which ran around the Great Hall. Marriage between an Infidel and a Christian Queen! It was unheard-of, yet the offer had been made. There was disquieting news, too. As soon as the rebuilding of Jaffa had begun, Saladin, then en-camped at Ascalon on the coast, had evacuated the town and returned to Jerusalem. He had left it of little use to the Crusaders, even thought it was a vital route between Egypt and Syria.

October slipped into November, and the heat was less. Huge fires now blazed in Shah'mat throughout the day and well into the night as chill desert winds penetrated the draughty castle. How much longer before Jerusalem was retaken, Karin asked herself day after day. How long before she became Rollo's wife? Time was dragging, and his reserved treatment of her, at first puzzling, now gave her cause for concern. Was he waiting for her to make the first move? Surely he could not expect her . . . ? As she found him watching her that night, she knew that that was indeed what he intended.

As he held out his goblet to a hovering servant, she took the jug from the man, saying quietly, 'I shall serve Lord Rollo myself.'

A gleam came into his eyes as she tipped wine into the silver vessel. He drank deeply and she topped it up, her eyes never leaving his face. Chavo nudged Siward's arm, and grinned. Following his gaze, the Norseman watched the silent encounter and felt a moment of envy. He had spoken the truth when he said that what he shared with Karin was nought but friendship . . . Would that he could share such with a woman of his own.

'I am tired. May I go to bed?' Karin asked, setting down the jug. She could say nothing more before all these watching eyes . . .

'As you wish,' Rollo replied in the same low tone. There was a surprised murmur as he bent and kissed her on the mouth, allowing his hand to linger against her breast. The response her lips gave him in that one short moment told him that this night would be different—if he chose to take the chance. He watched her ascend the stairs, never looking back at him, and felt a dryness in his mouth he could not quench with wine.

'No, not that—The white silk,' Karin said, when Celine brought her a nightgown. 'Then you may go to Chavo.'

'How do you know I go to him again?' Celine asked, raising an eyebrow. 'I have said nothing.'

'You are in love, as I am. When you have been with him, it is written in your eyes.'

'You have made your peace with *him*, then?'

'Tonight. I can do no more than I have. I do not know how.' Karin pulled on the full robe and secured it about her waist with a jewelled girdle. Her hair, loose about her shoulders, framed a pale face, with a hint of anxiety about the mouth. 'Go now, before he comes.'

She paced the room for almost two hours, remade the fire several times as the hours passed, and Rollo did not appear. He was not coming! In the early hours of the morning, with laughter still echoing from the Hall below, she climbed into bed, believing he had stayed to get drunk with his men again. She was almost asleep when she heard the door open and close. The bedcurtains she had pulled to keep out the draughts from the shuttered window were dragged back, and Rollo stood looking down at her, a candle in one hand. He was quite sober.

'I did not think you would still be awake.' He sounded uneasy . . . or was it unsure? Karin wondered, as she slowly sat up. He blew out the light when he saw that the flames dancing in the hearth illuminated the figure in the bed far better than a dozen candles. He caught his breath as he saw what she wore . . . something so sheer, so flimsy, that it hid nothing from his hungry eyes. 'I was not certain . . . You gave me the impression you would—might— welcome me. I had made up my mind that you would have to come to me . . .'

'That has not concerned you in the past.' Karin could have bitten off her tongue for her careless words, as he stiffened. 'Does it matter now? I am here. When I am your wife, it will matter not if I am unwilling. Why should it now? What do you want of me?'

'You know that well enough,' he whispered, sliding down over her, his hands drawing away the silk covering her body. She trembled and was immediately awakened by the touch of his hands against her skin, lightly running over her breasts, her thighs, between them. She sank beneath him onto the feather mattress as his lips closed over hers, parting them, drawing from them an instant response, just as they had down-stairs. 'Do you not hate me still for my rough treatment of you in Acre?'

'No. I have tried . . .' He was making it impossible to think, for he was kissing her face, her throat, her breasts, exploring her body with knowledgeable hands that made her breathing quicken in excitement at the pleasure she was experiencing. If she was different this night, then so was he. Gentle and con-siderate, seeking to please her and anticipating her needs, rather than his own as he had before. Words of love came to her lips, but she bit them back. If he did not believe her—and with his contempt of women, there was no reason why he should—she would ruin this night as the one before, and perhaps send him back into the old personality where lingered hatred and suspicion and mistrust.

'I wanted you to dislike me—to hate me,' Rollo whispered against the mane of red-gold hair. 'In that way it was easier for me to keep you in my mind where you belonged. In that way I had no fear that you would throw yourself at me with lying protestations of love in order to try and entrap me into marriage.'

'You are a cruel, mistrusting man,' she murmured, easing her lips from beneath his. 'Do you treat every woman so—so despicably?'

'You would not believe those who have done as I said—sworn they loved me after one night in their bed because I am a lord, with a title and lands. I have even had some hoping to thrust another man's bastard on me . . . God! You cannot know the tricks that can be conjured up to trick and trap a man.'

Karin lay still, her mind reeling. Her fingers stole slowly to the flatness of her stomach. She could not tell him now. But when? If she was right, then she carried his child from that wild night in Acre. She was at least three months pregnant, perhaps more. Thank God it did not show! But when it did, how would he react? Most men wanted a son and heir, even a daughter, to bounce on their knees and boast about to friends. But Rollo was not like other men.

'When—When Jerusalem is in Christian hands again, what then?' she asked hesitantly. He drew back from her, stripped off his shirt and then the rest of his clothes, and threw himself down beside her again. 'Shall we go to England—or remain here at Shah'mat?'

'So it's England that takes your fancy now, is it?' His voice was tinged with soft mockery, and she coloured in the flickering light as she caught the glitter in his eyes. 'I wondered how long it would take you to assess what you have.'

'I—I don't understand. Oh, you are insufferable! I don't care for your name or your money . . . or the estates I have in England. I would prefer to stay here.'

'Would you, now.' Rollo was taken aback. He had not expected that answer. To stay at Shah'mat—What an idea! They would be for ever under the eye of the Infidels, but he was learning to live with them. Why should he not stay here, where he felt most at home, and keep her with him. The two of them alone—apart from a couple of hundred of armed retainers . . . 'You really mean it, don't you?'

'Yes, if it is the only way to prove to you that I care nothing for your worldly goods,' she replied sincerely.

'Do you realise you are an heiress in your own right?'

'I have nothing. King Richard gave my lands to you.'

'And I return them to you, here and now. On our wedding day I shall have a paper drawn up to that effect. Sooner, if you prefer. Now what do you say? Do you still want to stay at Shah'mat with me?'

'I shall give the English estates to our daughter. Shah'mat must go of course to your son.'

'If Saladin's men don't lay siege to it within the next few months and topple the walls about our ears,' he chuckled, and then, as her words sank into him, she felt him stiffen. His hands became still on her body. 'What is this talk of children? I want no more complications in my life, do you hear? You are more than enough. Wherever I go, you will be with me, and that will not be possible with some babe clinging to your skirts.'

With a soft cry Karin turned her head away. His lips touched her cheek and found it wet with tears.

'What's this? Are you one of these women who must have children about them? Sweet Jesus, not yet, *Kutti*. Let me enjoy you a while longer before you become inaccessible to me. I want no children, and neither must you—yet.'

She protested half angrily as he thrust a knee between her legs and parted them, but his lips descended on hers to transport her to a world of infinite joy. His lips and hands sought, explored, tantalised every secret place until her body arched up to meet his for the final explosive culmination, which held her suspended as if in mid-air for one shattering moment before she descended to earth again, to fall asleep in his arms with him still over her.

'Mistress, there is a man who wishes to speak with you.' Karin turned from the window as Celine entered the solar, followed by a short little Arab who bowed respectfully before her.

'Mar'haba!'

'Mar'haba!' Karin replied, returning his Arabic greeting, but then she said in English, 'You wish to see me?'

'Why do you use the tongue of the Infidel?' the man

returned in stilted English, a frown crossing his pointed features. 'Have you succumbed so completely to the charms of this Frankish knight that you have forgotten who you are?'

Karin drew herself upright, her whole body stiffening at the man's rudeness. He was one of the many Arab servants that Rollo employed in the castle. She remembered seeing him tending the soldiers' horses, and sometimes serving the men when they ate and drank in the courtyard at night. There was disapproval of her not only in his voice, but in the small brown eyes which darted over her, and his lips curled at the sight of her western-style dress.

'I asked who you were! Give me an answer, or leave,' she snapped.

'I am Zolto. I bring a message from the Lord Ayub.'

She gasped, and sank onto a stool. Celine came to her and laid a hand on her shoulder. Ayub! How had he found her? And then, looking into the eyes of the man before her, she knew without a doubt that he was a spy. His work, his very nearness to the Crusaders, enabled him to overhear important conversations which he could send back to his master.

'Tell me,' she demanded through tight lips. Why was she even listening to him when she ought to denounce him to Rollo and have him killed for his betrayal? Yet Ayub was like a brother, even though she now knew he was not, and there was still love in her heart for him in that capacity. If only it were possible to see him again and explain what had happened to her . . . the love she now felt for Rollo, the child she suspected she carried. His child!

'My lord bids you be ready one week from today. When you ride on that day, he will be waiting with men to free you from this accursed Infidel who has abducted you, and to return you to Jyira.'

'You talk like a fool,' Karin interrupted, her features paling. 'I am not a prisoner. It was the Lord Badir who insisted I be returned to my own people. Do you hear that—the Franks are my people! I am where I belong, with the man I shall soon marry. Tell Lord Ayub I am well, and he should have no fears for my safety, but that I wish him not to risk his life unnecessarily. I am content here.'

'Traitorous bitch!' The words came as a growl through the man's clenched teeth. 'You have no choice in the matter. If you do not ride on the seventh day, I shall kill you myself!'

'Leave me!' Karin flung out a shaking hand towards the curtained doorway. 'Now, before I call for Lord Rollo and relate this conversation to him.'

'You would be dead before you could utter a word,' Zolto growled, and both women shrieked as he withdrew a wicked-looking dagger from inside his sleeve, where he had been holding it while they talked. 'The message I brought came from the Lord Ayub. My orders to kill you, should you refuse to comply with it, come from my true master, Rashid al-Din.'

'You are one of his men?' Karin grasped for the comfort of Celine's hand and held it tight. She had heard, as most people had in the Near East, of this man, more commonly known as 'The Old Man of the Mountain' and his followers. He was the leader of a Syrian revolutionary religious movement who dwelt

in a great fortress base at Alamut, in the defiles of
Lebanon. It was said that their name came from the
Arabic 'hashish', which many accused them of taking
in large quantities before they launched out on
another orgy of murder. For this was their trade, and
their weapon was a dagger. They were known as
Hashishin, 'Eaters of Hashish'.

Wide-eyed she watched the dagger slide slowly
back beneath his sleeve. She had to denounce him—
but how, without condemning herself to certain
death?

'In seven days . . .' Zolto said, backing away as
voices sounded from the stairway. She nodded. What
else could she do?

'What were you talking about to that little weasel?'
Rollo asked, coming into the room.

'I—I lost a piece of jewellery—a brooch. He found it
and returned it to me,' Karin faltered beneath his
penetrating gaze. He was wearing his chain-mail and
carrying a cloak. She seized on his attire eagerly as a
way of changing the subject. Realising she was still
clinging to Celine's hand, she dropped it, and asked,
'Are you leaving? Have you had word from Jaffa?'

'No. I go to escort some supply wagons on the last
part of the way here. Chavo tells me there has been a
great deal of activity among the Saracens this past
week. They grow too bold. They must be taught not to
come too close to Shah'mat.' He reproved himself for
disbelieving her tale. It could be true . . . but then why
was she so pale and agitated. He could see no piece of
jewellery anywhere. Why had she been clinging to her
maid's hand as if seeking, nay needing, reassurance?

'I shall be gone two days, or three at the most. I leave you in Siward's capable hands.'

'I have no plans to go anywhere but to Jerusalem, my lord,' she replied, forcing a smile to her lips.

'I would prefer you to remain within the walls of Shah'mat until I return. Not that I doubt your word, *Kutti*,' Rollo added, as she stiffened. 'I wish you to be safe, that's all.'

'As you wish.' Safe! She was in more danger if she remained at Shah'mat. What was she to do?

CHAPTER NINE

RICHARD'S ARMY was on the move once again. The negotiations with Saladin's brother al-Adil came to nothing, as both men knew they would. However, they gave time to both commanders: for Saladin to retire to Jerusalem and await the assault he knew must come, and for Richard to concentrate on the rebuilding of the forts and castles destroyed by the enemy from Jaffa to the Holy City, to ensure a firm line of communication between posts. Often the Lionheart himself led the patrol that drove off Saracen raiding-parties who harassed the soldiers as they worked. He had no fear for his own life, and his men loved him for his recklessness.

Rollo was full of the news when he returned. Watching his face one night as they all sat in the Great Hall, seeing the mounting excitement on not only his face but those of his men, Karin knew he would soon be leaving to join the others. With Saladin's forces concentrated in and around Jerusalem, Shah'mat was no longer in any danger. And he was growing restless for a fight—as they all were. She sensed it in him, in his manner which had begun to grow more distant, in his voice, now often abrupt and sarcastic as in the first days they had been together. And he no longer came to her every night.

Dear God, was he tiring of her? she thought, as he

laughed at a joke Chavo had made and drank deeply from the goblet in his hand. He was in a good mood, but she was not the cause of it. He hardly seemed aware she was beside him, and had not spoken more than a dozen words to her all evening. She could stand it no longer. Her head throbbed from the smoke of the fire and the wine she had drunk. It did not agree with her in her condition, and she must have no more of it.

She was sure now. How glad she was she carried the babe well. It still did not show; he would be away when it did. She rose to her feet to leave.

'Where are you going?' Rollo looked around. Even though he had been listening to Chavo, he was well aware of every movement, every look, she gave him. She was uneasy and he was to blame, but he could find no words to comfort her, nor to explain the terrible torment going on inside him. But for Richard's order that no women were to travel with the army, he would have taken her with him again, but if the fight was to be a long one, he did not want to subject her to the rigours of his uncertain life. He had trusted servants who would care for her—watch her—and ensure that she did not spend too much time with the Arab members of his household and, if she did, he would hear of it. Even now, after all these weeks of contentment, happiness such as he had thought never to know again, he still doubted her. It would be different in Jerusalem, he decided, when she wore his ring and bore his name. And then, when they returned to Shah'mat, he would try to put his thoughts, the complexity of his feelings for her, into words, and pray she would understand his misgivings.

'I have a headache. I am going to bed.'

'Then I shall not disturb you,' he returned, and gave Chavo his full attention again.

Karin could not sleep. She had undressed and climbed into bed, and Celine had made up the fire before leaving her. The room was warm and comfortable, but her thoughts would not allow her to rest. Two weeks had elapsed since the man Zolto had come to the solar and threatened her life if she did not ride on that seventh day. She had not, and now waited in an agony of suspense for the assassin's hand to strike, jumping at every shadow until her nerves were taut and frayed, ready to snap at the least little thing. Had Rollo sensed this, and thought it was because of him and the demands he had come to make upon her so regularly? Had she driven him into this distant mood?

Pulling on a robe, she sat by the shuttered window, her head leaning against the slats. She wanted to tell him about the child, but feared losing him if she did. He did not want the encumbrance of a baby . . . What would his son look like? Dark, like his father, she decided, with a firm chin and stubborn too. His eyes perhaps would be green—or blue as hers were. A daughter would inherit her nature, she hoped, and endear her father to her where her mother could not.

Restlessly she paced the room, trying to ease the nagging suspicion in her heart. He was tired of her now that the army was moving again. She had been a diversion which had occupied his time and prevented him from being bored, as Leila, the dancing-girl, had occupied him in Acre, and Lina, here at Shah'mat. He had discarded them both without remorse. Was he about to do the same with her? She heard footsteps in the corridor outside. In the stillness of the night, they heralded the approach of someone like the blowing of a trumpet. They halted outside the door, and she froze by the window as it slowly opened. Rollo stood there, gazing towards the bed. Seeing she was not there, his gaze swivelled around the room until it came to rest on her, clutching nervously at her robe.

'Can you not sleep either?' He came in, closing and bolting the door, she saw. He intended to stay. He always ensured that they were not disturbed. Which one of them was he saving from embarrassment? she now wondered, and reproved herself for such thoughts. 'How is your head?'

'Better.' He frowned at her stilted tones. 'I did not expect you . . .'

'A messenger came from the King. He wishes me to join him at Beit Nuba. I leave tomorrow—early.'

'But that is close to Jerusalem!'

'Ten or twelve miles. You will not have to wait much longer to be wed, *Kutti*,' he chuckled softly, advancing towards her. 'Are you not pleased? I shall send for you as soon as it is safe. Queen Berengaria and Joanna remain in Jaffa, but they, too, will come to Jerusalem when it is in our hands.'

'Tamir said it never would be again,' she reminded him, and he scowled at her words, angry she should remind him of such a stupid prophecy.

'I do not accept that. I cannot! Why else are we all here, risking our lives? I would prefer to be at Shah'mat, believe me. If only you would,' he added, coming still closer.

She stood quite still, mesmerised by the gleam in his eyes. If she did not look away, she would believe every word he said, allow him to use her still more, and then go off to his war and forget she ever existed.

'Damn it, woman, I am leaving tomorrow! Have you nothing to say to me? Wish me well, or curse me, for I sometimes think that is what you would prefer to do, rather than smile in that way you have . . . and tell me nothing with those guarded eyes.' He grasped her shoulders and shook her roughly, so that her head fell back, her loose hair falling like a cloud about her shoulders. He did not release her, but drew her to him, his lips seeking hers, his hands laying claim to her body beneath the thick velvet robe. She was stiff in his embrace for a moment only, then suddenly clung to him, seeking sanctuary from the darkness of her thoughts, and she heard him utter a low oath. He carried her to the bed, laid her down and then drew back, reaching into his surcoat. 'I have something for you. I intended to give it to you on our wedding day, in Jerusalem, but . . .' She lay still, not believing the reality of the pendant he fastened about her throat. On a heavy gold chain was suspended a pear-shaped sapphire, the size of a chicken's egg. Smaller stones surrounded it, seven in all.

'It—It is beautiful,' she said slowly, touching the cold stones which lay against her skin. He pulled away the robe, baring her shoulders and breasts, and sat back to admire his gift.

'Ay, it is, and it has a perfect setting. You are pleased with it, then?'

'How could I not be!' Impulsively she raised herself

and kissed him, forgetful of what she had been thinking earlier. How silly she had been! He was preoccupied with other things, plans for war which she
knew nothing of. He still wanted her! When he
reached for her again she gave herself without restraint, losing herself and her fears in a whirlwind
of wild passion that drained her, and brought her
peaceful sleep for the first time in many a long
night.

Rollo did not sleep, however, and was glad when
dawn came and he was able to leave her. He dressed
quickly and quietly and left the bedchamber. He met
Siward coming to wake him . . .

Karin stirred and stretched languidly . . . and then,
becoming aware that Rollo was not beside her, sat up,
her eyes sweeping the room. Had he left already?
Without saying goodbye? Or had the pendant been his
farewell? Likewise the hours of pleasure she had spent
in his arms? Grabbing up her robe, she ran to the door,
stole out into the corridor dark with shadows, for the
wall torches had all been extinguished, and along to
the staircase. From somewhere below she heard the
low murmur of voices, and, recognising them, began
to descend.

'I should tell her,' she heard Rollo say, and her steps
faltered.

'I shall do that, my lord. It will be better if it comes
from me.' It was Siward with him. Was he not going
with everyone else this morning? Rollo wore his mail;
his companion did not. What were they discussing in
such low tones, their faces so serious?

'Perhaps so. Get her on the first available ship, do

you understand me? She is not to be here when I return—whenever that is.'

'Are you sure?'

'I shall never have any peace while she is under my roof.' Rollo's tone became sharp and impatient. 'I will not have any woman thinking she owns me. Get her gone, Siward. I leave her in your hands. She trusts you . . .'

Tears blinding her vision, Karin stumbled back to her room. They were talking about her! The sapphire pendant lay on the table where she had laid it before he made love to her. She picked it up and squeezed the stones in the palm of her hand until the pain brought more tears. A wedding gift! A parting gift! He was tired of her, but he did not have the courage—the honesty —to send her away himself. He was leaving it to Siward, because she trusted him! On the first available ship! To England—where else?

She collapsed onto the bed in a fit of weeping, and did not even rouse herself when she heard the sound of the men assembling in the courtyard, and Rollo's command to move out. Did he expect her to be watching him . . . waving a farewell? He had given her his farewell last night—and his child to remind her of her misplaced love! How treacherous he was, how cruel! She had not suspected a thing as she lay in his arms. He was a past master at deception, and she had been his pawn . . . used and now discarded, as all his other women were in time.

There was someone by the door . . . a shadow which brought her to her knees, fear registering in her eyes. Zolto! Firelight flickered over the dagger in his hand. He had waited until Rollo had left. She knew that, before she could scream, his blade would be in her. As he approached the bed, she said in a calm voice,

'There is no need to kill me. Send a message to Lord Ayub. Tell him I am ready to leave Shah'mat.'

'Well?' Ayub stopped his pacing, and stared at the man who came into the room. 'Does she carry a child?'

'Ay, my lord. My estimation is that she is in her fourth month—or very near.'

'Is it possible to do something about it? She cannot have this child.'

'Possible, yes—but dangerous at this stage. The Lady Karin is quite adamant that she will have the child.'

When he strode into Karin's room, Ayub's rage had not diminished at the news. But to his surprise, instead of showing remorse or shame, she turned on him, her eyes blazing blue fire.

'How dare you subject me to the humiliation of an examination. I told you I am *enceinte*. That would have been enough, without being poked and prodded by that—that man!'

'It was necessary. The pregnancy cannot continue. You will not have a Frankish child,' Ayub declared. 'I shall not allow it.'

'I will.' Karin faced him unflinchingly. She had been preparing herself for this encounter ever since she arrived in Jyira the week before, and was resolved to fight tooth and nail to protect the unborn life within her. Her child—and Rollo's! No one would take that from her. 'I shall resist any attempt to force me to agree to such a monstrous suggestion. I want my baby, and I will have it.'

'The child of a man who raped you? A Frankish knight who has had more women than you have hairs on your head?' Ayub was beyond himself with rage. 'I did not bring you here to sire another man's bastard!'

'I thought you had rescued me because of the love you have for me as your sister,' Karin returned, tight-lipped. 'I know differently now. Celine was right—you have never thought of me in that way.'

'I shall cut out her tongue!' he threatened.

'Why? For speaking the truth? I will not marry you, Ayub. I do not love you in that way. It would be wrong,' she protested, trying to reach him.

'Do you love *him*? The father of your bastard?'

'Yes.' He struck her hard across one cheek. The blow rocked her on her feet, but she did not falter and break before him, even though tears started to her eyes. 'I shall always love him.'

'Then I shall bring you his head to remember him by,' Ayub snarled.

'I shall have his child.'

'You forget, woman, here I am master. I can do as I please with you and no one will lift a finger against me. I could have you tied to the bed and a potion poured down your throat to rid your body of his seed.'

'Yes,' she admitted quietly. 'You could, and I know you are capable of doing it. I shall make a bargain with you, Ayub. Allow me to have this child, and I shall stay with you—willingly. I swear it. I shall be—whatever you want me to be—wife, mistress—I care not any more what I am or where I am.'

Ayub frowned at her words. He wanted her badly enough to agree to anything. He had flown into a wild rage when she told him of the child. The thought of touching her while she carried it sickened him, and he had turned away from her, hating her and the man who had sired it. But later, when his temper had cooled, he realised the desire would always be in him.

'Very well. Have the child.' He caught her by the shoulders, his long manicured nails sinking into her soft skin. She barely concealed a shudder at the look in his eyes. How could a man change so? The love and affection he had once given her had turned into something too terrible to contemplate. 'And then I shall have you.'

He crushed her lips beneath his. The overpowering scent of musk from his skin and clothes made her feel nauseous, but she did not move, and offered no resistance. The life of her child depended on her obeying him in all things, she knew.

When he released her, his narrowed gaze bored into her pale face. 'I shall teach you a more responsive answer than that, Karin. In my arms you will forget your Christian lover. I advise you to put him out of your mind as quickly as possible, for I intend to kill him. He and his men are at Beit Nuba. They patrol the roads and keep away Saracen raiding-parties, so that the main army can reach there undamaged. I have seen him fight. It will be a good encounter between us, but I shall kill him . . . Perhaps I shall allow you to watch.'

*   *   *

'Gone?' The blood drained from Rollo's face. He sprang from the bed to stand before Siward, echoing again, 'Gone? Where, in God's name, could she go?'

'I know not, my lord, only that Celine and one of the Arab servants are also missing. A man called Zolto, one of the grooms, I believe.'

A terrible look came over Rollo's features. The green eyes became emerald flints as they stared at the Norseman. His hands clenched into tight fists.

'I placed her in your care, and you let that weasel take her from under your very nose. Are you blind? Deaf? How?'

'She—She went of her own free will, my lord, of that I am certain,' Siward said in defence of himself. 'I guarded her well, and Berta slept in her bedchamber along with the girl Celine. The woman must have been drugged, for I could not wake her on the morning of Lady Karin's disappearance. There were no signs of a struggle. The three of them must have gone over the wall to horses waiting below. I found a place where it was possible, and there were tracks below which led towards Jaffa.'

'You followed them?' Jaffa! She would not go there unless to seek the protection of Queen Berengaria, and why should she do that? The last night they had spent together she had shown no signs of discontent. On the contrary, she had made it more difficult for him to leave her!

'The sand obliterated them a mile from Shah'mat. We searched for two or three days, as far afield as the villages to the north, thirty-two miles away. No one had seen a woman of her description.'

Rollo swore vehemently, running a hand through his crisp black hair. Gone—and willingly! The bitch! She had been playing him like a fish on a line. No wonder she had been so willing that last time. He had suspected nothing! He still knew nothing about women and their devious ways—but he was learning. By God, he was learning!

'Shall I return to Shah'mat, my lord, and continue the search?'

'No. Stay here with me. She is long gone, to a place called Jyira with a man named Ayub!' Rollo returned, tight-lipped. 'When Jerusalem is ours, we shall go after her and take her back, and God help whoever gets in my way!'

'It is close to the Holy City?' Siward asked, and Rollo nodded, having studied his maps the very first time Karin had mentioned the name to him.

'On the outskirts. We ride through it to take Jerusalem.'

'And when we do?'

'They are mine! Both of them,' Rollo declared savagely, and Siward frowned at his manner.

'My lord, forgive me! But, if I am mistaken . . . If she did not go of her own free will . . .'

'She did. I know it. She went to him. I am a fool, and I admit it to you in my anger. I would not do so even before Chavo, who has seen me this way before, and heard me utter a terrible vow never again to trust a woman . . . yet I have done so again . . . and been betrayed again! You will not repeat this to anyone, or I will kill you,' Rollo muttered fiercely. 'She has taught me once and for all the stupidity of weakness. For her

. . .' He broke off, his face contorting with mounting fury.

Siward could never remember seeing him so affected by anything or anyone. The woman was dead if he found her, yet he still found himself saying, 'There were times when the two of you . . . seemed to share so much.'

Rollo wheeled on him, tight-lipped, eyes narrowed. 'Shared? I took—She gave nothing.'

'Perhaps that was the trouble.'

For a long moment Rollo's hand rested on the hilt of his dagger. It was in his mind to draw it and rip out the tongue of the man who dared place blame at his door! But gradually he calmed himself, although it was a great effort. Yes, he had taken, without thought for her . . . until those last few times when he had found himself seeking her company, her body, because of the change in him. A need that did not stem from lust or mere desire, but from something he had shared with only one other person. Even then, she had never understood the depths of his passions. With Karin he had found something different, more meaningful and fulfilling. Something he had always longed for, and thought never to find. And now she was gone . . . back to the man she called brother! Yet this man wanted her in his bed! If she had gone willingly, that meant she, too, wanted him in that way. His blood boiled at the thought of anyone else making love to her. She was his! She would remain his, even if he had to move heaven and earth to get to her and return her to Shah'mat!

*   *   *

Early in February, Ayub received a summons from Saladin himself, which could not be ignored. He was to go to Jerusalem, taking Karin with him. She was transported there inside a closed litter, so that her identity was kept secret. Day after day he had led his men out of Jyira to harass the Christians pouring into Beit Nuba, praying to Allah that he would encounter Rollo, but their paths never crossed. He saw as little as possible of Karin, unable to bear the sight of her growing big with the child of another man.

She bore without reproach his curtness, his anger and the terrible condemnation in his eyes each time he looked at her. Her health had not been good since returning to Jyira, and a heavy cold had left her feeling weak and listless. Celine fussed over her, slept at the foot of her bed as if afraid she might suddenly be whisked away again, made her eat and take nourishing goat's milk when all she wanted to do was lie abed, caring not what became of her. The child sapped what little strength remained after her illness, so that by the time the journey to Jerusalem was completed—short though it was—she was exhausted and had to be put to bed.

They stayed at the house of Ayub's uncle, Haroun. Karin had never liked the man, knowing he had never agreed with his brother Badir's taking a Christian girl into his family and treating her as his own daughter. She waited for the storm to be let loose on her head when Ayub told him of his own plans for her, but to her surprise he was not only pleasant, but went out of his way to see that she had everything she needed. A doctor came daily to the house until she began to grow stronger, and she was given a comfortable room overlooking gardens where sweet-smelling orange blossom invaded the air after heavy rain and brought its own special kind of perfume to linger about her bed.

It was three whole weeks after her arrival before she was well enough to keep the rendezvous with Saladin. Shrouded in a heavy cloak, and veiled, she followed Ayub into the audience-chamber where the Sultan of Syria and Egypt sat on a pile of brightly-coloured satin cushions beneath a striped silk canopy. On each side of him stood impassive-faced Nubian slaves, the bodyguard who never left him. She had once heard a rumour that even these faithful servants had a more powerful allegiance—to 'The Old Man of the Mountain' who, by a mere word, could command men to leap to their deaths from tall buildings or cliff-tops, to kill a friend without compunction—or a powerful enemy of Rashid al-Din whom he wanted to dispose of. She shuddered inwardly to think that this kind-faced man should die by the dagger of one of those murderous Hashishin.

Saladin looked up at the two figures prostrated before him, waved aside the servants close at hand, and ordered them to rise.

'Lord Badir always gave me to understand you were a jewel among women, Lady Alisandre, the most beautiful he possessed. It was a boast I have never forgotten. Please remove your veil so that I can look on your face.'

Karin heard Ayub draw a sharp breath at the request . . . and not only that! Saladin had called her

Alisandre, not Karin! He did not think of her as
Badir's daughter any more? He could see his chances
of persuading the Sultan to agree to the marriage
between them rapidly fading.

Loosening her cloak, Karin removed the flimsy
covering across her face. She had dressed with great
care, choosing a loose plain gown which did not reveal
her state of pregnancy. Not that it mattered, she
thought now, as Saladin's eyes scrutinised her pale
cheeks, still thin after the recent illness. She had the
feeling he had made it his business to know everything that had happened to her since she was
abandoned in Acre on his instructions.

'He was not wrong. But I do not see a bloom in your
cheeks to remind me of the blush of the first summer
rose.'

'I—I have been ill. But I am better now,' she added
quickly, as his eyes turned on the man beside her with
a silent accusation in them.

'And will continue to improve in the capable hands
of the Lord Ayub, I am sure. Soon you will be well
enough to be returned to the Duke of Aquitaine again
where you belong. There can be no marriage without a
bride, can there?' Saladin's tone was dry, and Karin
felt her senses spin. He did know!

'She cannot!' Ayub blurted out. 'I mean—gracious
lord, he has abandoned her. She has suffered at his
hands; she cannot be returned to such an ill-feeling
monster.'

'That is not what I have been told. Lord Ayub, out of
respect for your father, whom I considered my friend,
and the wise Tamir ibn Dak, who foretold this girl's

destiny, I have not ordered you to be arrested and flogged for your flagrant disobedience of my orders. Both men told you that she is to remain with the Franks. Your feelings are not to be considered in this matter, nor hers!' Saladin's hollow cheeks became tinged with grey. Karin thought how ill *he* looked. He looked far older than his fifty-four years, although she knew there was great strength and determination in the frail body concealed by a long robe which fastened at the neck and was totally bare of trimmings of any kind. He could have been some wise old professor, or doting father, instead of the most powerful man in the Muslim world.

'May I speak?' Karin asked softly. Ayub turned on her with an angry frown to remind her that, in his world, such boldness would be rewarded with a flogging. But Saladin nodded. He rang a small bell and ordered a servant to take Ayub to an adjoining ante-chamber and return him in fifteen minutes.

'Now come and sit down, child, and tell me what troubles you.' Saladin indicated that she should sit beside him, which she did tentatively, aware of a smile on the lined face. 'Is it not true that you carry the child of the one called the "Lord of Darkness"? That you lived with him at the place known as Shah'mat? The reports I received did not seem to indicate that you were there against your will. In fact I heard that, in taking you with him when he left Acre, he did in fact save your life.'

'Yes. And he fought for me when my identity was challenged by my cousin,' Karin confessed. 'In the beginning, everything that happened to me . . . was not to my liking. I sought to be free of him and to return to Jyira, to my brother.'

'The brother who now wishes to make you his wife.'

'The relationship between us has changed since Badir died, but I have agreed to wed him if he will allow me to have my child—and he has.'

'The child of a man you hate?' her companion asked with raised eyebrows, and she blushed. 'Now I see the first summer rose. As always, Badir was most eloquent in his descriptions. You are not unhappy, then, to become wife to Lord Ayub?'

'He will not let me go,' Karin whispered. 'I do not want it, but I wish my child to live. Besides, where would I go now? He spoke the truth when he said I had been abandoned . . . at least, I would have been.' Her tone growing bitter, she related what had passed between Rollo and Siward the morning he left Shah'mat. A frown turned to a look of anger as she spoke of Zolto, and the threat to her life should she not leave the castle and return to Ayub. 'I no longer know what I am, or where I belong.'

'Surely that is not the truth,' Saladin said gently, ringing for a servant to bring them hot coffee. When it arrived, she drank hers with appreciation, feeling the sweet liquid restore warmth to her cold limbs. It was a dismal day again and heavy rain had turned the city streets into rivers of mud. Beyond the walls, many of the *wadis* were flooded. She tried not to think of Rollo out there somewhere, in perpetual danger, telling herself not to waste her sympathy on a man who cared nothing for her.

'If you remain in Jyira, you will become a true
Muslim, the wife of Lord Ayub. Yet your child—your
first child at least—will be the offspring of a Frankish
knight. Will you ever forget him? Will you not wish
you had gone back whence you came—England—to
see for yourself the life you left five long years ago?
You have estates there, have you not? You are a
woman of wealth and importance in your own right.
The child should be raised as the son of a knight. The
way of the Franks is not our way, as you well know.
You have been among them again. Can you tell me, in
all honesty, that you would be happier in Jyira than
among your own?'

Karin bowed her head. She could not. She had not
considered what would have happened to her if
she had been put on that ship to England. Why, she
could have gone to her family home, and discovered
what kind of a woman Alisandre de Greville-Wynter
really was. Once installed there, she could forget Rollo and assume her rightful role as mistress.
With Hugo dead, there was no one to usurp her
claim.

'When the child is born, we shall speak of this
again,' Saladin said, bringing the interview to an end.
Though neither said anything, they both knew that
there was only one course of action for her to take.
'Until then, you will remain in the care of Lord Ayub,
here in Jerusalem. Tell him it is my wish that he show
you the house where you were found. It is time a key
was found to unlock your memory and give you
peace.'

'If only you and Richard Lionheart could sit like this

and talk,' Karin said impulsively. 'Perhaps you would both find peace, too.'

'*Insh'allah*. Who knows?'

The jubilant soldiers who had encamped at Beit Nuba, only twelve miles from Jerusalem itself, who had ridden out to gaze on the tall fortified walls and to renew their vows to take it from Infidel hands, were silent now, for the King had ordered a retreat, persuaded of the dangers which surrounded them all if he and the army continued to remain where they were. To lay siege to the city meant weeks or months of endless fighting, and he would undoubtedly be caught between the Saracens defending it and the army of Saladin coming up behind him from the coast.

And if Jerusalem fell? How many of the men with him, their pilgrimage completed, would remain to live in the Holy City and defend it against more attacks? Some of the disheartened men marched away from their goal to refortify and rebuild Ascalon, but not all went. Some, including the Duke of Burgundy and many of the French, retired to Jaffa, where the living was good and easy. Others returned to Acre. Money in the coffers was growing short, and when there was none to spare, many nobles drifted back to the larger towns and warred amongst themselves to relieve the boredom.

While work went on at Ascalon, Richard of England once more began negotiations with Saladin, which went on uneventfully throughout the months of February, March and April, 1192. Meanwhile news from England brought the Lionheart more worries.

His brother John, who had been left as Regent, was beginning to exceed his authority, and King Philip of France was once again raiding along the borders of the Lionheart's possessions in collusion with him. From all sides he seemed to be threatened. But if he left the Holy Land, who would take his place against Saladin? Conrad of Montferrat, ruler of Tyre, or Guy de Lusignan? Who would be the next ruler of Jerusalem? Guy was weak and men did not rally to him, while Conrad was strong and commanded many men in the field, although his methods were sometimes not to the liking of those about him.

In the end, despite the agreement made the previous year in Acre that Guy should rule the city, another decision was taken, in favour of Conrad. Before he had finished celebrating his triumph over his old enemy, however, he was assassinated by several unidentified men as he was returning home late one night. The blame was laid at many doors. Richard himself was suspected, also Guy, who hated him, but most people thought the followers of Rashid al-Din to be the culprits.

Richard saw at once the advantages of Conrad's sudden demise and arranged for his nephew, Henry, Count of Champagne, to marry Isabella, the twenty-one-year-old widow, the twice-married heiress to the kingdom. In Acre, one week after Conrad's death, they were wed, and Henry became the new Lord of Jerusalem.

Karin went often to the narrow cobbled street which housed the remains of her old home. Ayub had stub-

bornly refused to take her there at first until she had
threatened to send word to Saladin of his disobedience.
She knew, had she not been pregnant, he would have
beaten her for daring to blackmail him so blatantly.
The pathetic ruins were open to the sky. Beams,
blackened and charred by the roaring inferno which
had swept through it, lay on the ground. A band of
travelling merchants had housed their caravan in the
grounds, trampling down the flowers and the hordes
of weeds which grew untroubled over the high walls
and round the fountain, long since dry and fallen into
decay. There was an eeriness about the place that
made her shiver, but she overcame her natural
reticence and again—against his wishes—moved
slowly through the battered rooms, seeking to find
something which would bring a picture to her
mind.

It did not happen that first day, nor the second; but
gradually, as she made at least one pilgrimage a week
to the sad little street, it was as if a curtain began to lift
from her mind. She remembered how the flowerbeds
had been planted round the fountain, how the
honeysuckle had smelt in spring. How she and her
mother had sat beneath orange trees, preparing vegetables for dinner. Little things, seemingly of no con-
sequence, but they mattered. Alisandre was returning
to life, and she accepted that Saladin was right.
England was where she belonged. Even though she
did not want the estates for herself, she must accept
them for the son she would bear. It would be a boy,
she knew it. Strong and arrogant like his father . . .
and her heart would break each time she gazed on his

likeness, but she would also know joy, to have part of him with her always.

She said nothing to Ayub. He left her to her own devices, knowing nothing of what had passed while he was absent from the room and believing that, once she had borne the child, she would marry him. She would leave it to Saladin to tell him differently, she thought wisely, not wanting to risk his anger. She did not hate him for his treatment of her, the change in him from brother to prospective husband. It frightened her more than anything, but she was sad not to have realised his true feelings before, and thus averted pain to them both.

The child was heavy in her now, and quite vigorous with its movements. She tired easily and slept badly, her dreams of Shah'mat and the man who discarded her. Celine, who had insisted on accompanying her because of her condition, much to her joy, chided her for her terrible appetite. She had begun to experience nausea each time she ate any food, and at times could touch only water for a whole day. She felt sure that it was not so much the child within her who caused the problem, but her own poor state of health. With each passing day she grew weaker—more troubled in her mind—fearful of what lay ahead.

Doctors came to prod and examine her, leaving her different potions to ease the discomfort, but none did. It was the middle of May, when she was in her eighth month, that the pains started without warning. Her distressed cries brought Celine and her servants running into the room where she had been resting, to find her sprawled unconscious on the floor.

There was fire in her body—and it was no dream. She screamed as pain seared her limbs, gasped for breath, and screamed again. Was she being ripped apart? Dear heaven, she was losing the child!

'Hush, mistress, don't fight it yet . . .' Celine's voice, but sounding as if it was a hundred miles distant. The room was dark. She could not make out the faces bending over her. 'Try to rest—it is almost time . . .'

'Time,' she whispered, hope rising inside her. 'He is well? I fell . . .'

'He lives still,' Celine murmured, wishing that Ayub would not hover beside the bed, listening to every word. He had not wanted to be with her until now. Did he enjoy seeing her toss and turn in agony?

Karin drifted into a semi-conscious state, only to be dragged back to reality again as more pain came again and again until she thought she could bear it no longer.

'A boy, mistress!' Above Celine's joyous shout, she heard the lusty howl of a baby, and sank back amid the pillows, tears flooding her eyes.

'Give him to me! Let me hold him,' she pleaded. Her son! Rollo's son!

'Later. Do not be so impatient! I must wash him first and then you shall nurse him. Gently the maid smoothed Karin's wet hair away from her face, her eyes following the figure of Ayub and, beside him, the wet-nurse, who carried the small infant wrapped in clean cloths from the room. She knew something was terribly wrong, but there was nothing she could do about it. She had lied to her mistress, understanding that she must calm her, and allow her to sleep. Had Karin known that her faithful maid had not even been allowed to touch the child, there was no knowing what she might have done.

Three days later, when Karin came out of a deep sleep induced by an opiate, she was told that her son had not lived out the first hour of his tiny life.

While she lay in bed in Jerusalem in a state of shock, past caring for her own needs or those of anyone else, Rollo left Shah'mat with his men to join the King in an attack on the fortress of Darum, some twenty miles to the south of Ascalon. He had been at his castle since the retreat from Beit Nuba, a solitary, unapproachable figure who sought comfort in too much wine and the arms of any woman who took his fancy.

It was the general opinion that he had at last rid himself of the tawny-haired woman who had bewitched him, and was his own self again. In battle he was a veritable devil. At Shah'mat he was a bear, but one they knew, who trained them mercilessly, drank more than any of them and took his pick of the castle women. Only Siward and Chavo knew the loneliness dwelling within him, although not one word was spoken on the subject. Each at some time had seen him sitting in the solar where Karin had spent many of her days, his thoughts a thousand miles away.

He never spoke her name. Never mentioned her at all. Her bedchamber remained as it had been left when she fled that night, and it was kept locked, and he retained the key. Only they knew of the hours spent there too. Had they not both been so sure of his infallibility against the wiles of a beautiful woman, they might have suspected him of being in love!

The fighting which took place over the next five days was fierce and bloody. Darum, when it fell, was given to the new Lord of Jerusalem, even though he had arrived too late to be of help; spurred on by this new victory, talk once again turned to Jerusalem. With the improved weather, and Ascalon now a firm place to retreat to if necessary, the men pressed for a siege. A final decision was delayed by illness, which confined Richard to his tent for over a week. When he recovered, he had come to terms with the fact he must try again to retake the city. He announced that he would remain in the Holy Land until Easter of the following year, and preparations were begun immediately for the army to depart.

Rollo returned to Shah'mat with fresh supplies, reinforced the castle with more men, and rode on towards Jerusalem. He was scarcely out of sight of its walls, when they were attacked by Turkish cavalry. The last sight Siward had of him was of being felled from his horse with an arrow in one shoulder. He rallied the men and tried to chase after the retreating enemy, who had lifted their lord up behind one of them, but they were driven back. Though it was destined that Richard, King of England, would never set foot in Jerusalem, Rollo, Duke of Aquitaine, arrived there two days later.

'What is it, Celine? I said I didn't want to be disturbed,' Karin demanded, raising her head from the mound of pillows. She had had a bed made up for her in the gardens, beside an ornamental pool, so that she could lie there and listen to the murmur of the water. It was peaceful here, and no one troubled her, and it reminded her of Acre . . . of Rollo. Her son was dead. She was cursed! She had no reason to go to England now, nothing to live for.

The sun was warm on her face, but she hardly felt it. She was thin and pale and totally uninterested in what went on about her. Ayub's manner had changed considerably in the three weeks since that day. He was as kind and gentle as she had known him to be before, and he sent her little gifts of jewellery, spices, enamelled boxes inlaid with silver, hoping to please her. Nothing could drag her from the depths of despair. She had lost Rollo, and she had lost his child. Nothing could ever replace the emptiness inside her.

'A messenger brought this.' The maid handed over the parchment she held, and as Karin stared at the seal, added, 'It is from the great Saladin himself. You are honoured, mistress. Lord Ayub is longing to know what it contains, but he dared not take it from me. You have a powerful friend.'

In small, almost delicate, handwriting were the words: 'I send you what I believe you desire most in all the world. If I am wrong, then marry the Lord Ayub and allow him to avenge your wounded pride, and I shall hear no more of you. If my gift pleases you, then go with him and live in peace in the shadow of Almighty Allah.'

Karin gave a little gasp as she finished reading. Gift? Her heart thumped unsteadily as she anticipated what

he had sent. She took Celine's hand and rose to her
feet, a flush rising in her cheeks. Ayub saw it as he
confronted her at the entrance to the house, and his
mouth tightened.

'You know?'

'Is it possible?' She could not bring herself to say his
name.

'He was captured on his way to Jerusalem. At this
very moment I am entertaining him in the dungeons.
You may see him if you wish,' he said bleakly.

'Saladin shall hear of this,' she warned, and he
caught her by the wrist, his nails biting into her skin.

'Not from you. Your lover's life hangs in the
balance, as it is. Come, I want to be present at the
joyful reunion. Did he know about the child, by
the way?'

'No.' Karin stumbled after him, and heard Celine
cry out as a guard detained her when they reached the
door that led below to the dungeons. They had been
built originally as huge underground storerooms and
cellars, but Ayub's uncle, an ambitious man who
made enemies easily in his striving for power, had
found another use for most of them. 'You must not tell
him!'

Ayub stopped and shook her roughly until her hair
came loose from the pins securing it and fell about her
tortured features.

'By Allah, you love him still! You sicken me,
woman. Have you no shame?'

'Yes, I love him.' She was beyond lies, beyond
deception. She was no longer afraid of him, or of what
he might do if she went against him. She feared now

only for the man she loved. 'I did not say he loved me.
I know that is beyond him. A woman betrayed him
once. He cannot trust again.'

'I know only that he took what is mine,' he
thundered. 'Now you shall see how I deal with my
enemies.'

He dragged her after him down narrow corridors,
lighted only by pitch torches suspended from the
damp walls. The air was foul, and from behind barred
doors came the moans and pitiful cries of people
imprisoned beyond. Karin's eyes registered horror at
the sounds. She had never thought of Ayub in this
light before. How many of the poor wretches were
Christian prisoners taken in battle? She dared not
ask.

She was thrust through an open door, and fell
against the wall as he unexpectedly released her. The
room was stifling hot, and the smell of burning flesh
made her feel faint. Ayub grasped her loose hair and
jerked back her head, so that her eyes were directly in
line with the man hanging suspended in chains from
the opposite wall. He wore nothing but a pair of torn
breeches. His feet were bare and bleeding from treatment with the bastinado. The leather guards had been
ripped from his wrists, and the manacles were
fastened tightly over the scarred skin. Bright red
lash-marks seared his chest and shoulders, and there
was an arrow-wound in one shoulder. A massive giant
of a Nubian, his half-naked body gleaming in the light
of the blazing coals heaped into the brazier at his side,
applied a brand to Rollo's left arm, and she watched
the muscles knot as he fought to prevent himself from

crying out. Then, with a groan of agony, his head fell forward.

'If he dies, I shall die too,' she threatened, gagging at the smell which reached her nostrils. How brave he was! Lesser men would have screamed for mercy, but not him—not the Lord of Darkness! There was no weakness in him. But there was in her. She could not allow this to continue. 'I shall kill myself. You cannot watch me all the time, Ayub.'

'How can you love—that?' he demanded in astonishment. 'In another day I shall break him, and then you can have him—if he survives.'

'And Saladin? What will you tell him?' she challenged.

'You will tell him you did not want his gift—that you preferred me.'

'As my brother, I shall always love you. As my husband, I shall hate you.' He swore at her, and for a moment as his clenched fist was raised before her, she thought he meant to strike her. He let her go, shaking his head in incomprehension.

'I can give you anything you want—anything! I love you that much.'

'I love him enough to give myself to you in return for his life . . . his freedom,' Karin returned wearily. 'I have lost his child. Would you take the last remaining life left in my body by killing him? Is what you propose for me any worse than his actions? With him I was willing, Ayub.'

'So would you be with me—in time . . .'

'If he lives, nothing else matters,' she replied with a shrug of her thin shoulders. Looking at her, he thought she would break like a twig in his hands if he seized hold of her now. And all because of this Frankish knight!

'Woman! If only you loved me in that way,' he exclaimed, turning away from her. 'Leave me, I need to think. Ask nothing for him now. I shall tell you my decision later.'

'No, now!' Karin cried, afraid that the moment she was gone he would kill Rollo, or at least continue to torture him until he was reduced to an unrecognisable misshapen object to whom death would be a blessing. 'If you love me, then let him live!'

He signalled to a sentry, and she was dragged screaming from the cell, and carried back to her rooms when she refused to walk. When he came to her as it was growing dark, she was lying on the divan, where she had fallen in a fit of uncontrollable weeping.

'You can have him now,' was all he said, and then he turned on his heel and left her again.

Two men dragged him in and dropped the unconscious body on the floor with as much concern as they would have delivered a sack of grain. Karin threw herself beside him, and with Celine's help turned him over, touching his face with trembling hands, calling his name, burying her face against the black hair on his chest, still warm and matted with blood from fresh weals on his skin.

'*Kutti!*' A blooded hand fastened painfully over her shoulder, the fingers biting savagely into the uncovered skin as Rollo's pain-filled eyes looked up at her. 'You have long claws, even for a she-cat!'

A terrible look crossed his face. She gasped as his

fingers reached for her throat and closed about it, pressing agonisingly on her windpipe. He wanted to kill her! But why? Although not strong herself, it was not difficult to prise them away, for he was so very weak. She pressed her lips to the calloused fingers that sought to end her life, and the last thing he remembered before he faded into oblivion were her tears soaking his skin.

'Will he live?' Karin asked the doctor who turned away from Rollo's bed. He had lain there almost a week, while fever raged throughout his body. To her surprise, Ayub had not refused him medical attention, nor set extra guards upon her room to spy on them.

'If Allah wills it.'

'Or if the Lord Ayub wills he should die, he will,' she said angrily. 'You should know that this Frankish knight was sent to me by the Sultan Saladin himself. He would not be pleased to hear of his death at your hands. He must live.'

The man nodded, giving her a penetrating look, but she had no means of knowing if Ayub had given him any of his own instructions. He came the following day and the day after, and ten days after Rollo had been brought to her, there was a marked improvement in his condition. She was able to give him solid food instead of liquids, and he was more alert, watching her as she moved about the room or sat by the bed, although he pretended otherwise. He did not speak to her or acknowledge her in any way, but for the moment, even though it hurt, she chose to ignore it. When the time was right, they would talk.

Yet what was there really to say? She still did not know if Ayub intended him to leave. Was he to be snatched from her and returned to the dungeon again when his strength improved still more? Was this Ayub's way of breaking her to his will, by giving her what she wanted most for a brief while and then threatening to take it from her again—for ever?

She had had another bed brought into the room and made up close to where Rollo slept. Now that he was more coherent, she had ceased to provide the more intimate attentions for him that she had done when he was feverish. She had cared for him once before, and thought nothing of it while he was out of his mind, but when those green eyes were upon her, silent, accusing . . .

Again—of what? It was he who had wanted to send her away and after all the talk of marriage between them. How gullible she had been!

As she pushed away the plate of food before her, much of it untouched, a mocking voice behind her remarked,

'If you don't eat more than that, he won't be able to find you in your marriage bed!' She swung round, her cheeks blazing as she stared into Rollo's sardonic features. A fading lash-mark cut across one cheek from ear to mouth. She had seen him touch it once and smile strangely to himself, but he had never mentioned the pain his wounds must have given him, never thanked her for her care, although he had spoken quite respectfully to the doctor who attended him. 'You are going to marry him, I believe.'

She got up and went to the bed, ignoring the question, to look down at the plate he held. It was clean. At least *his* appetite had returned.

'There is no possibility of your fading away.'

'I shall be needing my strength, shall I not, for when your lover returns me to be entertained again.' He gave a harsh laugh, winced in pain, and laid a hand against his bandaged chest. 'What would I not give for my faithful axe now. They'd not take me down there alive, and that would surely spoil his fun!'

'I can try and get you a weapon if you are so eager to die, but there may be another way,' Karin returned, wishing he would not stare at her so searchingly. What did he seek in her face? 'Saladin sent you to me, do you know that? As a gift.'

'Sweet Jesus! Am I to be served up with an apple in my mouth? Oh, I forgot, Muslims don't eat pork.' There was no humour in the remark.

'I am glad to see that you are regaining the bite to your tongue, although you will need more than that to fight Ayub, if it comes to that. I do not know at this moment what he intends for either of us.'

'Why should he wish to harm you, his intended bride?' Rollo asked harshly. 'Do you think I have been lying here with my ears closed? Bedding you was all he talked about. The wedding is all that maid of yours can speak of.'

'Saladin will not agree to the match, if only I can reach him. I tried to send Celine with a message the other day, but it was intercepted, and Ayub threatened to have her head cut off if I tried again,' Karin cried, glaring at him. 'What do you care what happens to me? You had your fun, my lord, and then, when you tired of me, you decided to ship me off to England. Did you expect to visit me there and continue the relationship?'

'What are you saying, girl? Are you out of your mind?' Rollo tried to sit up, but was too weak, and collapsed onto the pillows again. 'What ship? Who told you such a lie?'

'I heard it from your own lips. Deny it if you can,' she challenged. 'The morning before you left, you ordered Siward to put me on the first available ship.'

'Not you! Damn it, not *you*! My God, is that what you have been thinking all this time? Is that why you left Shah'mat?' Rollo cried, this time managing to drag himself up onto one elbow. The blood drained from his face with the effort. 'Not you—Lina! I wanted us to be alone together at Shah'mat . . .'

Karin stood stock still, unable to believe her ears. Not her, but his old mistress! Not her! She had heard no name, but she had thought . . . He had been so distant those past days . . . Her face registered sudden alarm as he groaned and fell back.

'Celine! Come quickly, Help me!'

CHAPTER TEN

A HAND fastened over Karin's arm as she stood gazing down into the pool, lost in deep thought, and wheeled her about.

'Why have you been avoiding me?' Rollo demanded, his eyes searching her face. He had recovered from his faint to find Celine tending him, and when she was not at his side, other competent hands washed and re-dressed his wounds, but not Karin's. Nor did she return to sleep on the makeshift bed in his room. 'I have not seen you in almost a week.'

As he began to sway slightly, the colour, such as it was, ebbing from his cheeks, she guided him into the shade of the trees and sat him down on a stone seat beneath perfumed blossom. A silk surcoat barely covering his chest did not hide a heavily bandaged shoulder or the red weals across his neck and arms.

'What are you doing out of bed? You are not strong enough,' she chided, and he gave her a one-sided grin.

'There is a saying out here, that if Muhammad won't come to the mountain, it is the mighty mountain that must move. While I don't feel much like a tower of strength, I thought it was time to find out why you are deliberately avoiding me.' He still held fast to her hand, his fingers roving over the back of it and along the slender wrist almost absent-mindedly as he gazed at her, as often happened when they were alone together. The gentle caress brought a flush of colour to her cheeks, and he added with a frown. 'You are thinner than I remember.' And nervous, too, though he did not say so.

'I have been ill. Please let me go! If Ayub should see us like this . . .'

'Why should it bother you, if you do not care for him? Where did you go when you left me? To his bed?'

She gasped and flung back her head, blue fire blazing from her eyes. 'I needed time to think!'

'Are you not eager to have your revenge on me, now I am in your power? Or are you leaving that to him—the expert. I assure you he is!' His mouth tightened and the weal across one cheek grew taut and angry as he recalled those agonising hours of imprisonment and torture.

'I tried to stop him, but I am as much a prisoner here as you are,' Karin said. 'I have gone from one prison to another.'

'You thought of Shah'mat as a prison?' He sounded startled. 'I thought you were beginning to accept it . . . even to like the place?'

'Accept what? Guards at every door to watch me night and day? Siward to ride with me, so that I did not keep on riding . . . Not that I had anywhere to go.' She shrugged, which brought a frown to his features.

'Then why did you leave? The moment my back was turned, you ran.'

'I told you why! I heard you ordering Siward to send me away.'

'And I've told you I was not! Had I been planning

that, I would have taken you to Jaffa myself and put you on board a ship,' Rollo snapped, growing irritated as he considered his own stupidity. He should have confided in her. 'I had intended to, at first—take you to Jaffa, I mean—and wed you there instead of waiting for Jerusalem. I could not forget the old Teacher's words . . . that we shall never set foot in it again as rulers. But it was important to me to go there, to dress you in fine silks and jewels and present to you the King and Queen as the woman I had chosen to marry. And to return to the church where I made a vow many years ago. To stand once more in the sight of God and beg his forgiveness for my vehement words that day. Words spoken in anger and hate . . .'

'Because of your wife,' Karin whispered, and he nodded, pain lining his face. Unconsciously her hand stole to rest upon his arm, but he appeared not to notice.

'She betrayed my love, and I vowed never again to give any part of myself to another woman. I would take, as she had, but give nothing in return. I did not know what those words really meant until I met you, and the spell you wove about me enmeshed me like a spider's web. I could not escape from it, from my own feelings, or from you, nor could I find any way of unburdening the blackness in my heart. I sought to hold you in any way I could, without thought for the pain I caused you . . . and then, just when I began to accept that you would always be a part of my life, you were gone from Shah'mat, and I believed myself betrayed again. I swore in my heart to kill you if we ever met again.'

'You tried!' Tears sprang to her eyes. 'But you were too weak.'

'Merciful heaven, I remember!' His fingers stroked her throat, his expression shocked. It was obvious that he had not remembered the incident until now. And then he looked puzzled. 'And there were tears on my hand—your tears. Why did you weep for me, *Kutti*?'

'A touching scene, which I must curtail. There is a messenger from the Sultan Saladin to speak with you, Karin.' Ayub stood a few feet from them, his face impassive as he surveyed them. How long had he been there, watching, listening, Karin wondered as she came quickly to her feet. She heard Rollo mutter a fierce expletive beneath his breath, for the inopportune arrival delayed the answer on her lips, the words of love she had never had the courage to say to him before. Ayub stared at the tall figure, who also rose, and for a moment the two men faced each other in silence. Enemies in war. Enemies in love. 'You may stay, if she desires it.'

'Thank you, Ayub,' she said quietly, grateful for his placid manner. Placid in speech, perhaps, but not in the way he looked at her before he turned away and beckoned to a man standing in the room beyond.

The messenger was one of Saladin's personal guard. He ignored the man beside her, but greeted Karin in a friendly manner. Perhaps he was mindful of the time she had spent closeted alone with his master, she thought, as she held out her hand for a parchment.

'There is no written word, my lady. I am to ask you . . .' He paused, and looked significantly at Ayub. 'Shall I go on?'

'Yes,' she said firmly. Had Saladin guessed that she had not been allowed to send an answer thanking him for his gift, and in contacting her again in this manner was giving her an opportunity to break free of Ayub's hold? 'I have nothing to hide from anyone present.'

'My master, the Mighty Sultan Saladin, asks if you are not pleased with the gift he sent you, that you send him no word of thanks?'

Her guess had been right! Ayub's frozen features did not deter her from a direct and swift answer.

'Please convey to the gracious Sultan my apologies for my lack of courtesy. As you can see, my lord has now recovered, although it will be several weeks before he can travel.' She heard Rollo's sharp intake of breath beside her, slipped her fingers through his, and held them in an impulsive, daring gesture.

'That is the second question for which I require an answer. You intend to return with this man—to the place he calls Shah'mat?' The guard's gaze flickered momentarily over Rollo. He did not like what he heard, but it was none of his business, he was only a messenger. 'Or do you venture further afield and return to your own country?'

'We are to be married. I shall go where he goes—should the generosity of the great Saladin permit it.'

'I shall convey your replies to my master. My lord Ayub, I would speak with you for a moment also—alone.'

As the two men disappeared inside, Karin looked up into Rollo's grave face. He was free, did he not realise it? He was looking at her so strangely.

'Why did you do that?' he asked in a hollow tone. 'You could have been free of me for ever?'

'Oh, you blind fool!' She could have slapped him for not understanding. 'Will you never trust again? I love you! I was afraid to tell you before—afraid that you would use me again to ease the bitterness inside you. It became unbearable to know I could never have your heart—your love . . . but it does not matter now. I shall go with you wherever you wish—be whatever you wish. So long as I am with you, it matters not what I am . . .'

'It matters to me,' he said, gathering her to him with fierce possessiveness, regardless of the pain which tore through him as she was crushed against his still tender chest. 'Don't you realise what I have been trying in my clumsy way to tell you? I love you, too. I've fought against it, hurt you, cursed you, but I can't rid myself of it. I don't ever want to. Say it again— let me hear you say it again?' he whispered, still not believing that such a miracle could happen for him.

'Let me show you . . .' Karin lifted her lips and laid them against his. The fire which leapt unbidden fused them as one—forgetful of where they were, and of the sentries who watched from high above on the walls— unleashing upon them all the suppressed passion neither had acknowledged until this moment.

Rollo uttered a groan as he ran his fingers through her hair, losing himself in the wonder of her lips, willing, alive, seeking an answer from his. An answer he gave freely and without restraint. She strained against him, eager for his touch, as she, too, allowed the full flood of her emotions to consume her. He loved her!

'Rollo, put me down!' she gasped, as he swung her up into his arms, with an awkwardness that made her lock her hands behind his neck, fearful that he might stumble, and pitch them both onto the tiled patio.

'Be quiet, woman. I have no words to tell you how much you mean to me, but I can show you, so that you never doubt me again,' he whispered, brushing a bright red cheek with his lips. Celine ushered the servants from the room as he carried her inside and laid her on the bed. She protested, but not too vigorously, as he removed her robe and unfastened the jewelled bodice she wore, laying bare her breasts, for his mouth was on hers and she did not want to end the moment—not yet! She had to tell him about the child . . . She balked at revealing the terrible news . . . Yet, he had not wanted one, he had said. All the longing to possess part of him had been in her. All those hours of pain—all for nothing. Why was life so cruel?

Her hands stroked his hair and face, while he lost himself in the exploration of her body with his lips. He whispered sweet endearments and words of love which made her both blush and sigh with the desire to be back at Shah'mat with him. Alone, untroubled by the past. Together! Her fingers slid over his bronzed back, touching scars left by past battles, and the fresh scars not yet properly healed from the lash and branding-iron of Ayub's executioner. Gentle as her touch was, she felt him wince as she encountered the arrow-wound sustained when he was captured.

'You must not,' she whispered. 'Save your strength.

We shall have all the time in the world when we are at Shah'mat.'

'I have lain awake wanting the woman for over five months, and she says wait!' Rollo eased himself away from her with a grimace. 'But you are right. Despite all your excellent ministering, I am still as weak as a babe.'

'It will be better,' she added, knowing that she must tell him now, before the courage left her. 'For me also.'

His gaze bored into her face. Once again he was struck by the hollow look about the large blue eyes, the slenderness of the body pressed against his. At Shah'mat she had not looked like this. Silently he cursed himself for a fool. Illness? What kind of illness?

'You are right, *Kutti*, I am blind. What else did I not see at Shah'mat? That you carried my child in you?'

'How could I tell you, when you did not want a baby? I always seemed to hold you by a thin thread to me . . . and there were times, especially before I left, that you were so distant from me,' Karin answered, burying her head against his shoulder.

'Because of the devilish thoughts which plagued me. One day I was so sure of myself, and of you. The next, the doubts returned. What is it I do not know?'

'It is dead.' She could not look at him, as she felt him stiffen from the shock of her words. 'It was a boy.'

'It is God's judgment on me that it should happen.' Rollo's voice was strained, as he slowly forced himself to absorb the pain and silent grief of the discovery. A son! Gently he tilted back her head and kissed her quivering lips. 'We shall have another . . . and a daughter to inherit your estates in England. Was that not how you wanted it? You shall have everything you want. There is nothing I would deny you.'

'So long as I am at your side, I shall be happy,' Karin replied, heedless of the tears which came at his words. She had been too shocked to cry after the birth and loss of her baby, too occupied with Rollo to shed tears while she nursed him and paced the room at night while fever raged within his body. Now, secure, content in his arms, certain of his love and devotion, she gave way to them, allowing them to drain her, for she knew that, in his arms, no danger could touch her. He held her while she cried, and then, exhausted, slept.

From behind a latticed framework from which hung multi-coloured blooms and greenery, flowering in wild profusion in the warmth of the June air, Ayub acknowledged defeat. She had never been his; she never would be now. Short of killing the Frankish Crusader and continuing with his plans to marry her against her will, he must concede victory to the other man. She had never looked at him like that, with such tenderness and love in her eyes. Nor returned his kisses with such unrestrained ardour. He had watched them ever since they entered the room, and fought against the anger in him as Rollo touched her. For one mad moment his hand had been on his dagger—but what would he gain? A lifeless doll in his bed—provided that Saladin allowed him to live long enough to know her, which he doubted. The Sultan's orders had been quite explicit. They were to be allowed to leave as soon as the Duke of Aquitaine was well enough to ride, and provided with an escort until Shah'mat came in sight.

'Would that you loved me as you do him,' he whispered, as he turned away . . .

'Faith! My men will make fun of me when they see how you have addled my brain,' Rollo chuckled, leaning up on one elbow to watch Celine as she brushed Karin's hair. One hundred and fifty strokes every night and morning. How it gleamed in the lamplight. And then his smile faded as he remembered that they were to leave Jerusalem in the morning. He still did not trust Ayub or the men who were their constant guard, although none had given him cause for concern since the day Saladin's messenger had come to the house. 'Send her away, I want to be alone with you.'

Karin smiled at her maid and Celine hurriedly left them, no longer minding her mistress's preoccupation with the Crusader. She loved him, and she was so blissfully happy. Even the servants had remarked on his devotion to her and were amazed that this man of such infamous reputation—not only as a fighter, but as a merciless womaniser—should bow so meekly to the will of a slender, gentle young woman such as Karin. Perhaps these Christians were not so fearful as they were led to believe?

'Why should they laugh at you?' she asked softly, turning to look at him. Over a nightgown of yellow chiffon she wore a matching robe, sleeveless and open to the waist. The hunger in him intensified as his gaze wandered over the body he had denied himself for almost two weeks. His arm had become infected, and fever had taken hold of him again, only diminishing several days before. He still felt a little light-headed from the opiate which gave him blessed rest each night, but his strength was returning fast. With it came the desire he knew he must quench, here in this holiest of places, where he had once vowed never again to ache as he did now, to long for the touch of a woman's hands upon him, to feel her softness pleading with him to take her in love. Love! That was the miracle of it. She loved him! God strike him dead if he ever betrayed her as he had once been betrayed!

For two blissful weeks they had shared each other's company, day and night. By day they sat and talked and laughed together, and he grew to accept the wondrous thing that had befallen him. By night she slept by his side, sometimes curled in his arms, asking nothing from him in his weak state except that he be near her. And when he was feverish, she remained at his side to bathe his face with cooling water, whisper words of love and encouragement in his ear, and beg him to get well soon. She was in his thoughts every waking moment, in his sleep and in his dreams. Such pleasant dreams now, no longer nightmares, for either of them.

Accompanied by Ayub's guards, they walked in the streets of Jerusalem, she cloaked and veiled as was the custom for women, he in Arab garb. With their command of the language, no one questioned their identity. Now that she remembered more of the years she had lived here with her parents, she saw how different it was. Voices chattering in a dozen different languages no longer resounded in the streets. Once they had been full with merchants and customers bartering over the wares brought up on Egyptian caravans journeying through Tiberias to Damascus, to fill the warehouses of the cities with Tibetan musk, incense of Hadramaut and pungent oriental spices, ivory and precious stones, silks, and the glass in which the Damascenes were masters of the art. She showed him the house where she had lived with her mother and father, able to speak calmly now and without emotion of the great trials they had all suffered during the siege of the city. Of the fire which had swept through the house, destroying everything in its path, except her. Saved by Badir, and his son Ayub, as she lay trapped beneath a huge beam of wood.

She still could not remember everything. Of her homeland, very little, except for an old nursery song her nanny had sung to her as a child, and which she repeated to Rollo one night with great emotion. She recalled a place named Winchester, but, apart from that, England was strange to her. Her parents had come on a pilgrimage, hoping that a visit to this holy city would grant them the son they longed for. He knew her thoughts were of the son she had lost in childbirth and, if anything, it intensified the bond already between them. Caught up in the midst of a new jihad, Karin's father had stayed to defend Jerusalem and died in the attempt, his wife also.

Rollo was glad that she did not regret those years she had spent with Badir, for from her he learned what a wise and generous man he had been and an understanding of an alien faith. Ayub was a different matter, and he kept his own counsel about the man who had tried to take his beloved from him, and at whose hands he had suffered the most unspeakable torture. Yet, late at night, when he considered his own feelings, he admitted to himself that he would fight tooth and nail to keep her at his side if another man wanted her. Had he not wanted to kill her when he thought she had betrayed him?

'Why are we stopping here?' Karin looked up at the church in front of them with a puzzled frown as Rollo drew rein. The Church of the Holy Sepulchre had always been a very special place for pilgrims to pray, but not a man like Rollo. Why had he come here, of all places? There were only a few priests now, left to care for the shrine and to prevent it from being defiled by Muslim intruders. Along with the Jewish community, they had been the only ones allowed to stay when Saladin's army retook the Holy City.

'I have something important I must do,' Rollo murmured, lifting her to the ground. 'Today I shall make my peace with God—and with you, *Kutti.*'

He spoke briefly to the nearest guard, and although the man looked at him with some suspicion and motioned other men to take up positions on either side of the entrance, he did not try to prevent them from entering. They were Ayub's men, but she and Rollo were known to *Saladin*!

Karin was struck at once by the silence within, and the strange sense of peace which seemed to settle over her like a cloak. She did not understand what Rollo's words had meant, but sensing that they were of great importance to him, she allowed him to lead her down the darkened aisle to the altar where the

Madonna and child were. As the memory of the many times she had come here to pray with her parents returned to her, she sank to her knees, head bowed. To her amazement, Rollo joined her. She could not understand such reverence in him. He believed neither in God nor in man, only in the strength of his sword arm. How many times had he told her that!

'Oh, God, do not desert me in my hour of need, as I once deserted you.' There was such pain in his voice, that she instinctively reached out her hand and grasped one of his. His fingers closed tightly round hers, as if seeking reassurance. 'I kneel before you, the most humble of men, to beg your forgiveness and ask your blessing on this woman at my side. My words were foolish, spoken in anger and hatred—and desperation. I now have all that any man could want, and I fear to lose it as once before.'

Was he speaking of his wife? Karin wondered. She dared not utter a word, not even when she became aware that they were not alone. A figure in a brown robe had appeared through a side door and stood listening to Rollo's words. An old man, and in ill health, she saw, from the way he limped forward, his back bent almost double as if crushed by some enormous weight.

'You came back after all, my son. I prayed that you would.'

A slight smile touched Rollo's lips as he looked up and saw the man. Soon his nightmare would be over and he would be at peace with the world again.

'I am surprised you remember me, Father. I have changed.'

'As I have. How long has it been now . . . four years?'

'Nearer five. I have come back, as you said I would, to beg his forgiveness—and yours, for my blindness and arrogance. Bless me, for pity's sake. Take this burden from me, I can bear it no longer!'

It was a cry from a soul in anguish. Karin heard him utter a long sigh as the old man bent to lay a gnarled hand upon his dark head.

'Has the burden not already been lifted, my son, by the one who kneels beside you? Did you not say to me you would return only if you found a woman, true of heart and spirit, who would love you? In finding her—nay, believing in her love—you have gained God's absolution. Go in peace, with his blessing—and mine.'

Rollo began to rise, then faltered and looked down into Karin's upturned face. His fingers tightened still more over hers as a great joy rose in his heart. It was suddenly as if there was a choir of angels, rejoicing at the peace and tranquillity now within him.

'I promised you a great wedding, in this very place, with a King and Queen to see us wed, and great knights to dance at our wedding feast afterwards. Would you be very disappointed if it were not so? Wed me now, *Kutti*. Here and now! I have this fear still that you might be stolen from me.'

'Nought but death could do that,' she answered quietly. 'And even then I would still be with you in spirit. Are you sure, Rollo? Really sure? I shall never leave you, whatever I am—wife . . . mistress . . .'

'Not that.' His voice was momentarily harsh.
'Father, can you marry us? Is it possible?'

'To perform such a ceremony is one of the few
things I am able to do under the circumstances in
which I live. Saladin has not been able to take my faith
from me, or the power God gave me to do his will. It
shall be as you wish, my children.'

'Why so serious, my love?' Karin asked, coming into
the room to find Rollo slumped on the couch, a frown
furrowing his brows. It was a sultry night and she
tossed off her robe with a grimace and went to stand
by the open window.

'You will not dress like that at Shah'mat, I hope,' he
murmured, as his eyes devoured the slender body,
scarcely concealed by the transparency of the nightgown she wore, and she lowered her own before his
burning gaze. Even after all they had shared, she still
experienced moments of shyness. He laughed and
came to join her, sliding his hands up to cup her
breasts beneath the thin material. 'You have yet to
wear all the gowns I brought you at Shah'mat . . .
including your wedding gown. We shall have a very
great feast, and everyone will be there, as I promised.
You shall wear it for me then.'

Karin looked down at the ring on her finger—a
twisted rope of gold in which were set three perfectly
matched sapphires. To go with the pendant he
had given her, he said as he placed it on her finger.
Outside the doors of the church she knew Ayub's
guards waited . . . to separate them, perhaps,
or cut them down without mercy. But it was im-

material, for now she was one with the man she loved!

As she stared into the serene face of the Madonna, her nostrils filled with the heavy perfume of incense, she knew that she would bear Rollo another child, and, strangely, felt no pain or anger over the loss of her firstborn. As if he still lingered with her, but she had not even seen his tiny face. Had he looked like Rollo? Yet perhaps not to have seen him was a blessing. It would have been unbearable to remember something she could not have.

'At Shah'mat I shall wear whatever pleases my lord, but can I not indulge myself—just a little? Do I not please you now?' Karin asked, her eyes alight with devilry. She allowed her body to sink against his. He was stronger, she knew, and he wanted her, but she needed it to be the right time, when she was sure there were no more doubts or suspicions. Was it right now? Or was Shah'mat the setting where he would give her a child to prove her love?

'More than you will ever know,' Rollo answered softly. 'Have you forgiven me for Acre? I wanted you, and I am a man accustomed to taking what I want. You have changed me. I am as meek as a lamb when I am with you now.'

The gleam in his eyes told Karin he was not, nor ever would be, her slave, but he was trying to please her in every way possible, and she smiled at him tenderly.

'How I love you, my Lord of Darkness.' They kissed and stood close together on the balcony, content not to disturb the perfect silence of the night. However, after a while, she became aware that his thoughts were not on her any longer and looked up at the dark outline of his features. 'Have no fear I shall leave Shah'mat again,' she said, and the profile softened slightly.

'I do not, but I do fear for you there. I must leave you and rejoin the King and discover the present plans of the army. After he had taken Darum, he was desperate for reinforcements. He hopes for some Frenchmen from Acre and Tyre, but our numbers are sadly depleted. We should have tried for the city the last time. All or nothing! I think maybe ibn Dak was right, and we shall not take it again.'

'I would not have had you return here under such terrible circumstances. I shall never forgive Ayub for what he did to you. I have told him so.'

'He loves you, *Kutti*. I cannot say that I would not have acted exactly the same way had the positions been reversed,' he replied, and her eyes widened in surprise. He could speak thus after all the agony he had been forced to endure, the long weeks of raging fever, the wound in his shoulder which still troubled him? And the brand which would always scar his dark skin. 'I do not say that, given a sword in my hand, I would not kill him on the spot,' Rollo added, sensing her reaction. 'But I have come to understand him.'

'Would that the mighty Kings who wage this jihad could understand each other,' Karin said, a note of bitterness creeping into her tone. 'I do not want you to fight any more. Why should you? Why can you not stay at Shah'mat with me? Saladin has promised that, if there is a peace agreement soon, we shall be left alone. What more can we ask than to raise our children in peace, as we please?'

'If there is peace, I shall be the first one to lay aside my battle weapons,' he promised her truthfully. 'But until that day comes, I must be certain that Shah'mat is secure. My men do not know what has happened to me. If they have not been paid, they will have drifted back to the towns. For all I know, the place could be a ruin . . . Siward or Chavo dead, or gone to be with the King. There are things I have to do, and you must not ask from me what I cannot give—not yet. Be patient.

'I shall try, but if I ever lost you again . . .' His lips silenced her, and she clung to him, seized with a premonition of danger that made her tremble.

Rollo held her at arm's length, and stared angrily into her face. 'Is this frightened creature the proud woman who defied me at Acre? Battled for her very existence on the journey to Shah'mat? Laughed in the face of death when I was ill, and Siward threatened her life? Shame on you! I must leave Shah'mat in good, strong hands.' He lifted her hands to his lips, kissed them gently, then, turning them over, planted kisses on each of her palms. 'You are my wife now, *Kutti*. The Lady of Shah'mat!'

'Forgive me, I know your thoughts cannot always be of me, but I grow jealous when they are not,' Karin confessed, shamefaced. 'I want all of your time, all of your affection, all of your love.'

'The last you will always have. The others must rightfully be divided among those who have given me loyal service and who, I hope, will continue to do so when I return. One day,' his voice grew low, 'I shall deal personally with the man called Zolto. He will be an example to others who seek to betray my trust.'

'Be careful,' she warned. 'Rashid al-Din has many followers. They are spread far and wide, and no one ever knows who they are until it is too late. Is it not said that the Lord of Montferrat could have been killed by them? Give him no cause to bring down his wrath on you, I beg!'

'Two attempts have already been made on my life,' Rollo said, confessing for the first time that he, too, was possibly a victim of the dreaded Hashishin. 'I have no proof that they came from Rashid, but each time a dagger was used. It is their weapon, is it not?'

Wordlessly she nodded, afraid to speak lest the tremor in her voice proclaimed the alarm he had roused in her. How many more of his servants at Shah'mat could be commanded by the evil 'Old Man of the Mountain'?

'I shall leave Siward—nay, Chavo—to watch over you while I am away,' Rollo said, drawing her back into the room, running his hands over her body in a manner which told her he wanted to think of tomorrow no longer. 'It is time I forgave him for Acre—as you must.'

'How could I not? He has brought me happiness such as I have never known before,' she answered, freeing herself of the cumbersome nightgown and drawing him down beside her on the bed. Some while later she raised her head and looked into the dark face close to hers. 'Do you believe, as I do, that we were destined to be together? Tamir said the stars predicted it, and that was why I had to leave Badir and Ayub. I have often wondered what else they told him.'

'While I hold you in my arms, I believe anything you

ask of me,' Rollo chuckled, laying his cheek against hers. 'If it is written, who are we to argue with our fate?'

He thought of her words the next morning as he waited for her to show herself. She had left the room shortly after Celine had dressed her, and although the maid was mounted beside him and ready to leave, Karin had not appeared. He had never believed in destiny—or fate—until he came to the Holy Land, and had laughed at love potions and magic charms. He had not thought Tamir ibn Dak and his predictions amusing, but they were coming true. Despite everything which had come between them—Hugo, her own foolish deception, which he at least understood if he did not condone it, her flight from Shah'mat—they were together, and he would move heaven and earth to see she remained with him always. Short of death, nothing, he had vowed, would ever part them.

If it was in his power, he would give her all she asked in the way of money and jewels, fine clothes. He would take her where she wanted to go . . . yet he wondered if they would ever leave Shah'mat? It would be different there now—If they reached it alive!

From beneath hooded lids, he surveyed the escort provided to ride with them as far as the castle, twelve of Saladin's élite Turkish cavalry. He knew the like of them and their skill on horseback. They were worth four times their number in close combat. If their orders were to kill their companions, he and Karin would be ridden down and slaughtered without quarter. He looked down into the impassive face of Ayub, who stood beside Karin's mount. He, too, waited, arms folded over his chest. The enmity between them was like gathering thunder in the air, and Celine was beginning to look uneasy. Then her mistress appeared, enveloped in a white silk burnous.

'Where have you been?' Ayub demanded, and helped her to mount, ignoring Rollo, who was half out of the saddle with the same purpose. The latter re-seated himself with a scowl. Even now he did not like to see another man touching her—especially this one, who had been determined to subject her to his will by force. She brought out the worst in them both, he admitted to himself grudgingly, not liking the thought that if he had not taken her in Acre, things might have been different between them, and even less to her liking than that first time.

'I went to try and find the woman who was present when I—gave birth—to my baby,' Karin replied. 'The wet-nurse. Do you remember her, Ayub? I—I suppose it was silly of me. I wanted to hear from her own lips what he had looked like, and perhaps to see where he is buried. I am leaving part of me here. I thought I could bear it, but now . . .' Her voice broke, and Rollo leaned towards her with an oath, a hand upon her shoulder.

'Gently, *Kutti*! Do not distress yourself. The pain will fade in time, I promise,' he said gently. Ayub's mouth tightened as he watched her fingers touch his, lay her cheek against them. 'We *shall* have a son . . .'

Ayub stepped back, more perturbed by the scene that he cared to admit. 'Get you gone,' he ordered. 'Have no fear for your lives. These are not my men.'

His meaning was only too clear. Rollo gathered up the reins of his horse and kneed it forward as the first of the escort moved out into the street. Karin hung back, looking appealingly at the man she had known only as her brother for the past four years.

'Must we part like this, with hatred between us?' He gave a hollow laugh in reply.

'That is the trouble, Karin. I don't hate you, I wish to Allah I did, then I could kill you both with a clear conscience. Get you gone. You are his, now, or does it please you to twist the knife in me?'

'How can you say such a thing? You will always be my brother. When I think of you, I shall try not to remember the cruelty you have perpetrated on the body of the man I love. He was a rival—not an enemy.' She had bent towards him, a hand outstretched in a farewell gesture, but he ignored it, and she drew back, hurt by the rebuff. 'I shall think of the times we shared together in Jyira. Of the father and brother who will always remain with affection in my heart. May Allah watch over you, Ayub.'

'Damn you, go!' He was nearer to losing control than ever before. He brought his hand down hard on the rump of her horse, and it started after the others. He turned away and did not look round again until the gates of the garden were closed after the last horseman. His uncle Haroun stepped from the house and regarded him with a twisted smile. 'I warn you, say nothing!' Ayub snapped.

'Like a love-sick boy! It is well that I am here to show you how to rid your mind of her once and for all.'

'I never shall. She is part of me—as the child was

part of her. I should have let her see the grave. Perhaps it would have helped . . .'

'Grave?' Haroun echoed, and something in his voice made Ayub look at him with growing suspicion. 'Why do you think he lies buried beneath the ground?'

'You told me, when I returned to Karin's side to try and comfort her . . . You came and told me that the boy had not survived . . .'

'Do you think I would give up an opportunity to strike back at this Frank who killed my best men? Men sent to strike him down?'

'You!' Ayub gasped, stepping back in disgust as sudden dawning broke upon him. 'You—are one of al-Din's men? That—That crazy man?'

'Curb your insolent tongue, pup, or I'll have it cut out—and I could, too,' he added, as Ayub's hand fell to his sword. 'Every servant in this house is loyal to me, even those who came with you from Jyira. One word—and I could have your head on a spike over the door. I sometimes think it would give me pleasure. I have watched you with that Christian woman, and I wanted to vomit! The child will give me the revenge I seek—and you will help.'

'Where is he? Tell me, I demand it!' Ayub was no coward, nor was he a fool. If Haroun said that all the servants were loyal to him, he knew this must be true. The power of the Hashishin was absolute, and terrifying.

'Tomorrow you shall see him. I am sending you to Shah'mat with him. There will be a cause for celebration at the castle of the Lord of Darkness, do you not agree? Much eating and drinking and making free

with their painted whores—as he will with her. I want
you to have time to think of him with her . . .' Haroun
laughed as Ayub turned away, but he stopped before
he reached the house. Ayub had to know the where-
abouts of Karin's son, and protect him from whatever
was planned. Even if it meant his own life.

'The child will gain me access to Shah'mat,' he
returned with a shrug, meant to imply indifference.
He was not afraid for himself, and he did not care if
Rollo died, but Karin herself! 'What will that achieve?'

'You will arrive, no doubt, while they are still in
the aftermath of their orgy of wantonness,' his uncle
continued. They went into the house and made themselves comfortable on low divans. A servant brought
them refreshments, and Ayub had to fume inwardly
until Haroun spoke again. 'They will welcome you
with open arms when they see what you bring. You
will be accompanied only by a small force of men, so
that treachery cannot be suspected. The main force of
men will be waiting well out of sight for nightfall,
when you will, with the able assistance of my man
from Shah'mat, Zolto, administer a powerful drug to
the guards and see that the main gates are opened. I
shall lead my men in the attack. As a reward, I shall let
you slit the throat of the Frank, and have the woman.
This time, Saladin will not interfere. He will be blamed
for the massacre . . . He will be too busy trying to
appease the Lionheart, with whom he is at this very
moment negotiating peace terms, to worry himself
over you. Have her, and get her out of your system
. . . then keep her well hidden until we have driven
the rest of the army into the sea.'

He made it sound so possible, Ayub thought, forcing his expression to remain impassive while his mind reeled under the onslaught of the plan. It was ingenious—foolproof. No doubt there were other castle servants, besides Zolto, ready to kill at the slightest command and, in doing so, obtain for themselves in the after-life, promised them by their master, an eternity of pleasures. Those who obeyed him, and killed others and were themselves in turn killed, were truly blessed among men—or so they had been taught to believe. Such was the power of Rashid al-Din over his followers.

'The woman . . .' If only he did not want her so much! 'I can have her? She will not be harmed?'

'You will have to kill her husband, but that will not matter to you, will it?' Haroun murmured, lighting the slim-stemmed pipe which had just been brought to him. A sweet, sickly smell began to perfume the air as he smoked, and Ayub watched him settle more comfortably on the couch. But still those snake-eyes watched his every move. When the pipe was handed to him, he did not hesitate to take it. He had never used hashish before. He found it not unpleasant, and the thoughts in his mind began to fall into place, no longer disturbing him.

'I shall take her back to Jyira and keep her in seclusion, uncle.'

'Good. Let us go over it once more . . .'

Rollo knew where he would find her when he discovered she was no longer in her bedchamber. On entering the solar, as he expected, he saw her standing

by the huge window which looked out over the
vineyards and orchards in the direction of Jerusalem.
He also knew the thoughts that had been in her mind
and were still there as she turned to look up at him and
slip her hand through his.

'I love this view. I sat here the first time I came to
Shah'mat, and watched the sun go down, as it is doing
now.'

'But then your thoughts were on Acre, hating me for
bringing you here, not dwelling on the past and what
has been left behind us in Jerusalem,' he said quietly,
and she flushed at the accuracy with which he had
read the sadness in her. 'It is still the child, is it not?'

'Forgive me.' Karin knew she had been preoccupied
on the short journey back to Shah'mat, and when they
had arrived, she was so tired that he had to lift her
from the horse and carry her upstairs. Karin remembered him laying her down on something soft, his lips
lightly brushing her hair, and then nothing more until
she awoke late in the afternoon to the sounds of much
activity from outside and below.

Berta, acquainted with all the facts from Celine,
fussed over her with even more motherliness than
before, which did nothing to rouse her from her
morbidness. In Jerusalem she thought she had
accepted it, but now, here at Shah'mat, she knew she
had not. Part of her ached, and would always ache, for
what she had lost.

'Do you not believe me when I say there will be
another child?' Rollo asked, taking her by the shoulders and turning her to face him. He could not bear the
sadness in her eyes on a day when they should have

been alight with happiness. 'Do you believe how deeply I love you?'

'Yes! Oh, yes, I do!' she cried, aware of a flicker of pain in the depths of his own eyes. She was hurting him too with her manner, yet she could not shake it off. 'But—if only I could make you understand. The child was proof of my love.'

'Proof, woman? I have asked for no proof!' he said sharply. 'You have given me your love—given yourself totally.'

'As others have before me, whispering in your ear words of love that you knew to be meaningless. To have given you a child from our union . . .'

'I will hear no more of this nonsense,' Rollo said harshly, his fingers biting into her soft skin. 'Have you not suffered enough without torturing yourself in this way? No more of it, do you hear? Sweet, foolish woman!'

She managed a faint smile at his manner.

'I hear—and obey, my lord,' she murmured, and he bent and kissed her mouth tenderly, seeking to give her reassurance. 'Now, I am ready. Do I meet with your approval?'

She stepped back and allowed him to inspect her appearance. While she slept, Rollo's men had prepared a feast for the return of their lord and his lady. Siward and Chavo had proposed it, Rollo told her with a grin when he broke the news. It had barely aroused her interest, when it should have excited and pleased her to know how readily she was accepted among them. A great feast was to be held in the courtyard, with games and mock fights between the soldiers, who showed immense relief at Rollo's return, for they had almost given him up for dead. Only Siward's insistence that he was alive, together with the opening of one of Rollo's money-coffers to provide them with more ducats each, had induced them to stay. Not all had been so patient, but enough remained to man the garrison effectively. Rollo did not doubt that he could bring the others back with him when he returned from seeing the King and discussing the plans for the assault on Jerusalem.

She wore a gown of tortoiseshell silk, woven with gold flowers. About her slender hips rested a girdle of finely twisted gold to match the ring on her finger. Simple, but effective. She would have the eye of every man below on her when she appeared, he mused, and he would be jealously watching her until they could be alone together again. He felt, as she did, that every moment was precious to them and must not be wasted.

Her gleaming red-gold hair was loose about bare shoulders, crowned with a jewelled circlet he had brought her from Jaffa. He noticed that her colour had improved since he had come into the room, although she was still very pale, but perhaps, in all the merriment and fun, he would be the only one to notice.

'If I had not been such a fool, we could have shared moments like this many, many times . . .'

Karin laid a ringed finger against his lips, silencing him.

'No regrets. Let it all begin for us tonight, here at Shah'mat, my love.' Endearments came easily to her lips now, for she had lost all fear of him, abandoned all inhibitions. The night before they had left Jerusalem he had completely reassured her of the deep-fired passions which raged within him and had sought release in loving her and being loved in return. She had prayed to God to give her another child as Rollo lost himself in the worship of her body and had shown her warmth and tenderness beyond her wildest expectations.

She brightened with this thought in her mind, and took his hand again, thinking how handsome he looked in a white linen shirt beneath a dark green leather jerkin, opening over hide breeches. A gold buckle, bearing his crest, fastened the belt from which hung his sword and dagger.

'Come,' Rollo said with a smile. 'I am impatient to show my wife to those who wait below.'

Karin was amazed at the sight which awaited them in the enormous courtyard of Shah'mat. A table at one end was flanked by two longer ones on either side. On each was an abundance of rich food, ales and wines, and servants were hurrying backwards and forwards bringing more platters, more kegs and bottles, amid boisterous comments from the watching men and women and cheers of encouragement when more liquid refreshments appeared. Sweating men basted suckling pigs on a huge iron spit, quenching their thirsts from jugs always kept filled and within easy reach by hovering kitchen-lads.

As Rollo led her towards the top table, where his banner streamed in the wind over two carved chairs, a roar went up from the waiting men—and also growls of approval for the woman at his side, which he did not miss, although he chose to ignore the disturbing effect she had on them. She was his. He was sure of her, and had no need to be jealous. Let them look, for that was all they would ever do!

Karin could not count the number of chickens—roasted, fried, or cooked in aromatic sauces. Young lambs were portioned and garnished with garlic grown in the castle vegetable-gardens. She had seen for herself how self-sufficient Shah'mat was while Rollo had left her alone to go to Jaffa. All kinds of vegetables were grown; meat was salted down and stored in the outhouses for later use; garlic, onions, and many vegetables were dried and laid aside for the winter. The cellars were full of wine casks and barrels of ale, and some special wine that Rollo had brought from one of his many visits to Jerusalem before it fell into Saracen hands. All the stocks would be vastly depleted when this night was over, she thought, as he seated her beside him and stood surveying the crowd.

He was proud of her, and it showed—every man looking at them knew it.

'Men, you see before you the Lady of Shah'mat. My wife. You will show her the same loyalty and obedience that you do to me. Any man—or woman—that does not, will face me and answer for it.' Then his voice lost its gruffness, and a smile crossed his face. 'Now, seat yourselves and let us enjoy the evening.'

Siward, with Chavo behind him, came to the table and stood before it as a mass of bodies emerged on the other two, fighting for places on the wooden benches. After a few hectic minutes, with much shoving and jostling, not to mention much swearing under the breath, they were all miraculously seated and making the most of the food and drink before them.

'You are satisfied with it all, my lord?' Siward asked. Chavo hung back, Rollo noticed, as he nodded and voiced his approval. 'And you, my lady?'

'It—It is a feast fit for a queen,' Karin said, a tremor in her voice. 'I shall never forget this night, messires. How can I ever thank you?'

'I think you know how, gracious lady,' the Norseman replied, and she felt colour rise in her cheeks. Only he would ever be so bold as to speak to her thus!

'Chavo, what means this?' Rollo asked suddenly with a fierce frown. 'Why do you not wear my colours?' He was referring to the surcoat of black and silver worn by the men appointed as his personal Guard, which he should have donned as soon as they returned to Shah'mat. Since the battle of Arsuf, Chavo's first real engagement since being knighted, the young Gy Savennes, who had once served Hugo de Greville-Wynter, had been appointed Rollo's new squire. A capable lad, whom Rollo had liked on sight, he was fast proving himself worthy of the post to which he had been promoted.

'I am not—fit—to wear them, my lord. Not yet.' The young man looked decidedly uncomfortable as Rollo's pale eyes fixed themselves on him angrily. 'I know it is an honour, but after what happened—I mean, in Acre . . .'

'Messire Chavo!' Karin extended jewelled fingers towards him. He took and touched them lightly to his lips. Someone behind him laughed, until Rollo's icy gaze froze him into silence. 'Will you spoil a perfect evening for me?'

'No, my lady! I? How?'

'By refusing to wear your lord's colours, of course. Have you not earned them? I think so. Have you not brought us together?' she asked, lowering her voice. 'We shall forget how it happened, for I am well content to be here, with the past behind me. Go and change, and bring Celine to come and sit with us. And you, Siward, sit beside me. I owe you an apology for the way I took flight and left you to suffer your lord's anger.'

'Nay, my lady. I would suffer it a thousand times more to see such a light in your eyes,' came the quiet answer.

'You have too smooth a tongue sometimes,' Rollo muttered. 'If I were a jealous man . . .' His meaning was only too clear.

'Which you are not and never shall be, for you will have no cause,' Karin replied, laying a hand over his. 'Pour me some wine, husband! I begin to come alive.' The cloud of despondency was beginning to lift from her heart.

'No, not that,' Rollo said, as a servant began to pour red wine into the silver chalice before her. 'Where is the special wine I ordered?'

'Here, my lord.' A place was cleared on the table, not without some difficulty, for it was brimming over with all manner of delicacies which Karin could not wait to sample, for a small cask as yet unopened.

'Tonight we drink only this,' he said softly, as he

saw to the uncorking. 'My men would find it highly amusing to get me drunk tonight, and I have other plans. No one is to have an opportunity to doctor our drinks. You would be surprised at some of the tricks they get up to,' he added, as she lowered her eyes in embarrassment. 'We are considered to be newly wed, remember?'

He poured wine the colour of honey into the chalice, yet, when she held it to her lips, the colour deepened to a golden brown. It tasted vaguely of honey and spices, yet contained a richer quality that she could not define. It slid down her throat like nectar, and he looked please as she nodded approval.

'Is it a kind of mead?' she asked.

'I was given several casks of it by a grateful old Jew for whom I did a small service. I—rescued—him from a bunch of Templars, who thought it amusing to bait a Jew as there were no Saracens about to fight. He called it Muscatel, but he would not tell me what it contains, only that his people have drunk it on special occasions for many generations. And this is a very special occasion!'

When it grew dark, torches were lighted and set in wall-holders to illuminate the proceedings, although the company were enjoying themselves too much to care about the fading light. Sentries were changed at two-hourly intervals, so that every man was able to come to the table and take his fill of what he wished—food, wine, ale and women. Even Siward relented, and found himself one of the kitchen-maids to take off into a side room. Chavo and Celine remained only for a short while, he now attired in his correct livery, and she unable to take her eyes from him. Karin made up her mind that they must marry soon.

'That was kind of you,' Rollo said, an arm casually about her shoulders as he watched two of his German mercenaries wrestling each other. Both had consumed a fair amount of food and far too much ale, and eventually both gave up and resumed their seats to tackle more. 'Chavo, I mean. I must learn to ask, not always command, but in the field it must never be any other way.'

'He understands that.' She felt content, and languid with the wine she had drunk, and laid her head back against his shoulder. She cared not if anyone was watching. His lips brushed her cheek. His fingers caressed the smoothness of her shoulders above the sweeping neckline of her gown.

'Are you tired?' He had sat for almost an hour, listening to her tell of her meeting with Saladin to a soldier who had disbelieved the rumour he had heard. She had held every one of them spellbound, he realised, watching the hardened faces of professional soldiers and mercenaries as they absorbed every word she spoke. She not only told them of the Sultan, but of Jerusalem, too. Of the beautiful paved avenues of trees where Jesus had walked, of the Church of the Holy Sepulchre, the Wailing Wall where the Jews worshipped. A city of all faiths, for all faiths, was what she had said. Would that it were possible! Man's inhumanity to man would never allow it. He accepted, now, that Jerusalem would never again be under Christian rule. His crusade was over, and he would tell the King so, and then he would return to Shah'mat and the wife he adored with a passion that at times frightened him.

'Very. And you?' A soft smile touched her lips, acknowledging his unasked question. He rose, drawing her to her feet, waving back the men who began to rise, not too steadily, from their seats to escort them inside.

His arm tightly about her waist, he guided her to a side door, and they slipped away from the merry-making—which was to go on well into the early hours of the morning—to the quiet, peaceful sanctuary of Karin's bedchamber and a night of love and fulfilment and untold pleasures.

Karin stirred, as Rollo rolled away from her and slipped from the bed. Drowsily she raised herself on one elbow to see him hurriedly pulling on his clothing. It was barely light outside! Instinct raised alarm inside her.

'What is it?' she asked, and he wheeled on her, his features grim and unsmiling. What could he say? What he had feared had happened!

'We have unexpected visitors. Saracens at the gate. Quickly, dress yourself, but remain in the solar until you are told it is safe to show yourself.' He was his old masterful self again, and she responded instantly to the tone of command, throwing aside the bedclothes.

He was gone before she could question him further. Saracens at Shah'mat! Had they come as friends—or to attack? She hurriedly dressed and made her way to the solar, where minutes later she was joined by Celine and Berta, the latter for once silent, her tongue stilled by the thought of the castle under siege. If it came to that, they were more than capable of defending it until help came, she assured them, determined not to allow any of them to dwell on such lurid thoughts.

From the window she could see the courtyard, and her heart sank as she saw Rollo striding through the débris from the night before, rousing men none too gently with the toe of his boot. One of the tables had been overturned, and food was scattered everywhere, much to the delight of the many castle dogs and cats. Men were scrambling over prostrate bodies towards their posts, cursing and swearing at being caught unawares. Thank God Rollo had seen fit to change the sentries so regularly—at least *they* had been sober and alert! Even in the midst of possible danger, she could not help smiling as she gazed down at the chaotic scene. These tough, war-hardened men had given her a night she would never forget, and she would always think of them kindly after this. As for Rollo? He had shown her two men in one. She must learn to accept and to deal with both.

The air was filled with the sound of voices—orders being bellowed, sentries answering from their posts, and one above all others standing out in command as Rollo came to stand before the main gate, surrounded by at least two dozen of his archers, with bows drawn and aimed at the entrance. Siward stood to one side of him, Chavo to the other, and the last two of the Guard who had survived the battle of Arsuf in front of him.

'The gates are being opened,' Celine said, clutching at her arm. 'My lady, is he mad?'

'He knows very well what he is about,' Karin returned reprovingly, yet silently even she doubted the wisdom of admitting whoever was outside. 'How many are there, can you see? It is still so dark. There seem to be two, no three, horsemen—is that all? She gave a shaky laugh, brightening immediately. 'What have we been worrying about? Three men!'

'One of them is Lord Ayub,' Celine replied, stepping back from the window. 'Why has he followed you? Risking his life to come here!'

Karin could see no faces clearly. Unheeding of Rollo's warning to remain in the solar, she picked up her skirts and ran down the stairs. As she came to stand beside him, he said in a low tone, 'I told you to stay inside. I expect obedience from my wife.'

'My place is beside you,' she returned with a flash of spirit that brought a smile to the edge of his mouth. 'Is it really Ayub?'

'It would seem so. He craved admittance in order to bring us a belated wedding gift. I like it not. We are too vulnerable after last night.' Rollo stared at the men about him with a grimace. 'If it is a trap, we shall suffer for it.'

'He would do nothing to harm me, I am sure. Remember, we are under the protection of Saladin!' He only shrugged.

Her eyes fastened on the three horsemen who had reined in and were dismounting a few yards away. On all sides, armed men menaced them. It was Ayub, and one of the men accompanying him was Zolto. Rollo looked at her sharply as she caught her breath, the colour ebbing from her cheeks. The Hashishin were back! Suddenly she was very afraid!

'Zolto, ay, I see him too. He shall not leave here alive, that I can promise you,' Rollo growled, his hand reaching for his sword. To his men, he ordered, 'Stand aside.'

They fell back, forming two ranks on either side of him, so that he faced the men approaching. Ayub was carrying something concealed beneath his cloak, and Karin's hand stole to her breast, clenching there as she tried to master her apprehension. What was so important that he came to them like this? A wedding gift? He hated Rollo, and had not forgiven her for loving a Christian. His gaze was quite level and unafraid as he halted before them and salaamed. Rollo did not move or acknowledge the greeting. His eyes swept upwards to the high walls, scanning the sentry posts, the archers, ready and waiting.

Ayub said tonelessly, 'I have not come to kill you, but to bring you—no, bring her—what is rightfully hers.' Turning towards Karin, he threw open his cloak. As he did so, Rollo swept her to one side. Siward caught and held her fast, as he stepped in front of her so that his body shielded hers. His sword was clear of its scabbard, lifting towards the Saracen, when a faint cry from the bundle he held stopped the blade in mid-air. It was the cry of a baby!

'I have brought you your son, Karin,' Ayub said, a strange smile masking his features. 'I, too, believed him dead, but my uncle Haroun deceived us both. He is alive and well, and where he belongs. Take him. Have you no wish to gaze on his face?'

Karin was sagging in the arms that held her, near to fainting at his words. Her bewildered eyes saw Ayub

draw back the blanket from a round little face, puckered and wet with tears. Siward urged her gently
forward under Rollo's watchful gaze. She cried out
with joy as a pair of bright green eyes gazed up at her.
His eyes, but her hair. Tiny golden curls clinging
tightly to his little head. Her child! Rollo's child!

'Ayub . . .' Wordlessly she lifted the baby from its
wrappings and held it against her breast. Her son . . .
not dead! God had answered the prayers she had
offered up that day at the Church of the Holy Sepulchre—but in his own way. Tears streaming down
her cheeks, she turned to her husband, and saw the
mounting wonder on his face as he stared down at the
infant. Hesitantly he touched one cheek, and with a
gurgle of glee his fingers were caught and held by
minute replicas of his own. 'Your son, my beloved
husband. Proof of my love!'

The eyes Rollo lifted to Ayub's face burned with
anger. His fingers tightened round the hilt of his
sword. His son! And alive!

'You dog—to put her through this. I should kill
you!'

'No! He has brought our child to us, Rollo,' Karin
cried. 'Forgive him. I believe he thought it had died.
Do not shed his blood now . . . Not now!'

He hesitated, trembling with the desire to kill this
man who had inflicted terrible wounds on them both
and the longing to be at peace with all about him. The
three of them at Shah'mat. That was all he wanted. If
blood was spilled this day, deservedly or not, the
repercussions might well destroy all of his hopes—her
dreams—their life together.

Sheathing his weapon, he held out his arms, and Karin placed the baby in them.

'My son!' His voice rose to a great roar. 'The new Lord of Shah'mat.'

Cheers rose from all sides, and men craned their necks to glimpse the face of their lord's son. He did not have little horns, so perhaps their lord was human, after all. There had been times when many had doubted it! In the following moments of confusion, the shuffling of ranks and disorientation caused by the new arrival, the third member of Ayub's party melted into the crowd, edging his way towards the gate. A sentry who turned to challenge him died with a dagger in his heart before he could call out.

'Come!' Rollo stepped to one side, after returning his son to Karin's eager arms. 'We shall drink to the health of my son.' His look challenged Ayub to refuse.

'We shall all be dead before the wine touches our lips,' Ayub returned. He had sensed, rather than seen, his man slip away. Zolto had disappeared, too. His fingers rested on his curved sword, knowing that the next words he spoke could well bring the wrath of this man down upon his head. He would die bravely, in the sight of Allah, but he would not be a party to the cold-blooded murder of the woman he loved and an innocent babe. 'I am not alone. Outside your walls are a hundred men—Haroun's men, under the orders of Rashid al-Din. You know of him? Stay your hand, Frankish man,' he snapped, as Rollo's blade once more showed itself. 'Listen to me. I am here because it was the only way to bring the child back. Haroun would have killed it, had he not had a use for it.'

'To get you into the castle—now, while we are soft in the head with drink and food. You selected your time well!' There was murder on Rollo's face. One word from him, and he knew his men would fall upon this Infidel and cut him to pieces. The memory of the poor wretches they had brought up from the deep dungeons at Darum was still vividly clear in all their minds, and the need for revenge, great and hard to control. Captured at the fall of Jerusalem, they had been imprisoned and treated like animals ever since. Many were leprous, others had lost their sight from being kept in continual darkness. All were so weak that they could hardly stand. One word . . . Karin was looking at him pleadingly, but he ignored her silent entreaty. She had not seen them. Even he, who had suffered many indignities at the hands of the Saracens, felt sick at the sight of them.

'Haroun did. I do not expect you to believe it. Believe this, then—I love her too much to have her killed just to have my revenge on you.' Ayub had not known how it would be until that moment. When Haroun had unexpectedly altered the plan of attack, he had realised that he had been lied to from the start. Karin would not be spared, and if he interfered, he too would be killed. The commands of the 'Old Man of the Mountain' were never disobeyed. They had ridden throughout the night to reach Shah'mat before dawn. They were to open the gates and allow Haroun's men to pour in, to overpower the half-drunk garrison within. All were to be killed! They had lain outside the walls in the darkness, listening to the sounds of revelry within. He had imagined Karin in

Rollo's arms until the images almost drove him mad.
But, worse, was the image of her lying in a pool of
blood beside her husband and child, for that was how
it would be.

He smiled at Karin, standing shocked and white at
Rollo's side, unconsciously soothing the fretting child
in her arms even while she stared at him, disbelieving
what she had heard. He lifted his shoulders in a shrug
of acceptance.

'*Insh'allah*. It *was* written, Karin . . .'

She screamed as blood gushed from his lips. Slowly
he folded his hands about his waist and fell to his
knees, and she saw the dagger protruding from his
back. Men broke in all directions, but they did not
know whom they were seeking. Rollo did. One face—
that of the servant who had betrayed them all—Zolto!
But even as he started towards the man, Chavo came
from behind him and leaped up the steps two at a time
to sink his blade into the Saracen's chest.

'For Acre, my lord,' he said as he straightened, and
Rollo nodded. Momentarily their hands met and
clasped in friendship and understanding, and then
Rollo came bounding back down the steps to where
Karin stood beside Ayub's inert body. He had fallen
onto his face, and was still.

'He is dead,' she said. The baby in her arms whim-
pered, and she clutched him more tightly to her, her
eyes dull with the shock of what she had seen. Gently
he turned her about and gave her into Celine's care.
She could hear shouting, and men were running past
her towards the gates.

'This time, stay in the solar until I come,' he ordered,

and kissed her briefly on the lips. He would have liked to say more, but his men were waiting for him to lead them. As she passed through the main door into the castle, she heard his voice ring out loud and clear above the din with the resilience of a church bell, as he urged his men on to do battle.

It was over. Shah'mat had the stillness of death hanging over it. There were many of Rollo's men who did not survive the bloody engagement with the fanatical Arabs who repeatedly stormed the walls once they discovered that the gates were still securely bolted and found the bodies of two of their brethren tossed over the walls. The odds were equal, despite what had taken place at Shah'mat before Ayub's arrival. When it came to a good fight, the effects of drink was of no importance to Rollo's men. They reacted to the call to arms like the disciplined soldiers they were, and his training showed as they drove the enemy from the gates with deadly arrows which never missed their marks, and then swept out after them on horseback.

A mere handful of Haroun's men fled back to Jerusalem. He himself was not among them, having died beneath Rollo's axe. Rollo came to his wife in the solar, his face streaked with dirt and sweat, his hauberk bearing marks of battle. She went to him and laid her head against his shoulder and he held her in his arms, neither speaking. Celine, holding the baby, looked on, not daring to interrupt this moment for them to ask whether Chavo still lived. In one corner Berta now sobbed tears of relief, instead of terror, her huge frame still shaking from the sounds of fighting which had reduced her to a quivering jelly.

Karin had seen much of the fighting from the solar windows, moving from one to another, trying to keep track of Rollo's thatch of dark hair. Four hours had passed since Ayub had come, and the courtyard and olive groves beyond the walls were littered with the dead and dying. Her lord was alive! Once she had seen him sent reeling from his horse, and, in the mêlée of men around him, could not see him rise. For agonising minutes she clung to the window embrasure until she saw Chavo help him to remount. She raised her head and looked up into her husband's weary features.

'You are not hurt? I saw you fall . . .'

'No, love. The blow winded me, that's all.'

'Will they come back?' Drawing away from him, she fetched him wine and made him drink a whole glass, then refilled it. He drank that also with a grateful smile. It was the Muscatel they had been drinking the previous evening. 'I thought you would like to—relax—here for a while with our son,' she added, as he looked down into the courtyard.

'I have to see to my men first. No, I think not . . .'

'Of course! I shall come with you. We can turn some of the storerooms into a hospital for the wounded. Celine can help me to see to them. There are many hurt?' Killed, was what he knew she had wanted to ask. Was Shah'mat adequately defended? He nodded, and watched her straighten her shoulders as she steeled herself to go below and face the ghastly sight of arrow-wounds, limbs split asunder by axes, heads cleaved open by swords. He would never be as proud of her as he was at this moment. 'There is much to be done,' she said, as he remained silent. 'You must allow me to help.'

'As you told me earlier, by my side is where you belong.' He drew her to him again and looked down into her resolute face. 'Ayub came to warn us at the risk of his own life. I shall always remember that. He was a man of honour. A man I could respect. We must not think of him with anger in our hearts. His love for you was as great as mine. If I had been in his place, I would have done the same thing. He shall be laid to rest in the chapel vault. We shall tell our son when he is old enough to understand, of your brother the Lord Ayub, who saved his life and returned him to us when others sought to harm him. Perhaps he will learn, as we have, that though our faiths may be different, we are all brothers under the skin.'

'What shall we call our son?' Karin asked, as they walked hand in hand out into the sunlight. His words had brought her comfort, but still she could not allow herself to dwell on the sacrifice Ayub had made for her. There was too much to do for her to lose her composure now. The wounded needed her . . . Rollo needed her . . . their son would need her too when it was time for him to take food.

'One of my forebears was called Jarl. It means "Warrior". A good name for him, do you not think? My ancestry, like that of Siward, is Norse. They have always been warriors.'

'A fighter like his father? I want him to be a man of peace,' Karin protested.

'We shall call him Jarl,' Rollo insisted. 'You may choose the name for our daughter.'

Karin did not know what time it was when she wearily climbed the stairs to her bedchamber. She ached in every limb and her head was throbbing madly from the nauseating stench of blood and rotting flesh, but she had given way to none of the emotion which at times overtook her as she aided the physicians in their work, rolled bandages for hours on end, fed broth to those too weak to fend for themselves, and sat with the gravely injured and the dying, hoping that in some small way her presence helped them. Rollo came and went, never seeming to tire, and while he strived so ceaselessly to regain some order out of the chaos about them, she did the same.

But at last he detached her firmly from the side of a wounded man and told her to go to bed. She sent Celine and Berta away and sat by the cradle where her son slept peacefully, her aching head resting in her arms. How perfect he was. He had Rollo's nose . . . and perhaps her lips. The memory of the long weeks of agony she had endured after his birth faded away as she gazed down at the cherub-like face. Jarl. It was a proud name, with a ring of fierceness about it. Like his father—proud, strong, determined—and stubborn. What traits of hers had he inherited? Compassion, she hoped, and understanding. The ability to love.

When Rollo came into the room he found her by the window, gently rocking the cradle where the baby was making soft plaintive noises. She had discarded her beautiful gown that had been soiled with blood and dirt, and washed all traces of the battle from her skin, before she put on a loose robe, such as she had worn in Jerusalem. He watched her tickle the baby's chin, saw the curve of her breast as she swept back the long red-gold hair and slid the bolt home across the door.

He was bone-tired, barely able to strip off his mail, yet the sight of her looking so fresh and desirable over-rode it. His sword arm pained him greatly, still tender from the arrow-wound he had sustained. Karin saw him wince as he flexed it, came to him, and took the towel with which he had been attempting to wash himself.

'Come, let me.' She washed his body with the fresh water she had put ready for him, and carefully dried his skin, aware that he stiffened as she touched a grazed arm, a raw leg. He had not escaped totally unscathed; she saw that from the many cuts and abrasions.

'Enough, *Kutti*!' Rollo said, in a hoarse whisper. 'I am not made of stone.'

His fingers fastened in her hair, thrusting her head back for him to take possession of her mouth, waiting eagerly to be claimed. But as he slid the robe away from her, a cry came from the direction of the crib and she eased her mouth from his, protesting as he bared shoulders and breasts to his searching caresses.

'I must go to him.'

'Am I not needing your attention also? Your undivided attention? Have I lost you already?' he said with a mock scowl. Throwing himself down onto the bed, he watched her gather up the baby and rock him, and said condescendingly, 'I suppose I must learn to share you with him?'

'He has every reason to be fretful after all that has happened. So many strangers touching him, but none loving him as we do,' Karin reproved. 'He shall sleep between us tonight, so that he will know he is safe— and loved.'

She slipped in beside him, placing the baby alongside her, so that it rested against his chest. A soft smile of understanding touched her lips as Rollo muttered,

'This is the last time I allow anything to come between us—even him.' But then she saw he was smiling too, and that moment of apprehension fluttering inside her died. There was such tenderness and pride in his eyes that she wanted to weep. 'Come here, woman. At least let me hold you too.'

She moved herself into the circle of his arms and laid her cheek against the warmth of a solid shoulder. Rollo touched Jarl's curly hair and chuckled.

'He is handsome, is he not? Like his father?'

'And modest,' she answered, and a devilish light flickered in her eyes as she looked up at him. 'If only Chavo and Siward could see you now!'

Tugging back her head, Rollo took her mouth, silencing her, and she accepted the rebuke with a contented sigh and drew his hand across Jarl's tiny body to cup her breast. She sighed with pleasure as he pushed aside her robe and began to caress her again.

Resting snug and warm between them, Jarl yawned—and fell asleep.